STRATHARD

A Question of Choice

JEAN BISBEY

authorHOUSE®

AuthorHouse™ UK
1663 Liberty Drive
Bloomington, IN 47403 USA
www.authorhouse.co.uk
Phone: 0800.197.4150

Published by AuthorHouse 06/29/2017

ISBN: 978-1-5246-6705-4 (sc)
ISBN: 978-1-5246-6706-1 (hc)
ISBN: 978-1-5246-6704-7 (e)

Print information available on the last page.

Any people depicted in stock imagery provided by Thinkstock are models, and such images are being used for illustrative purposes only. Certain stock imagery © Thinkstock.

This book is printed on acid-free paper.

CHAPTER 1

I knew that if I lived to be 100 years old, I would never forget the day the seagulls got drunk and my brother Callum fished Big McGreegor's flies with a magnet and a piece of string.

That was in 1936 when I was twelve years old. Now I was 40 and, like the salmon in the River Ard, had journeyed back against a tide of difficulties to the land where I'd been spawned. I had a problem and here in this Scottish valley, cradled by mountains and washed by rivers, I hoped to solve it. As a child I'd imbibed the beauty of Strathard as naturally as I'd breathed its unpolluted air. As a woman, what virtues I possessed were nourished by its memories. Like a traveller needing a waymark, I needed those memories to sustain me in my choice of direction. I needed reassurance that my inclination to travel a certain path had substance and was not just a passing whim.

It was the screeching of the scavenging gulls above my head, flapping their way to the Firth which kick-started me back into the time of their drunken ancestors. As I made a pilgrimage to the old graveyard behind the church, about a mile from the hotel where I'd registered the previous evening, I shortened my stride on the hard macadamized road and sauntered across the grass verge to find a gap in the hawthorns that I might gaze upon the moors beyond.

I recalled one fine spring morning when I was twelve. My father had been chauffeuring the Laird to Inverness to meet a shooting party from The South. My mother was heavy with child. Grandpa had invited my younger brother Graham and myself to ride in the spring cart on his weekly jaunt to the hotel on the shores of the Firth. It was his custom to

1

transport deer carcasses, plucked chickens and skinned hares from the castle larder to the hotel next to the distillery. My older brother, Callum, after helping Grandpa load the spring cart, waved us cheerily on our way.

It was a sunny morning with a breeze barely ruffling my hair which was pulled back from my face, plaited and secured with neat green ribbons. I wore a green cotton dress with puff sleeves and a smocked bodice and on my feet I wore white ankle socks and stout brown brogues.

The Highland pony knew the day, the hour and the journey and what was expected of her. She clattered over the cobbles towards the creeper-covered archway separating Stable Square from the long winding driveway which led to Strathard Castle. Long before the castle could be sighted, we forked into a tributary pathway which wound between banks of rhododendron and azalea to the lodge gates and on to the road to Strathard village. It was the same road I was standing on now.

Tillytudlem's leisurely trot gave me time to pluck leaves from overhanging branches. I smiled fondly at my younger brother as I gave him some to feel. I watched him as he fingered the soft smooth leaves and, leaning towards him, let him rub them against my cheek. I laughed with him as he directed the rougher leaves at Grandpa who, in spite of the protection of moustache and beard, pretended alarm.

I nourished a fierce protective love for my younger brother who was both mentally and physically handicapped. The time I had caught the McGreegor twins imitating his shuffling walk, I discovered that I had a left hook worthy of respect. When it came into contact with Tam's button nose, no one was more surprised than I was. With the combination of red hair and strong left hook I was someone to be reckoned with.

I couldn't understand what God had been thinking of when He'd sent us Wee Graham. Young as I was, I felt the difference between my two brothers to be a travesty of justice. I had once asked my mother why Graham couldn't speak properly.

'It's God's will Jenny, and God knows best!'

I fared no better with my father.

'Why can't Graham walk properly, Father?'

'Some questions are better not asked!' my father had answered. Even Grandpa's dismissive 'You're too young to understand' hadn't helped.

I was always left frustrated. I wanted to understand things when the need arose and I didn't take kindly to having my questions shelved. I was particularly interested in God and his 'mysterious ways' which the minister called the tenets he couldn't properly explain. It didn't satisfy me. I needed a lot of convincing.

My grandfather pulled on Tillytudlem's reins as the sound of a motor car came fast upon our rear.

'Damned seasonals!' he muttered. 'Drunk wi' speed. They should never've done away wi' the twenty mile limit.'

As the car caught up with us it slowed to a crawl. It was a DeLauney Belleville, its round radiator decorated with the Scottish flag. When Grandpa saw the woman at the wheel, his face lit up.

'Miss Catriona,' he yelled as if she were a mile away. 'It's grand to see you back again.'

'It's good to be back, Donald McLeod. You're looking fit.'

'Not half as fit as you look bonny, Your Ladyship.'

'Flatterer,' smiled Miss Catriona as she gently moved ahead and away from us.

I was left with an impression of a wide-eyed beautiful woman looking as a bright flower must look to a bee. Certainly Grandpa hadn't been slow in buzzing in and as he began busily singing her praises I felt my first faint twinge of jealousy.

Catriona McKenzie, of whom I'd heard a lot but seldom seen, was the Laird's daughter who had married a 'gallivantin' millionaire', as Grandpa called her husband and she had gallivanted with him all over the world.

'You're very familiar with the gentry,' I now accused Grandpa who had always made such a to-do of seeing that Callum and me kept our proper distance.

'Ach! I knew her when she crawled around in her breeks. Besides, her faither and me fought the Boers thegether.'

'Just the two of you?'

'Less of your impudence. I'll have you know they'd never have managed in Africa without us.'

Grandpa had been a gamekeeper when he was younger and, as he kept insisting, it had been the gamekeeper's skill with the gun and the telescope and his expert knowledge of the rough terrain that provided the expertise needed for South African warfare. Very proud he was of his Lovat Scout association with the Laird. I realized that this special relationship seemed to give Grandpa a familiarity with the gentry denied to the rest of us.

I watched Graham's pleasure when the Firth came into view with its life of screaming gulls, sandy shore and sparkling waters dotted with fishing craft, with a backdrop of cloud-topped mountain peaks. He had seen it all many times before but the measure of his delight made each time seem like the first. I wondered if Her Ladyship had taken time to admire the view. I couldn't understand folk leaving Strathard for very long, least of all the folk that owned it. I knew I could never leave it. By just imagining such a possibility I felt a shiver of apprehension in spite of the sun's warmth.

The distillery next to the hotel was set well back from the road behind a large lawn which sloped gently seawards and was edged by a drystone dyke. While Grandpa and one of the hotel staff unloaded the cart, I helped my brother on to the dyke and sat beside him, my arm round his shoulder, happily observing the other onlookers, all waiting expectantly for the show to begin.

Grandpa soon appeared leading Tillytudlem. He tethered the pony, checked we were behaving ourselves then went to join the Laird who was sitting on his shooting stick clad in the small green check of the Strathard tweeds. There was a hum of interest as Jock Napier came out of the distillery. He was holding in each hand a double handful of bran mash which still contained potions of very potent liquid and he threw this to the seagulls flying over the lawn. They swooped on to the lawn and gobbled up the bran mash. The effect was almost instantaneous. They rolled on the ground. One or two tried to take off. They attempted a few flaps into the air before executing a half roll and landing on their backs. They took off again and performed three or four close loops. There were shrieks of laughter in which I joined, excitedly kicking the heels of my new brogues against the dyke and hugging Wee Graham in my delight at the crazy spectacle. I heard the laird's loud guffaw duetting with Grandpa's. I glanced towards the pair of them eyeing them fondly as their heads nodded in shared amusement.

Cutting across the laughter and spontaneous bursts of applause there was a loud shot and one of the gulls dropped to the ground to lie at the laird's feet.

There was a moment's stunned silence broken by a startled shriek and murmurs of concern. Drunk as they were, the other birds veered seawards, croaking in alarm. Astonished eyes were riveted on the marksman. He was so close to me that I was surprised I hadn't seen him take aim. It was Mr Stacey, Her Ladyship's gallivanting husband. He was in riding gear and was brandishing his crop to all and sundry. I heard Her Ladyship's swift intake of breath and saw her face ablaze with fury.

There was another shot. The bullet whistled past the heads of the spectators before finding its target. Vincent Stacey's riding cap was lifted from his head. Breathless, the crowd watched as the figure of Big McGreegor, the Strathard gamekeeper himself, stepped into the arena. I noticed that all that rush of blood had drained from Miss Catriona's face, leaving it as white as a bag of flour. The gamekeeper had made his mark in more ways than one! He'd shot the hat from the millionaire's head as casually as he would swipe a fly from a treacle tart. I held my breath as I saw Mr Stacey raise his gun and point it at Big McGreegor. Catriona rushed forward and grabbed her husband's arm but he was so drunk that without even the need of a push, he tumbled to the ground, landing bottoms up while his gun slipped from his fingers. Somebody laughed. Then others joined in. A sideways glance showed me that Her Ladyship was not amused! She was as agitated with anger as the Laird was with embarrassment. Her beautiful eyes were sparking a fury so intense that I wouldn't have been surprised to see Mr Stacey go up in smoke. The laird made a move to leave and Catriona was beside him in an instant, leaving Mr Stacey to make a melodramatic retreat as best he could.

'It's time we were gettin' back,' said Grandpa, his voice sounding like the snapping of dry twigs. Graham and I were unceremoniously bundled into the cart and Tillytudlem headed for home. I was ruffled at the sudden termination of my enjoyment.

'Why did Mr Stacey shoot the seagull?'

'He was drunk.'

'Why did Miss Catriona marry a man like Mr Stacey?' -

'She was gey young at the time.

I was younger than Her Ladyship but never in a thousand years would I have married Mr Stacey.

'And why—'

JEAN BISBEY

'Stop askin' your questions. It's questions, questions questions wi' you!' grumbled Grandpa.

'How am I ever going to get any answers then, if I don't ask questions?' I snapped as much as I dared while trying to glare at my grandfather and, at the same time, smile reassuringly at Wee Graham.

"Haven't I told you often enough that if you ask no questions you'll be told no lies?'

'And if I shut my mouth I'll catch no flies. I know.' I sighed, taking the hint.

We had climbed from the shore with the Firth now behind us and a view of the rolling moors ahead and the peaks of the high mountains in the distance beyond. Everywhere I looked was Strathard. My father had told me there were 30,000 acres of it, far more than my eyes could take in now. Besides the moors and mountains, it had two lochs, a river, forests, farms, deer, ptarmigan, pheasants and grouse – lots of grouse. The school, the church and most of the houses belonged to Strathard and of course the castle with its many rooms and turrets. How could all that, and a lot more besides, not be big enough for Her Ladyship without the need to gallivant round the world? By the look on Grandpa's face I decided I'd better not ask him.

Why? Why? Why? The story of my life! Asking questions was what had epitomized my childhood and I was still doing it!

I left the grass verge and resumed my journey along the road to the churchyard with the whispering ghosts on my shoulder.

The metal gates to the small granite-stoned church were open. I crunched my way along the gravel path encircling the church, noting the ancient slabs leaning against its walls, the profusion of weeds, the few memorial benches, chipped, with peeling paint, their metal feet and arms rusted. Here and there the colour of surviving Michaelmas daises and undisciplined clumps of montbretia relieved the general neglect. I could feel one ghost on my shoulder deeply disturbed by the scene; that of my late father-in-law, the Reverend Andrew Fraser. With an image of his righteous indignation I hastily turned my thoughts to my gentler ghosts. I was nearing their graves.

A gentle smirr of rain, like heaven's tears, washed my face in sympathy as I fingered the grooves of the inscription on my mother's headstone.

'In memory of Fiona McLeod dearly beloved wife of Angus and mother of Callum, Jenny and Graham

Died aged 42 on 14th April 1936.

Rest in Peace'

I'm sorry it didn't work out the way you wanted, Mother, I thought, remembering her deathbed wish which had so burdened me at that time. Next to my mother's grave was that of my grandfather, Donald McLeod, whose love, humour and wisdom had guided me gently through childhood, adolescence and to the fringe of womanhood.

Oblivious to the rain and the stark symbolism of the surrounding headstones I was remembering my return home from the distillery. Our living quarters had two storeys. Downstairs there was a large living room-cum- kitchen with a small stone-flagged scullery built on to the back. Upstairs, reached by a narrow winding ladder of a staircase leading from the kitchen, had once been haylofts. With the development of Home Farm and the advent of the motor car, the haylofts had been converted into sleeping quarters where one bedroom led into another. When I stepped into the house upon returning from the castle, my eyes flew to the box bed where I saw my mother. This bed was only used in emergencies.

My mother's eyes seemed too big for her face and there was a bright red patch on each cheek. Her hair was as damp with sweat as her mouth was parched with an unquenchable thirst. Father gazed at her helplessly. Callum was washing his hands at the sink.

I felt a sickness in the pit of my stomach. I rushed across the room.

'Mother!'

In response to my anguished cry she smiled gently and patted my hand. She tried to speak but her voice was so weak and the effort did nothing to calm me.

'I'll look after you,' I whispered. At that moment I would have gone to Hell and back for her.

'You'll have enough to do mindin' Graham,' said Father.

'I can do that too,' I answered, my eyes glued to my mother's face while grabbing the corner of the sheet to wipe the running sweat from her brow.

'You can do everything, I suppose,' said Callum, hanging the kitchen towel on the nail behind the door.

'Aye, if I have to,' I snapped.

'Now leave your mother to rest a bit and off you go and play, the pair of you.'

'But we've only just come in!'

'Then you can only just go back out!'

'I want to stay with you, Mother,' I pleaded.

'Do as I say, Jenny,' Father cautioned. 'Your mother's tired and could do without your girnin'.'

'Come on Jenny,' coaxed Callum. 'I've something to show you.'

I stubbornly ignored them both and bent over my mother. The red patches had drained, leaving her face as grey as the spilt ashes in the hearth.

'Mother, are you going to be all right?' It seemed an interminable time before she answered with barely a whisper.

'I'm just tired, lass.'

Then she cried out in pain. I grasped her hand as if by doing so I could channel the pain to myself. I felt Father's grip on my shoulder, preparing to pull me away.

'Bide a wee, Angus,' Mother gasped. 'Let Jenny feel the bairn. She's a real fighter.'

'But wife—'

'Go on Jenny,' Mother whispered. 'Put your hand on my stomach and feel how strong your wee sister is.'

Reluctantly and conscious of my disapproving father breathing down my neck, I placed a timid hand on my mother's swollen stomach only to snatch it back as I felt the movement of the life within.

'She's a strong one,' whispered Mother. Again I wiped the sweat from her face with a dry bit of the sheet. I couldn't bear to see her agony.

'She's not as strong as me,' I whispered fiercely. 'I'm very strong.'

Mother raised her arm, drawing her finger down my cheek.

'Dear wee Jenny. I can depend on you.'

I had to bend low to hear the words. 'I know you'll look after them all when I'm gone - keep them all together - and the bairn...'

Numbed, I watched as Mother's hand dropped like a leaden weight on the quilt.

'Father,' I gasped in alarm as mother's eyes closed and her breathing seemed to have stopped. But Father was already pushing me aside.

Everything happened at once. Mother moaned and Grandpa hurried in, calling that the doctor was here.

'Thank God,' breathed Father. I could hear the hooves of the doctor's little pony canter over the cobbles and stop at the kitchen door. I couldn't see my mother now. Both Grandpa and Father were between me and the bed. I hated the baby. We didn't need another one. We already had two boys and wasn't Grandpa always maintaining that one of my kind in the family was enough. I couldn't get to Mother. Father was too big and never even felt my hands on him. Grandpa kept getting in my way. The doctor had no sooner set foot in the house when he lifted me like a sack of potatoes and dumped me in the Square beside Callum.

'Take your sister for a walk - and make it a long one.'

Seeing our wretched faces he relented, placing a large hand on each head. 'If you really want to help, the pair of you, keep out of the way for a while. This is no place for bairns. Now, off you go.'

'Come on, Jenny,' said Callum. 'The doctor's right. There's nothing we can do just now.'

'You mind my mother now,' I commanded to the doctor's retreating back.

Grandpa, looking old and weary came out of the house and joined us. "Your mother's in God's hands now lass,' he consoled.

That was no comfort to me. I wasn't too sure about God. I'd appealed to Him before when I'd first realized that Graham wasn't like others. My appeals then hadn't done much good. Why should they do better now, I asked myself?

Like a symbolic gesture, banks of heavy cloud, in keeping with our mood, lowered above. We gave no thought to the likelihood of rain.

CHAPTER 2

We left Grandpa standing forlorn on the cobbles and made our way under the archway and out of the Square keeping clear of the main drive. Callum, his blond hair glistening with rain, led me through the wood of birches on whose furthest fringe stood Big McGreegor's hut. Foolishly we had not thought to bring coats and it never occurred to us to go back for them. Undeterred Callum urged me forward to the gamekeeper's hut.

'I'll help you on to the roof and we'll have a look at Big McGreegor's flies.'

I shivered, thrusting my chilling hands into the pockets of my thin cotton dress. I wasn't interested in McGreegor's flies. My mind was on my mother and what she had whispered to me.

Callum, always sensitive to my moods queried what was wrong.

'You don't think Mother's going to—'

He turned on me in a flash.

'No!' he shouted, then more quietly. 'No, she isn't, Jenny. Mother's having a baby, that's all, and she's had babies before.'

I looked at him, searching his face for reassurance. His eyes darkened before their long thick lashes dropped, obscuring any reassurance I was hoping for. He turned from me and, approaching the hut, called over his shoulder.

'Come on, let's look at McGreegor's flies.'

His words only succeeded in prompting another fear.

'Supposing he shoots us,' I said.

'It's game he shoots, not folk,' he snorted.

He dragged me on to the roof of Big McGreegor's hut while I scrambled for a foothold, slipped, grazing my knees on the rough wood. Lifting off the skylight window Callum placed it carefully to the side before kneeling down and beckoning me to join him. Gingerly I hunched by his side. We were both by now very wet, our hair clinging damply to our faces, our hands colouring with cold. I felt sure that if Big McGreegor caught us he would shoot at worst, or at best, skelp our backsides.

Together we peered into the interior of the gamekeeper's office where he did his accounts and official business and where he kept his flies and other items used by gamekeepers. Directly below was his desk on which lay dozens of coloured fishing flies. They were bright and glittered and looked most attractive. There were sandflies, ordinary brown trout, Loch Leven trout and rainbow trout wet flies.

Callum withdrew from his pocket a magnet and a length of string. He tied the string to the magnet which he carefully lowered until he made contact. He continued with the utmost care, one successful catch after another. Neither of us heard the gamekeeper's approach. He must have been standing there watching and waiting on the ground below.

Proud of his achievement, Callum offered the captured beauties for my inspection but try as he did, he elicited little enthusiasm. My thoughts were elsewhere. Sighing, Callum dropped the flies as carefully and accurately as he could. No damage had been done and the mix-up would give the keeper something to puzzle over. Smiling, he replaced the skylight window. Only when we were again on the ground did McGreegor make his presence known.

The keeper caught me as I swooned. When I opened my eyes, it was McGreegor's face I saw bending over me. His breath on my face was heavy with tobacco and his wet tweeds reeked of live dog and dead rabbit. His hands on my bare arms were rough. I was beginning a scream when he spoke.

'Steady lass. It's only me.' But I didn't relax until I felt reassured that he was neither going to shoot us nor skelp us.

'You're wanted back home,' said the keeper.

I felt a new terror. I looked at him. His voice was too gentle. His kindness worried me. By rights he should be ladling into us with his tongue. There must be something worse in store for us and I sensed that McGreegor knew about it.

'Come on Jenny,' said Callum. 'Maybe our wee sister's here.'

I was staring at McGreegor, trying to read his eyes but he seemed to be looking everywhere but at me. I felt sick. I was afraid to go home but wrapped in McGreegor's malodorous jacket I was hurried through the rain.

When we entered the house McGreegor's wife, Ella, met us inside the kitchen, carrying a bundle in her arms. In my drenched condition I must have looked like something the cat dragged in. Ella, showing immediate concern laid the baby in a dresser drawer drawn up before the fire and specially lined to receive it. She pulled a towel from the pulley.

'Let me rub that head o' hair. You'll catch pneumonia if we don't do something about the state you're in.'

My eyes flew to the box bed. It was empty. McGreegor's jacket dropped from my wet shoulders on to the kitchen floor. Ignoring Ella I called for my mother. Ella, still holding the towel expectantly, tried to hush me. Someone was coming downstairs. It was Grandpa. He stood looking at us, trying to speak but nothing was coming from his mouth. His wrinkled old cheeks were wet with tears. He put one arm round Callum's shoulders and held out his other to me. I ran to him and he didn't seem to notice or even care how wet we were.

'Hae you seen the bonnie bairn?' he asked in a shaky voice.

'Where's Mother, Grandpa?' It was Callum asking the question. I could only cling tight and try to ward off some terrible threat.

'Let me rub you down, Jenny,' pleaded Ella, tears running down her cheeks.

Grandpa held us hard for a minute then said gently, 'Your mither's in Heaven. She's wi' the Lord Jesus now, bless her soul. You two maun be brave.'

He nodded to McGreegor who handed Callum a towel which my brother took from him. Callum pulled off his shirt and began a vigorous scrubbing of body and head with the rough hessian. Under protest I suffered a similar rubbing from Ella and as soon as I could escape her rough treatment rejoined Grandpa. My brother and I both ignored the baby.

'Where's Wee Graham?' I choked, grabbing my grandfather's arm.

'Graham's gone to the manse. The minister's wife is kindly looking after him,' he said.

'I want Graham,' I sobbed.

'Hush Jenny,' said Grandpa. 'It wouldn't be fair to Graham. This is no place for him for a day or two. He's better where he is. He's being well taken care of.'

I wouldn't look at the baby. I followed Grandpa around, trying to force his attention on my fear. He said he'd make some tea. He lifted the large cast-iron kettle from the hob and filled it at the kitchen sink. With gentle prods of the poker he coaxed the flames from the smouldering peats. McGreegor had already left, having slipped away after a whispered word with Ella.

I gazed in sudden alarm at my father as he stumbled downstairs. In a few hours my tall handsome father had changed into a bowed and broken old man.

Mesmerized, I watched him sink into his chair in front of the fire, dropping his head between his hands. Ella hovered uncertainly but, after exchanging a look with Grandpa, resumed her attentions on the baby.

'The doctor said he'd be back directly,' Grandpa told my father as he poured tea. I watched as my father ran his fingers through his hair. He was dishevelled and his hands shook when he took the bowl of tea from Grandpa and raised it to his lips. The strong black liquid ran down his chin and spilled on to his pullover.

I felt a new wave of terror. This couldn't be Father sitting there so crumpled and helpless. Father would never let his tea dribble down his chin. Father never cried. Men didn't cry. It was as if a lump of jagged-edged coal had got stuck in my chest. I ran to him howling.

Father held me in his arms but my need and longing for my mother could not be assuaged. The baby began to cry. I hated that small mass of flesh writhing in the dresser drawer. I wanted to throw it on the fire and hear it screech as my heart was screeching, watch it suffer as I was suffering. The strength of my feelings frightened me. I watched Grandpa take it from Callum and shoogle it gently. I hid my face in Father's chest. Callum ran from the kitchen. I could hear his boots clattering across the cobbles as the rain rattled on the window panes.

'There, there,' soothed Grandpa, cradling the baby.

'There, there,' comforted Father while I sobbed in his arms and my mother lay cold and rigid in her bed upstairs.

There was a knock at the front door. Father gently pushed me aside and rose to answer. I was shocked to silence by the unexpected sight of the Laird and Her Ladyship standing there together in the kitchen. It was the first time they'd ever been in our house. For a few moments my curiosity won over my grief. Mercifully the baby had stopped crying. Grandpa laid her in her makeshift bed. I withdrew into the corner between the dresser and the scullery door while I watched the laird and Miss Catriona talking quietly with Father. Grandpa was rummaging in the dresser for a bottle. Then the doctor came back with Mrs McLaren. Following on his heels came the Reverend Fraser and his son and soon everyone seemed to be talking at once. I could feel Neil Fraser's eyes on me and I retreated further into the shadows. Horrified, I watched Callum come in and smile at the visitors, I saw Father pull himself together then talk to the Laird. I could hardly believe my eyes when I saw Grandpa measure drams with an exactitude generally accorded medicinal drugs.

How could they behave so ordinarily when upstairs Mother lay dead! Perhaps she wasn't dead! Panic-stricken, I thought of the possibilities of a mistake. Maybe while we all thought her dead, she was actually in a deep sleep, tired after the birth. In my imagination I had my mother screwed down in her coffin and buried alive. I broke out in a cold sweat. I had to make sure.

Carefully I skirted the room, keeping to the shadows. Unchecked, I reached the staircase and, once there, its narrow winding reaches to the rooms above afforded an easy escape, or so I thought at the time. I crept through my own room, then Callum's. On entering Grandpa's room which he shared with Graham, I hesitated but the need to see for myself that Mother was dead and not just in a deep sleep gave me the courage to go through the remaining door.

I stood for a moment, my breath coming in gasps. Gathering all my courage I approached the bed. I kept my eyes averted until I was by my mother's side. Only then did I look down upon her body. I held my breath. Mother looked beautiful. Her hair was unpinned and brushed, the long silky strands arranged neatly over her shoulders. Her hands were crossed on her breast. I dropped to my knees.

'Mother, Mother! Don't go away. Please don't go away.'

I lowered my lips to my mother's cheek. I wasn't prepared for the coldness of the body. Startled, I drew back then, hope gone, I surrendered to despair. My mother had gone away as she had said she would. She had gone into God's hands and would never come back to us. We would never see her again. They would put her in a coffin and bury her deep down in the earth and her flesh would crumble to dust. 'Dust to dust, ashes to ashes', the minister would say.

Tears rolled down my cheeks, over my chin, spilling on to the green cotton of my summer dress. My vision blurred. How were we ever going to manage without her! Instinctively, I reached for her hand, drawing it to my cheek and mingled with my pain was the memory of an earlier touch and the sound of my mother's voice as she had spoken just for me.

'I know you'll look after them all when I'm gone - keep them all together - and the baby—'

It was as if she were in the room with me. I could feel her touch on my face and on my hair and it was as if she was pressing me down, down, down with the weight of what she was asking.

It was all too much for me. I sobbed until I felt I must surely drown in my tears. I didn't hear Neil Fraser come into the room. When I found him standing in the doorway looking down on me I felt exposed. Any intruder on my grief would have been bad enough but Neil Fraser especially so.

'It is God's will,' he said just as his father kept saying from the pulpit. 'I will pray for you Jenny.'

He took a hesitant step towards me. I resented his presence. I resented his sanctimonious words as they rolled so glibly from his tongue. To me he was the symbol of God and I was once again angry with God. Neil Fraser had often claimed that he was the servant of God. I was angry with Neil Fraser.

It could have been what I needed to drag me back from my pit of despair but the consequences were unlooked for. I used Neil Fraser as a boxer might use a punch bag, swiping, thumping and pounding mercilessly, only my attack was of words and jibes and insults. But while every delivery bounced back upon myself Neil Fraser remained totally undamaged. I pushed past him and, blinded by tears, made my way back through the bedrooms to the top of the stairs. I missed my footing and hurtled to the kitchen below.

Now, as I stood alone in the church cemetery, I became aware that the rain had stopped. I felt the cold, wet granite of my mother's headstone beneath my hand and sensed a fleeting touch of eternity, that timeless reality where the limits of time and space are transcended and, like the symbol of the serpent with its tail in its mouth, end and beginning are one. I had brought some wild flowers, freshly picked earlier in the day and these I now laid on both graves. It was time to return to the hotel.

On leaving the graveyard and once more passing close to the church I thought again of my early antagonism to Neil, the Holy Willie of Strathard, or so I'd called my husband in 1936. He had carried a chip on his shoulder the size of the Corrie Cairn all because he'd had polio which forced him to hobble to school while others streaked. Unlike Wee Graham his limping bothered him badly. Certainly Neil Fraser had always seemed hell-bent on getting my dander up and he was still doing it!

Although a great deal of water had flowed under the bridge since I had married Neil Fraser, my memories had evoked the power of my early aversion to my husband as it had been all those years ago. Why had I chosen to marry him? At the time it had been a choice borne out of dramatic circumstances and against even more dramatic advice.

I lunched in the Strathard Arms then spent the rest of the day walking on the moors thinking about the decision I had come here to make. My problem was both simple and complicated. I had recently inherited one million pounds from Professor Hugh Hadley, my dear friend and guru, but on condition that the money was spent for the good of humanity. This condition, I knew, was a declaration of trust in me that I would honour his wishes. As guru and disciple, a strong relationship had been built between an eccentric esoteric and an enthusiastic idealist. Although the condition may have been part of his eccentricity and posed a problem for me, I felt honour bound to comply with his wishes.

My husband was a minister of the Church of Scotland. His answer to my problem was simple enough. He had a missionary fund for Africa, another for China, a number of parish poor and a nearby home for the disabled. What was I waiting for?

I didn't see it like that. My ideas were more complicated. How did one spend a million pounds for the good of humanity, I asked myself, and not for the first time. Of course, it would be so easy to top up Neil's missionary funds. That might be for the good of orphans, lepers and the like but what would that do for humanity? And surely the professor would be expecting more of me.

'All you need Jenny,' he'd said, 'is a challenge, a big challenge and your imagination.'

I had the challenge all right. He'd seen to that, but did I have the imagination equal to the challenge? He must have thought so. I was less certain. It was dusk when I returned to the hotel which I preferred to think of as the castle.

Strathard Castle was a pretentious monument to fame and fortune conceived by the laird's grandfather and built by imported Irish labour. It was about 400-500 feet above sea level, built in Scottish baronial style with pointed turrets, crow-stepped gables and overhanging caps. It had once been fronted with a large lawn and circular drive.

Sadly the drive was now cushioned in weeds, the lawn macadamized with painted white lines for parking vehicles. The borders were overgrown and the once imposing portico was in need of restoration. It was decayed grandeur at its worst. When the estate was broken up it had begun a new existence as a hotel where, for a brief spell, I had worked as a make-do secretary for an astrologer and her husband who had become my dearest friends and from whom I had parted in anger and sorrow.

The current proprietors were an American couple at present on a visit to their native land. Initially dedicated and awash with great ideas for Strathard, their interest in the hotel business had worsened with their experience of the Scottish climate and, in the words of Flora, the exuberant young receptionist, 'they were away oftener than they were here'. Flora was behind the reception desk, smiling brightly as I entered the main hall.

'Did you enjoy your walk, Mrs Fraser?' she asked.

'Yes thank you, Flora,' I smiled, pocketing the key to my room which she had taken from a row of hooks behind her.

'That man's on the prowl again,' she whispered leaning across the counter, her pouter pigeon chest swathed in cotton resting on the counter and, in answer to my raised brows, she continued.

'You know, the one everyone's talking about. It fair gives me the willies when I listen to them. Didn't you hear about him?' she added wondering at my silence and dramatizing her surprise. 'He keeps himself to himself,' and, reverting to a stage whisper, 'they say he wears a long cloak to his ankles and a big floppy-brimmed hat. Nobody's spoken to him. They say...' She cast a hasty glance around the deserted hall before continuing in the same conspiratorial whisper. 'That he's the devil in disguise.'

There's plenty of them around, I thought, especially in small communities where strangers were always under suspicion and none more so than strangers who kept themselves to themselves. What the locals didn't know they were quick to invent. I was faintly amused but tried not to let her see.

'I expect he just wants to be left in peace,' I said, feeling some sympathy for the poor devil.

Flora was not to be put off.

'But don't you think it's kind of queer wearing a long cloak and large floppy hat and not speaking to anybody?' She made an exaggerated moue.

It was obvious Flora was squeezing all the drama that she could from this unusual visitor to Strathard.

'I wouldn't worry about it, Flora,' I said, edging away from the reception desk but she seemed loath to let me escape.

'I'd run a mile if I saw him. They say he's on the prowl late at night. I'd be careful if I were you,' she cautioned. 'Don't go too far by yourself.'

'I won't,' I promised. Then to steer her mind from the subject I enquired about the old stables and flats about half a mile south of the castle, not telling her that it was the place where I'd first seen the light of day.

'I suppose you mean the old storerooms.'

'I suppose so,' I agreed. 'I believe they're quite interesting - architecturally,' I added as an inspired afterthought.

'I never kent that,' she said, her eyes widening, but there was no lasting interest. Her mind was still on the devil incarnate.

'Would it be all right if I had a look at them?'

'I expect so. There's no much in them now, things running down like.'

'Is there a key should I want to take a look inside?' I ventured.

'Ach, you won't need a key. As far as I know the doors are hanging off their hinges.'

My stomach lurched. Was I ready for this, I wondered. It was after dinner when I left the castle and made my way along the path which led to the crumbling archway. I passed beneath it, trying to believe, like a Zen master, that there was no yesterday, no tomorrow, only now. Yet here I was, digging into my subconscious like a fanatical archaeologist. I knew I had to view what was left of my birthplace. It had been the place where I had learned to love and had first experienced the need to hate.

CHAPTER 3

Flora had not exaggerated when she said the doors were hanging off their hinges. Entry was effortless. I was slightly put out by how small the rooms were. Had six of us once lived here together in harmony? I had no memory of feelings of confinement. Privacy had been important to all of us and now, walking through each room, carefully side-stepping broken furniture, rolls of frayed carpet, discarded boxes and household utensils, so rusted as to be almost unidentifiable, I marvelled at how we had, as a family, managed to enjoy so much privacy and domestic comfort. Here was the scullery, surprisingly still housing the original coal bunker. Here the sink in the kitchen, stained and rusted.

Dispassionately I wandered through the upstairs rooms, conscious of the dangers of dodgy floorboards until I completed my inspection in my parents' room. It was here, in this room, that I had thrown out God, the belief system which had sustained my family and friends but which had not been good enough for me. It had offered no logic, only a bag of contradictions. And yet ... my mother had been a confirmed witness. So too my upright and honest father, my straight-as-a-die brother and my dear wise old wily grandfather. They had felt no need to challenge the Bible and question the anomalies of life. What had made me different?

Carefully I picked my way back down the twisting stairs where my body had bounced and bumped its way to the kitchen and a roomful of visitors on the day of my mother's death. I sat on the bottom stair and recalled that time so long ago.

I had instinctively curled myself into a ball which protected my head and face from serious injury but I suffered a severe pounding on my back and buttocks. When I came to a halt one foot was twisted beneath me. Dr McLaren was first at my side.

'That was quite an entrance, Jenny,' he joked before turning serious and commencing his examination. I winced as he took my foot in his hands, twisting and prodding, raising and lowering, and systematically testing for breakages.

'Aha,' he murmured as he did the same with legs and arms and ran his knowing fingers down my spine. Then he relaxed, breathing an audible sigh of relief.

'No breakages but I can promise you some bruises,' he said, and after a searching look at my scowling face added, 'but I think you'll live.'

I took no comfort from the remark. Thoughts of Holy Willie and how I was going to kill him provided more satisfaction.

There were sighs of relief from the concerned onlookers and the anxious silence they'd maintained during the doctor's examination was relieved by quiet murmuring but I still carried the anger which had instigated my fall and was ready to swear that Holy Willie had pushed me. Maybe it was Grandpa's presence that kept me from going that far. The others now crowded round. I felt suffocated and began gasping for breath but kept one eye on Grandpa's ruthless look of suspicion. I saw Callum with the baby in the crook of an arm. Ella started fussing, saying if someone would carry me back up the stairs she'd settle me in my bed.

'You're coming back with me,' said the doctor. 'Mrs McLaren will look after you. Besides I want to keep you under observation for a day or two.'

Like a bug under a microscope, I thought unkindly but I later realized it was a ruse to get me away from the deathbed and its attendant miseries. I co-operated by making the most of my pain. I winced and bravely blinked back my tears. No doubt it was a way of engaging my emotions which were a seething cauldron of energies fast getting out of control. The Reverend Andrew Fraser now dominated the gathering. His large bulk, dog-collared and dark-suited rose stiffly from the chair and in appropriate sobriety addressed family and friends.

'Please be upstanding and let us join hands and hearts in prayer.'

Whatever comfort he might have had in mind was lost on me. The doctor had already seated me on a chair from which I declined to rise, making the most of the swelling already evident on my foot. My body ached with the hammering my tumble had inflicted but not as badly as I made out. The laird, with his customary dignity, joined the small circle of bowed heads and I noticed that Miss Catriona had taken the trouble to relieve Callum of the baby so that he could join the minister's circle.

'Come Jenny,' said Grandpa, his voice devoid of sympathy. 'Ye can lean on me.'

My grandfather was not easily fooled. On the point of weakening I saw Neil Fraser slip into the room. Without a glance at me he joined the circle. His apparent lack of concern infuriated me and I resisted Grandpa's offer of help and stuck stubbornly to my chair. Grandpa left me with unspoken reproof. I didn't care. Something was happening to me.

'Be with us Lord in the hour of our travail,' the minister intoned.

I could feel a fire kindling in my belly. I was experiencing a new energy, both powerful and attractive to my needs. I was beginning to hate. I hated God and I didn't care if he struck me down dead for my wickedness. He had plucked my mother from our midst when he could have managed fine without her.

'Into your hands dear God we commend her spirit.

Bestow thy blessing on this family in this their hour of grief.'

I hated the minister. He was asking God, not telling Him. Folk were always asking God for things they never got. Mostly they got things they hadn't asked for. It had happened to me often enough. I hated Callum for cuddling the baby and ignoring me. I hated Father for having recovered so quickly. But most of all I hated the baby. When Miss Catriona made to put her in my lap, offering her powdered perfume to my nose, her warm flesh to my hands and helpless presence to my sight, I pushed her away with more force than was needed. But the pivot of my hate turned on Holy Willie when he limped himself before me and began an apology for upsetting me, for saying anything that might have offended. Then I knew that what was happening to me was important. Though I couldn't have put a name to it. I was marvelling at the power of my aggression. Nor could I have analyzed or even understood it but I could feel it and intuitively I realized that I could push my demands to the limit with it.

For the next few weeks that's just what I did. I hated, I craved, I condemned and conditioned everything in my orbit. I was a sore trial to my elders and a challenge to the doctor's wife who was caring for me. I couldn't help myself. The devil was in the driving seat and it was easier to carry the hate than the sorrow and the grief.

Mrs McLaren understood something I didn't because my tears and tantrums were returned by kind words and warm embraces. The good doctor ignored them completely but gave the gravest attention to my injuries.

'You'd better stay here till after the funeral,' he advised and I knew it wasn't just my ankle he was considering. I attempted a mild protest.

'Does Graham no need me?' I asked as he prepared to examine my foot.

'He's being taken care of,' he said pulling a chair beside me and sitting down. 'Your aunt and uncle from Glasgow have arrived for the funeral. They're going to stay on for a while.'

My heart sank.

'They're going off to Canada to live,' he continued while I was tackling this uncomfortable piece of information.

I didn't much care for Aunt Sheena, my mother's sister. She was as different from Mother as was possible to imagine. She was a mothball to Mother's lavender, a piece of rough pottery to Mother's delicate porcelain, a peasant to a princess. I didn't care where she was going.

'I wish she was in Canada now,' I grumbled.

The doctor ignored this too. He was as good at ignoring some things as he was skilled at spotting others. 'Let's see that ankle,' he said.

I lifted my foot for his examination.

'You know where Canada is?' he asked, looking at me over the rim of his spectacles.

'Of course I do.'

As he tested my reflexes he proceeded to give me a rundown on the Canadian economy and why it was the best of places for my relations. Uncle Peter who made and sold sweeties in a room and kitchen of a Glasgow tenement had a promise of a real glass-fronted shop in Vancouver. They had good prospects, the doctor said.

'And so have you,' he added, giving me back my foot, and in a few days time we'll send you home. Your Aunt Sheena will take care of you and, if we ask nicely, maybe the schoolmaster will set you some problems to solve. That should keep you out of mischief.'

The next day Big McGreegor's son, Todd, arrived.

'The dominie's sent me with some homework for you,' he announced in his customary forthright fashion.

Although I was secretly pleased to see his stalwart figure and familiar cheeky grin, I pretended otherwise.

'I don't need any homework,' I said, ignoring the books he put on the table beside my chair.

'Clever clogs,' he scoffed. 'I suppose you think you're too good for homework.'

'You know as well as I do, Todd McGreegor, that I'm streets ahead of everyone else. I can afford to miss some schooling.'

'If I made up my mind I could knock spots off you.'

'You! Todd McGreegor, you never work hard at school.'

'Only because I can't be bothered. I've more important things to do.'

'Like making model aeroplanes?'

'What's wrong with that? Callum makes them, doesn't he?'

'Aye, but Callum's at university now studying to be a doctor. I can't see you ever getting to university.'

'Do you want these or don't you?' he said indicating the books at my side.

'I'll think about it.' I sat back in the armchair and gazed at the ceiling.

'Please yourself. I'm off,' he said grumpily. 'I came here to be nice to you but I can see that I'm wasting my time.'

He stamped to the door. On the point of departure he paused and, looking back over his shoulder, grinned his normal cheeky grin saying, 'I'll come again when you're in a better mood - clever clogs.'

I threw a cushion at him but it hit the door which he'd promptly closed behind him possibly guessing my intention. In spite of his inherent good nature which seldom left him, his visit only added to my depression. Ignoring the books by my side I indulged myself in some new hates. I hated Mr Ross, the schoolmaster, and I certainly hated Aunt Sheena.

I had reservations about Uncle Peter. He was kindly and always brought samples of his delicious wares with him when he visited Strathard.

My fast-accumulating hates might have gone on satisfying me if it hadn't been for my grandfather who very soon after the doctor had passed his verdict paid me a purposeful visit. I knew it was purposeful by the scowl on his face. I would have to be careful. It seemed I might be in for a dose of the 'Wisdom of the Ages', as Callum and I called Grandpa's periodic doses of moral instruction. Grandpa seldom went straight to the point.

'Callum will be back to the university next week. He's going to be sorely missed and by naebody more so than the bairn. She's to be called Moira - and there's nae need to purse your lips and wrinkle your nose. The bairn's a fact, Jenny McLeod, and ane you've to learn to face up to.'

I had difficulty looking him in the eyes.

'Like any bairn she has to be watered and fed and cleaned and cuddled and it doesn't happen a' by itsel', ye ken?'

'It's her fault that—'

'Stop your haverin' lass and use some o' the sense you were born with.' He stuck his empty pipe in his mouth.

Fishing his tobacco pouch from his pocket he continued. 'Your Aunt Sheena and Uncle Peter have stayed on since the funeral?'

This was the first reference to the funeral that I had heard. I hadn't wanted to go, nor had the doctor deemed it advisable.

He began stuffing the bowl of his pipe with tobacco while I pressed home my disapproval.

'And where am I supposed to sleep?'

'In the box bed,' he said, bending across the hearth for a taper.

A vision of my mother the last time I'd seen her alive lying in pain on that self-same bed horrified me.

'I can't!' I gasped.

'You surely can,' he said before applying the lighted taper to the tobacco and puffing in obvious satisfaction.

I drew the rich flavour of the tobacco into my nostrils finding some comfort in its familiarity and associations but I retreated into a sulky silence.

'Your Aunt Sheena has been a real help.'

I made no response but made a great thing of puffing the cushion on my chair.

'They're emigrating to Canada in a week or two. Your uncle has guid prospects in Canada.'

I remained silent, intent on tying my shoelaces.

For a few minutes he puffed away with enjoyment then, knocking his pipe on the hearth, said quietly, 'It was a fine funeral.'

I sat up and looked at Grandpa direct. 'I don't want to hear about it.'

'Jenny lass,' he said fingering the point of his well-trimmed beard. 'Your mother's in Heaven now.'

'And where's Heaven, Grandpa?' I asked throwing my head back and rolling my eyes to the ceiling.

He waved his pipe at me. 'It's young Neil you should be askin' that question of.'

I jumped out of my chair. 'Holy Willie!' I put all the disgust I could muster into my voice.

'Sit ye doon and listen to me, Jenny McLeod, who is never slow to complain when the McGreegor twins shout names after her wee brother.'

'That's different,' I said sulkily.

'Not a bit of it. Young Neil's mother would be just as hurt if she heard what you're callin' her lad, as you are hurt when the twins misca' our youngster. You don't have to live in a castle to have some breedin' ye ken, and folks wi' breedin' respect the dignity of their fellow man. Young Neil is a fine honest upstandin' cratur - a bit of a sober-sides I'll admit, but you wouldn't get him harmin' man, fowl or beast.'

'He's so sanctimonious.'

Grandpa's eyes opened wide in feigned astonishment. 'Sanctimonious, you say. Now there's a fine word for you. What does it mean?'

'You know fine what it means. He's always praying, thinks God can do no wrong. Always telling me how I should feel. He's not interested in how I really feel.'

'To my mind,' ruminated Grandpa, 'that doesn't sound like an excuse for being rude.' Then without warning he changed tack.

'And when are ye thinkin' o' comin' hame? I fairly miss you.'

When I saw him eyeing me fondly I felt my new powerful energy fast dissipating while another more familiar one sneaked in to take its place. In a flash I was in his arms and sobbing on his jacket. It seemed that if I couldn't have the hate I'd just have to try and suffer the grief.

To my surprise, after the first few minutes of angst, I felt better. My grandfather had worked his usual magic. My spirits lifted and I now felt ready to move on.

It was only when the McLarens waved us off and Tillytudlem headed for home that my relief in going there began to waver. Would I be expected to look after the baby? Aunt Sheena and Uncle Peter would be going to Canada. Callum would be going to university. Father would be working. There would only be Grandpa and me and of course, there would be Wee Graham to mind. I'd soon be going back to school myself. I didn't mind looking after Graham but I was determined to have nothing to do with the baby. I thought I'd make this clear to Grandpa from the start.

'Do you understand?' I asked after giving him a rundown of my feelings.

'Aye, I understand fine. You can't abide the bairn. You blame her for losin' your mother and as far as you're concerned she can go to the devil.'

'I didn't say that.'

'As good as. Still, it's a' for the best. I shouldn't think you'd worry ower much if we let the bairn go.'

'Go where?'

'Your aunt and uncle want to take her tae Canada.'

'They can't!' I gasped.

'They can, ye ken. That's if we a' agree to it.' 'I don't agree.'

'I thocht you'd be glad to be rid o' her.'

'Well you thocht wrong.'

That's when I realized the seat of my real fears. It was the memory of my mother's deathbed expectations of me that somehow I would look after them all and keep them all together, even the baby. I was convinced that I had made her this promise and the magnitude of it I had yet to face. So far I hadn't been able to voice my fears and now, when my grandfather might have been prepared to listen I couldn't find the words.

'If you could but hear yersel', he was saying to me. 'One minute you want this, the next minute you want that. I don't think you ken whit you want.'

'I ken fine what I don't want and that's the bairn.'

'Weel then, let the bairn go. You'll soon get used to the idea,' said Grandpa, 'they're no leavin' for Canada for a wee while yet.'

On reaching home we found Aunt Sheena nursing Moira and at the same time chastising Graham.

'You dirty wee thing,' she was saying as we walked into the kitchen. The saliva was running down Graham's chin and he had wet his pants. My temper flared.

'He can't help it,' I yelled.

'Then it's time he did,' she replied putting Moira's bottle on the fender before throwing the baby over one shoulder to break wind. 'That one needs some handling, that's no mistake,' she said nodding her head at Graham.

The same head was topped by a black velour hat perched on top of severely dressed iron-grey hair and was secured by an enormously dangerous looking hat pin. Her black dress was covered by a floral pinny and bib and her feet were encased in black buttoned-up boots.

'We handle him all he needs,' I shouted at her, 'and we don't need any handling of yours.'

'Jenny!' warned Grandpa. 'Apologize to your aunt at once.'

'Why?' I saw his face harden.

'Because I say so.'

'You heard what—'

Jenny!' There was no escape. I apologized through clenched teeth.

'You don't seem to have improved much over the years,' commented Aunt Sheena running her eyes over the length and breadth of me. 'You always were too big for your boots.'

Wee Graham was upset and needed no second bidding to follow me upstairs where I cleaned him and changed his clothes. His face brightened when I suggested a walk. I took his hand and together, without a word to the prim figure now cooing softly at the bundle in her arms, we walked out of the house into the sunshine and under the archway whose covering creeper was now blushing at the edges. I made for the river, helping Graham to pick white clover and milkwort. There were blackberries and wild raspberries in abundance.

Graham wanted to paddle and I indulged him, taking off my own socks to wipe his feet dry when he'd had enough. His legs were skin and bone. I thought of Callum's sturdy limbs and how handsome and healthy he always looked. I tried to hide my rush of tears from Graham as I fitted his socks round his ankle bones and witnessed his delight so disproportionate to his pleasure. He'd never be strong like Callum, nor clever, and I felt acutely the pathos of his circumstances. I had a momentary vision of what life was going to be like for him as he got older and of the attention he was always going to need, but that was another of those thoughts that had to be pushed out of mind. I was fast discovering that there were some things that were just too much to handle. I'd even lost the spirit to handle the reception we received on returning home.

'Have you no sense young madam than to go swimming with the likes of him?'

My guts screwed but I managed to stay calm. 'We were only paddling.'

'Paddling, swimming, whatever! The last thing you should be doing is encouraging someone like him to go into the water. Before you know it he'll be getting himself drowned. You're completely irresponsible.'

My spirits plummeted. This was something I could do without. Callum was no help either. At the first opportunity while taking a walk together, I tackled him.

'Do you want the baby to go to Canada?' I asked.

'It isn't up to me. I'll only be here at weekends and when I go to university, not even then.'

'But Mother—'

'Mother would want the best for her. Aunt Sheena is Mother's sister and she has the means to bring her up so that she won't want for anything.'

That wasn't what I wanted to say. I had wanted to tell him of Mother's death wish but it didn't seem the right time after all. I wanted rid of this growing burden of guilt. I wanted to ask Callum what would happen if I didn't keep Mother's death-bed wish. Had I promised her? I couldn't remember. It was bad enough just knowing what she wanted.

We had been walking through the wood bound on the further side by a drystone dyke. About to skim over the dyke to take a short cut home, we stopped suddenly. Lower down the field was the tall, broad-shouldered frame of the gamekeeper. His back was towards us and by his side was the slim figure of a woman.

'That's Her Ladyship,' I hissed.

'Sh!' warned Callum.

As we watched, McGreegor turned towards Catriona and after a minute's conversation he pulled her against him and bending his head covered her mouth with his own.

'Did you see that?' I gasped.

'I did not,' said Callum, 'and neither did you.' 'But—'

'It's none of our business. I don't want to hear another word.'

We ducked our heads and made a detour back home in silence. Callum could maybe stop me talking about what we had just witnessed but he couldn't stop me thinking. What would Ella say if she knew her man was kissing another woman and what would Mr Stacey do if he knew his woman was kissing another man and that the man was the same one who had taken a pot-shot at him not so long ago? And Todd! Unexpectedly, I wished I had been nicer to Todd.

CHAPTER 4

While I had been sitting hunched on the bottom step just inside the kitchen, lost in painful memories of almost 30 years gone by, it had grown dark. I was cold and cramped. I was confused by the unfamiliar shadows of the room. I had lost any sense of direction and was slow to focus. Gradually what light there was from the stars shone through the window aperture. After a few stretches to restore circulation I cautiously picked my way towards the grey shape which looked like a door.

My reminiscences had done nothing more than depress me. Was this really the way to sort out one's life, I wondered. Was I being as stupid as my husband had declared? I tripped over some wooden obstruction and only saved myself from falling in the nick of time. While taking a few steadying breaths a shadow seemed to flit across the window. Imagination? Then I heard what could only be a horse's hoof on the cobbles. That wasn't imagination. That was real. I stood still, straining my ears, feeling my racing heart send blood coursing to my scalp. This was eerie. The long silence which followed was as unnerving as the strange sound. Why should a horse be here?

I waited a few minutes more when I could hear nothing but the distant sound of a dog barking. I gave myself a mental shake and threaded my way towards the doorway around a seemingly endless trail of dangers. When I stepped outside there was no sign of anyone.

I chided myself. That's what comes of listening to Flora's prattle. I'd be telling myself next that it was the devil in a cloak and floppy hat. I set out for the hotel at a brisk trot but kept looking anxiously around convincing myself that I was being watched. Thankfully I reached the drive and hurried to the portico and brightly lit hall.

I decided that I couldn't put off phoning my husband. He would have finished his Wednesday Bible class by now and be waiting for a phone call. What was I to tell him? Certainly not what he wanted to know because I didn't know myself yet.

There was only the telephone at the desk available and it was too near the garrulous Flora but at least this would have the advantage of being a good excuse for impersonal chit-chat only. Come to think of it, that was all Neil and I managed now.

As expected, Flora kept within earshot.

'When are you coming home?' he wanted to know. 'I've barely arrived.'

'Don't know why you're there at all. Don't know what you expect to find there.'

'It's all changed,' I commented.

'What did you expect? Have you been to the kirk yet?'

I couldn't enlarge on this because of Flora's cocked ears. For some time now my husband had hankered to return to his father's old church and I'd had my work cut out dissuading him.

'I can't talk now but I'll write soon.'

We exchanged a few desultory remarks and then I rang off. We had said nothing.

I went to bed early, having decided that I'd take a good look around the estate, or what had once been the estate, in the morning. I wasn't tired though, and in spite of myself could not check my compulsive memories.

My aunt and uncle's visit, I recalled, had stretched from weeks to months through spring and well into summer. I had been made to do my share of watering, feeding and cleaning Moira but I refused to cuddle. 'Thrawn' was what Grandpa called me.

For a time I had managed to forget my mother's last words to me but the worry and the fear of them was festering in my subconscious. The more I tried to smother them out of existence the more often they asserted themselves in terrifying nightmares. Sometimes I'd scream everyone out of their beds in the middle of the night. Sometimes I'd dislike my aunt so much I'd wish all sorts of mishaps upon her. I'd often tremble at my daring.

Father was no help. In fact, he was worse than useless and had been spending more and more time at the Strathard Arms. Seldom a night had passed but he drank there, often not getting home until the rest of us were in bed and he would frequently fall asleep in the kitchen chair. At first I used to keep awake listening for his feet on the cobbles, waiting for him to come in and pass by my bed, hoping for some attention and reassurance. I never got it. Instead I was forced to lie in the box bed pretending to sleep while, reeking of whisky, he snored the night away in his chair.

His work was suffering. Grandpa was constantly covering for him. As well as doing most of the household chores, grooming the horses and minding Graham, he was doing Father's work of washing and polishing the castle cars and sometimes chauffeuring the laird while Father was recovering from a worse than usual hangover.

'You should be downright ashamed of yourself,' Aunt Sheena stormed at him one morning when, coming downstairs, she found him lying on the floor having been sick on the rag rug before he'd managed to reach the kitchen sink. 'Fiona will be turning in her grave, God rest her soul.'

I lay in misery unable to shut my ears to their arguments.

'No good will come of it,' she harped on. 'If you're not careful you'll end up in the gutter.'

'Stop nagging, woman,' said Father beginning to clean up his mess.

She Ignored his remark and continued her tirade.

'You're fit for nothing getting. It's wicked letting the laird down the way you do. When the laird gets to hear of your drunken state - and get to hear he will, take my word for it - he'll soon find another chauffeur, and where would you a' be then, might I ask?' She sniffed in derision.

Father stamped out of the house. 'See to the waen, woman,' he yelled as Moira howled from her pram.

The day of departure eventually arrived. I stood in the kitchen watching Uncle Peter come down the stairs with Aunt Sheena behind him carrying Moira. I moved closer to Callum holding Wee Graham tightly by the hand. At that moment, seeing them stuffed and starched in their finery and Moira expensively bundled in a white angora shawl knitted painstakingly by Aunt Sheena, I didn't know what I felt most - relief to be quit of them or anger at Father who was showing signs of changing his mind. Grandpa who would be saying his goodbyes at the station was in the Square harnessing Tillytudlem to the trap.

Hands clenched at my side I watched Callum receiving a handshake and a peck on the cheek before extending his own hand to pat the baby's head. I could almost hear Father beside him saying, as he offered the baby a large horny finger to clutch, am I doing the right thing?

It'll soon be over, my mind said, while my body accommodated another feeling, a prick of conscience, immediately smothered by my aunt's parting shot.

'As for you, young lady, you'd do well to mind your manners. "Dogs bark as they are bred" ye ken? I'll see this yin kens better.'

I was so mad and miserable I made short shrift of saying goodbye to my uncle. I would be sorry later. He was a kind and gentle man.

Although I was glad that Moira had gone out of my life, the continuing nightmares proved she was still a threat to my peace of mind.

'I can depend on you ... keep them all together and the bairn,' Mother had said and for weeks after Moira had been taken away from us and was beginning a new life in Canada her power over me got mightier. I blamed her for my nightmares and dreaded going to bed.

It was inevitable that my school work suffered and after a particularly undistinguished day at my lessons the master asked me to wait behind while he dismissed the rest of the school.

'Is something bothering you?' he asked, not unkindly. 'Things aren't that easy,' I mumbled transferring my satchel from one hand to the other.

'I can appreciate that and I've made allowances but giving up on your schooling isn't the answer. Being satisfied to grovel around in the dark isn't the answer either.'

The master was perched on the corner of his desk with his arms across his chest. I laid my satchel carefully on my desk, giving him grudging attention.

I looked at his shiny suit with the frayed cuffs then raised my gaze to meet those challenging eyes.

'It's not escape you should be looking for, Jenny. It's opportunity. Look for your source of power and tap into it.'

'I thought you didn't believe in God,' I accused once again reaching for my satchel.

'Who said anything about God?'

'Tapping into a source of power and all that stuff.'

33

'I'm talking about your mind.'

He slipped from his desk and stood towering above me.

'Open it! There's more than one god out there and they're all worth getting to know. In time you can take your pick or if you find none of them to your liking you can aye invent one of your own.'

'And how am I to find all these gods, as if one to contend with isn't bad enough? Besides I don't know where to look.'

'For pity's sake, Jenny, you can start by getting back into stride with your lessons. You can't go on resting on your laurels.'

I was the most promising pupil the school had ever had, so I'd been told often enough. I was top in every subject and had been for some time. There had never been a serious rival.

'Todd's creeping up on you,' warned the master, beginnng to order his desk.

'He'll never catch me up,' I declared, grabbing my satchel and slipping my arms in the straps.

'Don't you be too sure, Jenny McLeod. There's more to Todd McGreegor than meets the eye.'

My satchel now securely on my shoulders, I left in a sulk.

I supposed it was time to knuckle down but it wasn't easy. I was just beginning to realize how useful Aunt Sheena had been. Grandpa took on as many of the domestic chores as he could but Graham was the escalating problem. His life seemed to be spent trying to possess my time and attention completely. Mother's death, followed by my aunt's antagonism, had affected my younger brother badly. The only time he was prepared to let me be was if Neil Fraser was around. It would seem that his short stay at the manse after our mother's death and until after the funeral had established a bond between them.

There had been something in the schoolmaster's remarks about Todd McGreegor after all. I watched him closely. He began to take his school work seriously. His marks shot up and I knew that if I didn't look out I'd be ousted from my top dog status. Todd was a year older than me but as I was considered advanced for my years we were taught in the same group.

There began a deadly contest between us in which the schoolmaster and most of the class participated. The class split into two camps. My camp was heavily outnumbered. This only served to make me more determined than ever to retain the position I'd always thought would never be threatened.

The master decided to cash in on a wonderful opportunity for progress, leading the contest on from Todd versus me to Todd's camp followers versus mine. He spurred us on until we were like bees in a honey pot abuzz with meaningful effort. After one particularly bracing lesson the master arced an arm to include the lavish display of our many efforts brightening the classroom walls.

'This all began,' he queried, 'from what?'

'A miracle, sir?' said Todd.

Everyone laughed while Todd beamed in acknowledgement.

'You might say that,' smiled Mr Ross. 'But it was much more simple than that.' We cocked our ears. 'It began with an idea. Todd's idea! Yes. Todd had an idea, or to put it plainly, a thought, a special thought.'

'Had I?' Todd's eyes widened in feigned surprise as he scanned the admiring audience.

The master, thumbs stuck behind his braces, left his desk and faced Todd whose face was alight with his cheeky grin.

'Didn't you say to yourself Todd, "I think I'll do better at my lessons. I'll begin by paying attention in class and doing my homework. I'll try to get good marks." Am I right Todd?'

A sea of faces swept from teacher to Todd.

'I had only one idea,' grinned Todd, 'and that was to be better than Jenny McLeod. I was getting fed up with her superior airs. I just thought she needed bringing down a peg or two.'

There was a resounding cheer from the class and the schoolmaster smiled, saying, 'But the only way you could do that was to work harder yourself, eh? And incidentally, Jenny is still ahead of you.'

'But not for much longer, sir.'

The McGreegor camp cheered which set up a chorus of jeers from camp McLeod.

'But you see what I'm getting at,' said Mr Ross. 'The power of thought! Never underestimate it!' Every eye kept tagging him as he paced the classroom floor. 'Everything has its beginnings in thought. Somebody has to think of building a castle before it can be built. Someone has to think of saying something before it can be said. Someone has to think of working before any work is done. Our thoughts are what we call cause and what happens because of them is called effect.'

The schoolmaster had a way of making me sprout wings and fly high in my imagination. I found his ideas irresistible. They touched upon a secret part of me.

'Remember this, children. It's our thoughts which prompt our actions.' Pacing his words slowly and deliberately he continued. 'Sow an act, and you will reap a habit. Sow a habit, and you will reap a destiny, because habits build character. This is the sequence: an act, a habit, a character, and a destiny. You are the creator of yourself.'* He paused to let this idea sink in. 'So you see, Todd's thought had a spin-off on us all and changed our lessons from boredom to enthusiasm, from having to work to wanting to work.' He paused at my desk and when he continued he seemed to be talking directly to me.

'You can change anything you like by the power of thought.'

There was a hushed stillness broken only by a songbird on the tree outside the window.

'Sir,' I ventured. 'Can a thought change God?'

There was a subdued titter at this strange turn in the conversation. I didn't care because I had faith that the master would take my question seriously.

'Yes, Jenny. I think it could. Your thought makes your God. God is different to different people depending on their thoughts.'

Tam McGreegor had had enough!

'Whit's she on aboot talking about God and Heaven? I expect it's because her mither's deid.'

His twin brother was out of his seat in a flash. He grabbed Tam by the scruff of the neck hauling hir from his seat before delivering a punch on the nose Tam reeled. Mr Ross quickly intervened. I sat oper mouthed and amazed like a Guinevere witnessing a jous for her favour. I was the cause and Tam's bloody nose was the effect. All I needed was a floral tribute to thro' at the feet of my Sir Lancelot. By one swift involuntary action Todd McGreegor had defended my honour. From a teasing tormentor, then serious rival, he'd donned the mantle of Knight Errant and had astonishingly attained, in my eyes at least, the grandeur of hero status.

From that day on I looked at Todd with new interest and respect. I sought his company whenever I could1 asked his advice, shared my ideas and even shared my lunch-box so lovingly packed by Grandpa when Todd had already eaten his. It wasn't long before we took to walking together and talking about our lessons and other things. His response to my onslaught of advances was never short of chivalrous. I adored him.

Somewhere in the hotel a door slammed. It jolted me to wakefulness. I had been treading the borderland of sleep. Now it beckoned fully. From all my memories I chose the image I wanted to take with me into that little death. I went hand in hand with Todd McGreegor, the lad with the curly hair, the laughing eyes and cheeky grin. For the first time since learning of my inheritance I smiled in happiness and slept soundly until the cockerel heralded the dawn.

CHAPTER 5

A glance at my watch told me it was too early to leave my bed. I turned over but in spite of being comfortable, sleep did not return. I let my thoughts return to Todd, wrapping them around my spirit as snugly as I wrapped the blankets tighter to my body.

I was back in Strathard more than a year after my mother's death. Todd and I had just finished a study lesson with the schoolmaster. We were walking home together through the wood when we saw Todd's father and Catriona in one of the lower fields. McGreegor had his arm around Her Ladyship who was aiming a gun at a target perched on the branch of a tree.

'He's giving her lessons,' mumbled Todd when there was no way he could pretend he hadn't seen them.

Not knowing what to say I said nothing. Although I was growing up fast and learning about the world even faster I didn't know how to handle a situation like this. What I did know as I scrambled through the bracken after Todd, was that just such a situation changed him from a jolly companion to a surly brow-furrowed boy kicking at every tuft of grass he could find and swearing at a rabbit who shot past his feet.

Seeing his normally genial face downcast with embarrassment I had the strongest urge to put my arms round him and hold him close. It had been a long time since I'd been cuddled unless you counted Graham. My imagination was finding fresh fields in the thought of a different kind of cuddle. I enjoyed being close to Todd. I liked his boyish strength, his fresh open face and his smile which began in his eyes. He was never moody and always quick to see the funny side of things. He could make me laugh and he could also make me stamp my feet. I stretched out my hand with a wish to comfort but, as if guessing my intention, he shied away then tore recklessly ahead. I tried to keep up but leg weary and panting for breath I lost him. I returned home feeling like a maiden scorned.

When I arrived Callum was wiping Graham's face while Grandpa was putting his slippers and some of his toys in a bag.

'What's happening? Where's Graham going?' I asked in alarm.

'Dinna fash yersel',' said Grandpa. Callum's taking him to the manse. Neil says he'll look after him for the day.'

My first reaction was annoyance, not far short of anger but Callum, sensing this, intervened.

'Graham loves being with Neil, Jenny, and both you and Grandpa aren't averse to the benefit.'

I checked my angry retort. I looked at Graham and for the first time noticed that his hair needed cutting. The bloom had faded from his cheeks. He was thinner and more restless. I sighed and for the umpteenth time wondered how my mother had managed to do everything needed and always be there for us.

'I suppose you're right. I am rather a beast where Neil's concerned and he has been good with Graham.'

'Neil likes you, Jenny.'

'Neil is a soldier of Christ and only wants to convert me. He can't accept the fact that I don't think the way he does and he thinks he can make me. I'm convinced he's targeted me for the first of the sinners he is dedicated to save.'

'You know what I think?' said Callum.

'No, what do you think?'

'I think you're afraid of Neil. You cannot cope with anyone who doesn't think the way you do.'

'Rubbish!' I said, but to myself I wondered. Maybe I was a little afraid of him. He was so sure of everything that scared me to bits but I'd be a fool not to be grateful to him for looking after Graham as often as he did. I wouldn't be able to give so much time to my lessons otherwise. I hugged Graham fondly then waved my brothers off.

'Make sure you help Grandpa with the housework,' said Callum. He had disappeared before I could retort.

I went inside and stood looking round the kitchen and noticed sights for a long time ignored. The kitchen range hadn't been black-leaded since Mother had gone. The windows were smeared. There were pans under the sink awaiting a good scrub. The mantelpiece was dusty. The rugs needed beating and the brass scuttle could do with polishing. As my eyes travelled the length and breadth of the kitchen my spirits sank. My mother would be ashamed of the state the house was in and what would she think of Graham. She would be disappointed in me and no doubt she would be looking kindly on Neil Fraser who gave so much of his time to Graham. For my mother's sake I would try to think more kindly of the minister's son.

While Grandpa went off to do some outside jobs I rolled up my sleeves and set to. Callum, having delivered Graham at the manse came back some time later and, after congratulating me on my hard work, said he'd help me make a rabbit stew.

Suddenly, overwhelmingly, I was overcome with sadness and, flopping on to the fender stool, I began to blubber.

'Oh Callum! I do miss Mother!' I said searching my pockets for a handkerchief.

Callum handed me his handkerchief. "I know. We all do. I'll speak to Father about getting some help with the housework.'

'It's not that. Besides, we can't afford it,' I sniffed, wiping the tears on my cheek. 'And Grandpa's a great help.'

Callum sat on the opposite stool looking serious.

'I'm worried about Grandpa. He's beginning to go downhill. I think he's doing too much,' he said.

Panic signals! It seemed to me that we were living under constant threat, swinging from one crisis to another. Was there to be no end to it?

'As a matter of fact,' said Callum, 'I'm going to find a job in Edinburgh.'

'What, sort of job?' I asked, forgetting my own distress. 'Anything that pays.'

'But you're going to be a doctor!'

'I'm going to get a job!'

'You're going to do no such thing!' It was Grandpa booming from the doorway. He strode grim-faced into the kitchen, taking up a challenging stance before his grandson.

'Get any sic notion right out o' your heid!'

Callum rose to his feet.

'It will be years before I can earn any money.' He spoke defiantly.

'We're no worse off now than we were before - as far as money is concerned,' said Grandpa.

Callum took a step closer. 'But suppose Father loses his job, and the way he's behaving he's going the right way about it. He practically lives in the Strathard Arms and the whisky isn't given away for nothing.'

'Don't be disrespectful,' said Grandpa unwaveringly. 'We'll cross that bridge should we ever meet it.'

Was it my imagination or was he really looking older? As if to refute this he again dominated the conversation by drawing on his authority and subjecting Callum to further censure.

'As for you, young Callum, I don't want to hear another word about looking for a job. You're the ane aye shootin' off your tongue about the depression and the dole queues. I wad hae thought you'd consider your chances o' findin' work in Edinburgh finished afore they even started.'

Fetching his pipe from the rack he sat down heavily in his rocking chair.

'I'll join the Air Force if they'll have me,' said Callum. 'I'll be eighteen next birthday and if Father loses his job at least it will be one mouth less to feed.'

Grandpa struggled between anger and exasperation.

'Stop your damned heroics and put your mind tae doctorin'.' He hadn't finished. 'Oh aye. I ken whit you'd rather be gettin' up to. It widna be to dae wi these socialist papers ye keep bringin' hame. You're in Edinburgh tae learn doctorin' no the politics and the like. The dominie has a lot to answer for!'

He began stuffing tobacco into the bowl of his pipe as if that was the end of the matter.

The schoolmaster's influence over his pupils had long been a bone of contention with Grandpa and a bone that he regularly chewed with Callum whose teeth kept gnashing at it now.

'The dominie's a free thinker and considers it his right to challenge the status quo,' he asserted.

The pipe was pointed at Callum like an accusing finger.

'Free thinkin'! That's what you ca' it, is it? I ca' it radicalism.'

Grandpa's dander was up. To him Archie Ross was a cultural sniper shooting off all the decencies of the Scottish feudal system. He had no tolerance for the schoolmaster's political colour. According to Grandpa Archie Ross didn't know what was good for him or for his charges. Grandpa believed that the aristocracy had been born to lead and he had never tired of telling Callum and me that if we had any' sense, we'd show a bit more appreciation of having the honour of serving them. Archie Ross, on the other hand, had some high-flown notion of equality and, according to Grandpa, instead of concentrating his teaching on the three Rs, spent his time - and the laird's money - on filling his pupils' heads with broken glass.

I looked at those two adversaries, Grandpa like fire in his wrath, Callum maintaining a stubborn front. I was seeing a side of my brother that bothered me. Rightly or wrongly he was giving me more heavy emotional baggage to lug around, more uncertainties to live with, more confusions! So long as he was in Edinburgh I could see him regularly. Once in the Air Force he could be sent anywhere. Was that what he wanted? He was certainly doing his best to convince our grandfather that this was exactly what he wanted.

'Things change Grandpa,' said Callum with strained patience.

'And so do folk - and no always for the best!' The taper was lit and the puffing commenced.

There was little patience in Grandpa's argument. The feud had ended as quickly as it had begun but as far as I was concerned the damage was done.

Our insecurity had again been highlighted and for the next few days my imagination went into top gear. To make matters worse Graham fell sick and we had to call in Dr McLaren.

'He's stretching a bit,' said the doctor. 'His body's changing fast and it needs time to adjust.' He prescribed a tonic. 'I'll make it a big one,' he said to Grandpa, 'and you could take a spoonful or two yourself. You look as if you could do with it.'

Words, worries and fears! The pattern was becoming very familiar. I had to learn to accept the words, ignore the worries and hope that the fears would not materialize. Little did I know that before the day had finished my fears would again become nightmares.

Callum made some pretext to get me out of the house. I covered his footsteps in silence, conscious of the resolution in his stride, the ramrod back and the feeling of determined intent being demonstrated. He didn't halt until we reached one of the many rickety bridges to be found spanning the river. Leaning one elbow on its wooden rail he turned towards me. 'There's something I think you should know,' he said.

His eyes had darkened, taking on the reflection of the peaty water beneath. His determination was emphasized by the firm set jaw and unsmiling mouth.

'Good or bad?' I leaned on the rail, my eyes on a leaf being borne on the water to an unknown destination.

'It depends on the way you look on it.'

The leaf was followed by others and I was reminded that this was the beginning of autumn. I turned to look at my brother.

'That means bad.'

'For you maybe but for somebody else good - very good.' He avoided my eyes. His determination was cracking and I could detect a creeping discomfort. The stretch of water below us was known as Black Rock Pool, the deepest part of the 30-mile stretch of the small river. It was here that the salmon rested under the large boulders and with patient baiting could often be coaxed out of their hiding places. Callum was sinking into silence as I waited for an explanation of his words.

'Well? Tell me,' I baited.

'You know how Neil is gey fond of Graham,' he said straightening to face me.

'I suppose,' frowning.

'He's been making enquiries in Edinburgh. Since he's studying for the cloth, and with his father being already a minister of the kirk, they know all the important kirk people in the capital. They know where to go for advice and help and they know what help is available.'

'Stop hedging and get on with it,' I said, tossing my plaits off my face.

'This last week in Edinburgh he's been finding out what help there might be for Graham.'

More alarm bells! Callum hurried on, his voice dropping to a murmur. I edged closer to him.

'It seems the Church of Scotland has a home in Edinburgh for people such as Graham.'

'People such as Graham,' I echoed taking a backward step.

My brother just didn't know the best way of saying what had to be said but that one phrase told me everything. 'Peole such as Graham! I held my panic at bay allowing my easy temper full reign.

If red hair was linked with temper then it had to be noted that my hair was very very red.

'What gives Neil Fraser the right to make such enquiries?'

'It seems Catriona asked him to. It was her idea. She feels it is too much to ask of you and Grandpa to look after Graham. His condition is not going to improve as he grows older.'

Whoever painted the devil's eyes red had got it right!

I glared at my brother. My mind was racing ahead. Thoughts! Deeds! Destinies! Wasn't that what the master had said? Was Graham's destiny going to be decided by a thought in the mind of Her Ladyship, a thought among her other thoughts busily mucking up other people's destinies.

"People such as Graham" as you put it, get in the way of the rest of us. Is that what she thinks? They demand too much from us, make life difficult for us, tire us out. Better to get rid of them - in the nicest possible way, of course. They have special homes for "people such as Graham" and, of course, since Neil Fraser's mixed up in it they must be godly homes administered by godly people. What I want to know is why God made "people such as Graham" in the first place?'

It was the question I'd been asking for as long as I could remember and it was a question nobody could answer. I felt confused but greater than my confusion was my anger.

'It's God again,' I said to an uncomfortably bemused Callum. 'It's God behind it. Bugger God! Bugger Neil Fraser! Bugger Catriona McKenzie!' I choked on my curses and fought tears of rage but my brother was not giving sympathy. He turned on me.

'You must stop this nonsense about God. You can't seem to say anything without bringing God into it. It's becoming an obsession with you. It's unhealthy.'

Callum's temper was outstripping his concern and had the desired effect of both calming and shaming me. It was true what he said. Most of my contemporaries were obsessed with toys and boys or trains, football or fighting games but I was obsessed with God. Their obsessions were acceptable. It was all right to fantasize about boys or fighting toys but you were considered queer or quirky to wonder what life was all about.

According to Dr McLaren it was Graham's body that was growing out of reach of his mind. According to my reckoning it was my mistrust of the world which was growing and playing havoc with my judgement. I think I left my childhood forever on the bridge at Black Rock Pool and was being plunged by cataclysmic events into the deeper waters of the adult. But, I thought, as I followed Callum back home, was I adult enough to deal with this calamity? And Mother! Far from keeping the family all together I seemed to be losing them one by one.

CHAPTER 6

They were all in the kitchen waiting for us. The Reverend Andrew Fraser held the floor, emphasizing some point with outstretched arms and upturned palms, his head thrown back. All good theatre. Neil stood leaning against the table, his bad leg outstretched, his eyes turning on me as I entered. I felt them boring into my skull, searching out my thoughts and no doubt finding them not to his liking. He looked displeased but then he generally did when he looked at me. I went straight to my grandfather who was rocking gently in his chair. Father stood beside him and made the unusual gesture of placing an arm around my shoulders.

The talking had stopped when we appeared. It was obvious that I had been the subject of their conversation and my father's protective arm did nothing to allay my fears. I could guess what had been the substance of their conversation. How will she take it? Will she make it difficult for us? You know how attached she is to the child. It is for the child's own good. She must be made to see that. Oh yes, I had absorbed the substance of their argument before a word was addressed to me.

'Where's Graham?' I asked.

'Ella's looking after him for a while,' said Father.

'Has Callum put you in the picture about Wee Graham then?' asked the Reverend Fraser.

'Callum has told me you intend taking him from us and putting him in a home.'

'Come, come Jenny. We are doing your family a great service. Your young brother will not always be young. His needs are going to increase as he grows into manhood and you won't be able to cope.'

I moved from Father to confront the minister full face.

'We love him. I thought the kirk preached the power of love and that it could move mountains,' I challenged, unmoved by ministerial compassion.

'That's faith,' replied Neil casually, still leaning his weight on the table.

I turned to look at him.

'It's faith,' he took pains to explain, 'that can remove mountains, not love.'

I threw him a look of contempt. I resented his correction but then I resented everything about this person.

'Grandpa?' I pleaded, dropping on my knees beside him while he changed his unlit pipe from one hand to the other, feeling in his pockets for his tobacco pouch. I had seldom seen him so obviously discomfited.

'Wi' the best will in the world lass, I canna give him a' the attention he needs.'

'Tell Jenny about the place Graham's going to,' said the minister to his son in placatory tones.

I rounded on him. 'I don't want to hear it. I don't want Graham to leave Strathard.'

'We can visit him often,' said Father, moving towards me. 'He's no likely to forget us, ye ken?'

'More likely you'll forget him,' I said, backing away. 'It'll be easy enough when you won't need to put yourself out for him.'

Callum spoke. 'This has all been a shock for Jenny. We shouldn't have sprung it on her like this.'

'It was Her Ladyship's idea,' said the minister in honeyed tones.

'So that makes it all right, does it?' I scoffed. I felt stiff and angular in my belligerence.

I didn't fail to notice the disapproval in the eyes of both men of the cloth at my outburst. The minister took considerable pains to inform me how magnanimous it was of Her Ladyship to consider mine and my family's welfare, not to mention the long-term benefits for Graham. Neil, taking his cue from his father, made a determined effort to be patient with me, explaining in what wonderful manner this would all happen. Encouraged by my silence he painted a reassuring picture of the 'home' and the people who ran it - all God-fearing Christians. Grandpa, who had found his pouch, was thumbing tobacco into the bowl of his pipe.

He nodded gently as Neil spoke. My heart sank and Callum looked as miserable as I felt.

They were ranged against me. I wanted to fight. I had the feelings but I didn't have the words. I had thought our love for Graham was all the argument I'd need but it wasn't enough. Graham's needs were too many. Everything they said about his physical demands increasing with age and his lack of simple, self-sustaining skills was true. We didn't have the right kind of support system needed. What could an old man, a heartbroken father, an absent brother and myself do for Graham, both now and in the years to come. I looked at them, all so sure that sending Graham to a home was the best thing for him and the rest of us. How was that to be measured against the loss of his happy, sunny-natured and lovable personality? Then my heart did a funny little leap. That might have been true once. His had been the light that shone the brightest in our home. But could that be said of him now? Recent images clicked in my mind - unkempt hair, palour, wet pants and tears, a sum total of pitiful dependency. Could that be right for him?

The fight went out of me. I could be as brave as Mother might have wished but there was no way I could keep them all together. I fled from the room. The nearest refuge was the coach-house and here I indulged in a dollop of self-pity, convincing myself that I had failed my mother once again. It was all my fault! When Neil Fraser joined me I was in no mood to be civil.

'I hope you're satisfied,' I accused, conscious of my red-rimmed eyes and how unattractive I must look to him. One plait had lost its ribbon.

'Look at you,' he scoffed. 'Crying like a spoilt brat. Tears of self-pity. When are you going to grow up, Jenny McLeod?'

There was neither pity nor sympathy in his voice. I met his contemptuous look with shattering dismay.

'You realize,' he continued coldly, 'that your attitude is totally selfish. You're not thinking of Graham's welfare. You're only concerned with yourself.'

It wasn't criticism I needed then but comfort. I yearned for my mother, anguished at my helplessness to do what she had asked but I could never explain this to Neil Fraser. I made the mistake of trying to defend myself.

'I love Wee Graham. It's only natural I don't want to lose him.'

'If you love Graham you will do what is best for him.'

'And you're so sure you know what's best for him? You talk like God Almighty Himself.'

'You should be ashamed of your blasphemous tongue.'

I wanted to hit him. He was being unfair, unjust and lacking in the charity he was supposed to preach. I realized that not only did I dislike Neil Fraser but, as Callum had so rightly guessed, I was also afraid of him. He exercised a power over me. His call to perfection only served to exaggerate my uncertainty and shortcomings. His air of righteousness and voiced piety shrivelled any trust in God I might have been prepared to foster.

'I only want to help you, Jenny, believe me.'

'Why?'

'Because I ... I ... like you - a lot.'

I couldn't believe what I was hearing. It didn't make sense and it didn't particularly please me. He embarrassed me. He opened his mouth as if to say more then, changing his mind, he turned and limped from the coach-house. I watched him go with a mixture of relief and frustration. The last thing I wanted to do was to join the group of antagonists in the kitchen. I would go to Todd.

When I arrived at the keeper's cottage the twins were alone. Todd was constructing a model aeroplane with his meccano set while Tam was on the point of leaving for the castle kennels to help exercise the dogs. He invited me along but it was Todd I had come to see.

'You're as bad as Callum,' I said making a circuit round the table where Todd was working. 'His room is full of aeroplanes. What's so special about aeroplanes?' 'They're the transport of the future. As soon as I'm old enough I'm going to learn to fly them.'

I admired the way his hair flopped over his forehead.

'Callum wants to join the Air Force. He's threatening to leave university,' I said looking at his hands caressing a metal wing.

'He wants to go to Spain,' said Todd. 'So do I and so does the dominie.'

I wanted him to hold my hand as lovingly.

'I've never heard the dominie talk about Spain.'

'It's man's talk - at woodwork lessons while you lassies are sewing your baggy knickers.'

'What else does he tell you?' I listened with greater attention.

'All he talks about is the Spanish Civil War. His brother has just come back from Spain.'

'What was he doing in Spain if there was a war on?' His eyes left his model and turned on me.

'He was a freedom fighter. He smuggled himself into the country and joined the Spanish Army. When a bullet got stuck in his chest he joined the refugees.' His attention went back to the nuts and bolts.

Without looking up he said, 'Eventually he got to Marseilles, smuggled himself into a British freighter and got back home to improve his health.'

I passed him the screwdriver. He nodded his thanks saying, 'As soon as he's well enough he's going back and I'll tell you this, Jenny McLeod, I wish I was going with him.'

'Don't be daft!'

Carefully Todd attached a strip of metal to the second wing of his model, securing it with a deft twist of the screwdriver.

'The dominic thinks that there will be another world war in a year or two, maybe less.'

I remembered Callum say much the same to Grandpa who only told him to stop babbling and not to read so many socialist papers. Spain was a long way from Strathard and the troubles of Spain seemed very remote to me. I '. couldn't imagine the worries of life in Spain affecting the quiet tenor of life in the Scottish Highlands.

'Freedom fighters,' repeated Todd, obviously fond of the expression, 'that's what the dominic says they're called.'

Although it sounded exciting and quite romantic it was far too remote for me to worry about. Besides I had bigger worries of my own, and remembering them now, I lost interest in Todd's account of the Spanish Civil War. He noticed my withdrawal and without interrupting a detailed appraisal of the now completed model aeroplane he changed the subject.

'And who stole your scone then? You've a face as long as a flittin'.'

Hoping for an ally I told him about the plans for Graham, not forgetting the part Miss Catriona had played.

'They've got a point,' he said whooshing his model into a nose dive over the table. I felt like tearing it from his hands.

'And so have you,' he added as if divining my thoughts. Very carefully he placed the model at a safe distance before turning to look at me.

'It seems to me that folk who should know better take a bit too much upon themselves.'

I wondered again how much Todd suspected regarding his father and Her Ladyship. I lost interest and, seeing a box of flies on the dresser, changed the subject.

'Are you going to be a gamekeeper when you leave school, Todd?' I asked, extracting what I thought might be a sandfly.

'No fear! That's Tam's job. He's the one who wants to follow in my father's footsteps.'

'And what about you?'

'I'm going to be a freedom fighter. Tell you what Jenny...' He turned to face me taking the fly and returning it to the box. 'Let's go to Spain together. With your red hair and caury fist and my aeroplanes we'd soon scare the living daylight out of the Fascisto. How about it?'

'You'd better not let your father hear you talking like that.'

'I don't care what he thinks.'

That furrowed brow again and withdrawal of good cheer. Quickly I changed the subject again, this time inspired by a framed photograph of the twins.

'What's it like being a twin, Todd?'

'All right, I suppose,' shrugging his shoulders.

'Does Tam feel like your other half?'

'No! I'm me and Tam's Tam. We're different.' He began clearing the table.

'But it's a wee bit more than just brothers surely. You must feel closer.'

'I don't know what you're going on about. After all, we're no identical.'

'No. You're better looking,' I said with a grin, 'and cleverer - but no as clever as me, mind.'

'That's what you think. I'll leave you standing next term.'

'Want a bet?'

'You're on.'

I helped him clear up.

We grinned at each other and for some blessed moments I was the happiest girl on earth. I felt bolstered enough now to stand up to Neil the next time we met.

He cornered me in the coach-house while I was fetching straw for the pony and continued the contention about Graham.

'You think of nobody but yourself,' he argued.

'I know Graham better than you do,' I retorted. 'Besides he needs us. We're his family. All he's got.'

'And all he's ever likely to get, but it isn't enough.'

'I don't want to talk about it.'

'You're afraid you might be forced to see reason.'

'No one will force me to see anything,' I snapped, plucking straw from my hair.

'Graham needs special help,' he said.

'We'll give him all the help he needs.'

He wouldn't give up.

'You don't even know what he needs,' I said, trying to push past.

'And you do?' he asked scathingly.

'Of course,' I answered with casual confidence.

'I work with children such as Graham,' he said.

'Children such as Graham!' I shrieked, throwing decorum to the wind and straw into his face. 'You make me want to spew!'

He removed the straw and replied with exaggerated calm. 'You are vulgar as well as selfish.'

'So you keep telling me.'

I wanted to howl. We were alone in the coach-house, the air redolent of oil, grease, horse and straw but as he closed in on me, or so it seemed, I was more keenly conscious of the smell of tweed and soap and a faint whiff of disinfectant from a handkerchief the tip of which protruded from the breast pocket of his jacket. I bit my lip to keep me from rushing from his presence. I forced myself to look eyeball to eyeball.

'Would you like me to pray that you may have guidance in this matter?' he asked.

'Heaven forbid!' I glared at him. 'You and your praying! You think it's the answer to everything.'

'It generally is.'

I took a deep breath. 'Graham stays and you can tell God that I say so.'

He shook his head slowly from side to side conveying with the gesture, I supposed, that I was obviously a hopeless case.

I was like any animal when her cub is threatened. My recent experience of the power of aggression had served me well. I knew what belligerence could do, what blackmail was capable of. I bullied my family mercilessly. It had to be what I wanted. I knew best. It didn't matter that Callum's absence at university denied that line of support or that Father's constant drinking threw a heavy burden on Grandpa.

Somehow we would manage. Grandpa and I between us would hold the fort. Graham must stay. I think they feared I'd have a breakdown if I didn't have my way. My behaviour was maniacal enough to justify their fears. I won, or at least forced them to compromise. He could stay a little longer to see how things went.

Graham stayed and things settled down. Somehow we managed thanks mostly to Grandpa.

I threw myself into my lessons. The growing rivalry between Todd and me was motivation enough. Our efforts seemed to work as an inspiration on the schoolmaster. Now that Todd was operating in top gear there wasn't much to pick and choose between the pair of us and, without our realizing it, the master had gradually dispensed with the need for graded marking and focused our efforts on the real rewards to be enjoyed from the work itself.

It wasn't long before we were staying behind after school for extra lessons. We could ask the schoolmaster anything. We were fertile ground for the seeds of his cherished beliefs. Out of his hard work and our attentiveness were borne two little pink socialists dedicated to changing the world. He dealt with our questions socratically, forcing us to think for ourselves and discouraging us to take his word for it. Although I had always been one for questioning, my experience in Strathard village school put the seal on my future life. From then on I accepted nothing at face value. I became a dedicated seeker of the truth.

CHAPTER 7

Seeker after the truth! Such was my waking thought, my prompt to return to the present, the now, the big problem, the reason for being back in Strathatd. The phrase reiterated in my mind as I rose from my bed. Life was beginning to stir around the hotel. I could hear voices, plumbing noises, animals and doors banging.

There was the smell of a big fry-up for breakfast wafting from the kitchen below. I washed and dressed, remembering that Mr Ross had told Todd and me that truth is what compels.

'It's that something inside you,' he told us. 'It's just a matter of uncovering it.' Easier said than done. After brushing my tangled hair and tying it back from my face I went in search of breakfast, thinking of my husband. I could never remember him searching for truth. He'd been born with it. His religion was his truth and nothing but the truth. If the Bible said so then it was so. No argument!

When I reached Reception I found Flora in a tizz. She had received a letter from the owners of the hotel who had returned from America and were expecting to be in Strathard in a few days.

'We haven't done half the things we were supposed to,' she wailed.

'A case of when the cat's away,' I suggested with a smile.

'It's the maids. They need a kick up the backside. They were supposed to spring clean all the bedrooms. They've hardly begun.' She drew her fingers through her bobbed hair. 'And Jock was to have painted the ceiling in the conference hall.'

'Where's that?' I asked, suddenly alert.

'You ken, that big barn of a place in the end wing there,' indicating the direction with a nod.

'You mean the-' I stopped myself on the verge of revealing a familiarity with the building I didn't want her to know I had. Fortunately she was still busy coming to terms with the unexpected shock of her employers' imminent return. Instead of asking if the 'barn of a place' was what had once been the castle ballroom I asked instead if I might have a peep in the 'barn', my interest being purely architectural, of course.

'Help yourself. Along there.' Another nod of the head. 'You can't miss it. The door's open.'

I knew exactly where it was and, quietly excited, I made my way there. The said Jock had made a statement of intent if some paint tins and brushes were anything to go by. There was no sign of the man himself. Obviously the news hadn't yet reached him. There was an extension ladder across the floor, a trestle table still to be mounted and a paint-spattered stool. I was glad of the stool when my memories began crowding in on me. This was where, all those years ago, I had humiliated Neil Fraser as revenge for the scathing remarks he'd regularly inflicted on me. The dull empty barn disappeared and I was back in the first day of 1938. New Year's Day, the day of the castle ball, the one day in the year when we could mix freely with the gentry.

'We can't go to the ball,' I said to my father, aghast at his suggestion. 'Not this year.'

'What for no!' said Father. 'You deserve some cheering up. You've had a sair time.'

I was torn between a great happiness at this unexpected kindness and a greater worry about enjoying ourselves so soon after our bereavement.

'What do you think, Callum? Will you be taking your sister to the Ne'erday ball?' asked Father.

'We'll all go,' said Grandpa.

'What about Graham?' I asked.

'I'll look after Graham,' said Father.

'But you'll be—' I stopped myself.

'I'll be drunken-fu'?' laughed Father. 'Oh, I suspect I'll manage to stay sober for one night.'

I was relieved to hear it.

On the night of the ball I was in a dither of excitement. Resplendent in a new dress and my mother's sash, duly shortened, I studied my reflection. I liked what I saw except for one thing. My hair. I was too old for plaits. Then it happened again, that short sharp pain when something triggered off a memory of my mother. She would have known what to do with it. Although it was red it was also abundant, too abundant I thought for me to fashion it on top of my head, or anywhere else for that matter. I tried it with clips, with ribbons, with combs but it always ended up looking like a floor mop. There was no one to help me with this. Resigned to the plaits I began brushing out the tangles I'd managed to create. When I'd finished it hung to my shoulders, soft as silk and shining like a newly minted penny. It was mostly straight but with all the brushing it had acquired a slight wave and the ends were easily coaxed into a page-boy curve. About to begin plaiting, I changed my mind. I'd wear it as it was.

I joined the others downstairs. Father inspected us proudly. Grandpa and Callum were in the McLeod tartan kilts and I was, after a brief consultation and some generous approval, given permission to leave my hair unbound.

'Off you go and enjoy yourself,' said Father heartily.

'Will you be all right, Father?'

'Don't you worry about me, lass.'

I wore a red cape over my white satin and, one arm linked with Grandpa and the other with Callum, I set off through the archway and down the drive. Instead of disappearing into the secluded secondary paths as we normally did, we walked straight down the centre of the main drive.

As we turned the final bend in the drive, the splendour of the castle stood before us. I stared at the beauty of fashioned stone and illumined windows. The pointed turrets enhanced the three-storeyed central block which was dominated by a huge-columned portico. A winged Cupid, poised to shoot his arrow to the stars, graced the circular lawn in front. The drive was a Piccadilly of cars and carriages. The laird was waiting to welcome us as we stepped inside.

The ballroom was magnificent. It was lofty and spacious and I stood on the threshold with racing heart. Rustling silks and shimmering satins were enhanced by jewels sparkling in the light from the crystal chandelier. Tartans were everywhere - on floors, windows and decorative shields. They were swinging from waists and draped over shoulders, colouring the scene with magnificence.

On the walls among the hunting trophies were stag heads and five or six wild cats. Suspended from the high ceiling was a stuffed golden eagle with an eight foot wingspan - a spectacular adornment. It was perfect.

Fiddles and accordion were warming up while dancers were already forming on the floor. McGreegor was there and in his clan tartan he made every other male look ordinary. No other figure could have shown the Highland dress to such advantage. Beside him Ella looked like a wee brown speckled hen. The twins, smaller versions of their handsome father, made straight towards me and claimed the dance now forming on the floor. It was the 'Dashing White Sergeant' and as the opening chords sounded I ran with them to help form a set.

The music went into full swing. It was the music of the folk, programmed to set us clapping and hooching in delight. Happy music, lifting the heart with the feet, joining the young with the old, linking the present with the past. Kilts swirled from the hips, sporrans bounced as the bodies moved in rhythm and delight. The dance ended with a resounding chord. There were bows and curtsies and a lot of laughing before the music struck up again.

There followed an evening of pleasure where the colour, sounds and sights of revelry, the excellent food, drink and entente cordiale enfolded everyone present in its magical spell.

But it was a magic not without its dangers. Spells could be broken and it was no thanks to McGreegor and Miss Catriona that the evening didn't turn sour. It riled me no end to see how they were flirting. They never touched, except their fingers when they happened to be dancing in the same set, but they never seemed to be more than a foot apart all night. I could see the twins watching their father and I knew that Ella was noticing every move they made. The trouble was it was a situation that depended on guesswork. You couldn't actually say they were behaving badly. Of course, Callum and I knew something that neither Ella nor the twins knew. We'd seen them kissing. I looked at Callum now to determine what he might be thinking but he was helping Neil Fraser hold up the ballroom wall. Their posture seemed slovenly and they irritated me. So too did Vincent Stacey who was strutting around like the popinjay he was, greeting everyone with a flourish ofgestures and a garble of words. I wondered how much he was guessing and how much he'd already seen.

I could see Neil Fraser looking at him; that is, when he wasn't looking at me. I'd been aware of the son of the manse watching me from the minute I arrived. He hadn't danced or talked with anyone except Callum. I wondered why he'd bothered to come. He was the only male not wearing the kilt. I guessed it was because of his gammy leg which made me wonder just how gammy it really was. I felt tempted to find out and put this sober saint to the test. I waited until the next ladies' choice and, taking a deep breath, made my determined way across the hail to stand before him. I steeled myself against his air of disdain, my behaviour compelled by an urge to challenge whatever it was his arrogance was declaring.

'May I have the pleasure of this dance?' I asked dropping a half curtsy.
'I don't dance.'
'If you're not sure of the steps I'll help you.'
'It isn't that.'
Callum intervened.
'I'll dance with you,' he offered, extending an arm to me. 'We make a dashing couple in the Gay Gordons, remember?'
'It's Ladies' Choice,' I said, still sweetly, 'and I've chosen Neil.'

He was about to say more but Neil rose to my challenge with neither good grace nor gratitude.

'I doubt if we'll make a dashing couple,' he said, his voice laden with sarcasm, 'but as you wish.'

I exulted at my victory. I'd forced him to do what he didn't want and now I'd find out what sort of dancer he was.

It was painfully obvious from his first step. He had no idea of the sequence of the dance. Nor would the knowing have helped. He could barely keep himself upright and his lame leg seemed to shoot out in all directions. In my consternation I made to withdraw from the dance, suggesting we find something to eat but he held my hand in a vice-like grip forcing me to join in his undignified charade. I had asked for it and he was determined I would get it. It was difficult to say which of us felt the more humiliated. I could feel my face burning with both anger and shame. I wanted to run but the painful grip on my fingers prevented this. Things might have been much worse if a disturbance hadn't arisen on the other side of the ballroom. I learned later that Stacey had challenged McGreegor to a duel and only the laird's intervention had nipped that little melodrama in the bud. We endured to the end of the dance when my partner's grip was released and Neil Fraser limped away lèaving me to mixed feelings of triumph and self-disgust. The sparkle had gone out of the evening for me. Although I was ashamed of the part I'd played in Neil's public humiliation I was confused at the satisfaction his distress had given me. Not even dancing again with Todd helped, especially when his thoughts were more on his father than on me. The evening was spoiled and when Grandpa said it was time to go home I wasn't sorry.

A quick glance round the ballroom showed that there was no sign of Neil Fraser and I was glad about that too. I wasn't sure how I was ever going to face him again.

Callum said he'd stay a while longer so Grandpa and I said our thanks to the laird and Miss Catriona. I noticed all the McGreegors had disappeared and that Vincent Stacey was drinking himself under the table.

This wonderful castle life was all an illusion. The master had spent a long time explaining that word. Now my feelings were explaining things clearer than his words ever could. I followed Grandpa from the ballroom on to the paved terrace. The garden was awash with yellow moonlight. I felt a spasm of envy. It was all so lovely but it wasn't ours and never could be. You'd think the night's activities would have brought the gentry closer but all it had done was to put them and all that belonged to them, meaning Strathard, as far out of our reach as the yellow moon in the inky sky. Some day we were going to have to live without this. We were only here as long as we were needed. We were the tools of the aristocracy, as I'd heard Callum once say when he thought Grandpa wasn't listening. We would be dispensed with when worn out or no longer needed. If the laird should decide that he no longer needed a chauffeur then there would be no reason for our being in Strathard or, what was more likely, if Father went on the way he was doing with the drinking, we'd be dispensed with even sooner. I shivered, drawing my cape closer around me, asking again why? Why? Why was the daughter of the laird born into this splendour while old Kirsty Colquhoun earned her bread raking the chippings on the castle drive into geometrical patterns only to have them repeatedly savaged by the gentry's cars? It didn't make sense.

As I entered the house I gasped in horror. Grandpa, close on my heels, cannoned into me. My father was slumped in his chair, his stockinged feet on the fender stool with an empty bottle of whisky on the floor beside him. The place reeked of alcohol. The smell in the room was enough to make your stomach turn. Graham was crying soundlessly in the corner, his nightshirt sodden where he'd wet himself. There was no guard on the fire whose embers were still aglow. Some small lumps of coal had fallen on the hearth, undersides grey and hot. In my rage I could have swept them with my bare hands in the direction of my father. Instead, I rushed at him and with clenched fists began pummelling his chest. He jerked up in astonishment, lifting an arm to shield himself from my flaying arms. Grandpa grabbed me from behind and tried to stop me, but to no avail. I fought in a frenzy, until Father, although stupid with drink, began to resist. He grabbed both my wrists, holding them in a vice-like grip until I screamed in pain and fury. My rage was spent as quickly as it had been roused and I collapsed on the floor wailing for my mother. My need for her was absolute and in utter desolation I kept calling her name.

I'd forgotten Graham. We'd all forgotten Graham. We'd also forgotten to close the door when we came in. Graham had fled and when we rushed outside he was nowhere to be seen. A new and more terrible panic seized me, worse than any nightmare, and a terrible thought took possession of me. This was God's punishment. I'd insulted and humiliated Neil Fraser. I'd been dancing and enjoying myself when I should have been looking after my little brother. Ever since my mother died I had ignored and insulted God. Even before then I had been less than respectful to Him. I felt God was wreaking vengeance for my sins. I was brought suddenly. to earth again when my father hit the air, reeling and tripping over his own feet, colliding with me in a way that would have been comical if not so tragic. Grandpa followed him from the house and helped steady us both. I turned to him.

'Where can he have gone?'

'No far,' he said, 'I'll go round the buildings. You make for the castle and you'd better fetch Callum.'

As I raced through the wood my thoughts focused on the river. Graham loved the water. I covered the ground where I often took him for a walk, calling his name without halt. When I reached the water's edge I had to force my thoughts from the direction they were taking. The river was a ribbon of moonlight but I had no eyes for its beauty. I could only feel its cold and watery depth. Aunt Sheena had been right. I should never have encouraged Graham's love of water. It was all my fault.

Callum! I must find Callum! I raced back to the main pathway. As I neared the castle I could hear the music. I remembered how much Graham loved music. Perhaps I would find him in the ballroom. The thought of my brother, trembling with fear and clad in sodden nightshirt, tore sobs from my throat. I rounded a corner and stopped dead in my tracks. Limping towards me was Neil Fraser with Graham in his arms. Even in my anguish I could feel sympathy for Neil's slow and painful progress but it was pushed aside in the immensity of my relief. I rushed forward and caught Graham in my arms. He was wrapped in Neil's coat and relinquished to me without protest. I hugged him, covering his face with kisses, unheeding of his weight. At the same time I was thanking God and silently vowing to heed this terrible fright as a warning.

I heard a yell behind me. Grandpa and Father joined us making sure for themselves that Graham was unhurt. Grandpa wrapped his own coat round Graham's legs while Father, who had miraculously sobered up, prepared to carry him home. By the time any of us thought fit to thank Neil Fraser he had disappeared. We hadn't seen him or heard him leave. It was as if he'd dissolved into thin air. I was feeling sick and cold as I tagged at the tail of our little procession heading home. I knew it wasn't just because of the scare I'd just had or the cold of the rising wind. It was the desolation inside me, the feeling of impotence against the mighty powers of the unknown. It made it no better that it had been Neil Fraser who had delivered me from the horrors of my plight.

The outcome of this was that I had lost my case for Graham staying with us. Neil's point had been proven and he made the most of it. Without delay, arrangements were made for my brother's admission to the Church of Scotland home designed specially for 'people such as Graham'.

Neil drove him to Edinburgh. Father went with him. I was invited but refused. Unpityingly Neil looked on at my distress as I held my brother close before they took him from me and bundled him into the car. Smitten again by the hand of God! I hated God. I hated Neil Fraser.

CHAPTER 8

'Are you all right, Missus?' The voice came from a long way off. Slowly I focused on the source. A man in dungarees and a tartan tam-o'-shanter stood before me, his pleasant features serious with concern.

'Yes. I'm fine, thanks,' I smiled.

'You looked as if you were awa' wi' the fairies.'

'Maybe I was,' I said lightly, rising from the stool. 'You must be Jock.' I offered my hand.

'Aye, I am that. An' you, I take it, are the lady frae Edinburgh, a minister's wife I'm told.'

'I am that.'

'The minister isna wi' you then?'

Afraid this was the onset of an interrogation to satisfy the local curiosity, I turned to leave but Jock didn't seem in any hurry to begin his decorating.

'Is the minister's kirk in Edinburgh then?'

'It is.' Then not to seem too grudging added, 'in Morningside district. You'll have your work cut out,' I added, 'if you have to decorate this hall before your employers arrive.'

'If it's no finished then it's no finished,' he said beginning to construct the trestle table. 'For a' they'll care. Absentee landlords I think they're called,' adding, 'Will you be staying long?'

As long as it takes, I said to myself, but aloud only, 'Not long.'

Anticipating a follow-up I wished him well in his work, said there would be no breakfast left if I didn't get to the dining-room and managed to reach the door.

'Hae ye seen the devil?' he called as he began adjusting the extension ladder.

I turned and looked at him, saw his wide grin and was beginning to wonder if I was still away with the fairies. 'That's what they call him.'

'Who?'

Ye ken, the queer body wi' the big hat who only comes out at night. Sometimes in the early mornin' too mind,' he added with another grin. 'When I last saw him he was on a horse galloping on the moors.'

'I expect he'll present himself at the village store in due course,' I suggested. 'I take it he eats like the rest of us.'

'I wouldna bet on it,' said Jock. 'I wonder what his game is.'

'Maybe he just wants to be left to himself,' I suggested. 'Or stalking his prey,' said Jock. 'Maybe he's a vampire.' 'Now who's awa' wi' the fairies?' I laughed.

Intrigued as I was, I had problems of my own to solve. I knew what fanciful interpretations the valley folk could put on ordinary events. They hated nothing more than being left in ignorance of the comings and goings of folk, especially strangers. I had no doubt that my own movements were being closely monitored. What would they say, I wondered, if they were to see me galloping over the moors in the early hours?

As I ate my kipper in solitary splendour in the dining-room I considered it wasn't such a bad idea. There must be somewhere I could hire a horse for the day and gallop on the moor. If I were to meet the devil it would be no different from meeting the ghosts I knew would still haunt me there. But I had to meet those ghosts, to fit them into the jigsaw of my life, that is if I were to make the decision I'd come here to make. Flora, on her way to the kitchen, paused for a moment at my table.

'You found the conference room then?'

'And Jock,' I said, folding my napkin.

'I hope he's getting on with the painting,' she said stacking my empty plate on her tray. Then conversationally, 'It's a fine morning.'

'It must be lovely on the moors on a morning like this,' I said. 'I'm beginning to wish I'd a horse. It seems good riding country.'

She made to laugh then stopped herself, perhaps sensing that I wasn't entirely joking.

Jock could find you a horse, that is, if you really wanted one. If there's a problem then Jock's your man.'

I made light of it but I knew the prospect of a day on the moors was gripping me.

'I used to ride a lot when I was young,' I said. 'It just seems a pity not to make the most of the moors when they're out there.'

She took a long hard look at me and I was beginning to wish I'd never brought the subject up. The last thing I wanted was to encourage Flora's curiosity.

'Give me five minutes,' she said. 'Pour yourself another cuppa till I come back.'

She almost ran out of the dining-room. I guessed she was racing along to the conference room to see her Jock. Sure enough, in five minutes exactly she was back telling me I only had to name the day and the time and the horse would be waiting for me.

I was beginning to have second thoughts but seeing her pleasure in having granted my wish I hadn't the heart to refuse.

'Shall we say tomorrow morning, after breakfast?' 'Couldn't be better. It will make sure that lump o' butter starts his decorating early.'

And so it was arranged.

I decided to write to Neil. That way there would be no need to phone again. I determined to get it over with. I returned to my room and settled in the chair by the window, writing pad on my lap and pen in my hand.

My husband had dedicated his life to the good of humanity and, with missionary zeal, had made many worthy suggestions as to how I should spend my inheritance. The trouble was that he and I didn't quite see eye to eye about what was the best good for humanity. His concerns were for the homeless, the hungry, the infirm or insane. He crusaded for reparations for the ravages of wars and eco disasters. He supported the need for repairing cracks in churches and cathedrals, for more beds in hospitals and more hospitals. He was totally involved with his congregation raising enough money to resuscitate the church organ now on its last gasp. I myself had helped considerably, even with enthusiasm. So where was my problem? Where indeed?

My problem was that this colossal legacy had been entrusted to me by someone who had saved me from my own particular hunger and homelessness.

Money had played no part in this. The changes wrought in me through association with my benefactor were not of physical hunger or homelessness but were changes in my attitudes and beliefs.

I sat in my chair looking at, but not seeing, the growing shadows on the lawn, the herbaceous borders rich in colour from which emerged the sleek form of a black cat. I saw it freeze in its path, then cautiously drop to the ground, waiting and watchful. A garden warbler, darting among stems and leaves, was unaware of the danger. I waited, fascinated and helpless to intervene. It was an easy conquest. I watched as the cat struck. The young Jenny McLeod would have asked Why? Why did God allow it to happen? The older Jenny McLeod did not need to ask why. She knew why - or thought she did. Bird, cat, Callum and Graham blurred together in my subconscious in a strange but significant perfection. Gradually the lawn, shadows and shrubs disappeared and in their stead I saw again the day they unclasped Graham from my arms and took him to Edinburgh.

When my young brother left home he had been skin and bones. His naturally happy disposition had been threatened by stress. That was the image over which I'd agonized the weeks and months before I saw him again. Callum had constantly reassured me that he was well and happy but I thought that was only intended to make me feel better.

On our first visit to see Graham, Grandpa and I travelled to Edinburgh by train. We were expecting to find Callum waiting for us at Waverley Station. There was no Callum but a few minutes later Neil Fraser arrived, limping awkwardly along the platform.

'Don't look so disappointed,' Neil said before I had time to say anything.

He had immediately picked up my annoyance which I tried too late to conceal.

'Let me carry your bag,' he offered. Reluctantly I relinquished my bag which contained a few treats for Graham.

'Callum is at a lecture. He sends his apologies.'

Then he ignored me and turned his attention on Grandpa, helping him climb the long steep flight of steps to Princes Street.

'Wait till you get your breath back,' he suggested to Grandpa.

Panting after the unusual exertion Grandpa responded to the kindness with a rueful smile. It did not take him long to recover and we made our way to the stop where we boarded a tramcar that would take us to Graham's new home. The tram deposited us in a residential area on the outskirts of the city. It was a short walk to our destination. The home had a pleasing approach but I was unconcerned with its tree-lined sweeping driveway, its mullioned windows set in red sandstone or the large lions chiselled in stone and staged on either side of the oak-studded doors. I was trying to still my racing heart. Would Graham remember me? It was a long time. Had he pined for me? Worse! Had he forgotten me?

The matron met us in the hall, welcoming us with a warm smile. I could hear a piano playing which seemed to be coming from upstairs.

'It's music time,' said Matron. 'Neil, take our visitors to the music room. They might enjoy watching the children at their lesson. We can have tea afterwards.'

The door of the music room was wide open. I stopped short at the scene within. What I saw had such an impact that I was not prepared for the desolation that swept over me. I seemed to have been transported to some alien world frequented by strange creatures. There were about 40 children of all ages, shapes and sizes. They were not like other children. They were all, to a greater or lesser degree children 'such as Graham' that Callum had referred to. There were Down's Syndrome sufferers, dwarfs, hydrocephalics and cripples of all kinds. The pianist was hammering a marching tune and every child followed every other child in a circle, some waving, some clapping, all laughing with every appearance of enjoyment. Another adult was on guard ready to catch any tottering casualty. I'd forgotten Wee Graham. They were all of them Graham. In a quick flash of insight I suddenly realized the world into which Graham had been born. Then I focused on him. I didn't expect him to show signs of recognition and he didn't, although he beamed a radiant smile in our direction, but I noticed that they were all beaming at everyone, in every direction. They were enjoying the music and the movement and just being. I had a terrible feeling of loss. I turned away, choking on my sobs. Neil followed me.

'Why do you always run away?' he asked, offering me his handkerchief.

'Why don't you leave me alone?' I replied, refusing it.

'They're happy. Graham's happy. Why doesn't that make you happy?' he persisted.

'Let me ask you a question,' I said. My tears of sorrow had turned to tears of rage. The more I fumed the more sardonic his expression became. I wanted to hurt him as I was being hurt. I wanted to diminish him as I felt I was being diminished. I genuinely wanted to know the answer to all of it.

'You talk about a just and loving God,' I said in a none-too-steady voice. 'If He is so just and so loving why does He allow these children to suffer?'

'Are they suffering? Are they unhappy? It strikes me you're a lot unhappier than they are.'

'You still haven't answered my question.'

'God has a purpose, Jenny. We must have faith in Him. Why don't you return to the Church?'

His self-righteousness did nothing to calm me. 'That's no answer.'

'It will have to do for now. The music has stopped and Graham will be waiting for you. Come.'

Graham, when we returned to the music room, was on Grandpa's lap with his arms around his neck. Grandpa saw us first.

'Here's Jenny,' he told Graham, gently lowering him to the floor.

'Chenny!' I opened my arms as he ran to me. I had my Graham back again. He had gained weight and had colour back in his cheeks. He hugged as lovingly as ever but was also happy to unlock himself from my arms and join his friends then run back again for more spoiling. He took us to his room and showed us his toys. He took, us to a room where they painted and showed us his pictures on the wall. We had to see the kitchen where some of the older children were helping to prepare tea. I gave him the few presents I'd brought which he immediately shared with others and he insisted on wearing the gloves I had knitted him. We were joined by Matron who gave us a wonderful report on his progress.

'Aye, you can say that the proof o' the puddin' is in the eatin' o't,' said Grandpa. 'The bairn's happy. We've nothing to fret about and we should be thankin' the Lord for His goodness. It doesn't do to neglect such things.'

I stole a glance at him out of the corner of my eye and found him doing the same to me.

'Aye, ye may look,' he said, 'but your neglect o' the Kirk hasna escaped my attention. A wee prayer noo and again does no harm. Besides it gey often pays to keep on the safe side.'

I brought myself back to my hotel room, sitting on the chair by the window, the writing paper on my lap, the pencil still in my hand. I focused on the lawn outside. Both cat and bird had gone but a bundle of feathers, lying still in the breathless air, assured me that I hadn't dreamed the killing.

I turned my attention to the pad on my knee. 'My Dear Neil,' I wrote. Sighing I continued.,'I'm sorry if I was not communicative last night but as you may have gathered, phoning from here is no small feat. I'd better stick to a few words on paper. I say a few because I am still in shock I think at the enormity of the responsibility the professor has left me. I am not thinking logically yet. I seem to be waiting. I have a gut feeling that I shall find the answer here in Strathard. Gut feeling is all I have and I know with what scant sympathy you will look upon that. I would ask your forbearance. When I have the answer I shall do nothing until I speak first with you. I'm afraid you would be saddened by the general neglect of Strathard and in particular the poorly maintained churchyard. I do not think you would find it such a good idea to return here to minister, after all. I trust all is well.

Your wife, Jenny.'

I signed it, folded the paper, placed it in an envelope which I duly addressed and stamped.

I decided I would walk into the village and post it. I might lunch in the Strathard Arms where I could decide what to do with the rest of the day.

I spent the afternoon on the shores of the Firth watching the play of sun on water, listening to sighings of the incoming tide. The magic of the sea did me good. I breathed deeply, wanting to milk joy from every moment. I resisted the prompts of memory. Tomorrow would be time enough for that. For the rest of this day I would absorb Strathard as it is and not as remembered. It had changed little. There were a few more shops in the village, more vehicles on the street, unsightly TV aerials pointing to the sky but the sea was the same and the gulls winging above it. I drew in the old, familiar smells of seaweed and fish, and feasted my eyes on the mountains beyond which were always my symbol of strength and constancy.

I remembered a concealed spot a good half mile along the headland. It would be rough walking but I had the time. When I rounded the headland

I saw him, sprawled on the shore. He had discarded the long cloak and was using it as a headrest but his face was concealed by the wide-brimmed hat. The crunch of the pebbles startled him. He shot upright, his hat tilting slightly. For a split second I glimpsed his face. In that infinitesimal moment of time I learned his secret.

There were no horns of a devil here. There was no evil. Only ugliness which was being so zealously shielded from human eyes. Beneath that flopping wideawake hat was a deformed face. There was no time for detail but little time was needed to find the answer to the question everyone was asking.

I could feel my compassion streaming from the depths of me and eddying towards him. With one hand securing his hat he bent and, after lifting his cloak, turned from me and walked away. He did not hurry but his decisiveness told me he wanted nothing from me.

Standing alone again surrounded by the beauty of land and seascape I felt bereft, as if I had lost my identity under that wide-brimmed hat. I began to walk in the opposite direction and went on walking and thinking of humanity and the endless problems it seemed to pose. For the good of humanity, the professor had ordained. Where did one begin? I was just an ordinary person, born with red hair and a temper, a mind that queried and a heart that yearned. What could I do for humanity? What could a mere million pounds do?

Much later, too wearied even to feel hungry I returned to my hotel room and lay on my bed. I relaxed and gradually began to feel the quick little throb of something akin to joy. It's all mixed up together I thought. Life is one, all is one. Amidst the sorrow is the beauty in the midst of the sadness is the joy. Quietly I began to consider my amazing response to this stranger with a life I couldn't begin to imagine. But in that moment he was one with me and creation. He was me. I was him. It was, to me, a miracle of divine awareness and it was mighty powerful. I was convinced that the experience was important. My intuition was not deceiving me. I knew I could make of it what I would. I knew that I must treasure this moment because only too soon it would recede. If the stranger was a tragic victim of a catastrophe he was no more or no less than the victims whom Neil championed. Why had they not moved me as this man had done?

I lay awake well into the night. I saw the stars appear, watched the moon ride on jagged clouds, watched the hotel lights extinguished one by one, heard the screech of an owl and the spitting of a cat. There was a blast of music which was immediately switched off. Then there was silence.

I could listen for a whisper because answers come in whispers and my intuition was telling me that I would catch that whisper soon.

CHAPTER 9

When I woke next morning I decided to make a full day of it as, with a little persuasion from Flora, the hotel cook prepared some parcels of food which I slipped into my saddle-bag. It was a fine morning with excellent prospects for the day. Jock offered me a bonnet in case I got sunstroke. I accepted, settling it over my long thick red hair which I wore tied back with a tartan ribbon confiscated from a tin of shortbread. Jock and Flora waved me off. I was beginning to enjoy myself.

'We'll see you when we see you,' smiled Flora.

'Don't wait up for me,' I joked.

'Look out for the devil,' yelled Jock when Betsy and I were half way down the drive.

The devil I will, I thought. I pointed Betsy's nose to the moors. She was a docile creature who would give me no trouble. The first whiff of moorland air sent my memory scuttling back through the years to a day such as this, a special day of the year - the 'Glorious Twelfth', the first day of the grouse shooting in August 1938.

At that time with all the schoolmaster's talk about the Spanish Civil War, the word gun to me was more associated with Jews, political dissenters, the weak and the no-longer-useful, rather than with grouse. I was no longer sure if I wanted to witness the gunning of the birds. The schoolmaster himself was always a regular gun on the 'Glorious Twelfth' and when I asked him to square this with his principles he gave us a lesson on the balance of nature and the need for culling. Although this belief was supported by Todd and Callum I was tempted to debate the matter but I resisted because Neil Fraser was voicing his usual diatribe on the wickedness of blood sports. So deepseated was my antagonism for this guardian of the faith that I felt a constant urge to oppose everything he preached.

While the twins would be going with the beaters and be subject to the instructions of their father, I would be going to join Grandpa and Callum who would be with the other guns and loaders assembling on the castle courtyard.

Tam was in his element. As the three of us met early in the morning on a rise outside the castle grounds, known locally as Hirplin' Hill, he told us about the work he'd done with his father.

'The rain didn't harm the birds,' he told us as we trudged up the hill, watching the slivers of light gradually widen on the horizon. 'The hens were in fine fettle before laying and the rain was too late to flood their nests. The chicks hatched all right and besides, all those crow traps I helped Father set up did a good job and what with rootin' the foxes and snarin' the hares, we successfully controlled the vermin. Aye, it's been a good season so far and it should be a fine shoot the day. There's no mist, thank God, and even the wind's in the right direction.'

Todd winked at me as Tam, as well as taking on his father's words, seemed to do likewise with his appearance, pulled his body to maximum height and stretched his stride. I winked back, enjoying our intimacy and wishing it could be like this forever.

As Tam strode ahead Todd and I stood for a few minutes on top of the rise enjoying the daybreak, eyes skimming on the rounded contours of the moors and following the ribbon of road where soon the shooting-brakes would carry the guns and their loaders to the first of the drives. I pictured the grouse sitting at peace among the heather tussocks, their colourful plumage protecting them from the early morning nip. They would have to take their chances with the guns. I almost wished that I might not witness their deaths but the thought touched me lightly.

From Hirplin' Hill we made our way to the castle courtyard where the guns had already assembled and where Big McGreegor organized the draw for positions. Grandpa was chatting with the laird. Mr Stacey was there laughing with one of the castle guests. Rab Gillespie, the head gardener, Archie Ross, the schoolmaster, and MacVicar, the session clerk, made the other three guns. McGreegor would be with the beaters.

Grandpa drew 'butt 2' and after McGreegor gave some further instructions about the drives we set off. I was instructed to stay close. The shooting-brakes took us part of the way and we walked the remaining distance to the first line of butts. The first drive was from the high ground downwind. The air enlivened me. The reds and mauves of the heather delighted my eyes which swept from the cotton-wool clouds over the undulating ground peopled only by the familiar figures of friends and neighbours.

As we trudged on foot to the higher ground, Grandpa and Callum scanned the sky for likely predators while I plodded behind until we reached the first line of butts.

Stacey and his friend were moving ahead to the first butt. I disliked their swaggering and swanky attire so out of keeping with the small green checked Strathard tweeds worn by the other men.

While Grandpa settled himself on his shooting stick, removing his cap to swipe at the pestering midges, I watched Callum organize his cartridges for correct and easy loading, remove the guns from the gun sleeves and prepare to load. I felt Callum's excitement as keenly as I appreciated Grandpa's serenity. By contrast Mr Stacey's high-spirited frolicking with his friend seemed out of place.

It would be some time before shooting commenced. Grandpa puffed contentedly on his pipe - to get rid of the midges, or so he said. I was keeping alert - as I'd been instructed - for signs of activity beyond the butt.

'And I don't mean the butt beyond,' said Grandpa, nodding towards Mr Stacey's friend who was laughing as his host aimed his gun towards the distant line of beaters which McGreegor was busily organizing. Callum focused his attention on the job at hand.

'You're well advanced for your age,' praised Grandpa adding wickedly, 'The Spaniards don't know what they're missing.'

Callum ignored the good-humoured taunt and went on with his loading.

There was a shot and Grandpa's gun instinctively flew to his shoulder. A single had escaped Stacey's gun. Grandpa took it from behind. Then a pair came swinging round the hill. Grandpa, on the limits of his swing, took them in front. There was no time for conversation after that. A covey streaked across the heather and this time Grandpa swore while wide-eyed,

I watched Stacey as he threw back his head and lifted a flask to his lips. After a long swig he drew the back of his hand across his mouth and offered the flask to his friend.

McGreegor had given the signal for the guns to move on. Realizing that Grandpa and Callum were already yards ahead, I raced after them. They trudged steadily on towards the next line of butts. The sun beat fierce on my face. I could feel the pull of my calf muscles while my tongue licked the salt sweat from my upper lip. I'd forgotten my compassion for the grouse.

Clad in kilt and sweater and long woollen socks, topped by buttoned-up boots, I trailed behind Callum whose garb consisted of cloth cap, knee-length trousers, an old tweed jacket and laced-up boots. By now I was as keen as everyone to bag as many grouse as possible. Mother's death, Graham and Moira were a world away. It was as if they had never been. I missed nothing of my new experience. Now and again I was encouraged to do some picking but mostly I was happy to watch and listen.

Grandpa's luck was still holding but Mr Stacey, according to Callum, was becoming greedy. He was taking long shots at birds he should have left for other guns. He was also, it seemed, becoming careless and swinging round too far. After McGreegor's signal at the end of the next drive, we watched aghast as the millionaire fired a shot in the keeper's direction.

'He's hell-bent on killing that man,' said Grandpa.

Stacey's hip flask was already uncorked and halfway to his mouth. Watching him, I couldn't understand why Miss Catriona had married him.

It was a relief when, after the third drive, we made our way towards the picnic which two servants from the castle were tending. I kept close to Grandpa and Callum who joined Rab Gillespie and his loader. I was surprised to find how hungry I was. Even Mr Stacey could do nothing to dispel my appetite for the venison sandwiches, game pies, plum tarts and the other delectables from the castle kitchens. The younger set of beaters, egged on by the boisterous Tam, were engaging in a tug-of-war.

An ugly scene was brewing between McGreegor and Stacey, the former insisting that the latter retire.

'Can he do that?' I asked Callum in a whisper.

'McGreegor is in complete command,' muttered Callum. 'If he thinks anyone's a danger, he can ask them to leave.'

'But not Mr Stacey, surely?' I said.

'Especially Mr Stacey,' said Callum, biting into his sandwich.

Stacey was mocking McGreegor who turned from him in disgust. He walked past the servants now packing the empty picnic baskets into one of the shooting-brakes. The tug-of-war teams were yelling good-humoured abuse at each other. In the midst of this Miss Catriona arrived in her DeLauney. She was in tweeds and brogues with a jaunty cap covering her braided hair. She parked a few yards from McGreegor and with one hand on the car bonnet stood scanning the shooting company scattered around in little groups.

'Here's trouble,' said Grandpa. 'Look at Stacey,' said Callum.

I looked. Arm raised, head bent back, he held a hip flask to his mouth which he drained before grabbing his gun and tottering off towards his wife. She turned to look at him and said something which seemed to enrage him. He tried to grab her arm. She pulled it away and they quarrelled. It was impossible to hear what they were saying. The tug-of-war was reaching its climax and the cries of the contestants and supporting onlookers drowned all other sounds. With a disdainful look at her husband Miss Catriona walked towards McGreegor who was watching the contest.

The game was over and Tam's team were victorious. Tam raised his arms above his head in triumph while the onlookers applauded. At the same moment Stacey aimed his gun at McGreegor. Tam, arms still aloft, ran forwards into the line of fire. He took the bullet in the chest. He dropped to the ground. He didn't stand a chance.

For a second the world seemed to stand still. Callum gasped, Grandpa groaned and Rab Gillespie swore while jumping to his feet. The doctor was already bent over Tam but everyone knew Tam was dead.

Archie Ross, Rab Gillespie and their two loaders were restraining McGreegor from rushing at Stacey. With amazing self-possession Catriona, with the help of others, bundled her drunken spouse into the DeLauney then took the wheel and sped him out of McGreegor's reach. It took half a dozen men to keep him from the vehicle. When it was out of sight he collapsed beside Tam's body howling like an animal caught in a snare. It was pitiful to witness.

'Tak' Jenny back to the hoose,' said Grandpa to Callum.

'Todd! Where's Todd?' I cried. I saw him standing as if carved in stone. His eyes were glazed as they stared at the still, silent body of his twin. Dr McLaren was on the point of covering Tam with a rug that someone had fetched from one of the shooting-brakes. I reached Todd a second before the schoolmaster.

'Oh Todd! Todd!' It was all I could say. Slowly he turned his head and looked at me. His eyes were glazed, his face ashen white and his lips etched in a straight, hard line. I don't believe that he saw me. I was now crying unreservedly.

'Oh Todd.' There were no words. Nothing but his name and his shock and his pain. Mr Ross's arm was round his shoulder. Gently he led him away to one of the shooting-brakes.

'Come on Jenny,' said Callum.

There was no stemming my sobs, no calming my bewilderment. Callum put both arms around me, holding me tight while the sobs began to rack my body. The others were being gently shepherded from the scene of desolation towards the shooting-brakes while the laird and the other guns waited to enter two cars which seemed to have arrived from nowhere.

Somebody, it seemed, was getting things organized.

Without realizing it I'd heeled Betsy into a gallop and, as the vision of that long-ago moorland tragedy slowly faded, I focused on the empty moors stretched before me. Exhilaration soon gave way to exhaustion. It was so long since I'd sat on a horse it was beginning to tell. I was hot. I was sore but I was happy in spite of the sad associations. It had been so long ago. How different things might have been.

I needed a rest. We had arrived at a small stream with some shrubs close by that would provide a little shade from the glaring heat of the sun. What better place to stop and eat my packed lunch. I dismounted carefully and unhooked the saddle-bag. A pat on Betsy's rump gave her the signal to enjoy her rest too. She'd be all right, I decided. Very docile. Unlikely to set off at a gallop particularly if she knew that I kept the titbits. She mouthed one daintily from my hand, tossed her mane in thanks and then grazed.

The sandwiches were delicious. The juicy apple to follow like nectar. I tested Betsy's obedience with the core. Hearing her name she cantered happily towards me and took the proferred reward.

'Good girl.' I buried my nose in her neck. 'Ten more minutes. Be a good girl now and don't go away.'

Using my jacket as a pillow I stretched out on the grass, my face shaded by the shrubs, and stretched my aching limbs. I was glad to be where I was. If I pretended really hard I could feel I'd never been away. This was the same sky, same moors, same running water and scents of heather. The manse in Edinburgh was in another existence, not real. It had surely not been a week ago when I was rehearsing in the Women's Guild Dramatic Society for the annual show - proceeds for the African Missionary Fund, of course. The Sunday school, the children's choir, the church services, the pulpit, the minister were all unreal, remote, in a far off place of no significance.

This was real. My solitude, my sky, my moors, my Strathard, my real people. The only problem was that they were all ghosts, disturbing, coming en masse to haunt me, especially Todd. Come to think of it, his ghost had never left me. Hadn't I a suitcase crammed with letters to him hidden in the attic of the manse. Admittedly I had not thought of these letters for many years but before I married Neil and more especially after, I could never bring myself to destroy them. Tam, Todd, or the injustice of the Spanish Civil War. Where did they all fit in, in the scheme of things? I wriggled around until I was as comfortable as the grassy earth would allow, took a slanted look at Betsy, happily nibbling grass and let my mind wander back in time once more.

CHAPTER 10

Tam's death put a different complexion on our thinking. I searched the works of philosopher, poet and sage for enlightenment. As a natural consequence of all that had happened to me since my mother's death I was becoming obsessed by injustice, in my own life and in the lives of others around me. Why Tam? Why Graham? Why me? I had to find a way of coming to terms with what was happening to me and the people I loved. I suppose it was because of my obsession with injustice that my imagination was sparked by the master's reports on the Spanish Civil War.

By the winter of 1938 hope was lessening for the People's Government in Spain. Not even the heroism of the International Brigade had been enough to save the Spanish democracy. It had no chance against the capitalists and appeasers who, being terrified of the spread of communism, provided the money and the weapons for the Nazis and Fascists to employ and do their dirty work for them. The dominie's brother kept sending reports from the battleground describing the bloody events which certainly kindled the sparks of my socialist beginnings.

Todd and Callum were as emotionally involved as I was. My interest fed my obsession with the concept of 'injustice', lending conviction to my quarrel with God. Todd's involvement served as a channel of release for his angst at the manner of his brother's death. He could not bear to talk about Tam but could give his tongue Un bridled liberty to decry the despotism in Spain. Callum, although none of us realized it at the time, was limbering up for future combat. In our various ways we were all driven to excess. It hadn't gone unnoticed. The schoolmaster had been warned more than once that his curriculum activities overreached the requirements of the pupils of the Strathard estate and that when his contract required renewal at the end of the school year his appointment would be reconsidered.

Miss Catriona was in America with her husband who was banned at his peril from ever setting foot in Scotland again.

The laird, according to Grandpa, was a broken man who had retired completely from public life, seeing few people other than Grandpa. Together they had stormed the defences of the Boers and together they were building their own defences around the heartbreak and desolation of the terrible event of August 1938.

Todd offered the scantiest information about his parents but along with shreds picked up here and there, we learned that his father was now completely submissive to his wife. Ella had put her foot down about prosecuting Stacey, taking the view that it was McGreegor's behaviour, in the first place, that had brought about their downfall and their son's death. Ella - wee hen-speckled Ella - had emerged the strong one, sparing her spouse neither guilt nor repentance and the future, whatever it might hold for the McGreegor clan, would be determined by her. I was appalled at how easily Stacey had escaped prosecution and could not understand Ella's magnanimity or McGreegor's surrender to it. I had little sympathy for McGreegor and even less for Catriona. My sympathy was for Todd but he was shutting me out.

'Gie the lad time,' said Grandpa when he found me moping and, in his usual way, prised out my thinking like a winkle from its shell. '"There's a time to every purpose",' he quoted, 'and this is the lad's time to mourn.'

I wiped the last mug and plate with exaggerated deliberation.

'I only want to help him,' I huffed.

Grandpa sighed with feigned patience.

'Sometimes you can help most by doing nothing.'

I knew it was more than that. I needed Todd for my own ends. I needed the stimulation he provided. I needed to know how he was feeling. I needed to identify with those needs. Since the day in the classroom when he pulled his twin from his chair and punched him on the chin for upsetting me, he had been my hero, but I was discovering that a hero was a remote figure, a little god. I wanted nothing to do with a god, little or otherwise. I wanted the nearness of flesh and blood. I wanted Todd and to feel him close. I had the awakening of a woman in every sense of the word and I had a huge void waiting to be filled. Todd and I thought the same way, liked the same things. Why was he shutting me out?

I was sleeping badly again. Nothing was going right. The castle was empty, the estate running down, the schoolmaster uncharacteristically uncommunicative. Callum was unsettled, even Grandpa was distracted and not much help, and Todd had cut me off.

One night while tossing and turning in bed I heard a thud on the window-pane. I lay stock-still. I was just beginning to think I had imagined the thud and that it had probably been the thudding in my head which my restless body had induced, when it happened again. Someone was pitching earth at the window. Curious, I rose and looked out. There was just enough moon clear of the heavy clouds to show a dark figure below, head tilted back. It was Todd. When he saw me he raised a finger to his lips and with the other arm beckoned me to join him. Now the thudding was coming from my heart. I pushed my feet into my slippers, threw a shawl over my shoulders and crept downstairs. Grandpa was already in bed and Father, back on the drink again, hadn't come home yet.

'I haven't long,' began Todd as I followed him to the back of the building where we would be safe from discovery. We could see each other clearly in the moonlight. He lifted his hand and touched my hair.

'I couldn't leave without saying goodbye,' he whispered.

He had to repeat it before I took in its meaning. 'Where are you going?'

'I'm running away. I'll never come back.'

Was it fear or anger that threatened and sharpened the cry?

'Why? Where? You can't!'

'I must. Father and Mother are leaving. They're going to some estate in Aberdeenshire but worst of all, Father told me he has fixed a job for me too as a pony boy. I don't want to work on the land, never did and never will.'

'Where will you go?' It was happening all over again. Someone I loved was leaving me. For a moment the moon was hidden in cloud and the darkness was nothing beside that spreading inside me. When he next spoke his voice was rough with suppressed excitement.

'I'm going with Mr Ross to join his brother in Spain. We're leaving in an hour. I've packed some things and they're in his car now.'

The cloud had passed and now the moon, more foe than friend, highlighted the loved and handsome face I'd thought would be there forever.

I caught his arm. 'They'll catch you and make you come back.'

'I've left a letter for my father. So has the dominie.'

'Archie Ross is a wicked man. He can't do this to you.' I was bordering on hysterics.

'I told him that if he wouldn't take me with him I'd run away anyhow.'

'Your father won't allow it.'

'Father won't worry. Mr Ross said he'd explained everything to him and I expect he'll be relieved to be rid of me.' The light was bright enough for me to see the jutting chin and determined mouth. Never had he looked so splendidly handsome.

I wanted to imprison him, protect him, fend off demons and slay dragons.

Todd, losing a little of his decisiveness, began stubbing his toe on the tufted grass muttering self-consciously. 'Noo dinna start greetin', Jenny.'

'Who's greetin? What makes you think I'd shed a tear for you, Todd McGreegor? You're nothing but a bloody fool as Grandpa would be the first to say. You're as daft as a brush, I say.'

'I like you better when you're riled. Your face gets as red as your hair.'

'If you knew what was good for you you'd, you'd...' But I couldn't go on. The moon was playing tricks now. Todd's face became an impassive mask in which only his eyes were fired like beacons against the pallor of his skin. I felt frightened. Then he grinned. The mask slipped and I saw my beloved Todd again. He placed his hands on my shoulders.

'I think you're great, Jenny McLeod and I'm never going to forget you.'

'I should hope not.' I was crying.

'Now you are greetin' and greetin' for me.' His voice was gentle. 'I'll be back,' then cheekily, 'after I've sorted out the Fascists.'

Impulsively I kissed him. For a moment he stiffened in embarrassment then lifting his hands to my hair tugged it gently, his grin hiding any deeper feelings he may have had.

'Look after yourself, Todd.' I wanted him to go and quickly but his hand on my arm halted my flight.

'There's something else, Jenny. Another reason why I had to see you.'

I turned to face him dismayed by his seriousness. 'The estate's to be broken up and sold. The laird's already sold off some of the farms. Things are going to be different here for you.'

I began to shake. His concern was immediate.

'You'd better get back inside. You're shivering.'

My voice seemed to come from a great distance.

'Father will lose his job.' The moon disappeared behind a cloud. 'We'll have no home.' I felt as dark as the night around me.

My mouth was dry and a knot tightened in my throat. 'I'm sorry to be the one to tell you, Jenny.'

'Do you have to run away, Todd?'

'Aye. And the sooner I go the better.'

'Take me with you.'

'Now who's as daft as a brush?'

He leaned towards me and kissed me on the lips. Then he was gone.

Turning back to the house I went to my room and lay in an agony of cold and fear. I heard my father return from the village. Soon he'd come stumbling past my bed without a glance in my direction. Now I knew why he'd started drinking again. Now I knew what all the whisperings had been about. Now I knew that the world was a cruel and frightening place and that I'd just said goodbye to the one person who'd helped colour it brighter for me. What was going to happen to us? Where would we go? What would we do? Mother! Mother! Why did you go away and leave me? No! You didn't want to go. God took you.

I turned on my back, staring into the darkness. There is no God I decided with a reassuring conviction. It's better that there is no God. Life's just a game of chance.

That night I had the nightmare of all nightmares in which I was running for my life. No matter how hard I ran I got nowhere. I was under the illusion of covering distance but seemed grounded to one spot. My screams woke me. When I shot up from my pillow in terror I saw Grandpa shuffling to my bedside tuttutting and shaking his head.

'What a kerfuffle!' he said testily but his hands on my forehead were gentle.

'You're fevered And what's all this about keepin' a' ... thegither?

'Who told you that?' I gasped.

'You did. You've been shouting in your sleep about keepin' somethin' thegither. Whit's that supposed to mean?'

I turned my head on the pillow and looked up at my grandfather seeing him with new eyes. This old man, I realized, was not just Grandpa who'd loved me from my cradle, he was all the wisdom of the ages, the manifestation of Christian values I'd been taught, the rock of ages I'd sung about. He was my friend and had always been there when I needed him. I needed him now. With unimaginable relief I told him about my mother's death wish. How could I do what my mother had asked? How could I keep the family together?

'It was bad enough before,' I told him, 'but a thousand times worse now. It's impossible, I can't do it Grandpa.'

I struggled upright in my bed unconscious of the cold. I half made to rise but was firmly restrained.

'Dinna fash yersel' lass. Nothing's ever as bad as it seems. Now settle down and let me ask ye something.'

I lay back on my pillow while he reached for and held my hand.

'Do you think for one minute that your mither would willingly put sic a burden on your back?'

'Those were her words. I swear it.'

'It was love she was talkin' aboot, lass. For folk to be thegither doesn't mean that they aye need to be in touching distance. It is possible to be thegither with someone on the other side o' the world. Love keeps folk thegither wherever they are. Your mither kent that. When she said she could depend on you to keep us a' thegither she was telling you that she knew you had mair than enough love in your heart to do just that. God rest her soul.'

I felt like Christian must have done when his burden dropped from his shoulders. Then I remembered something.

'Noo, what's the matter?'

'Moira,' I whispered. 'I've never loved her.'

He sighed. 'Ye can begin by just keepin' her in mind.

Noo, isn't it time ye went back tae sleep?'

But I wasn't finished. 'I hear the estate's being broken up and sold.'

'And who told you that?'

'Todd when he came to see me tonight to tell me that he was running away to Spain with the dominie to be a freedom fighter.' I decided to tell Grandpa all that Todd had told me - about his father's new job and about

McGreegor getting him fixed as a pony boy and him not being interested, and about the dominie and the plans for both of them to leave Strathard.

'The dominie has a lot to answer for,' he mumbled.

'What's going to happen to us all Grandpa?' I repeated.

'It's time I was in bed. It's tiring work answering your questions.'

'Grandpa!'

'We'll talk about it, Jenny, but no the noo. We need oor sleep. Anyway there's still a lot undecided. Time enough for decisions.'

'But we will talk about it!' I was telling, not asking. He grunted as he tucked me in and in spite of my worry I slept immediately.

Soon the break-up of the estate was the main talking point of tenants and workers. Everyone knew it would happen. The question was when? It was nearly six months since Todd had left Strathard. The only news of the outside world I received was from Callum. Things were not going well for the people of Spain nor, as I learned, for the people of Czechoslovakia or Poland or indeed for any of the European countries. Neville Chamberlain was doing his best to appease Hitler and this made Callum angry.

For months now Callum's weekend visits were times of tension. He had become more and more withdrawn. He'd take off alone on moorland walks. The few tentative offers I made to accompany him were politely rejected. His mood spread among us like an infectious disease. Father's temper was more than usually short. The only time he eased up was when a letter arrived from Canada. They came regularly with photographs and paper cuttings which I generally ignored. When the atmosphere became too highly charged between Callum and Father, Grandpa would take himself off to the kennels which were being quickly and severely culled in the general run down of the estate and he'd come home lacking his customary good humour. We were all saturated with our own miseries and tempers were short. Callum raging about Hitler didn't help matters.

'Ye'd think ye wanted a war,' growled Grandpa.

'I don't want to see Hitler marching down Princes Street,' grumbled Callum.

'Ach awa' and stop your haverin'!' said Grandpa. 'Ye dinna ken whit ye're talkin' aboot.'

'I read the papers. I listen to the wireless. I go to the political meetings,' said Callum, using the floor like a stage in a theatre. Father, taking up the drama, turned on him.

'And do you read your lesson books and listen to your professors?'

Callum sulked, addressing the family audience at large.

'What good will that do if there's going to be a war?'

'Folk'll still be sick and need doctorin', war or no war,' said Grandpa from his rocking chair. And on it went!

As the summer wore on and the estate was wound down, the tension became unbearable. Father hardly spoke but at least he had stopped wearing out the path to the Strathard Arms. He had less and less work to do. The laird had retired completely from social life. There was very little chauffeuring needed. What there was did little to reassure us. Instead of meeting shooting parties at the station, Father told us about lean-faced business- men in pin-striped suits and stiff white collars being taken to meet the laird and his lawyer.

In the midst of all this a letter arrived for me. It had a foreign stamp and was addressed in Todd's familiar scrawl. I carried it to my room where no one could see how my fingers were all thumbs as I slit the envelope, and how my breath kept catching in my throat as I hungrily scanned the contents. The rest of the world slipped away as my eyes travelled the pages. Todd wrote as he would have spoken with an easy warm style. Even the grimmest of his accounts were leavened with his wry humour.

'...trekking o'er the mountains was no great shakes, not when you've spent all your life climbing the local bens and tramping the moors. It was having to act like a half-baked deaf mute that took the biscuit. You know I'm no mute even if at times I might have seemed half-baked but the funny thing is, I enjoyed every minute of it. Even when we eventually joined the refugees and dodged the gunfire I managed to remind myself that I was dumb and dim-witted...'

I read on, feeling alternately scared and excited, alive and quickened by Todd's graphic descriptions. '...the hills are pretty barren, not like our green and purple ones, less friendly, especially when the shooting here is for real. Now I know how the grouse must feel. The most difficult time was in the dark, but I discovered my sight made up for my lack of hearing and speech! I have the eyes of a cat and was often a help to the others.

Sometimes we would come to a bridge which had been blown up and the smell of rotting animals was a fair scunner. There were plenty of friendly Spaniards willing to help us on our way and I must have been a source of embarrassment to them because after one look, they'd turn their eyes away. I became so cross-eyed and gapiflg mouthed that I just hoped the wind wouldn't change and I'd stay like that...'

I was glad to laugh and for a brief moment when my eyes strayed from the letter to the mirror on the wall before me I was surprised to see my heightened colour and wondered why my hair was not on end because my scalp tingled so.

'...It wasn't long before I realized that Archie Ross, was getting worried and not just for me. We hadn't done any fighting for Spain yet. His brother, who is a big chief in the underground here, had arranged our illegal entry but the way things were going I think Archie began to think we had left it a bit late. The Nationalists - Franco's rebels - were sweeping everything before them and in spite of the wonderful International Brigade it became pretty certain that the Frente Popular (how do you like my Spanish?) were done for. Even Kurt (Archie's brother - his code name, I think) thought it was time we did a bunk. Archie decided that we'd probably be needed back in Britain. He is convinced that when this show is over, ours will begin...'

I thought of Callum and what he'd said about the traitor Chamberlain. Would there really be a war, I wondered.

'...It would be nice to be myself again but it wasn't easy to switch to being normal. To tell you the truth, Jenny, I don't know what normal is any more...'

I thought that normal was the last word I'd use for Todd. He had become my hero when, in a little country classroom he first raised his fist to his twin in my defence but within the last few minutes he'd taken on the stature of a Titan. I flushed with pride. Todd McGreegor of Strathard, barely 16 years old, being smuggled into Spain as a deaf-mute by a Scottish schoolmaster and his brother who probably had found it less trouble on their consciences to smuggle him in than to leave him fretting behind.

'...and what about you, Jenny. I hope you're keeping the red flag flying in the valley and remembering all that the dominie taught us. He's different here, Jenny. Still great, but different. Sometimes I find him looking at me as if he didn't know who I was and what the heck I was doing there. I sometimes wonder that myself. But I wouldn't have it any other way. I never want to return to Strathard. There's only one reason that I should and that would be to see you again. One day I might do just that and we can talk the hind legs off a donkey.'

'I've so much to tell you Todd,' I whispered aloud before realizing that I wouldn't be able to tell him. The letter contained no address where he could be contacted. My spirits plummeted as my mind absorbed the fact that Todd McGreegor, so close to my heart, couldn't be further from my reach. It was one more denial in my ever-increasing circles of desire.

CHAPTER 11

Todd's letter was beginning to split along the creases. I carried it everywhere and had reread it until I knew it by heart. I let Callum read it.

'Brave don't you think?' I asked him.

'Or foolhardy,' he replied.

I read parts of it to Grandpa who just shook his head, tutted and said that no good would come of it.

Neil Fraser was ordained and took up his pastoral duties in a Presbyterian church in Edinburgh. He was now where he had always wanted to be. Callum, on the other hand, had reached a significant crossroad in his life. His disenchantment with the appeasement policy kick-started a revolution in all our lives. It began when we were seated round the table at supper.

'Are you saying that you want a war?' growled Father, holding out his plate for replenishment.

'No, but Hitler certainly does, and God only knows what is going to make him stop.' He raised a forkful of shepherd's pie to his mouth.

'Mind your tongue,' warned Grandpa, more upset than angry.

Callum ignored him and continued addressing Father. 'He doesn't believe we'll try to stop him and the way our government's behaving he's not far wrong.'

'We can't afford to go to war,' said Father, lifting the end of a loaf to clean his plate.

Callum rounded on him. 'We can't afford not to!' He pushed back his chair as if to leave the table and his face was flushed, eyes blazing, his hair on end from running his fingers through it in exasperation. I was annoyed.

We had enough problems without Callum bringing more. I asked him if he'd finished his meal. I too was ignored.

'Nothing is going to stop Hitler and before you know it this country will be at war.'

'And you'd like that, wouldn't you?' said Father. 'That's just what you're waiting for, I suppose. It would be just the excuse you need to leave your learnin' and go and get yourself killed. Is that what you want? Is that the best you can do for our situation?'

Things were getting ugly. Callum was acting completely out of character. His plate was only half empty but so agitated was he that he rose, and standing behind his chair, faced Father across the kitchen table, ignoring Grandpa's further pleas for calm and my concern about his dinner.

'You're the one to talk,' he charged Father. 'What have you ever done for our situation, as you call it, apart from feeling damned sorry for yourself and getting drunk?'

There was a stunned silence. Grandpa replaced his knife and fork, shaking his head from side to side while Father slowly rose from his chair and towered above Callum. Like stags in combat they edged closer. I looked on in horror. This was something that hadn't just happened to either of them. I lost my appetite.

What grotesque thoughts had been burrowing in each of their minds, slowly fermenting until this moment when the lid blew off. This explosion of frayed tempers and hurtling accusations was the outward signal of inner torment.

'Has it never occurred to you,' asked Callum, glaring at Father, 'that the laird uses you. Only when he's sold the last stick and stone of this place will he stop using you because he'll have no need of you, or Grandpa or any of us. He won't care where we go or what happens to us.'

'That's not true,' interrupted Grandpa.

Again Callum ignored him, continuing his attack oil Father.

'When were you ever able to decide what you wanted tc, do or where you wanted to go? The laird paid you a pits tance which made you his slave. You weren't even allowed to fight for your country in the last war. He saw to that He believed he needed you more than your country did.'

Father flinched, his face suffused in angry hues.

'Callum!' I pleaded, feeling sick. 'Finish your supper please. I want to wash up.' He paid no heed to my distress. We were seeing a side of my brother never before suspected.

'Does the laird care? Of course he doesn't.' He was expostulating like a soapbox orator.

Father's face hardened, his eyes glinting like steel. His voice, when he spoke, was as brittle.

'Sit down!' he ordered.

My grandfather's head jerked up from his chest while Callum, bracing himself, remained on his feet. Father repeated his command and Callum's hands which had been tightly gripping the back of his chair, relaxed.

Pulling it from under the table he did as he'd been ordered but managed to maintain his air of defiance.

Father now took centre stage.

'First of a',' he said, slipping into the idiom as he usually did when roused, 'if providing steady work which I happen to enjoy and a hoose for my wife, faither and three bairns is what you Ca' using me then I've no shame or discomfort in having been used.

'As for His Grace being the means of exempting me from the battlefields, I've no regrets on that score. We're not a' like the creatures that canna get to the cliff edge fast enough. I've no doubt I'd fight as weel as the next man if I had to but I've been lucky, thanks to the laird. There's plenty, like yourself, only too ready to fodder the guns.'

'That's neither true nor fair,' protested Callum half rising again and pushing back his chair.

'Sit doon!' Father shouted and like a well-trained pup, Callum did as he was told. He opened his mouth to speak but Father silenced him.

'You say, wi' the arrogance o' your superior learning, that the laird doesn't care what happens to us.'

Callum flushed. I sat on the fender stool beside my father. He had also left his dinner and was sitting on his rocker, gazing into the fire.

'It's not the laird personally I was objecting to,' said Callum.

'That's not the way I heard you,' said Father. 'If saying he doesn't care what happens isn't being personal, I don't know what is.'

'I was meaning the feudal system, the class divisions, the unfair distribution of wealth and opportunity.'

90

'I ken fine what you were meaning. You don't like anyone being better off than yourself. The politics of envy it's known as. Did the dominie mention that?'

Both Grandpa and I had stopped our pleas for calm. This was a battle between father and son which brooked no interference. Callum made another attempt to get on to his feet.

'Wait,' said Father. 'I haven't finished with you.' His eyes swept towards Grandpa and me, including us in the delivery of his next words. 'It's time you a' knew the way the wind's blowin'. He placed his chair carefully under the table, momentarily pausing before again pacing the floor. He stuck a finger under his shirt collar stud as if clearing a passageway for his next words.

'His Grace has found a job that would be mine for the taking. Oh aye,' he said, looking from one to the other of us. 'You may look surprised. The laird actually caring what happens to us! That's flummoxed you,' he added turning to Callum. He thumbed his braces. 'That makes think, does it no?' He let his words sink in before continuing. 'It sounds a fine job, a bit of everything in a place up north. He's closely acquainted with the landlord has accepted his recommendation, even allowing for the three of you.'

He paused now, put both his palms down on the table and looked at each of us in turn. Grandpa was the first to speak.

'Och aye,' he said softly as he began filling his pipe 'That sounds fine, just fine.'

I was at a loss to know what to say, aware of Father's need of a job and hesitant about saying the wrong thing to upset him further. Callum's dark mood was still stamped on his face. His heavy frown and troubled eyes gave no indication of pleasure in the news.

'Weel,' said Father with rising impatience. 'You're none of you what I'd say dancing a jig about my news.'

'What about Graham?' I managed to say.

'What about him?' said Father.

'We can't just go up north and leave him here.'

'Graham's fine where he is.'

'But suppose there's a war,' I said in desperation.

'We get enough o' that kind o' talk from your brother without you starting.'

'And Callum won't manage home for the weekends,' I added. 'He'll have to stay in Edinburgh.'

Callum, who hadn't said a word since Father's startling announcement seemed to draw himself back from a distance and rejoin us.

'I'm pleased for you, Father,' he began. 'It makes it easier to say what I have to say to you and the others,' indicating grandfather and myself with an inclination of the head. Instinctively, I prepared myself for another shock.

'I've volunteered for the Air Force,' he said. 'I didn't want to say anything until I'd been accepted.'

He'd shed his arrogance, his confession now matched with an air of contrition which seemed to emphasize his youth and vulnerability.

'You're a fool,' said Father, 'but I kent fine it would happen sooner or later.'

Grandpa, laying his pipe on the stove, reached for his stick and struggled to rise. Callum made to help him but he was waved off.

'I'd've thocht you'd rather cure folk than kill them,' he grunted. 'Don't you want to be a doctor?'

'I don't ever want to be a doctor.'

At a stroke my own misery was forgotten.

Callum was now drained of colour. His eyes looked startling against his pallor and I noticed that a shadow of facial hair edged his upper lip and chin.

'I've never mentioned it,' said Callum, 'but I hate the medical school. I've hated every minute of it and the pity is I didn't realize it till I thought it was too late to do anything about it. I'm just not cut out to be a doctor.'

'Why, in the name o' the wee man didn't you tell us this before?' stormed Father.

'I didn't want to disappoint you, I suppose.' For a moment he hung his head but it was no indication of shame. His colour was still high, his jaw set and he was aware of the bombshell he'd just delivered. We were astounded and choked for words. Grandpa was the first to recover.

'So the war you're so sure is comin' is an excuse. You're escaping into the Air Force.'

'I've always been interested in planes,' said Callum. 'For a long time now I've wanted nothing more than to learn to fly them. But it isn't only that. I truly believe there is going to be a war soon and fighting the Nazis is going to be the most important thing in the world. I had to do what I've done.'

'You're as bad as Todd McGreegor,' said Father.

At the mention of Todd's name my misery returned full blast. Todd, I felt, would be stupid enough to get himself killed and even if he didn't and we weren't here but somewhere 'up north' if he ever came back home he'd never find me. I had an urge to run from the room and dig a hole to crawl into. Only the memory of Neil Fraser's scorn at this need of mine to run away from scenes of stress restrained me. 'When are you going to grow up, Jenny McLeod?' was what he'd said the last time I'd done it.

I rose and began clearing the table. There was obviously going to be no more food eaten tonight. My grand father was making us tea. Just as it was my way to ruin for cover, making tea was his way of coping with difficult situations. Now watching his painstaking preparation helped restrain my impulse.

'When do you go then - to your Air Force?' he wa asking Callum.

'I have to report to the Recruitment Centre on Monday morning. I'll have to leave by tomorrow's afternoon train.'

'And where would this Centre be then?'

'On the outskirts of London.'

I sensed Callum looking at me but couldn't bring myself to meet his eyes. Instead I concentrated on Grandpa as he spooned tea from caddy to pot.

'I'll likely be there for a few months. I'll be back home before you all move north, I expect.' His voice tapered into silence.

To me London was synonymous with Mars, a place afar, out of my orbit. Now Callum was on course to go there. I was about to lose him as I'd lost Mother, Graham and Todd, even Moira. Father's next words did nothing to reassure me.

'We won't be going up north,' he said. 'I told the laird I wouldn't be wantin' his job because I had other plans.'

I was flabbergasted. Grandpa, apparently unperturbed, began pouring the tea.

Father walked to the dresser and took a letter from one of the drawers. Taking it out of its envelope he unfolded the crisp pages, shuffling them to find what he was looking for. On the point of reading aloud he changed his mind, throwing the letter and envelope on to the kitchen table.

'You can read it for yourselves after,' he said, 'but the thing is when I wrote to Canada and told them about the break-up of the estate your

Uncle Peter wrote back to say that he wants me to join him in Canada and begin a new life there. He guarantees me work when I get there in his own shop which is fast becoming a factory. His sweeties are gey popular in Canada, he tells me.'

It was a long speech for Father. Grandpa was spooning sugar into the cups. Callum's face gave away nothing while I wanted to run to a hole in the ground. Almost peadingly Father continued. 'He says once I find my feet I'll likely want to turn to my ain kind of work with machines. He says there are plenty opportunities if one is prepared to work hard. What's mair,' he offered into the continued silence, 'he says accommodation is no problem. So what do you say?'

Like a defendant pleading his cause, he looked at us, the jury, who were, to all appearances, struck dumb.

'So Jenny,' he concluded. 'How do you like the idea of a new life in Canada and the chance of gettin' to know your bonnie wee sister?'

He went back to the dresser drawer and found a photograph. He put it into my trembling hands. Moira, whom I had last seen as a baby, had developed into a strikingly beautiful child with Mother's dark brown eyes and chestnut hair.

My heart sank. It might as well have been a death warrant. This wasn't just my young sister I was looking at. It was a reminder of a not-so-recent past and painful time whose bruises I still bore. I had never allowed this child whom I blamed for my mother's death, into the fabric of my make-up. I had considered her, and still did, an outcast.

I believed that because of her I had lost my own childhood, and any rapport I might have had with God and the angels had been destroyed the day she breathed life and my mother expired. The threat of 'up north' was bad enough but the thought of Canada and Aunt Sheena and the child Moira was inconceivable.

'Your grandfather will come with us, of course, and to set your mind at rest, as soon as we are settled in a place o' our own, we'll arrange, some way or another, to have Graham join us - if it's in his interest, of course. We must always consider that first. So, what do you say?'

I looked helplessly at my grandfather who came to m side and took the photograph from my none too stead hands. He placed a mug of tea on the table motioning me to join him there. In his characteristic way he took control of the situation. I think we were all glad of the tea ritual. It was like a moment of holding one's breath. and concentrating on the edge of a diving board before' taking the plunge. Grandpa, as always, proved the life-saver, rescuing us all from saying things we might later regret.

'Tell me, Angus,' he said, addressing my father who was looking anxiously from one face to the other, 'how long is it since you kent aboot a' these grand plans?'

Father considered a moment. 'For about ten days,' he replied before lifting his mug to his lips.

'Ali wee!, we've just had about ten minutes,' said Grandpa. 'We're goin' to need more time to get used to the idea.'

'Don't you like the idea?' insisted Father.

'Noo haud yer horses,' said Grandpa. 'I suggest we tak' this slow and steady. It's a fine idea. You're still a young man and could dae weel for yersel but I'm up and o'er the hill and won't see three score years and ten again. What wad a be doin' trampsin' off to Canada?'

'But you'll have to come with us,' said Father. 'This place is no going to be our home for much longer. You'll have nowhere to stay.'

'Noo, that's jist whaur ye'r wrong.'

He got the immediate attention his words provoked.

'Callum's had his say and although I think he's a bit headstrong I can understand him. I'm no that old that I can't mind wantin' to save the world when I went wi' His Grace to fight the Boers.'

I could hear a soft sigh of relief escape Callum's lips. Grandpa sat back more comfortably in his chair before continuing. 'You've had your say so let me have mine. I can tell young Callum here, that in spite of what he might think to the contrary, His Grace does have our interest at heart.

'The system, as he calls it, is no a' bad. This place has to go. That's all in the deals at present bein' negotiated but there is one place that the new owners can't have and the laird has offered it to me for the rest o' my clays.' He smiled with sly satisfaction.

'What place are you talking about?' asked Father.

'Broom Cottage.'

I pictured the small whitewashed cottage on a rise above the shore road about a mile outside the village. In spring its garden was a riot of yellow daffodils, heathers and shrubs of golden broom. The cottage had stood empty for the past year, its elderly tenant having passed away in an Edinburgh nursing home. It was one of the few 'grace and favour' cottages of the laird and his father before him. Now it was to be the home of my grandfather for as long as he wished or the Almighty permitted.

I glanced at the faces before me. Grandpa looked serenely untroubled while in contrast Father's confident air was visibly slipping. Callum was looking at me.

Jenny?' he said.

They were all looking at me. A dog barking in the distance emphasized the silence. I felt outside myself, conscious that destiny was at work again. They were waiting for me to say something. Decisions seemed pointless. What difference would it make? I was no better equipped to say what I wanted now than when they'd 'consulted' me about Graham leaving home, yet here they were all expecting me to comment on this latest thunderbolt. I was learning.

I rose and carried my empty mug to the kitchen sink, amazed at how removed I was from the situation. I felt I was up above looking down at myself performing in a play.

'Have you nothing to say for yourself?' asked Father.

I looked at him, carefully choosing my words. 'Not at the moment,' I replied. 'As Grandpa says we need more time to think about it. I'll let you know when I've given the matter more thought.'

I turned and left the house but not before seeing a look of something which might have been approval in my grandfather's eyes. I still needed a bolt-hole which in this case was the stable. I sought its sanctuary. I haven't really changed I thought, my throat constricting with suppressed sobs. The only difference is that this time instead of running away I walked.

Then it hit me. On the point of giving way to tears and nursing my ego and blaming others for my troubles, I remembered that I had a choice. I could opt for a good cry and wrap myself in self-pity or I could refuse to act the victim. Fine, I told myself, you are not the heroine in some Greek tragedy. You are only a motherless child having a rough time and learning rather painfully about growing up.

So? Grow up, Jenny McLeod! Face reality. It's all a question of choice.

CHAPTER 12

The train was late. It was the train that was to transport Callum into a life in which I'd have no part. Grandpa and I had accompanied him to the station to see him off. Father was driving the laird to Aberdeen so could not be with us.

It was a fine day - sunny, windless, the air heavy with perfume from the scents of foliage and flowers, and hot enough to blister the paint on the station yard gate.

We were the only people in sight except for Dick, the elderly stationmaster, who shuffled out of his office and made his way towards a line of sherry casks further down the platform. Grandpa nodded in his direction.

'Dick's the only man I know who chews Black Twist tobacco and can spit from one platform to another through a hole in his teeth,' he said admiringly.

I caught Callum's eye and it was a relief to share a smile. If this was Grandpa's way of cheering us up I was grateful. He struggled to his feet and went off to have a blather with Dick.

Callum and I also rose from the rustic bench where we'd been sitting and began pacing the platform. Pigeons on the lookout for crumbs, dodged in our path. Margarets and marigolds offered splashes of colour in their wooden tubs, and the hedges were bloodied with hardy fuchsias. It was wasted on us. We were both in that state of longing for, and dreading, the train's arrival.

'I wish it hadn't been the threat of war that made you confess about no liking the doctoring.'

'Occasionally it takes something drastic to make our minds up for us,' he said.

'I wish you weren't going so soon.'

'A lot of wishing, Jenny. What about yourself?' 'There's no question of my going to Canada, not even to save hurting Father. I'm not as noble as you.'

The train's whistle sounded in the distance. Callum turned to me.

'You're wasting your talents, Jenny. Get yourself sorted out. Canada would offer great opportunities. Promise me you'll think again.'

Reluctantly I promised. I kicked a stone across the platform while Callum collected his small suitcase from the bench.

'One more thing,' he whispered before the others came within earshot. 'If you're ever in trouble, go to Neil. He's very fond of you. You could do worse.'

The train screeched to a halt belching clouds of steam.

'But I don't even like him,' I screamed.

Dick had the carriage door open. Grandpa delivered some snatch of his timeless wisdom to Callum as they gripped hands. Dick impatiently waved Callum on board.

'Goodbye Callum. Take care,' was as much as I could manage as we embraced.

'I'll write as soon as I can.'

'Just mind that you do,' said Grandpa before the door slammed and Dick blew his whistle and waved his flag. Grandpa put an arm round my shoulder and we stood watching and waving, shielding our eyes from the sun's glare and straining for the last sight of Callum hanging out of the carriage window.

'He'll be back afore long,' consoled Grandpa. 'You'll see. Now let's get on wi' the rest o' the day.'

It took more than the 'rest o' the day' for things to start happening. The laird moved out of the castle and into his shooting lodge at the other end of the valley and although, as yet, the new owners had not moved in, there was a lot of coming and going at the castle. It seemed most of the furnishings were being sent to auction and a regular stream of workers made their way up and down the main driveway.

We had decided to keep ourselves well out of the way, and besides, we had our own comings and goings. I busied myself in the daytime helping Jimmy the painter decorate Broom Cottage and at night wrote letters to Callum, Father and Todd. I described everything to Todd. Nothing was happening in my life that I didn't tell Todd about. Grandpa concentrated on collecting all sorts of creatures. The lifetime use of an adjoining field came with the cottage and he was planning to have his menagerie introduced before we moved in. Father gave up pleading with Grandpa and me to go with him to Canada and was busy arranging his journey.

Busy as we were, we were overjoyed when Callum came home on a short leave. He had completed his basic training at the RAF Reception Centre and, after an aptitude test, was sent for gunnery training somewhere in the English Midlands. Immediately afterwards he was transferred to an Operational Training Unit. Only after his training there was he given one short leave. He was a different Callum when he came home. His usual reticence was gone. He seemed more confident and was full of his new life, full of enthusiasm that now at long last he would be flying for real. His basic training would be converted to practice in the air.

'But it's still just target towing,' he said, his eyes glowing as we walked together on the moor. 'When war comes it'll be the real thing.'

I was thrilled that we were enjoying long walks together again like the old days but my enjoyment was marred when I thought about his possible involvement in the real thing. When the time came for him to leave I looked at my brother standing in the kitchen, handsome in his rough serge uniform. His field service cap tilted on his blond waves gave him a jaunty air. His highly polished leather boots, shining brass buttons and buckle added to the overall appearance. He looked happier, more confident than I'd ever seen him. I was happy for him. Only the brass bullet badge he wore on his sleeve reminded me of his vulnerability. As a newly fledged air gunner the bullet was for man, not grouse.

Only too soon the day came for leaving the Square. Father helped Grandpa and me move to Broom Cottage and stayed with us for a few days. Callum had already returned to his unit. The day came when, with mixed feelings, I watched my father pack his pitifully few belongings, and leave on the first leg of his journey. Only when he boarded the train for Inverness and we made solemn promises to keep in touch did our guards fall and we clung to each other in tears. I made a vow then that I'd do my utmost to 'keep us a' thegither' in the way my Grandpa had so comfortingly interpreted my mother's words. Solemn vows were made to keep in touch. None of us was hopeful that we would all be together again but we encouraged each other to think

Broom Cottage, our new home, brought a whole new lifestyle for Grandpa and me. First came the chickens. Next my grandfather acquired a lamb which had to be hand fed and practically house-trained. Then a pig and a dairy cow called Maggie. They were all refugees from Home Farm which had been hived off. He grew vegetables and acquired some fruit bushes. The resulting produce, together with newly laid eggs, he sold locally and he gradually built up a tidy little business. He seemed to have lost twenty years and to me this was wonderful to behold.

Wonderful too were the views of the Firth from my bedroom window. The elevated site of the pleasant property was in sharp contrast to the Square enclosure. For a time Grandpa and I were so busy that we had little outside contact but we did hear, in true Strathardian fashion, that the new owners were about to open their hotel to the public. Already, it seemed, the Village Gossip Society had them tabbed as heathens. According to the rumours the woman was a strange foreigner and the man wore brass curtain rings in his ears.

To my surprise, one bright sunny morning, I opened the door of Broom Cottage to a man of medium height with long grey hair brushed into a pony tail and tied severely back from a finely chiselled face. His eyes, startlingly blue against his tanned skin, were penetrating but held no threat. As they met mine they smiled, lighting his face with friendliness. A tiny gold ring was embedded in each ear lobe and round his neck he wore a gold chain. He introduced himself.

'I'm Guy Mason and you must be Jenny McLeod. I'm the owner of the new hotel. I need help,' he said with a smile. 'I need someone who knows the area and the people in it, and who can help smooth out the changeover. You come highly recommended and sound, from all accounts, just the person for the job. Are you interested?'

I was fascinated and invited him into the house, but he declined saying that he had to get back to his wife who was holding the fort and would be wondering where he was.

'I'm not looking for a job,' I said without conviction because already the thought excited me. A job could be just what I needed but I was canny. 'I'd have to talk to my grandfather and, of course,' I added hastily, 'find out a bit more about it.'

'Of course. Why don't you come to the hotel and meet my wife and we can talk more about it?'

'You mean now?'

'Why not? If it's convenient. I can take you and bring you back.'

Grandpa had gone off to the kennels 'to see a man about a dog' he'd said mysteriously. I decided to go.

It seemed strange seeing the main drive again and the castle façade looked exactly the same. But that was all. Somewhat shocked, I stood just inside the hall. The tartans and stag heads, guns and shields were gone. I gazed at the white walls, modern furnishings, the long snake-like counter with rows of keys on hooks on the wall behind it. And behind it too was Guy Mason's wife.

'Theresa!' said Guy. 'Here is the wonderful Jenny McLeod we've heard so much about, dropped fresh from heaven.'

'Our lucky star,' smiled this amazing stranger who turned a dazzling smile on me. I was entranced. Theresa Mason, as she came to meet me, took my breath away. She was like no one I had ever known or could have ever imagined. If I'd thought Guy Mason was unusual, his wife was extraordinary.

She was a little round ball of a woman with round, wide-apart eyes, round mouth, round fleshy arms protruding from a round red gown which clung to round buttocks then fell in soft folds to the ground, leaving only enough room to allow the toes of red sequinned slippers to emerge. Jewels sparkled from throat, wrists and fingers while two blood-red gems dangled on gold chains from her small round ears. Her hair was black - bouncy round ringlets, swept from her brow with a red silk bandanna.

I couldn't tear my eyes away from her. Her sparkling jewels seemed to emanate from a source of fire that trapped me in its warmth. I was pulled roughly against her body which exuded a musky perfume - heady and disturbing.

'You are most welcome, Jenny McLeod,' she breathed huskily, her voice coloured with a hint of accent. She kissed me lightly on my cheek. I felt no embarrassment, responding happily to her generosity.

'Come! We shall have tea in my studio.' With her bejewelled hand on my elbow she led the way from the hall to one of the other public rooms on ground level whose windows offered a view of the rose garden. Stepping into the studio was like entering the pages of Aladdin. The laird with all his many treasures had never revealed a room such as this. I was 'dumfoonered!' as Grandpa might say. As I looked around me, slowly taking in the scene, my wonder grew. The initial impression I'd had of roundness was further emphasized here. A round, highly polished table dominated the centre of the floor. On the table was a round velvet cloth upon which stood a crystal ball. Chime bells tinkled in the breeze from the open windows which offered a splendid view of the garden beyond. The air was thick with incense and candles burned on an alcove shelf.

On another shelf was a splendid armillary sphere flanked by two globes - one terrestrial and one celestial. On top of a grand piano was a collection of small statues none of which I recognized. The schoolmaster's instruction fell short in the visual arts.

The one touch of normality was the tea trolley placed in the window bay. It was laden with a silver tea set, plates of sandwiches and a layered cake of summer fruits and cream topped with peaks of snowy meringue. Theresa began dispensing cups, saucers and plates, unfolded round paper napkins and spread them on our knees. I needed little encouragement to tuck in. The cake tasted as delicious as it looked. The tea was perfumed and not like any I had drunk before.

'We three are going to be great friends, Jenny McLeod. We are of the tribe of Joseph.'

'She means we are on the same wavelength,' explained Guy. 'She likes talking in riddles.'

Theresa continued talking in riddles. 'I'd hazard a guess that Jenny is fire with an earthly façade.'

'Water,' said Guy.

'No, not water. Too much passion. Definitely fire.' I looked helplessly from one to the other.

'Sorry, Jenny,' explained Guy. 'You must forgive my wife. She gets carried away at times. Fire person doesn't mean a tendency to arson. She's talking planetary influence.'

'You've lost me,' I said.

'Theresa is an astrologer.'

The only reference to astrology I'd ever come across was in Sir Walter Scott's Guy Mannering where an elderly stranger returned some Scottish hospitality by predicting the future of his host's newborn son, giving dire warnings for his future.

'Oh, you're a fortune-teller,' I exclaimed.

'I am not a common or garden fortune-teller. I reveal through the planets strengths and weaknesses, and can teach how to make the best of these and of course warn, of the pitfalls. I cannot predict eventual outcomes. That is entirely up to the individual.'

Although genuinely amazed at this turn in conversation, I began to giggle. On seeing her puzzled expression, I quickly apologized.

'I'm not laughing at what you're saying. I find it fascinating. I was thinking of someone I know who is a very strong and devout Christian and was imagining his horror at the very idea of astrologers playing God.'

'Much of the Bible is best interpreted by the use of astrology and much is incomprehensible without it. I will introduce you to the ancient discipline of astrology. I will interpret your natal chart. You would like that, Jenny,' she said, taking my hand and turning it palm upwards. She gazed intently at its network of lines and intersections. I tried not to smile at the gravity of her expression.

'I see a long life but not always a happy one. I see high peaks and deep valleys. Beware of someone who wants to imprison you. Yours is a free spirit. You cannot be caged. You need to fly. Someone is trying to clip your wings. Be on your guard.'

Gradually a new routine was established. It became the pattern that every weekday I would set off for the castle, which I refused to call a hotel, to spend the morning filing and typing letters. Guy had loaned me an old Underwood machine on which I assiduously practised touch-typing. It had so much of my concentrated attention that very soon I was improving my speed and accuracy in leaps and bounds.

After I'd been working for the Masons for a few months I returned to Broom Cottage one day to find Grandpa in a state of euphoria. He produced from his pocket a tiny half-blind, half-bald, wriggling pup. This was the last of the litter which had been born in the castle kennels.

'What'! l we call him?' he asked as I took the pup in my hands to begin bonding with some cooing and kissing. I held the warm little bundle against my face, sniffing the smell of earth and straw he'd carried with him from the kennels, his tiny tongue tickling my face as he tried to scramble up my chest.

'Let's call him Busdubh, after his little black cheeks,' I replied.

As the days and weeks sped by Grandpa, who had spent his life training animals and children, became putty in Busdubh's paws. The pup was untrainable according to my grandfather but it was my guess that at this stage in his life he needed something to spoil rotten and Busdubh took full advantage.

Each day I grew happier. I loved my two lives. There was the busy domestic life Grandpa and I built up between us when I had the added satisfaction of seeing his health improve and his wits regain their singular sharpness. When he left the cottage with Tillytudlem pulling the spring cart it was to trade in eggs or homegrown vegetables, not to moon over family affairs.

My other life, working for Guy and Theresa at the castle, was a source of joy. I had an easy rapport with Guy. With him I talked typing and shorthand. I planned and put into operation a filing system. I provided local information about people, places and events and what I didn't know I found out. I answered his telephone, typed his letters, accompanied him to meet local people and see places of interest. When we weren't working I would talk about my family. This helped me to exorcize many ghosts. I could talk about my mother without pain now and it eased my guilt to talk about Graham. Guy provided a patient, attentive, sympathetic ear.

With Theresa it was different. Here my talk was all astrology. She began plying me with books on the subject. There were books on the history of this ancient science and its guiding principles. There were books on its symbolic significance related to the real world. It was new and mysterious, complicated yet stunningly simple when one pieced its jigsaw pieces of information together. I came to appreciate that it was the yardstick of all Theresa's activities and she would consult her ephemeris as the Reverend Andrew Fraser might seek guidance from the Bible.

One of my duties was to keep her diary updated. I noticed that her appointments were growing at a phenomenal rate and it was only when she asked me to type her letters that I learned why. Theresa was running a lucra-' tive business on the side. People, mostly women, were coming from as far away as London and Glasgow to have their fortune told, as they put it. Many of them stayed overnight which was good advertising for the hotel. Theresa Mason was more of the fortune-teller than she would admit.

But there was a seriously intellectual side to her business too. She'd often go off on lecture tours and there was a weekend when a coach-load of people came to hear her at the hotel. Needless to say, this did not go unnoticed in the village.

However there was another, more threatening, aspect of her mediumship. In the village store or post office or in any place where two or three were gathered together the tongues wagged and always about the same thing.

'Scandalous! It shouldn't be allowed among decent God-fearing folk.'

'A pair of heathens. Mark my word, no good will come of it.'

'Nothing short of blasphemy!'

At first I was included in the conversations but, being quick to refute everything they said, I soon got the cold shoulder. The next stage was inevitable. It was decided that I was tarred with the same brush and since, like the Masons, I no longer went to church, I too was in league with the devil. I tried not to let it bother me. Working for Guy and Theresa Mason was the best thing that had ever happened to me and I wasn't going to let village gossip-mongers take that away.

One day after a morning's work in the castle, I decided to do some shopping. I was ignored everywhere I met people, whether they were alone or in groups. My salutations were not acknowledged neither by word nor gesture. My emotions shot from initial astonishment to fermenting anger. I was ready to explode when I reached Broom Cottage and found myself confronted by the Reverend Andrew Fraser.

'The minister wants a word wi' ye,' said Grandpa. 'I'll leave you to it.'

'Sit down Jenny,' said Reverend Fraser. 'I've something I feel it my duty to say to you.'

I knew what was coming.

'There are unsavoury tales about these strange people at the castle. I hear they are godless and I worry for your soul.'

There was certainly no beating about the bush with the reverend. I waited for him to continue.

'It is not a proper place for you to be spending so much of your time. When were you last at church service?' His voice rose in anger as he spoke.

'At Tam's funeral,' I replied.

'Your poor mother will be turning in her grave at such lack of reverence to the Lord.'

He couldn't have said anything more likely to raise my hackles.

'The Masons are good people,' I said. 'Maybe they don't attend church but they are good-living folk and they have been especially kind to me.'

'From all I hear of their goings-on, they worship the devil.'

'I have never heard that word cross their lips,' I replied hastening to add 'and you're a one to talk of the devil. You're forever bringing him with you into the pulpit.' Then I held my breath.

'It's just as I suspected,' said the minister in shocked tones. 'They are leading you from the path of righteousness. They are tainting you. For the sake of your mother in heaven I forbid you to continue working for them.'

My anger was too powerful to bottle. 'Leave my mother out of this. I've found more consideration and respect from the Masons than I have from anyone else in this place. What's God ever done for me anyway? Why should I bother with him?'

The minister seemed unable to voice the horror written on his face. His next words were already hanging in the air between us before he gave them utterance. 'I shall pray for you, my child.'

This only fuelled my rage. I heard Grandpa return and only his grip on my arm stopped me voicing further abuse.

'Apologize to the minister' he said quietly.

'No. He should apologize to me. He has no right to tell me who I should see and who I shouldn't.'

'The minister's only thinking of your own good,' argued Grandpa.

The minister was having difficulty coming to terms with this doubtless unprecedented defiance of his authority and seemed unable to cope.

'I shall herd Maggie for you,' I said. I was glad to leave them but I had no intention of leaving in any way that would be misinterpreted. The problem was theirs, not mine.

But of course it didn't take long for the implication of my lapse in manners to hit me. The strength of my feelings was no excuse for rudeness.

I herded Maggie into the makeshift cowshed and left her for Grandpa to milk later. I would apologize but only for my shortcomings in proper conduct, certainly not for my lack of faith. However the minister had left in high dudgeon according to Grandpa.

'The minister's right,' he said lacing his boots to go to the cowshed. 'This job's no right for ye. It's changing you.'

'I'm growing up,' I said beginning to set the table for lunch. 'Is that so surprising?'

'What surprises me is how you can be interested in a' the rubbish that woman tells you.'

'What rubbish?'

'A' that rigmarole about the stars.'

'The planets actually.'

'Whatever. It's still rubbish and a' against the teaching in the Bible.'

'You don't know what she talks about so I don't see how you can rightly judge. And that goes for the minister too.'

'Ah weel. Maybe she'll tell him. He's gone there to warn her to leave you alone.'

I contained my temper and carried on preparing our lunch.

In the afternoon I helped Grandpa in the vegetable garden listening with only part of my mind to incidents from his morning's trade route. The rest of my mind was on Theresa and the minister, wondering what he had said to her and wanting to run to the castle and ask. With difficulty I decided to wait until the next morning.

In the evening I did what I did every evening. I wrote letters to Father and Callum, but mostly to Todd. There was hardly an evening when I didn't write something to him. His postcards although few and far between were the highlight of my life and were carefully treasured. My letters to him soon piled so high that I had to divide them into manageable bundles that I kept in a suitcase under my bed. I had a dream that one day he would come back to Strathard and we would read them together.

CHAPTER 13

The next morning I left early for work. Theresa's instruction notes were on my desk. They were brief and to the point: 'Come to my studio.' That was all. No please, or, if it is convenient. But it was good enough for me. Any time in Theresa's company was time well spent.

'Sit down, Jenny. No, not in the armchair, but here at the table,' was her greeting.

I complied. Theresa sat opposite. Her hair was hidden by a red scarf tied at the back of her head. She had a spread of papers before her on the table, one of which portrayed my birth chart and a host of glyphs not entirely strange to me now.

'This,' she began, tapping a painted fingernail on the birth chart, 'is the book of your life; the sacred text.'

'My natal chart?'

'Just so, and I think the time has come for you to know its contents.' She rose and, almost gliding to the fireplace, struck a match and lit a candle. I wanted to ask her what had transpired between the minister and herself but she began on my chart. I curbed my impatience.

'As a fiery Aries,' she began, 'you are idealistic, inquisitive, impulsive but,' and here she paused significantly, with the moon in Libra opposite your sun you've had your fair share of troubles. There is a great struggle between two polarities.'

'What does that mean?' I asked, my mind more on the Reverend Fraser.

'The influence of the moon in your chart is extraordinary. The moon is a selfish planet. It trivializes, keeps you in its grip, deflects you from your true purpose.'

'And what's that?' I found it difficult to take her seriously and felt distracted by the sickly scent from the lighted candle.

'Your sun is in the 12th house, the house where the true self is allowed to shine through.'

It meant little to me.

'Jupiter, the planet of opportunity is very strong in your chart. Jupiter is the opener of doors. But the moon aspects are so strong and the moon creates ritual circles around life, offering security aids which only means that doors don't open.'

Her earrings were beginning to have a hypnotic effect on me.

'Even Venus,' she continued, 'the planet of love and values, has a difficult aspect with Saturn, the planet which creates limitation and formalities.'

'Doesn't sound too good,' I said nonchalantly.

'This is serious stuff, Jenny. Treat it as such.'

I straightened myself in my chair and, as Grandpa might have said, wiped the silly grin off my face. Theresa dropped her unsmiling eyes and continued.

'Saturn is in the house of relationships and Saturn, remember, is the planet of boundaries, not only between one person and another but between the inner life and the outer life, between flow and form. Because you have been so polarized, your life needs balance in one-to-one relationships. The selfish moon and disciplining Saturn have worked together and conspired against you.'

'Stop please, Theresa. I really don't know what you're talking about. Where's all this leading?'

'That's up to you,' she said with a dismissive flick of her hand. 'Now, because you have Taurus rising, you present yourself to the world as solid and stable, confident and dependable. The real you however, is somewhat more vulnerable. The moon is so strong in your chart.'

'I thought the moon was feminine, endearing and all that,' I challenged.

'It also constantly offers you reassurances but in the wrong things. It forces you to run around in circles and plays on your emotions. But with the sun in the 12th house in trine with Neptune and Jupiter, you must aim for higher things.'

'Tell me how,' I pleaded, spreading my arms and raising my eyes to the suspended planets.

'The greatest challenge in your chart,' she continued, 'is the polarity between sun and moon in the house of relationships. There is someone trying to clip your wings. Believe in yourself, Jenny. Beware of those who want to change you.'

'Like the Reverend Andrew Fraser?' I asked.

'And his son,' she answered. Her face was inscrutable.

'How do you know?' I asked.

'Isn't he always telling you what you should do and what you should think, even how you ought to feel?'

'Aren't you?'

'No! No! No! What I am telling you is think for yourself. I am telling you to believe no one but to listen to everyone. I am telling you to keep an open mind. Life, is a many-splendoured thing and we have our own splendid place in it. I can tell you, more as a friend than as an astrologer, that Neil Fraser is not the one for you.'

'I could have told you that without a crystal ball,' I retaliated. 'I can think of no one less likely to be for me.' Although I sounded defiant I felt disturbed.

'Good. Just remember that. Now Jenny, very soon there is going to be a war. There's nothing more certain. I doubt if people will want to come here on holiday. We will remain for as long as we can but most likely the hotel will be requisitioned for a hospital or a training centre. You are going to be bereft of a job, I'm afraid. I want you to think carefully of alternatives.'

'Won't you and Guy still be here?'

'I doubt it. There will be nothing for us here. We will have to wait and see what our options might be. Now listen to me. No matter what happens, believe in yourself, Jenny. There is a great future for you if you make the right choices.'

'But how can I be sure they are right?' I asked, slightly irritated.

'You can't, but you will always know when they are not right. Whenever in doubt, listen to yourself and take heed. Now let's cheer up. There isn't a war yet and I sent the minister off with his tail between his legs so he won't be bothering you again.'

As the summer of 1939 unrolled, it became noticeable that bookings for the hotel were falling and many of those made were being cancelled. It was of course obvious why. Life was being dominated by the threat of war. What had, months before, been a cloud on the horizon, was now blotting the daylight from the sky.

Callum had been posted as crew to a squadron, officially ready for action. Now, at last, it was the real thing for him! On 3 September 1939 war was declared. In Broom Cottage this meant ensuring efficient blackout and leaving two gas masks in their cardboard boxes lying at the ready. Only six weeks later two bombs fell from enemy aircraft east of the Forth Bridge. The war had come to Edinburgh. I returned from the castle one morning to find Neil Fraser in Broom Cottage drinking tea with my grandfather. He was wearing his dark suit and dog collar. On the sofa beside him was his soft hat, rolled umbrella and gas mask. It gave me a jolt. I'd been lulled into thinking he'd left my life for good.

'Is anything wrong?' I asked

'Why should there be anything wrong?' With a few words the brick wall was up again between us.

'Just a thought,' I shrugged.

'Weel you thocht wrong,' said Grandpa. 'Neil's come to offer you a lift to Edinburgh tomorrow to see Graham, if that's agreeable to you, unless of course you're bent or going to the castle.'

'I'm not needed tomorrow. Are you coming too?' asked my grandfather.

'I canna leave the animals.'

'I'll take you another time, Mr McLeod,' Neil promised.

He rose awkwardly to his feet. I averted my eyes, moving to place my purse on the sideboard.

'I'll be here at seven,' he said, collecting his belongings.

'I'll see you to the gate,' said Grandpa while I turned my attention to preparing lunch.

'Till the morning,' I replied.

I was waiting on the doorstep when he arrived the next morning. I slipped quickly into the passenger seat before he had a chance to struggle out.

Grandpa followed with a lunch basket I had packed earlier and which I took from him placing it on the back seat. He waved us off and, with a degree of unease, I settled myself wondering how we were going to fare cooped up together for the next few hours.

I needn't have worried. Neil Fraser was someone whose heart was in what he had chosen to do. He loved his pastoral work and needed little persuasion to talk about it. He spared me his sermons but went into great detail about his wide range of activities. He was happy and comfortable in his large manse and well cared for by his housekeeper, Mrs Martin. I much preferred this enthusiastic Neil Fraser to the Neil I was used to. I relaxed into my seat and, by the time we stopped for lunch, our conversation seemed set on a well-oiled track.

We had waited until we were on the outskirsts, of the city before stopping for refreshment. We chose to eat in the car on high ground and could see the distant chimneys and spires against the sky. Ahead was a bustling city but here, in this quiet country road, all was peace. I was no longer so self-consciously aware of my companion. I was experiencing a new side to this dour Scot which was interesting and somehow reassuring.

'You will be delighted with Graham's progress,' he said before biting into a sandwich.

'More little accomplishments?' I asked.

'Hardly little. He enjoys painting, weaving, a little cooking and he's very happy. Everyone is very fond of Graham and of course, being Graham he is fond of everyone.' Neil smiled as if he'd explained everything.

'I can't help feeling that I am no more nor less to him than all the other people he meets. I've lost our special bond.'

'Nonsense! His eyes light up every time I say your name, and that is often,' he added with what I supposed was a reassuring smile. I did not feel reassured.

'I'm often tormented with the thought that if we'd kept him with us the bond would have held. Would he have been even happier, I wonder?'

'Graham thrives on love. Does it matter whose?' asked Neil.

'Of course it does. It should be our love, my love.'

'It sounds as if it matters to you more than Graham.' I detected a hint of the old censure in his voice.

'It may sound like that. I appreciate that he is well cared for. He has been taught and developed within the boundaries of his physical limitations, but I can't help feeling that he has lost what his family might have given him and which he once knew.'

'I seem to remember that it was the limitations of the family which was the reason for Graham being moved in the first place. They haven't changed.'

'I've lost him,' I could only repeat.

He was silent for so long that I wondered if I had offended him. I began to clear the remnants of ourlunch when his hand stayed my arm.

'Perhaps not, Jenny.' I waited, conscious of his change of attitude.

'I wasn't going to mention this so soon.' He seemed uncomfortable as if he didn't know how to say what he had to say.

'Perhaps you haven't lost him. There's a chance that Graham may have to return to you. No, don't say anything yet. Just listen. It is going to become practically impossible for the home to keep functioning as the war proceeds. In the first place it isn't considered safe to keep the residents in the city if enemy aircraft is overhead. Already Edinburgh has experienced its first bombing, little as it was. It could be worse next time but apart from that the staff intend dispersing for a variety of reasons and there will be no replacements. They have already begun enquiries among families. I volunteered to look after Graham's interests.'

I didn't know what to say. I didn't know what to think. I didn't know how I felt. That familiar giant cloud of uncertainty and confusion was there again leaving me helpless in its wake. I had to get out of the car. Neil followed and stood beside me as we looked across the adjoining fields towards the craggy heap of the castle rock in the distance.

'It might not be as difficult as you think,' he suggested.

'How can you know what I think?'

'Perhaps I can't, but at least let me tell you what I've been thinking,' he said. 'I can find you work in Edinburgh and Graham and you and your grandfather can live with us at the manse. I will be there to look after you all and Mrs Martin will help look after Graham.'

'I already have a job, remember?'

'With that ungodly couple at the hotel?'

'That ungodly couple, as you call them, are my dearest friends.'

'From all I've been hearing they are everything you should steer clear of.'

'Maybe they don't go to church but I've never heard them revile anyone who does.'

'Not going to church isn't what I have against them.'

'What then?'

'The silly notions they're teaching you.'

'You mean the ancient discipline of astrology?'

'It's bunkum Jenny. It's ridiculous to imagine one's life is determined by a few planets. The Bible is the one true guide for living. You must believe that, Jenny.'

'I don't must believe anything,' I said. 'A belief enforced is no belief at all.'

'Listen to me Jenny. Astrology cannot be proved.'

'Nor can God,' I retaliated, 'but it helps you understand yourself and for that reason alone it is relevant. Properly understood it gives insight.'

'And you understand it properly?'

'Of course not. It would take years but I feel it. It fits. It makes sense to me.'

We stood silent but the tension between us was palpable. Then he spoke.

'I don't know what to do about you.'

I followed him back to the car. Once in, he turned to me.

'Think about Graham but don't decide yet. Remember what I've said.'

'Grandpa won't leave Broom Cottage and I won't ever leave my grandfather. Graham must come to us.'

'Jenny—'

'I don't want to talk about it just now. Let's go.' I concentrated my gaze on the distant spires.

He hesitated for a second before turning the ignition, releasing the handbrake and letting in the clutch.

Graham was ten years old. He was tall like Father and Callum and seemed all arms and legs. This did not suit his childish behaviour and sometimes I had to chide myself for shivers of embarrassment. This saddened me, especially when I remembered how proud I was of Callum, handsome in his RAF uniform.

I spent an hour with Graham, playing his games, admiring his craftwork, tasting the biscuits he'd helped make. I left him with his carer and made my way to the Matron's office. Yes, Graham was happy and active and loving but what now struck me was that he was also tireless. I felt drained of energy but I knew that it wasn'i entirely due to the demands of Graham. It was just as much due to the new load on my shoulders.

'The minister has told you then?' said Matron raising her brow in question while motioning me to a chair. I nodded.

'I would have written,' she said, 'but the Reverend Fraser requested I didn't. He wanted to tell you himself.

It won't be tomorrow, you know,' she added quickly in response I suppose to my weariness.

'How long?'

'It's hard to say. A month maybe; perhaps two. Will that be all right?'

'I should think so.'

'He is very good, a lovely boy,' she said, 'but it's only fair to warn you he needs almost constant attention. If his interest is kept alive there are no problems. He depends on having others around, others who will participate with him. They're all spoiled for that here, I'm afraid.'

'I can see that.' I tried to look cheerful.

Neil arrived to take me to the station and we said our goodbyes. It had been agreed that I'd return home by rail. The train was already on the platform getting up steam, hissing with satisfaction as the fireman shovelled in coals. There was just time to board and say a quick goodbye.

'I'll be in Strathard in a few days. I'll come and see you both then.'

'Fine - and Neil.' 'Yes.'

'Thanks.'

He stood back as the train took up the rhythm of departure. I raised my hand then sat in the far corner, the empty lunch basket on the seat beside me and an overload of confusion in my head waiting to be confronted.

CHAPTER 14

I didn't tell Grandpa immediately. I decided to tell no one until I had adjusted to the idea of living for 24 hours a day with Graham. My emotional release came through penning my feelings to Todd. His postcards kept arriving from time to time but never contained what I wanted to see most - a contact address. Neil arrived sooner than I expected and I still hadn't told anyone. He didn't seem too pleased.

'I'll tell your grandfather,' he offered.

'No. I will.'

'When?'

'Tomorrow after work.' It was late and I made that my excuse.

The next morning while I was having breakfast Grandpa collected eggs from the scattered depositories. There was a hungry bleating outside and a yapping puppy round my ankles, both of whom I ignored until I finished eating. I remember the sun filtering through the branches of the rowan trees outside the window and a robin perched on the sill waiting for crumbs. I pushed away my porridge, still hot from the stove and Maggie's warm sweet milk. Among the day's mail was a postcard in familiar handwriting addressed to me. It was from Archie Ross. 'Todd made me promise,' it began, 'that if he ever flew out and didn't return I was to let you know. I am more sorry than I can say to be the bearer of this sad news but I must do as he wished.' It was signed Archie Ross. There was nothing else, no contact address and it was impossible even to decipher the postmark.

I felt totally numb. I stuffed the card in the pocket of my skirt and collected my bicycle from the shed. The lamb dashed into the kitchen when

I opened the door and was immediately challenged by the pup. Doubtless they would both be on a chair by now, tongues reaching to the yellow jug of Maggie's milk. I heard Grandpa's call as he saw me mount my bicycle. I waved, not stopping to speak. This must have seemed puzzling to Grandpa. Nothing seemed puzzling or unusual to me on that journey. The waters of the Firth were still there, white-crested waves heaving shorewards. The sun shone, seagulls flew in croaking concern for food. People waved and I waved back. The postman came out of the lodge gates as I turned into the castle drive. Dismounting, I took my usual short cut through the wood. It was a mistake. It took me past McGreegor's hut and near enough to the keeper's cottage. My limbs trembled and it was as much as I could do to finish my journey to the castle. Reaching my office I automatically set out my working tools and collected documents for typing from the files. I dropped a file. Its contents scattered on the floor, and stooping to retrieve them, I must have passed out. When I awoke Guy was bending over me, his face showing concern.

'Hey! What's this then? Did you come to work without eating breakfast?' He kept his tone light and helped me to my feet. 'I think you'd better sit down for a minute.'

'I'm all right.'

. 'If you say so, but you could give me an excuse for another cup of tea if you'd let me put the kettle on.'

'What is it about cups of tea that are so vital in emergencies?' I tried to keep my own voice light.

'Is this an emergency then?'

'Of course not.'

But that was the lie of my life! Somehow I got through the morning, not appreciating that neither Guy nor Theresa were never far away. When I didn't hear the phone one or other of them was always close enough to answer it. It was Theresa who made the mid-morning tea, poured mine and carried it away ten minutes later untouched. It was Guy who decided we'd done enough work for that morning and, since he was going into the village anyway, offered me a lift.

I politely declined and, smiling brightly, waved to them as I set off home for lunch and the afternoon's routine. Grandpa wasn't at home when I arrived. There was a note to say he'd gone on his trade route. He'd taken Busdubh.

I set to, feeding the animals, oblivious to the call on my patience as I bottlefed the lamb. I was unaware of time. I was experiencing a quickening awareness of every job on hand. I scattered chicken feed with infinite care making certain each clucking bundle received its fair share. I waited until the pig had nosed the potato peelings and cabbage leaves before herding Maggie, who was exploring the furthest corner of the neighbouring field. There was no pup to feed, but the day being sunny with a fresh wind blowing from the sea, I washed her blanket, scrubbing it vigorously on the washboard.

I moved from chore to chore with no desire for rest or food, concentrating only on the task of the moment until the sun reached its final hour. I had so disciplined myself to writing regularly at this time that it was natural for me to pull my suitcase from under my bed and carry it to the kitchen table. As I snapped open the locks I heard a hammering on the door which was wide open.

Neil Fraser came into the kitchen. I became acutely aware of the stillness and the creeping darkness outside. After a quick look round Neil came to the table where I was standing, my fingers poised over the small metal knobs of my suitcase.

'Is your grandfather around?'

I stared at his face, anxious and pale.

'I don't know.' I had, as yet, no inkling of the ominous.

'Where might he be?' he asked with the insistence I so disliked.

'I've no idea. I think he must be somewhere with Busdubh.'

His voice thickened in intensity. 'No one's seen him on his rounds today.'

The numbness which had blocked my mental awareness all day was wearing thin.

'When did you last see your grandfather?' he asked, stepping closer.

'This morning.' I could feel the beginning of a great discomfort but deliberately blocked my thoughts.

'Haven't you been worried?' His look was too searching and I tried to move away.

'No. I didn't realize it was so long.'

Then I felt the pressure of his fingers on my arm. At the same time another pain began to emerge and a great confusion from which I tried to escape. His face was inches from my own. I sensed his concern.

'You'd better sit down, Jenny.' He pulled a chair from under the table. I sensed something terrible had happened and was glad to be seated.

'Your grandfather's pony and cart, still laden with produce, was discovered on the Kennel Brae early this morning He's disappeared'

His face blurred while his voice disappeared. I fainted.

Neil revived me with a splash of cold water from the tap. His face swam into vision, drawn in concern.

'Easy now,' he said. 'Drink this.'

He handed me a glass of water but my hand trembled so much I couldn't hold it. With one arm supporting me, he gently tipped the water between my lips. Conscious ness wasreturning and with it fear.

'I must find Grandpa.'

'We will, Jenny. There's already a search on hand. Guy Mason's organizing it. When you're ready we'll go to the castle.'

But I was on my feet and making for the door. He caught up with me, steadying me; halting my headlong rush.

'Steady on, Jenny. Let's not think the worst.'

I was aware of the softer tones, the kinder glance. I was also aware that something was terribly wrong, but all that had to wait. The overriding compulsion was to find my grandfather. Neil steered me to his car and we headed for the castle.

There was a full-scale search in progress when we arrived. Theresa came to comfort immediately.

'Bear up, Jenny. Everything possible is being done. We'll find him.'

Neil, frowning, stood looking as I took comfort in her arms.

A man in oilskins and waders marched into the hail calling to Guy.

'We're going to try the river now. We've managed to lay our hands on some drag hooks. The trouble is the light. It's dark out there and it might be better to wait till morning.'

'No!' The yell was wrung from me. I rushed to him followed closely by Theresa and Neil. 'Try now, please. Don't wait till morning. I'll come with you.'

The man looked uncertain, glancing at Guy for guidance.

'Is that such a good idea?' said Guy.

'I must be there.' This time it was Neil's arm that went across my shoulders.

'There's no moon,' insisted the man who must have been the leader of the search party.

'I could take my car as near as possible and we could use its lights,' suggested Neil.

I moved closer to him.

'Better still,' said Guy. 'We could bring the truck from our garage and use the dynamo. It only arrived last week.'

'What about the blackout?' said Theresa.

'We could put a hood of sorts on the light,' said Neil. He was already moving to the door. In need of action I followed, feeling convinced that all the time we stood talking, my grandfather could be in dire peril.

I stood with Neil watching the volunteers attaching lengths of rope to the drag hooks, choosing their positions and casting and dragging, I felt that time was hardly moving. The men toiled unceasingly with the weight of the anchoring hooks and, every time they dragged to the riverbank, I held my breath and clung to Neil.

'They'll find nothing here,' he said to me as they, began to drag Black Rock Pool. 'It just doesn't make sense. Why should he leave the cart halfway up Kennel Brae and then walk more than a mile to the river, and early in the morning too? It doesn't make sense.' He turned to me. 'You're shivering. Here, have my jacket.' He struggled out of his tweed jacket before draping it over my shoulders. 'They shouldn't be long. It's not a very big pool.'

'It's very deep,' I whispered, comforted by the jacket's warmth.

The men were working systematically from both banks of the river. They seemed to cast effortlessly although the heavy metal hooks needed a team of men to drag their scrapings from the bed of the river to the banks. The light from the dynamo had been carefully shielded but there was enough light to keep track of the silently powerful figures as they cast and dragged, cast and dragged.

I was barely aware of Neil's arm round my shoulder. He kept telling me they would find nothing. I wanted to believe him. I had to believe him. There would have been no reason for Grandpa to be near the river unless …unless… I had a new thought.

'There's only one reason why Grandpa would leave his loaded cart on the Brae.'

'Why?' Neil looked at me, drawing closer.

'The pup, of course. It's so undisciplined. He'd take off after the smell of his own breath and lead Grandpa a right song and dance. He's been doing that since they got together. But the river's the last place it would go to. They must be in the woods or the moors, the kennels themselves perhaps,' I said, my desperation showing.

'They've all been searched, lass,' said the leader who'd been watching the rescue proceedings and been standing within earshot. 'This is our last chance.'

I wouldn't listen to him. I wanted to go to the exact Spot where the cart had been abandoned.

'Not tonight,' said Neil. 'We'll go first thing in the morning.'

'I must go now,' I insisted, turning to him.

'It will be too dark to see anything.'

'Please Neil. If you won't take me I'll walk.'

We looked at each other. He, silent, composed, attentive. I, desperate and demanding.

'Come,' he said.

I clung to him as we scrambled up the river bank and stepped our way carefully through the wooded fringe to where Neil had left his car on one of the woodland drives. His lameness was slowing him down. I was in the car first quivering with impatience until he joined me.

'We must find him,' I kept repeating as I peered helplessly out of the car window. 'Oh God, let him be found. Please, please God let him be found. I'll do anything God if only you will let him be found.' I hardly knew I was voicing my prayers.

Neil said nothing but from his nearness I drew strength. He drove to the Brae and stopped the car. We alighted and Neil led me to the spot where the cart had been abandoned. We stood in the darkness saying nothing. I was still wearing his jacket which I hugged closer to my body. He was right, of course. It was too dark to distinguish anything but the silhouette of the kennel buildings on the brow of the rise, dark shadows of tree clumps and the snaking lines of the dykes.

'This place is rabbit infested,' I said, 'and there's still strong smell of dog. Don't forget this is where Busdub was born. The place would attract him like a magne,; would a pin. I can imagine him jumping from the car and making a beeline for the kennels. Grandpa woul call him but he could call to the kye came hame and it would make no difference. Busdubh is a law unto himself.'

'You heard what the man said, Jenny. The place has thoroughly searched and, according to Guy, more than once.'

'I know.'

'Let's go back to the castle. It's getting late,' he suggested.

I stood my ground.

'Why would Grandpa be on this Brae? Where would he be making for?' I was speaking my thoughts. 'It doesn't lead to the castle or the village and there's no one living in the kennel bothy now. There's only the odd: job man's bothy on the loch road about a mile on. He's still living there and still doing odd jobs around the estate.'

'Would he be having deliveries from your grandfather?'

'He might have been. Grandpa and he are old friends.'

'That would explain the cart being here and perhaps your notion of the pup's behaviour might be right.'

'He might have fallen and hurt himself, broken a leg or something. Maybe he's lying somewhere and can't move.'

'They'd have found him and the pup would be sure to make its presence known. Remember what Guy said. Every woodland path and cover has been systematically searched. They've even had shooting brakes over the moors.'

The life went out of me. Neil led me back to the car and finding a rug tucked it round me. He also found another jacket which he donned. In spite of the rug and the shelter the car provided, my teeth chattered.

'Oh God, I can't bear this. If anything terrible has happened to Grandpa it is my fault. What was I thinking of. Oh dear God, let him be found.'

Neil's arms were round me, holding me tight, stilling my tremors. He spoke into my ear as I lay huddled against his body warmth.

'When it comes to the crunch Jenny, to bleak despair, we always turn to God for help. Everyone does it. Do you realize you've been doing just that all night – calling on Him, pleading with Him, praying and yes, bargaining with Him?'

I lay still in his arms, grateful for their protection, afraid to leave the shelter they provided.

'Shall we pray together Jenny?'

Previous to that night I would have recoiled at such a suggestion, curled with embarrassment and indignation. I would have vented my righteous indignation on Neil Fraser and his sanctimonious airs. Now I sat straight, my throat raw with dry sobs and nodded. I freed my arms from the blanket and clasped my hands together.

'I'd like that. Please pray for us, Neil.'

We bowed our heads. Neil offered a prayer. Without exchanging another word we returned to the castle hotel.

CHAPTER 15

'They're going to resume the search at first light,' Guy told me. 'There's little more they can do now.'

'I must go home,' I said. They looked at me. 'I haven't shut up the animals,' I explained.

'I'll take you,' said Neil, 'but you can't stay there alone. You could come back to the manse with me.'

'Bring her back here,' said Theresa. 'She can stay here as long as necessary.'

They were talking as if I wasn't there Upset as I was, I sensed the mutual antipathy.

My mother will look after you,' said Neil appealing to me

'I wouldn't want to disturb her, Neil. It's kind of you but I'd better come back here'

I followed him to the car. I was still wearing his jacket and I sank my face into the upturned collar as we stepped into the cold night air. He didn't wait to tuck the rug round me. After opening the passenger door for me he cranked the car which immediately sprang into life.

When the car turned into the gates of Broom Cottage there seemed to be chickens everywhere. I grabbed a bucketful of food from inside the kitchen door and with encouraging clucks tempted them back to their coops. I soon had them safe. Ducking under the washing, hanging limp and ghostly on the line, I returned indoors where Neil had lit the lamp. I gazed in consternation at the scene confronting me.

The lamb, who had enjoyed the freedom of the house 11 day, must have at some time knocked my suitcase from the table. It had spilled its contents on the floor, which was awash with page after page of my letters to Todd. Gazing at the scattered sheets the thoughts I had buried all day exploded, leaving me powerless.

Neil, his lame leg splayed out, was on his other knee gathering up the pages. I dropped on to a chair, my hand clutching the card which I had earlier stashed into my skirt pocket.

'Oh God!'

Neil looked up at me.

'You can hardly blame God for this,' he said. 'Are you writing a book or something?'

There was no lightness of voice.

'They're letters.' I hardly recognized my own voice.

'I can see that,' he said, adding, 'still to be posted.'

'They're letters to Todd McGreegor.'

'Oh.' He looked up briefly then continued collecting the pages.

'I couldn't post them. I had no address.'

'But you still wrote them.'

'Yes. He sent me a postcard now and again but never put a contact address on them.' I was struggling with the pain of remembrance.

'It would seem you had a lot to tell him.' His voice seemed far away and I spoke as if to myself.

'I told him everything. I've written to him practically every day since he left.'

'Why?'

I looked at the bent head with hair so thick nothing of the scalp was visible.

'I wanted, needed to share everything with Todd, as we were beginning to do before he left. He was my best friend. I ... I ... was very fond of him. I missed him. I think I loved him.'

Neil rose slowly and faced me.

'For goodness sake, Jenny. You were children.'

The pain could no longer be contained. I felt the tears sting my eyes. I was too overwrought to control them. They ran down my cheeks in continuous streams, splashing on Archie Ross's card which I held in my hands.

'How ridiculous can you get! You were both still wet around the ears. You've let your imagination run away with you and all this,' waving a hand at the letters now piled on the table, 'only shows where it's led you - into a fantasy land. Todd McGreegor was a selfish, unthinking child to run out on his parents the way he did. I should think you are well rid of him and if you take my advice you'll burn this lot.'

I looked at him, not recognizing the person who had so recently comforted me and spoken kindly. At that moment my emotional weight left no room for anger.

'I shouldn't have said that,' he relented but with no hint of remorse in his voice. He probably had realized how little it fitted his Christian principles.

'It doesn't matter,' I said. 'Nothing you might say can make any difference now. Todd is dead.'

I handed him the schoolmaster's card. He looked at it for a long time, his face inscrutable then, placing it with the pages on the table, turned to face me.

'I am sorry. It's a tragedy which needn't have happened.'

'You mean he asked for it.'

'I mean I am sorry.'

It was small comfort.

'I suppose you also think that Grandpa's disappearance needn't have happened if I'd been thinking more of him than of myself. You must think I'm an unlucky person to have around.'

'I think we should get you back to the hotel.'

'I don't want to go.' I began making an attempt to return the letters to the suitcase.

'You are going,' he said, his voice steely. 'You are not staying here on your own. Will the lamb be all right?'

'All the animals will need to be fed in the morning.'

'I'll come and do it.'

'Shouldn't you be in Edinburgh?'

'My father's gone to look after things for me. I'm here as long as you need me.'

'I need you,' I said, but there was no feeling behind the words.

'Come!' he ordered, 'there's nothing more we can do here tonight.'

The only thing I could do was to follow him.

Dr McLaren was at the castle when we arrived. He offered me something to help me sleep which I refused. I had to be awake with the first light. I was going to find my grandfather.

Sleep was impossible. No previous nightmare had prepared me for this long night of fear and desperation. My imagination saw my grandfather in a variety of dire circumstances, alone, injured and in pain. I imagined I could hear him calling me but even in my jumbled thinking I knew this to be fanciful. I kept up a litany of prayers to God. I even bargained my soul with Him.

After hours of twisting and turning I rose from my dishevelled bed and padded to the window looking out on a strip of lawn with tidy herbaceous borders just discernible in the starlight. The bedroom was on the ground floor in the west wing of the castle. It was an area I had become familiar with since working there. I had discovered that a gap in the far bordering hedge led to a shingled pathway which made a short cut to the kennels, so avoiding the castle drives. I had often used it and as soon as the first glimmer of dawn streaked the horizon I dressed hurriedly. The room could no longer contain me. My invocations were being gradually replaced by a different kind of mumbo-jumbo. I was fuelling anger. I had to be angry. Not with God. I felt I could no longer afford to take that risk. I was so full of a fear that could not be assuaged by religious incantation alone. Standing by the bedroom window, trying to distinguish the shadows outside had called to mind the night I had looked out of another window and seen Todd gesticulating for me to join him. I saw him. I could almost believe he was there, outside and waiting for me. I knew he wasn't but, I was tormented by wondering where he was. I saw him with a bullet in his chest, the way Tam had died. I saw him in flames, trapped in a small machine hurtling to the ground, leaving a trail of fire in its wake. I imagined him being tortured and heroically submitting rather than betray.

I crushed the master's card in my hand venting all of my anger on him. A few cruel uncosseted words were all he had thought to send me. Was that all I meant to him? Was that all Todd had meant to him? If it hadn't been for Archie Ross, Todd would still be alive. Neil was right. This was a tragedy that shouldn't have happened. I hated the master then for his stark and fateful message and for leaving me with no means of responding.

I had to find my grandfather. He was the only person in the world who understood me. I couldn't remember a time, until now, when he hadn't been there when I needed him.

It was a sash window, easily raised enough to throw one leg over the sill, duck my head, follow with the other leg and stretch my body through before dropping noiselessly on to one of the borders a few feet below.

I wasn't going to wait for the others. I would find my grandfather. God was on my side, I felt. He'd lead me to him. Was this faith? Was this what Neil went on about? Why was I so certain that I would find him? With this certainty my senses quickened.

Once through the gap in the hedge I took to my heels and didn't stop until I was clear of the castle, the woods and about 200 yards from the kennels. I didn't feel that I'd been awake all night. My adrenalin flowed fast and I was prepared to search all day if I had to. I wouldn't give up.

As I neared the long stone building which had once been the castle laundry but, like the kennels, was now an empty shell, I stopped to draw breath. A few feet beyond I saw a barrel on the corner of the ice house.

The ice house was dug into the ground. The ice was carted from the loch to this building and deposited far underground where, because it was so cold, it remained all summer. This meant the castle had ice all the year round.

We used to visit it with Duffy, the odd-job man, and coax him to let us in. It was a scary place. There was a gap of four feet between the outside of the building and the ice. This kept it cold and frozen. There was a plank from the side across to the ice. It was very dark and to us as children, this four feet gap looked bottomless. There was a drop of thirty feet underneath. When I discovered that I never walked the plank again.

As I drew alongside the door I heard a whimper. I held my breath and waited. There it was again and it was coming from the ice house. I ran to the door which had always been kept locked and put my ear to the keyhole. The door gave way to my body and swung open. It was pitch dark inside and freezing cold. I heard it again, the quiet whimper of a dog. That was Busdubh whimpering. My grandfather must be with him 30 feet below unprotected in the dark and cold. I could feel myself begin to sway and realized my danger.

'Grandpa!' I screamed. Busdubh managed an answering bark but there was no human response. I called again and again, at the same time looking for the plank of wood. There was none. I saw only the yawning four-foot gap and imagined the 30-foot drop. By now my feet, fingers and face were freezing but the cold struck deeper, paralyzing me with fear.

Busdubh's whimpers were punctuated by feeble barks but there was still no sound of a human voice. I knew I must control my panic and act quickly. There was no way I could reach man and dog at the bottom of the pit. I knew I had to get help and the nearest, I quickly decided, was Duffy whose bothy was about 200 yards further on, between loch and ice house which had served him well in the old days and which I prayed and hoped would serve me well now. He would know how to reach Grandpa while I ran to the castle for the rescue team.

As I ran to Duffy's house I concentrated on the rescue, keeping other thoughts at bay. It was possible that Grandpa hadn't heard my call. Perhaps he was sleeping. Some inner protective mechanism protected me from any other option.

There was a light in Duffy's window. Rasping for breath, I hammered on the door calling his name. I didn't have to wait long.

'Jenny lass! Whit's a-dae?'

'Grandpa - I've found him. He's in the ice house - with Busdubh - no plank.'

'Steady lass. Come and tak' a seat.'

'No ... no Duffy. I must run to the castle and tell them. Will you go to the ice house? I think they've fallen down the gap.' My voice rose hysterically.

'You're runnin' nowhere. You're fair done in as it is.'

As he was speaking he dug a whistle from his trouser pocket and, running outside, began blowing a series of short sharp blasts. He stopped long enough to put a jacket on top of his singlet.

'There's nae need for ye to wear yersel oot. We'll go thegither tae the ice hoose and fetch the ithers wi' the whistle. We'll soon hae your Grandpa oot. Dinna be feart.'

'The plank,' I gasped.

'Nae need. They'll bring a ladder and ropes.'

It seemed that the rescue plans were thorough. It was just as he said. By the time we were back at the ice house, the rescuers were in sight. They were armed, as he had predicted, with ladder and ropes, blankets and Dr McLaren. Neil was with them.

Duffy took charge. After a consultation with the doctor and the men who had dragged the river, the ladder was lowered down the 30-foot drop. Busdubh's whimpers continued. Duffy and the leader of the team descended the ladder. The doctor remained on top, his bag close by.

Neil joined me. I wanted to feel him hold me, his arms a protection against the terrifying fears in my grip but, although he stood close and murmured a few words of comfort, he didn't touch me. I had never needed comfort more than I needed it then.

It seemed an interminable time before the rescue was complete. Busdubh was the first face arising from the depths. One of the rescuers took him from an extended arm which immediately disappeared. A few minutes later the team leader reached the top of the ladder with my grandfather draped over his shoulder. His body hung limp and apparently lifeless. A body of men closed in on the scene. When I made a move to join them Neil gripped me with both hands on my arms.

'Not yet Jenny.'

'I must.'

'Give the doctor a bit of space.'

'Let me go,' I hissed, escaping his hold and racing to the doctor. The men parted to let me through. I saw my grandfather stretched on a pile of blankets, the doctor on his knees beside him. I stood watching, waiting for a verdict. Busdubh had already been carried from the scene. The doctor removed his stethoscope from his ears, signed to the waiting men who moved in a body with stretcher and more blankets. Then he saw me.

'He's unconscious, Jenny,' he said.

'Where are they taking him?' I demanded.

'To the castle. It's nearest.'

'Is he going to be all right?'

'I don't know, Jenny.' He sighed. 'He's a frail old man.'

'Only in body,' I said angrily. 'He's tough inside.'

'I'll grant you that. We'll do everything possible. The rest will be up to God.'

Thus began my biggest tussle with God, and God won! My grandfather never left the Strathard Castle Hotel alive. For three days he hovered between two worlds slipping from one to another with alarming ease. I stayed with him. Others, of whom I was hardly aware, came and went. I was with him in his few lucid awakenings when he recognized me.

When he slipped into another level of consciousness he took me with him. All my life his words and humour, smiles, guiles and a great tenderness had been his gifts to me. Now I was being carried along by a feeling of ineffable peace and wonder. As he hovered on the brink of departure he offered me an occasional glimpse of another world. I could feel an energy emanate from the frail body stretched between the sheets. It afforded me a strange comfort. It was as if my beloved grandfather was bestowing on me his final blessing. There was no struggle, no signs of distress; only peace.

On the evening of the third day his eyes opened wide. I felt him respond to the pressure of my hand on his and thought I detected an answering flicker in those grey eyes which had watched over me all my life. When his eyes closed I sat in stillness allowing my thoughts to pass unhindered through my mind, catching only the odd one and looking at it with love but emotional detachment. He could not be just nothing any more. There would be no sense in that. There would be no hope for anything if I were to believe that. There had to be an answer and I would never stop searching for it.

Was he with God? Had God been trying to tell me something all these years and I had not listened? Well, I was listening now! It was time that I gave God a chance. Was that what Grandpa had been telling me? Was that why I felt so close to him now? Was Grandpa with God and was God with me? Were we all one and the same? All rhetorical questions for which there could be no answers.

I don't remember how long I sat there.

The door opened and Neil Fraser came in. He looked at my grandfather then he looked at me. Our eyes locked and in that moment I felt that this was the man who would lead me on the right path to God. That was the destiny divined for me and there was no escaping. Like God, Neil Fraser should have his chance.

CHAPTER 16

Callum managed to get compassionate leave for the funeral. There was no way Father could travel across the Atlantic in war time. He had written at length to both of us demanding to be told everything. He wanted me to do my utmost to find some means of joining him in Canada. So far only Neil and myself knew about Graham having to leave the home. I had begged Neil to keep the matter between ourselves until after the funeral. I was particularly emphatic about keeping the news from Callum, to which Neil agreed with the greatest reluctance. Only the fact that Callum was now on active service persuaded him, for Callum's sake, to keep him in ignorance. In exchange, he extracted from me the promise to consider his offer previously made about joining him at the manse in Edinburgh. I decided to put this on the back burner.

The laird, who had insisted on taking care of all the, expenses, came to the funeral.

In sombre black, with Callum smart and handsome in his Air Force blue by my side, I followed the coffin down the aisle taking my place in the front pew. The church was packed with people from the valley and beyond. It was a great comfort to us. Neil, in ministerial robes, was waiting at the altar to receive the coffin. The church was heavy with scent, the music from the organ was gentle and solemn while the autumn sun filtering through the stained glass cast a beneficent light on the polished wood and brass. The peace that had enveloped me when my grandfather finally left this world for another was still with me. I was happy to think that he was now with Mother and Tam and Todd. My eyes never left Neil's face during the service. His words were comforting and his quiet and dignified manner sustained my calm. It seemed fitting that it should be Neil who bestowed the final blessing on my grandfather.

After the burial service in the churchyard we all proceeded to the hotel where Guy and Theresa had drinks and a buffet meal waiting for us.

'I hope you will come back to the castle, sir,' Callum asked the laird when he offered us his condolences outside the church.

The laird looked at us both without speaking.

'Please,' I pleaded.

'For a wee while then,' he replied gently.

I was glad. It was important to me that the laird should make his final gesture of farewell to my grandfather in the place where the old alliance had been forged. It was important that all the people, old and young, gentry and servants alike, who had known my grandfather and loved him, should be there to show their respect.

In the castle's Great Hall I mingled dutifully, making sure hunger was satisfied and thirst assuaged, accepting words of condolence and exchanging reminiscences about my grandfather.

'A word, Jenny.'

I turned. It was Neil's mother, tall, gaunt and stiff-lipped. She was neatly clad in black with the briefest relief of white around the collar. A small black felt hat was pinned securely on her head. Her iron-grey hair was drawn severely back from her face, secured in a bun, its shape discernible beneath the felt.

'You will be coming to us,' she said to my surprise. 'You can't stay by yourself in Broom Cottage and you certainly can't stay here with them.'

With the last word she threw a malicious look at Guy and Theresa who were busily replenishing plates. Then, creeping nearer whispered to me: 'I have a room ready for you, my dear. The minister is in full agreement.'

I looked wildly round for Callum. He was in the far corner of the hall in conversation with Duffy and Neil and was not looking my way.

'That's very kind,' I said quickly adding, 'but Theresa and Guy have been most kind. I wouldn't want to seem ungrateful.'

She snorted, tossing her head like a nettled nag. 'Neil is expecting you. He feels you will be safer with us.'

I wondered what drastic fate they imagined might await me here.

'I thank you for your kind offer Mrs Fraser,' I repeated, 'but I cannot just walk out on the Masons. Besides, I am still working for them.' I tried to back away but her body still inclined towards me.

'I know I shouldn't say it, today of all days.' She lowered her voice conspiratorially. 'You are doing your reputation no good by associating with people such as these.'

Her beady eyes rolled towards the Masons. Neil had joined us. I turned to him in relief.

'She won't come,' his mother informed him before he had time to say a word.

'I'm sorry to hear that,' he said, looking at me.

'It would seem rude to the Masons,' I explained. 'As a matter of fact I would really much rather stay on in Broom Cottage but everyone disagrees with that.'

'I should think so too,' Neil replied. 'You cannot be left alone at a time like this and there's no necessity for you to be there. I believe Callum has arranged with Duffy to find new homes for the livestock. Duffy's going to keep Busdubh himself.'

I nodded, glad to get on to another subject.

'I must say Jenny,' said Neil's mother, 'you are very cool and confident under the circumstances. It doesn't seem right somehow.'

'I think Father is looking for you,' Neil informed his mother. 'He's just gone into the garden.'

With another snort and toss of her head Mrs Fraser made for the door. I had to stop myself thanking Neil for his ruse.

'Are you all right?' he asked.

'I'm fine, but I must speak to Callum. He will be leaving in less than an hour.'

At that moment Callum turned. Seeing me he excused himself from Duffy and came across to join us, weaving his way between conversing groups seated on chairs and sofas or on their feet awkwardly balancing plates and glasses. He finally made it to us.

'Will you excuse us, Neil,' he said. 'I'd like some time with Jenny before I leave.'

For the first time since Grandpa died I felt the stirring of a great and terrible grief. I preceded Callum from the hail passing Theresa who sent an understanding smile in my direction and led him to my office where we carefully closed the door behind us.

Callum held out his arms. I fell into them, letting the tears come.

'You were wonderful,' he kept saying as he hugged me. 'I was so proud of you.'

As I fought for control he held me, patting my back, smoothing my hair and being the big brother so needed at that moment.

'I wish you didn't have to go,' I mumbled accepting the handkerchief he offered and beginning a tentative repair of my ravaged face.

'But I have,' he said firmly, 'and before I do I want you to promise me something.'

I turned from him, blew my nose, pushed the soiled handkerchief into my jacket pocket and waited.

'I want you to promise to let Neil help you. He has told me that he has offered you refuge in Edinburgh, helping his housekeeper. Accept, Jenny. You won't be alone and you will be near Graham.'

'I won't be alone here. I have Theresa and Guy.'

Callum frowned. 'I'm not sure about them. I've heard so much about them.'

'Gossip, silly idle gossip. You've heard about them from me too. Surely you can trust what I say rather than a lot of gossip-mongers.'

'Neil hasn't a very high opinion of them.'

'Neil's prejudiced. To him any religious dissenter is suspect. Surely everyone is entitled to have their own beliefs regardless. Didn't the dominie make us both aware of that?'

'That's as may be,' said Callum. He looked so serious and uncomfortable. I couldn't bear it.

'Don't worry,' I reassured him. 'I don't hold it against Neil. I understand him now. His religion is everything to him. He lives, and I think would be ready to die, for it.'

'I'd feel a lot better if I knew you were with him. He would always take care of you. Please promise you will accept his offer of a roof over your head.'

I thought of my brother going off to war, worried about me and found the words to reassure him easier than I had thought.

'I promise. I'll accept Neil's offer and join him in Edinburgh.'

Callum's relief was instantaneous, expressing itself in a smile that filled his face.

'That's the best news I've had. It's something I've always wanted. I can go back now with peace of mind and know you're going to be safe.'

He opened his arms and enclosed me in a bear hug. I pulled free and, grabbing his lapels, pushed my face close to his.

'And there's one thing you must promise me, Callum McLeod.'

His eyebrows shot up but he was still smiling.

'Promise you will come back. Promise you will survive this war no matter how long and hard it is. Promise me.'

He caught the intensity of my feelings.

'I promise. I will survive this war and I will come back to you, Jenny McLeod.'

We held each other tightly. I was the first to speak. 'I'll say goodbye here. You will be gone when I go back to the hail.'

'If you want it that way.'

'I do.'

After he left me I sat at my desk, feelingless, just wondering what force was pushing me the way I seemed to be going, wondering why I couldn't think logically. I had made a pact with God and I intended to keep it. There was only one person who could show me how. I waited and, when I heard the knock on the door, I knew who it was.

I rose as he entered. He came straight to the point.

'I've been speaking to Callum.'

I nodded.

'He suggested that you might have something to say to me?'

'It will mean a great deal to Callum if I accept your hospitality in Edinburgh.'

'And you Jenny? What will it mean to you?'

'Security,' I replied promptly. 'For me and for Graham.'

'I want to look after you both,' he answered, 'but I want to do it properly. I know you are young and headstrong and I know we do not agree about many things, but I don't remember a time when I wasn't glad to be with you. I've watched you grow from a happy, carefree child, before your mother died, to a troubled woman. I've always admired your spirit and great courage when times have been bad and I've always wanted to help you. If you decide to come to my home in Edinburgh I want it to be as my wife. I want to marry you. I promise to take care of you and Graham. I want to get you away from here as soon as possible.'

I wanted to love and understand God and if marrying Neil Fraser would help me do this I would be the surest convert he ever had, sculpting myself to be a pillar of his church.

'I am grateful to you Neil. I don't know how I coulc have managed without you these past weeks. You hav helped me see things differently. I want to believe. want to love God as you do. I have castigated Him for sc long but I can see now how wrong I have been. I kno' you can help me. I would like to marry you and I promise I will be a good and dutiful wife. I will help you in your work and do my utmost to be a worthy Christian.'

I waited, wondering why I didn't feel more excited. My words, I was convinced, must have sounded like lines from a play.

He took both my hands and looked at me.

'You have made the right decision, Jenny.'

I wanted to believe him. On impulse I moved closer. After a moment's hesitation he placed his hands on my shoulders and brushed my lips with a kiss. Brief as this was I could feel tension under the surface. I felt agitated and didn't know why.

He looked almost relieved when there was a knock on the door. Theresa opened the door and her large curious eyes swept across the room coming to rest on our flushed faces.

'Am I intruding?' she queried arching her dark eyebrows. 'I just wanted a word with Jenny.'

'I'm just leaving,' said Neil.

'Not on my account, please.'

Ignoring the remark Neil turned to me. 'I'll see you later and we can make arrangements.'

I nodded then watched him limp across the room.

The door had hardly closed before Theresa jumped on me.

'I know what's going on, Jenny.' 'You do?'

'He's not the man for you.' 'Theresa,' I began.

'He wants you to go to Edinburgh, doesn't he?' 'He wants to marry me.'

'No! Jenny, No! No! No!'

'I've made up my mind.'

'You've lost your mind,' she wailed. Then, closing her eyes, she took a deep breath. When she opened them again they were almost pleading. She spoke in a quiet voice.

'Can we talk?'

'I've been away from my friends too long as it is.' 'They're all right. This is important and I promise it won't take long.'

Grudgingly I agreed to listen. We sat down facing each other and she came straight to the point.

'When one is deeply grieving one ought not make big decisions, Jenny.'

'You won't make me change my mind, Theresa.'

'I've done a progressed map for you for this year.

What it shows should not be ignored.'

I didn't have Theresa's strength of conviction in astrology. I had found it intellectually stimulating but in spite of respecting her sincerity and being impressed by her persuasive expertise, I had not been able to commit myself

Especially now, on being turned towards God, I was less than ever inclined to give it credence.

'Do. you want to hear about it?'

'Progress map? I've forgotten what it means,' I stalled.

'Then let me remind you.' Patiently Theresa explained that research had proved that the changes of aspect of the planets following birth progress in the rhythm of a year for a day.

'Understand?' To my still rather hesitant response she added. 'It means that the aspects formed between planets on, let's say, the fourth day after birth actually act on the individual in the fourth year of his life, and so on.'

I nodded and she continued to explain.

'You will be seventeen on your next birthday, so by charting the planets' positions seventeen minutes after your birth time, I can tell you the influences for the future and,' she added meaningfully, 'I think you should listen.'

'Theresa, I appreciate your concern but really I thinl you are wasting your time.'

'Listen to me, Jenny. Mercury is opposite Jupiter Mistakes can easily be made and, without due care, so too can wrong judgements and a taking of high risks. Your moon, of which I've warned you already, is in opposition to Mars, your powerful ruler. There are so many unfortunate aspects together. It's a dire warning, jenny. Take heed.'

It was all becoming too technical for me and Theresa was obviously carried away by her own enthusiasm.

'Stop!' I ordered, adding no doubt from my subconscious, 'I don't care about astrology. I don't want to hear any more.'

Theresa's mouth dropped open as she looked at me in dismay. I wanted to laugh but found I couldn't. It all seemed so deadly serious.

'Haven't you been listening to me, Jenny?'

'Of course I have.'

She looked at me, her eyes narrowed, her mouth now in a thin straight line.

'Can I ask you a question?'

'If you like.' I turned from her and moved to the window.

'What do you really feel about Neil Fraser?'

I watched as some guests were leaving the hotel, thinking I should be down there.

'I respect him. I understand him better now. I can rely on him.'

'Is that all?'

I turned to her, surprised by her insistence. 'I think that's quite a lot.'

'Rubbish. Does he make you laugh?'

I made no attempt to hide my annoyance. 'What's that got to do with it?'

'Everything.'

'Don't be ridiculous. You are wasting your time.' I moved towards the door. She forestalled me.

'Do you feel the same about Neil Fraser as you felt bout your Spanish freedom fighter?'

'That was different.' I tried to sidestep her but she refused to give way.

. 'You once told me you loved your freedom fighter.' 'I was only a child then.'

'You are still a child, Jenny.'

My hurt showed and she was immediately contrite but the damage was done.

'Forgive me, dear. You are more mature than some people twice your age. If it's fear of being alone,' she said, 'come with Guy and me to London. We will look after you.'

'It isn't that,' I tried to explain. 'I really want to marry Neil. I want to be a true Christian. I want to love God. I know Neil will help me.'

There was a new harshness in her voice as she answered.

'He might have you singing in his church but he'll never make your heart sing. You are an Aries for goodness sake. You were born to be a leader not a slave. Your soul has to be free, Jenny. You must know that. It has been flapping its wings for a long time now. Neil Fraser will lock it in a cage. He will stitch your mind and clip your wings and turn your laughter to tears.'

'Stop it!' I was angry. No matter how well meaning Theresa might be she had, I believed, overstepped the mark. I jumped to my feet again.

'How can you say such things? Neil Fraser is a man of God.'

'And you know all about God,' she concluded.

I flinched.

'I'm sorry Jenny. Forgive me please. I shouldn't have said that.'

It was not going to be easy to forgive Theresa for her cruelty. I decided I'd rather spend the night at the manse after all.

We parted in anger and abject sorrow.

CHAPTER 17

Neil and I were married on Callum's next leave, a week after my seventeenth birthday. It was a subdued affair.: We had so recently buried my grandfather. Callum was on leave from the Air Force before rejoining his squadron for active service. My commitment to God had not been taken lightly. I had dedicated myself to Christian service. Never had there been a more aspiring sinner in repentance. Nor had I given my other vows lightly. I had promised to love, honour and obey my husband. To that I was also committed.

After our wedding feast in the North British Hotel, Neil and I saw Callum off at the station.

'Remember you promised not to get yourself killed,' I smiled through my tears.

'I'll be back,' he reassured.

'Just mind that you do.' I sounded so much like Grandpa that we both chuckled. He shook hands with Neil who promised to take care of me and Graham, who was to join us soon.

Neil and I had agreed to forego a honeymoon. There was a war on and there was much to be done. We took a tram to the manse - a large, granite-stoned house on the outskirts of the city standing cheek by jowl to the church, its oak door approached by a shingled drive. Neil pulled the bell handle before opening the door.

'Mrs Martin,' he called as he preceded me into the large, if rather gloomy, hall. 'We're here.'

There was a strong smell of furniture polish and carbolic but no flowers. Sombre portraits of previous ministers frowned upon us from the walls. The panelling was dark and unrelieved. There seemed to be a great many doors. They were all closed. The stairs to the floor above were uncarpeted. On the landing a tall, stiff-backed, heavily starched figure appeared.

'Come and meet Mrs Fraser,' called my husband. The figure glided downstairs like an apparition and I found myself shaking a stiff, cold, friendless hand. I shivered but managed a smile of sorts as Neil introduced us. The voice was equally cold and on meeting the expressionless eyes, my spirits dropped.

It was a relief to find a blazing fire in the room into which we were led.

'You'll be wanting some tea,' she said, addressing Neil and indicating a small side table laid with tea tray, crockery and a plate of scones.

'Just the thing,' said Neil heartily, 'but I think Jenny will want to freshen up first. Will you show her to her room?'

I felt deflated. This was not the homecoming I'd imagined. Meekly, I followed the gaunt figure upstairs, my hand clenching the handle of my personal valise. I felt no better when she opened a door at the head of the stairs, only pausing long enough to say that she'd taken the liberty of turning down my bed.

I entered the bedroom and looked with dismay at the single bed in the corner whose spread had been folded back and the white starched pillow puffed above the turned down sheets.

'I'll go and put the kettle on,' she said as she stiffly withdrew. It was not my imagination that detected the first glimmer of expression to escape those eyes. It was not kindly. I don't know how long I stood there trying to reason what this meant. There must be a mistake. I was Neil's wife, not just a cousin on a visit from the country. Yes, it was a horribly embarrassing mistake. It certainly couldn't be a joke. That woman wouldn't know what a joke was and anyway Neil would surely have prepared me for single rooms if that was his intention.

Was that his intention? Was this to be the tenor of our marriage? Was I to spend my nights here, alone in this cold comfortless room? Dismayed, I looked at the wooden floor, uncovered except for a concessionary rag rug at my bedside. The bedside table had a small low-wattage lamp. There was a walnut wardrobe, a tallboy and dressing-table devoid of ornamentation, its cracked mirror reflecting the colourless walls. No flowers or pictures;

Cold! Cold! There was a fireplace, screened with a framed peacock of stone mosaic in an iron frame and id front of the fire stood the only chair in the room. I found the bathroom at the end of the landing. I splashed cold water on my face relieved to find a clean towel. I brushed my hair vigorously, girded my loins and returned downstairs to the room where I hoped to find tea, Neil, and an explanation.

He was waiting for me and smiled as I entered. I allowed my spirits to rise. He didn't speak until I had poured the tea.

'It may not be as you expected, Jenny, but it is for the best. You will rest tonight and tomorrow night we will confirm our marriage vows.'

Could there ever have been a less romantic speech a bride could hear from her groom on her wedding night? It wasn't confirmation or even consummation that was my greatest need. I yearned for the close comfort of loving arms, the reassuring words of a new husband in whom I had placed my trust. He wasn't cold. One might say he was concerned but his matter-of-factness left me cold and confused.

'Are we to sleep in separate bedrooms?' I managed to ask in a croaking voice.

'Yes, but I shall visit you of course, as often as it takes.'

'Takes? For what?' I gasped.

'For procreation,' he replied without a blink. I was speechless, almost dropping the teapot in my consternation.

'It's not what we want that's important, Jenny,' my husband continued. 'It's what God wants and, according to the Bible, love between man and wife is for procreation.'

'Surely there's more to it than that?' I blurted. 'That's Old Testament lore and has nothing to do with the teachings of Christ.'

His face hardened and I was reminded of the old Neil whom I'd despised for so long. The life went out of me and he responded quickly.

'Don't look so tragic.'

Joining me on the sofa he took one of my hands in both of his.

'I will look after you. You will come to no harm, my dear. I will guide you to God and help you tame your waywardness. You know I have always dreamed of you sharing the love of God with me. That is what you want too, is it not?'

'Of course it is but—'

'There are no buts,' he said releasing my hand. 'It is the greatest challenge life can offer. Be guided by me, Jenny. We will serve the Lord together. You will have no time for moping. You will help me with my parish work. Soon Graham will be with us and he will need much of our time and we shall pray that we are blessed with many children of our own. There are no buts.'

There was a knock on the door.

'Come in, Mrs Martin,' Neil called.

The housekeeper entered the room, closing the door behind her. She stood before us, long-skirted and high-collared in sombre black, clasping a Bible to her bosom. Neil turned to me.

'We have a nightly reading before retiring. I have assured Mrs Martin that she is welcome to continue participating.'

I looked bleakly at the gaunt features, wondering what thoughts lurked behind her expressionless eyes.

The heavy furniture pressed in on me. It wasn't just the thick chenille curtains that kept out the light. The grandfather clock in the corner chimed ten. Taking one of a number of Bibles from the bookcase Neil handed it to me. This, I thought, was not the time for defiance.

And so we read and I kept repeating to myself, 'Let it be! Let it be!' - the next best thing to a mantra. After all, I wanted to learn, I reminded myself. I wanted to be guided. I knew that I must give God a chance.

I learned to submit to the evening readings, the Bible classes, the Prayer Meetings and Sunday schools. I planned a systematic attack on reading the Bible. I consciously bent my will to treading various paths of righteousness, the path of humility, perseverance and self-denial, and I managed fairly well because they were all directed from the head. I found that with constant perseverance I was more disciplined and my knowledge of the scriptures grew.

Where matters of the heart were concerned, progress was not so easy. After my wedding night of rejection and loneliness I submitted to the marriage-bed manoeuvres as dictated by Neil.

After the ten sonorous chimes of the grandfather clock and our devotional Bible reading I would go meekly to my room and, with bent knees and clasped hands, seek the help that Neil assured God would provide, to carry on in my chosen path. Then I would climb into bed and lie there waiting until Neil slipped silently in beside me to begin a ritualistic attempt at procreation. We never spoke. We worked in the dark with neither compliance nor complaint. We never saw each other's nakedness. We were blinded by our ignorance but guided by our instinct. He was never rough. Nor was he tender. His hands explored my body but he wasn't interested in my mind or my emotions. Even so, I gradually drew a strange physical comfort from his body. I went along with it. Neil had no imagination but I had enough of my own which I used to elevate his fumblings into fantasies to satisfy my needs. Fortunately I felt no revulsion and, striving in the silence and the dark, the time eventually came when I achieved an orgasm. I knew, after that first orgasm that I would conceive. Exhausted and exultant I hugged my husband almost as if I loved him and showered his face with kisses. His response, like his climaxes, was controlled.

When the pregnancy was confirmed I kept the knowledge to myself. My joy was so intense that I wanted to guard it against any intrusion and I suspected when Neil knew I was pregnant that the little ardour he had would cool. I changed from a martyr to a messenger of joy. Everything I saw and touched became beautiful. God was good. At last he was on my side. Neil had been right. Joy was to be found in the love of God. The change in me must have shown. People were responding differently. Neil, on his nightly pilgrimages, was staying longer. I was always tender with him and, although I silenced my cries at orgasm, I could never control the unbridled passions of my body. He was learning how better to accommodate them.

However, such pleasures as I'd garnered couldn't last. Sadly my secret was exposed and, as I had feared, life changed. Between us we had achieved God's purpose. What was a great joy to me was a grim satisfaction to Neil. The nocturnal visits ceased. He had done his bit. The rest was up to God - and me.

I missed the physical contact of his body which I had so well manipulated for my own enjoyment, but I refused to be downcast. Inside me there was another more important contact and it was one which made my heart sing.

I discovered that I didn't miss Neil's nightly visits. Indeed I was glad to be without them. During the day I kept busy organizing war efforts.

I steered knitting and sewing committees, compiled general knowledge quizzes and organized sales. I helped transform our flower and shrub grounds into vegetable plots. I accompanied Neil on some of his pastoral visits and generally offered my services where needed. Mrs Martin ensured I had no housework to do. She ran the manse with efficiency and rarely had to consult me. When she came to realize that I was no threat to her authority she became less hostile. As the life within me developed my happiness burgeoned. I was more relaxed and rather pleased with my new harmony with God.

On the fifth month of my pregnancy Graham joined us. Neil and I had visited him often in preparation for this occasion. His settling in was easy, made more so by Neil's consistent devotion and the housekeeper's unstinting help. Watching them I saw Christian service at its best. This only made the stark contrast of Neil's attitude to me and the housekeeper's scathing outlook on parish life in general, more difficult to understand.

Although I had been awaiting Graham's arrival with excitement and trepidation, my fears were unfounded. The 'home' had given him a great deal of help and support. His activities were limited, but what he was able to do, he did well. Physically he still needed help and here Mrs Martin came up trumps. Sometimes, seeing them together, I felt pangs of guilt. I was the one Graham should be dependent on, not a stranger. Sadly, I was forced to admit, it was I who had become the stranger. I had lost my special relationship with my little brother and he seemed none the worse for it. Neil had been right. Much of my earlier wishes had been for myself.

I don't know when it was planted but a new fear began to grow in my mind. Watching Graham's dependency and infantile reactions, I began to wonder if his condition was genetic? We shared genes. Could my child be a victim of the same fate? I prayed to God for the baby's health.

Mrs Martin's Christian charity now extended to bringing me an early morning cup of tea. One day she woke me earlier than usual but in place of a cup of tea she brought a small yellow envelope. With Father being out of the country, Callum had registered me as next of kin. My hands shook as I took the telegram and tore it open. It was from the War Office.

'With regret I have to inform you it began.

Mrs Martin lifted it from the floor where it had fallen from my trembling hands.

'Shall I fetch the minister?' she asked. Without waiting for an answer she scurried off.

Callum was missing, presumed killed. His plane had failed to return having been shot down over enemy territory. I fastened on to the word missing. Callum was not dead. He was missing. Callum would return. He had promised. By the time Neil reached my room I had regained my composure. I was on my feet preparing to dress. He read the telegram then looked at me.

'Are you all right?'

'Of course. It says he's missing, doesn't it? He's not dead.'

'Jenny, you must prepare yourself for the worst. When you have dressed we'll slip into church and pray for courage.'

A spurt of anger, resonant of earlier days, leaped from somewhere in the depths of me.

'It's faith we need, not courage,' I replied testily. I was aware of the housekeeper hovering in the background.

'Don't bother with morning tea, Mrs Martin. I'll be down for breakfast in five minutes. I expect Graham needs you now.'

A frown of annoyance flitted across the housekeeper's face but she left quietly.

'Don't try to hide your feelings, Jenny,' said Neil.

'What do you care about my feelings?' I retorted. 'You don't normally bother to find out what they are or which of them I might be hiding.'

'Jenny!' He seemed torn between controlled anger and dutiful concern.

'Callum's not dead,' I said dully. 'Now if you will leave me I'll get dressed.'

'And come with me to church?' he persisted.

'Do you think your prayers will have a better chance of being heard there?'

'Our prayers,' he corrected with his sanctimonious air of old.

'I'll do my own praying and in my own way,' I mumbled. 'Leave me please. It's time I was dressed and I'm hungry. I'm eating for two now, or had you forgotten?' We had turned back the clock.

'I'll be waiting for you in church,' he said as he left my bedroom.

When he closed the door behind him I slumped down on my bed overwhelmed by a concoction of anger, dread, guilt and contrition.

'What now God?' I muttered through my teeth. 'Are you testing me?' I felt the movement of my child in my belly I found myself resorting once more to pleading, near bargaining. 'Dear God, don't let this harm my child. Please, please, give me courage. Let me believe Callum is alive.'

I dressed myself, told Mrs Martin to hold breakfast, walked down the garden path, unlatched the wooden gate and entered the hallowed ground of the church. Neil was on his knees before the altar. Not trusting myself to kneel I sat on a front pew and bowed my head. My thoughts were splintered by conflicting images. I remembered the time I learned of Todd's death and how

I had pictured his blazing plane spouting smoke and flames spiralling to earth with Todd slumped low in the cockpit. With an enormous effort of will I conjured images of Callum escaping death and the enemy, and returning against all odds to safety. I vowed to hold fast to that image and no other. Callum was presumed missing. Callum was not reported dead.

CHAPTER 18

To occupy my mind I spent the afternoon in the church hall helping to sort jumble for a sale scheduled for the next day. I came across a book on astrology. Thumbing through it memories of Theresa came flooding back, bringing in their wake a sadness for friendship long lost. Impulsively I slipped it into the pocket of my smock, afterwards sneaking it home and into my bedroom.

As my pregnancy progressed I spent more and more time there. Neil's days were occupied by his pastoral and war work. I'd made no friends in the parish. I was lonely, worried about Callum and easily irritated by the demands of Graham. My husband's initial pleasure at the prospect of fatherhood was no longer in evidence. From his viewpoint I was doing the job for which I was made. He let me get on with it assuming I was without distress or discomfort, assured no doubt by the presence of Mrs Martin who was given responsibility for my comforts.

I began longing for the moment when I would hold my baby in my arms. My baby! My own flesh and blood! Someone I could love with every fibre of my being and who would need me, want me, love me.

If the calculations were right the baby was going to be a Sagittarian. The thought delighted me. I pored over the little book that I had purloined. According to the astrological inferences my child would be pleasant, cheerful, optimistic and likeable. I had already made up my mind that I was going to have a daughter. I read on. She would live an exciting life, travelling and exploring, making new friends wherever she happened to be. I sighed wistfully. She would be as I wished I had been, do all the things I'd love to have done. Like me she would be fire but I was determined that her fire would burn bright and not be easily dampened or flare out of control under provocation. I determined that she would grow up to be outgoing, balanced and, as the sages so aptly put it, have the ability to transcend the play of opposites. She would not be bigoted like her father or easily hoodwinked like her mother. She would learn to be discriminating, impeccably mannered and compassionate.

One afternoon, while reading my astrology book, I dozed off. When I woke Mrs Martin was at my bedside, a cup of tea in one hand and my book in the other. Her brows were knitted in disapproval. Carefully she set down the cup and saucer on my bedside table but I noticed that she was keeping a firm grip on the book. Her tongue was clicking and she eyed me as she would a wayward child. Ignoring the tea I held out my hand for the book. The tongue clicked at double speed and the head rolled from side to side.

"You're supposed to sleep when you come to bed, not read. Unless of course,' she added, 'it is the Good Book itself you would be reading. I don't think the minister would approve of this." She brandished the book in the air like some exhibition of war spoils. I knew only too well how disapproving the minister was likely to be.

'Let me have it, Mrs Martin, please,' I demanded but she was adamant. I was angry. How dare she!

'Mrs Martin,' I repeated with more emphasis. 'It isn't your book.'

'And is it yours?' she retorted eyeing me now with undisguised suspicion. Strictly speaking of course it wasn't but before I could struggle into a more commanding position she had gone, carrying my book off in spiteful triumph.

'Bugger you!' I exploded. I stopped myself wondering what God would think of me. To my horror I realized that I didn't give a damn what God might think. It was what I was thinking that mattered. I was thinking that trouble lay ahead.

It didn't take the housekeeper long to do her Christian duty. After supper Neil invited me to his study. I was more distraught than I realized. My instinct told me there could be a confrontation. My reason told me I should be on my guard but my caution went to the wind. Like the growth of the baby in my womb I realized that I had been nurturing a resentment that not even the very best of my intentions could have prevented escaping if sufficiently goaded.

'This grieves me Jenny,' he began. 'I thought you had seen the folly of reading books like this.' He held the little astrology book in his hand and began pointing it at me. 'There should be no room in your mind for such rubbish.'

I had no intention of defending astrology. I had every intention of defending my right to read it and think about it.

'What are you afraid of, Neil?' Even as I spoke I knew this was a question I should have asked long ago.

'Me! Afraid?' He looked and sounded mystified at such a question.

'Are you afraid your beliefs might not bear the comparison?'

He bridled. 'I have nothing to fear from my beliefs.'

'Then why so tense? Why on the defensive?'

'Don't be impertinent.' His expression was scornful.

I felt goaded. 'Must you be so condemnatory? Can't we discuss this like adults?'

'There's nothing to discuss.'

'You try to censor my reading like some Ancient Roman magistrate and you say there is nothing to discuss.'

He became all minister, reseating himself and changing scorn to contempt.

'I am advising you, not censoring you. It is for your own good.'

'What is the danger exactly?' I was nursing my temper.

'Corruption! That is the danger. These perfidious ideas damage the developing soul. They obstruct the way to glory. They are contrary to everything the Bible teaches. They are blasphemous and I forbid you to read about them.'

'Don't be so melodramatic,' I said witheringly, at the same time knowing instinctively that this was the wrong response. I was seeing a side of my husband long suspected but never illustrated so powerfully before. He was a mindless fanatic, a bigot without the charitable virtues which his calling purported to convey. He was a Pharisee such as he decried in his sermons. He was a wowser, a pulpiteer and he was my husband. There was a cataclysmic gulf between us.

'I thought you wanted my guidance,' he said.

'Your guidance yes, but not your bullying.'

'I have the right.'

151

My temper exploded. 'You have no such right. You are being childish, illogical, selfish and unreasonable. Yes, unreasonable.'

"Have you quite finished?' The scorn had returned. 'I'd like my book please.'

I felt adamant.

He went white with rage. I thought for one wild moment that he might strike me then he turned to the fire, looked at the book and glanced at me before tossing it into the flames.

Suddenly my heavy weight became unbearable. I wanted to collapse on to a chair. Instead I turned and slowly, blindly, made my way to the door. He made no attempt to stop me. The only sound was from the spitting coals.

I groped my way to my room and sat heavily on my bed. I could hardly breathe. I struggled for calm but I couldn't stop my thoughts churning. Why was he so dogmatic? How could he condemn astrology without knowing a thing about it? I wasn't asking him to embrace it. I myself didn't but I respected its tradition. It was a very ancient discipline, predating the gospels. Surely he was intelligent enough to be aware of the folly of being overzealous in defence of his own beliefs. Why didn't he examine them more stringently? There were just as many perplexities involved in the Christian creed but that was no excuse for dismissing it in its entirety. Or, did the same creed present no contradiction, no problems and puzzles, no leaps of faith to Neil Fraser? Was he so sure, that he could be contemptuous of everything else?

I was already contrite about my handling of the confrontation. Yet I was confused about how otherwise I could have responded to his absolutism. It didn't tie up with what I considered central to Christ's teachings. He could be cruel. Did he know he was being cruel? He was not a bad man. Was it only with me that he was cold, often calculating, happy to distance himself when it suited him? Or was it his fundamentalism?

My instinct for survival was paramount and I knew that if I were to survive I must control this renewed antipathy to my husband. To visualize a life of prolonged stress I had to take control. I determined to think more of his goodness. I must think of him with Graham and his parishioners in need, his unsung kindness and his many attempts to please. I must learn to be more tolerant of his arrogance and bigotr and to dwell less on these lonely nights in bed. It was hard to nurture any tenderness for him when I never felt his arms around me and experienced only the rarest moments of spontaneous affection.

I consoled myself with the thought that when the baby arrived Neil would be different. Perhaps then I could allow myself to hope for renewed intimacy and have another opportunity to break down the dividing wall he seemed intent on building.

One night at our nightly devotions I had the feeling that Mrs Martin's attention was more on me than on the reading. I couldn't rid myself of the feeling that I was being hemmed in.

I had made a bid for favour with God, a chance to settle for past misgivings, a hope for enlightenment. It wasn't happening. I had felt more enlightened after one good working session with the schoolmaster or after a stimulating conversation with Theresa. With Neil my life now was more fragmented, my will never in repose, always battling in a cheerless crusade. My only joy was the miracle that was happening inside me. I willed my baby to move that I might feel her physical existence.

At last I was free to go to my room. I had barely, divested myself of the restrictions of my clothes and wrapped myself in my dressing-gown when there was a tap on my door. It was Mrs Martin carrying a mug of warm milk.

'I thought you might be ready for a warm drink,' she said.

I felt such a rush of gratitude I almost wept.

'Sit here,' she said puffing the cushion on the one chair in the room, 'and while you drink it I'll fetch a pig for the bed. I've left the water on the boil.'

I couldn't speak. Cupping my hands round the warm mug gave me the glow of comfort I badly needed. When the housekeeper returned to slip the heated bottle between my sheets I tried to thank her. She cut me short.

'You're nearing your time. You can't be too careful. We want a fine healthy bairn do we no?'

'Yes indeed,' I smiled. 'I can't wait till my baby's in my arms.'

'All in God's good time,' she said as she took the empty mug from my hands.

I felt such gratitude for her kindness I was prompted to get closer.

'How much does God mean to you?' I asked.

She looked faintly puzzled for a moment then replied in her crisp tones, 'God's God. Now get into bed and you'll feel better in the morning.'

'Mrs Martin,' I called as her hand gripped the brass door knob. She turned her head towards me. 'Thank you.' I smiled warmly then slid down and curled my toes round the pig. I thought I heard a click of the tongue but she managed a half-contorted smile as she left me to my thoughts.

'So God's God! Just like that,' I said aloud. I wished it were so simple. I was glad of the warmth in my bed. God is Mrs Martin tonight I thought in appreciation. I closed my eyes and did what I'd been doing since my pregnancy had been confirmed. I visualized my child cradled in my arms. I conjured her baby flesh and felt its warmth on my breast. On the brink of sleep I was returned to full consciousness by a series of kicks against the lining of my womb. It was an exquisite pain. I felt the impulse to share my child with Neil. He should not miss this. He was her father. I felt sure he'd find the same joy in feeling the reality of his child.

I groped for the bedside light, pushed my feet into my moccasins and stumbled across the landing to his room.

He was asleep, his arms spread outside the bedclothes looking a little like a child himself with his long lashes edging his cheek bone and his hair dark against the whiteness of the pillow.

Placing a hand on his shoulder I spoke his name. He was slow to surface and the baby was kicking hard. 'Neil. Wake up.'

'Jenny. What on earth!'

'Can I come into bed - please?'

'Whatever for? Don't you know what the time is?'

'I want you to feel the baby.' I was excited. I could feel the sweat on my brow. I was already pulling back the bed clothes when he shot up.

'For pity's sake,' he fumed. 'Are you out of your mind?'

'I thought you would like to feel the baby's movements.'

'Pull yourself together and go back to bed.'

'It's a miracle, Neil.'

'It's unseemly. Go back to bed. I've a funeral in the morning. I need my sleep - and so do you.'

At that moment I hated him. He was joyless. This feeling sustained me on my exit from his room and the cold comfortless journey back to my own bed. I groped for Mrs Martin's pig and hugged it to my body. I began a slow count to hold my anger at bay. The child was still. I waited anxiously for the next kick. It never came. I didn't sleep until dawn. When I finally awoke it was almost midday and there was a mug of cold tea on my bedside table and a cold hot water bottle at my back.

I experienced a new energy, borne of my distress. It kept me active hosting the sewing bees, knitting balaclavas and packing parcels for the Red Cross. When Mrs Martin wasn't with Graham she was there somewhere within call. She never fussed but she had an uncanny sense of knowing what I needed and seldom failed to supply it whether it be comfort, company or just solitude. She appeared at my bed one morning with a letter in her hand. Normally she delivered all mail to my husband's study but this one she brought direct to me.

My stomach lurched. Callum!

'Don't go, Mrs Martin,' I beseeched the retreating figure. She came back to the bed and plumped my pillow, placing it behind me as I struggled to a sitting position. It was impossible to keep calm as I fumbled with the envelope. The housekeeper took it from my trembling hands, slit it open with her thumb and returned it to me.

Callum was safe. Although shot down over enemy territory he had found his way to the border of a neutral country and had eventually been shipped home. He assured me that he was still in one piece but had suffered some eye damage, nothing too serious but enough to be withdrawn from active service. However he was still badly needed for training work. He was expecting to have some embarkation leave when we could be together before he left the country. I read every word to the housekeeper. Suddenly I felt a massive blow to my stomach and fainted.

I came to in the ambulance. Neil was crouched over me. Even in my blurred consciousness I was aware that he was more with God in prayer than with me in my pain.

CHAPTER 19

I remembered nothing of hospital admission or of the operating theatre. When I regained consciousness I was in a cot with iron bars and sterile coverings. I was in a long ward with beds arranged down both walls. It was night. A nurse in starched uniform sat before a table, her head bent over sheaves of papers. The light from the shaded lamp cast her shadow on the wall. The only sound was from the slow progress of another nurse pushing a trolley from bed to bed, dispensing pills. For some minutes I struggled to make sense of my surroundings and what I was doing there. The sudden recollection of my unborn child trapped my breath in my throat. My eyes dropped to the starched coverlet on my bed. My stomach had flattened. In panic, still gasping for breath I pushed my hand under the tightly tucked covers to feel if my eyes were perhaps deceiving me. As I half raised myself from my pillow the pains were like branding irons. I moaned. The nurse at the table shot up and quietly padded towards me. She drew the curtains round my bed before telling me brusquely to lie still or I'd make matters worse.

'My baby' I managed to rasp. 'Where is she? Can I have her?'

The nurse didn't look at me, giving all her attention to a watch in one hand and feeling my pulse with the other. 'Sh! Don't excite yourself. It's bad for you.'

I pulled my wrist from her cool professional grip and hissing like an alley cat threw it against her white starched apron. She didn't bat an eyelid but in a gentler tone of voice again asked for calm saying she would call the doctor.

'You can talk to him and,' she added as an afterthought, 'your husband is in the waiting room. I'll tell him he can come in now.'

I didn't want my husband. I wanted my baby. She had come and I hadn't been there with her. She left the cubicle then returned with Neil who seated himself on the chair by my locker and reached for my hand.

'I'm sorry, Jenny.'

His voice was flat and meaningless. I shrank beneath the covers, ensnared in the black cloud of depression he'd brought in with him and tried to rid it of significance.

'You must be brave, Jenny. She - the baby - never lived. She was dead, stillborn, they told me. There was no time. They had to deliver her - a Caesarian.'

His words were flat, delivered without feeling. I tried to lift my arm which seemed anchored to the bedclothes. My voice was paralyzed by shock but when he stretched his hand towards me I was galvanized.

'I want to see her,' I gasped. 'Why won't they bring her to me? I must see her, hold her, touch her.'

His words were clipped.

'Don't you understand? She was stillborn.'

'But she is here,' I wailed. 'I must hold her. Don't you understand?'

'God has his reasons, Jenny.'

I felt repulsed by the comment. 'I swear to God,' I gasped, 'if you don't bring me my baby I will get out of this bed and find her myself. I must hold her.'

'Don't you understand? She's dead ... dead. You can't see her.'

His face, transmogrified by the turmoil of my senses into a hideous mask of evil, terrified me. I screamed. Immediately both nurse and doctor were at my bedside. I berated the nurse who attempted to calm me. The doctor, syringe in hand, grasped my arm and mercilessly shot the needle into my vein. I kept up a wailing demand to see my baby until the blackness which Neil hac brought with him was no longer a threat but an invitation. I turned from my husband and was swallowed into oblivion.

There was more agony to come. The following day the doctor told me that there could be no more children, They had cut away my womanhood. I was unable to conceive.

In the days to follow I was inconsolable. Neither matron's professional brusqueness nor the doctor's kindness could quieten my heightening agitation and my conviction that they were accessories to the murder of my daughter and conspirators in the execution of my tortured soul. I could hardly bear to look at Neil. I resolutely shut my ears to his prayers. Perhaps if there had been some shared misery in his voice, a kind gesture, gentle reassurance, I would have found some solace. If misery touched him he hid it. If he'd had any promptings to kindness he killed them cold. All he had to offer were his prayers which were as acceptable to me as hay to a dead donkey. Without Callum I might never have surfaced from my misery.

'Someone to see you Mrs Fraser,' smiled the junior nurse as she smoothed my coverlet and gently beckoned me from the land of beyond. I turned my head but kept my eyes closed until I heard my brother's voice. For the next few minutes I could do nothing but let the tears of misery and joy pour down my cheeks while his warm embrace and silent understanding began the long process of healing.

'They should never have taken her away like that.'

'I know.'

'I only wanted to hold her; look upon her face.'

'I know, Jenny.'

'They had no right.'

'Indeed they hadn't.'

'Why did they do it?'

'Probably thought it was for the best.'

'How do they know what's best? I wanted her so much.'

'There, there,' he soothed. 'Cry as much as you want.'

I was back in my childhood, in my father's arms. 'There, there,' he'd sobbed in his effort to relieve the trauma of my mother's death.

'There, there,' repeated Callum.

To him I could expose my anguish and have it accepted, recognized and acknowledged with no attempt made to pass it on to the will of God or my own inadequacies. I was given the sympathy I had craved, freely given and, from that, my strength and perspective slowly returned. The doctor, I felt, had failed me. Neil had failed me. God was no longer in the reckoning as far as I was concerned. He was a spent force, a nothing, a no-thing. I was on my own. The thought brought a blessed relief. Perhaps now, without

God's lurking presence and without Neil's unremitting insistence on this presence, I would somehow find myself, the real me who knew what she wanted and where she wanted to go. Perhaps the loss of my baby was the catalyst that enabled me to break free of that caged imprisonment of which Theresa had prophesied.

I felt free of my husband. He had lost the power to hurt or persuade. He would never be able to hurt me again. From that certainty of knowledge my strength returned.

A week later I was back in the manse. Against my husband's wishes I refused to stay in bed. Each morning I rose early and, as much as my painful wounds would allow, went on solitary walks or worked in the garden. The advantages were physical but there was no solace for the soul. I fended off all efforts of condolence gradually creating a reputation for myself as a heartless lump of stone. I made feeble excuses for opting out of clubs and meetings, and feigned headaches on Sunday services. I was hardly proud of myself but paddling a lonely raft on a turbulent sea, it was the only way I knew how to keep afloat.

'The poor minister,' I imagined them saying. 'I don't know how he puts up with it.'

I knew he wasn't putting up with it at all well. After the initial shock of my defiance Neil showed constrained signs of anger. I took grim satisfaction from my detachment. I did wonder how he was facing the prospect of no possible procreation, no sex. It had not been mentioned and I assumed that the doctor had informed him. I did not ask because I did not care.

I knew the time had come for me to make a statement. This I did a week after my return from hospital on the last stroke of ten when the housekeeper, Bible in hand, entered the parlour and Neil rose to fetch his own. My despondency had rendered me fearless.

'I hope you will excuse me,' I said rising primly and moving towards the door. For a moment I thought Neil was going to let me leave without a challenge, but as I reached the door he jumped to his feet, almost knocking over his chair.

'Wait!'

I turned, raising my brows, totally unperturbed, and waited.

'Where do you think you're going?'

In deliberately marked contrast to his raised voice I spoke quietly. 'I'm going to bed.'

'You can't go to bed now, not before Bible reading.'

I felt so detached I could regard his outburst as funny. 'I think I can,' I said quietly.

'I say you can't,' he responded with angry emphasis. Mrs Martin looked set in stone. My husband was more agitated than I had ever seen him.

'Good night, Neil, and to you too, Mrs Martin.' I even managed a phoney smile.

'Didn't you hear me?' He made no attempt to conceal his anger and to her credit the housekeeper was beginning to show signs of embarrassment.

'I think I'd better go,' she offered, clasping her Bible and springing to her feet.'

But he would not permit either of us to leave the room. I called his bluff and, seeing the involuntary lift of his arm, I sensed the danger but stood my ground. 'If you wish me to remain you will have to physically restrain me.'

An agonized expression flitted across his face as he dropped his arm to his side. I knew then what it was costing him to hold back and almost felt sorry for him. He was not equipped to cope with this unexpected defiance. At that moment I was not Jenny, his wife, but some colossal threat to his authority.

Trying to avoid contact I managed to open the door and, leaving the room, went upstairs. I sat on my bed dry-eyed and empty of emotion. I wanted no more Bible readings.

The next morning there was no mention of the previous evening's confrontation. Neil was in a continuous sulk, at least with me. With Mrs Martin he was polite and with Graham he was his usual reassuring and kindly self. Neil's relationship with Graham made it very difficult for me to hate him as much as I needed to. Never once had I heard an impatient or unkind word escape him in his dealings with my brother. He could never have pretended the love he levelled at my young brother. If the virtues of his Christianity were dependent on this alone he would be considered saintly. It was a contradiction that I found difficult to accept.

Callum visited the next day wishing to see as much of us as possible before his imminent drafting overseas. I was afraid he might guess the constraint between Neil and myself. I needn't have worried. My brother was in an unusually talkative mood. There was a rumour that Canada might be his destination.

'Perhaps you'll be able to visit Father,' I said as we sat in the parlour after a frugal wartime lunch enlivened by some chocolate Callum had brought.

'You can rest assured it won't be for the want of trying,' he said as he declined an offer of chocolate for himself. 'I'm dying to meet Moira,' he added. Realizing that our young sister was someone I didn't like to talk about, he looked at me anxiously.

I smiled. 'It's all right. Father sends us photographs. She is very pretty.'

'And spunky too, I hope,' he said including Neil in his smile.

'Not too spunky,' muttered Neil who was grimly stirring his sugarless tea.

'Oh I don't know,' laughed Callum. 'I like them spunky. Jenny was always spunky and still is, if recent events are anything to go by.'

He smiled fondly on me. Darling Callum, I thought. Still as sensitive and caring as ever. The war has not destroyed you.

'I only wish,' he was saying as he laid his empty cup carefully on its saucer, 'that I could take you in my pocket, Jenny, but,' he laughed almost too heartily, 'I don't think Neil would allow that.'

Neil made no comment but if Callum noticed he gave no sign. To cover my own embarrassment I fussed around the sideboard refilling the teapot.

'One thing you can be sure of,' he said to Neil as I rejoined them, 'is that when it's all over there are going to be big changes. For one thing I think you'll find your pews less occupied.'

'Meaning?' Neil asked stiffly eyeing him over the rim of his teacup.

'Meaning that life in the trenches has given any idea of a good God a bit of a bashing,' replied Callum.

'I'd have thought the opposite,' said Neil unperturbed. 'Life in the trenches would bring God closer to man, I'd have thought.'

Callum passed me his cup for a refill. I could see the puzzlement in his eyes.

'You're joking of course,' he said to Neil.

'Would I joke about such a matter?' I saw Callum's flush under the impact of Neil's scorn.

'No, of course not. I just find that idea a bit difficult to work out,' he murmured almost apologetically.

That's exactly the effect Neil has on people, I thought with kindling insight. On the face of it he is the epitome of respectability and good sense and when he decides to offer his extreme ideas people begin to think there's something they've been missing in the argument. He is, I thought, the most contradictory figure I've ever known.

An uncomfortable silence was broken by Neil.

'We are all sinners and never more so when battling against the will of God.' He did not look at me but I guessed what he was thinking and it wasn't about the horrors of the trenches.

Watching Callum I could see the first glimmer of suspicion that everything was not as it should be. I managed a reassuring smile in his direction and quickly he changed the subject.

'By the way, Jenny, I see your old friend's in Edinburgh just now.'

'I don't know who you're talking about,' I said, genuinely puzzled.

'The fortune-teller from the hotel,' Callum said having no notion of the bombshell he was dropping.

'Theresa,' I gasped. 'Theresa in town!'

'She's billed for a lecture on astrology somewhere in the New Town.'

Jenny has no interest in that nonsense now, said Neil.

I bit my tongue. I wanted to challenge his assumption.

Only the fact that it was probably Callum's last visit kept me from saying anything that might give him cause for worry. I also wanted to express my pleasure that Theresa was near. Hearing her name touched a part of me which I thought was dead and buried. Theresa! It conjured pleasure, interest, stimulation and joy in companionship.

Already my mind was busily scheming to contrive a meeting.

I steered the conversation to Graham, expressing regret that he was not present. Mrs Martin had taken him shopping for new shoes.

Callum began expressing his own regret when Neil interrupted taking us both unaware.

'Before you go,' he suggested, 'would you like to come with me to the church and seek God's blessing and protection?'

I looked at my brother who was looking at me. We had shared our scepticism in the early days and I had no reason to think he had changed his mind. But I knew that he thought I had. After all, I had married the church and had made no secret that I wanted to serve God. I could feel his reluctance although good breeding, as Grandpa would have called it, ensured he gave no sign of it. Our grandfather would have been proud of him.

'Of course,' he replied to Neil. 'It is kind of you.' Jenny?' asked Neil.

'I'll wash up,' I said gently enough to give no offence to either man.

'Can we have a walk together before I go,' whispered Callum as Neil led the way from the parlour.

I nodded and watched them cross the garden towards the wooden gate into the churchyard. I busied myself with the washing up until they returned. As he was leaving Callum asked if I'd walk him to the gate. I could feel Neil's eyes on us both as we left the manse and Callum, hand on my arm, steered me through the gate and into the churchyard. He led me to a quiet corner shaded by a giant oak.

We stood quietly for a few moments with Callum holding my hand. I had an overwhelming feeling that my brother was creating something of significance for me.

Soon he told me. 'You have been denied something rightly yours, Jenny.' I knew what he meant. I had never dared put it into words myself but had carried the torment ceaselessly. 'You need to say goodbye. Your daughter may have been stillborn - I think that's what they Call it - but to you she lived. You felt her in your womb. You felt her move as you have told me. You need to say goodbye in your own way. We can say it now, Jenny. We cannot dig an empty grave but we can make her mark on the tree. Somewhere you can come and find solace when you feel the need.'

I had always loved my brother but never more than at that moment. I nodded, tears of gratitude blurring my vision. These I blinked away and quivered my heartfelt thanks. How well he knew me and this knowledge was a comfort.

'What name would you have given my niece?' he asked deliberately keeping his voice light.

'I think our mother's name,' I whispered.

He nodded. 'Fiona. Yes, that's good. Let's find the place where I can scratch it on the tree. It won't mind I'm sure. In fact it will be honoured.' We both smiled and, after he'd carved my daughter's name where only we might look for it, we stood in silence. What might have been a sorrowful moment for me became a moment full of joy.

Callum left and my joy sustained me throughout the day. It was almost tangible and I knew that it would be there in many guises if I kept searching. I renewed my vow to go my chosen path knowing that it would bring conflict with Neil.

I was already in bed when the clock struck ten that evening but I might as well have been in the parlour since I suffered every minute of their devotions in my mind. The prospect of my future being a succession of ten o'clocks hiding in my bedroom was bleak indeed. My spirit may have made a bid for freedom but until my mind could be quit of the grooves it had dug for itself, I'd never be really free. Surely I could find some way out of this impasse. My thoughts turned to Theresa and made up my mind to contact her as soon as possible. When I recalled our many hours together working, laughing, learning, I was quietened along to the borderland ol sleep only to be suddenly jolted back by a knock on my door followed by the figure of my husband, Bible clutched in hand.

'I'm sorry you saw fit to absent yourself again from our devotional readings.'

I said nothing but pulled the blankets up to my chin. 'Perhaps you'd like me to read a passage to you now to prepare your mind for sleep.'

'I think not Neil.'

'I thought you wanted to be with God Jenny.'

'Sometimes we want things that are not right for us,' I replied. 'I thought I wanted God but I really want myself.'

'You're talking your usual rubbish.'

'I realize it is difficult for you to understand. Indeed, I'm just beginning to understand myself. All I know is that there is joy out there and I want to find it. I've had enough of your God's doom and gloom. There must be other ways of worshipping. You make it all so tedious Neil, so soul-destroying. I have tried to share your beliefs, really tried, but I'd be a hypocrite to go on pretending what I do not feel. I want to find out for myself, in my own way.'

'And how do you propose to do that?'

'I don't know but I'll find a way.'

'Satan's way.'

I slid further into the sheets, pulling the blanket close to my chin wishing he'd leave. He moved closer.

'You need God, Jenny. I will never give up until you offer yourself to Him completely.'

Such was the power of his words that I felt a depression like an amorphous weight on my body.

'You were happy when with child,' he said, almost like a lost little boy.

I closed my eyes and silently screamed. I willed him to go.

'I think we should begin procreating again.'

I shot up and looked at him with horror. He didn't know! He had never been told! I expected any moment to see some visible signs of the monster he became to me then. All I saw was a stiff-backed, thin-lipped, steely-eyed bigot who had to justify his beliefs by any means. I realized I wasn't afraid of him. I was only beginning to really understand him and wondered how on earth I could learn to cope. Suddenly I was glad of my infertility. I would never want Neil to be the father of a child of mine. I laughed hysterically then watched with dismay as his anger blazed.

'You are my wife,' he whispered with such ferocity that my laughter turned to a scream.

He grabbed both my arms and leaned over me, forcing me back on my pillows. I glared back at him, more shocked than afraid.

'It is our God-given right,' he said between his teeth.

'You will have to force me,' I said. 'Is that what you want?' I was damned if I was going to tell him.

His grip on my arms tightened. I suffered the pain, determined to make it as difficult as possible for him. After a long hard glance I felt his resolve weaken. His anger subsided as quickly as it had flared. He left me bruised in body and spirit. I imagined him returning to his room, collapsing on his knees and confessing his fall from grace. Let him drown in his illusions I thought. Let him roast in the fire of his perverted passions. Let him rot in a pit of his own creation. But of course I didn't convince myself. The trouble with Neil was that he wasn't all bad. In fact he wasn't bad at all. We just saw life and love and death and eternity differently. We were like oil and water. We just didn't mix.

I would gladly have left him, walked away from the manse and the church, distanced myself from the life of hypocrisy I was living. But I had nowhere to go. I had no money of my own, no family near enough to run t Then there was Graham. He was still my responsibility even if I had shouldered this on Neil and Mrs Martin. Courage was needed but I shied from a courage of endurance. I had endured enough. I needed a different kind of courage. Not for me the courage of Joshua 'not to be afraid or to be dismayed for the Lord my God is with me'. Rather of Virgil who promised my courage would be the way to the stars.

I turned on my back and looked at the stars framed by my window and resolved that somehow the next day I would find Theresa.

CHAPTER 20

'You like our library?'

I turned from the book I was skimming to meet a friendly scrutiny from a pair of sparkling eyes. My unhesitating response to the medium-sized, middle-aged gentleman with grey hair and lengthy beard was to reciprocate with a friendly smile.

'Hugh Hadley.'

I took the extended hand. 'Jenny Fraser,' I replied, returning his firm grip.

'You're impressed with our library?' he repeated.

'I'm flabbergasted.' My eyes made a full sweep of ceiling-to-floor shelves overspilling with books of all sorts, shapes and conditions.

'What sort of library is this?' I asked.

'A library for the broad-minded,' he answered. 'If you want to know about the esoteric it is all here - sacred geometry, shamanism, Gnosticism, Jesus, Buddha, Blake, Crawley and Cayce - to name but a few. If you are interested in the welfare of your body there's holistic medicine, yoga and the chakras. If it's stimulation for broadening the mind there's all the sciences, philosophies and religions or, as I dare to suspect in your case, the quest of the soul, it's there too. The Holy Grail, the Knights Templar, Freemasonry and magic. Here you will find Tennyson, Masefield, Einsten and Krishnamurti. Around you is the knowledge and the wisdom of the ancients. Here you can, if you persist, find your truth.'

'Stop,' I pleaded, holding up a hand as if to ward off an attack. 'There's so much.'

'And more,' he said with a wide sweep of his arm.

'And truth; it's here?' I asked.

'Everyone's truth is here.'

'Isn't it the same for everyone - truth after all is truth is truth?' I asked, enjoying this unexpected verbal exchange.

'There are as many truths as there are seekers of truth,' Hugh Hadley answered, 'but only one will work for you and even then, just one at a time. You can change it when you outgrow it or find, like a coat, it doesn't fit.'

'That sounds rather fickle - that it's all right to change your truth just like a garment of clothing,' I challenged.

'Would you go on wearing a coat that no longer fits?' 'That's different surely.'

'Surely not. Truth changes all the time as does our body and mind. Why not our spirit, the true home of truth? How else could we grow and develop if we got stuck in the same spot for ever? As knowledge increases, attitudes change, perceptions sharpen or deepen et cetera. One's beliefs expand or are shaken out of all recognition and somehow we have to fit this in to our day to day existence. This library contains the wisdom of the ages. You can learn how to do it, if you keep looking, or you can leave it alone.'

'A question of choice,' I commented.

'Everything is. For instance you chose to be here tonight, probably instigated by circumstances way back in your life.'

'That doesn't sound like choice. More like a foregone conclusion.'

I looked more closely at this strange, yet strangely familiar man. I had one of my feelings of knowing without knowing why I knew that he was going to be significant, just as Theresa was significant.

We were in a Georgian house in a terrace of other Georgian houses in the New Town of Edinburgh. I had managed to track Theresa's whereabouts to this mansion which I learned was the headquarters of a theosophical society about which I knew nothing. All I had learned was that every week the society had a meeting at which various experts lectured to the members of the society. I had noted from the programmes on the notice board that the lectures were wide-ranging. At first glance they seemed to indicate a synthesis of the sciences, philosophies and the arts, with a distinctly esoteric core.

Earlier, when I arrived at the front door there was no one greeting arrivals so I followed printed notices, finding my own way upstairs to the lecture room where Theresa was billed to speak. I was not prepared for the intimacy of the surroundings, having imagined some large hail where I could slip into the back and listen unobserved. I was nervous, not knowing how Theresa might receive me. I had been pinning such hopes on seeing her again but flinched at the thought of a possible rejection. There still being some minutes to go before the meeting was due to start, I left the lecture hall and wandered into a room which I had seen from the landing was a library of sorts. I'd been immediately struck by the wide-ranging collection of books. In fact I would go as far as to say that I'd been completely bowled over by the titles with which I was now confronted.

Hugh Hadley, looking at the book I held now commented. 'You are interested in reincarnation?'

I flushed. 'I have been wondering about it,' I confessed, 'but the idea is so revolutionary to my way of thinking,' I added almost apologetically.

'Maybe your way of thinking needs some new clothes. You could try this for size. See if it fits,' he suggested laying a finger on the book in my hand.

'I'm a minister's wife, for goodness sake,' trying to laugh off the suggestion.

'The concept of Christ is much broader than is generally credited and I rather think that eternal Heaven and everlasting Hell are unpopular nowadays. Now, in the, pages of this book which you have chosen to inspect and which I recommend, you will find a more inspiring attempt to explain the anomalies and inequalities of life.'

My senses quickened. Hadn't that been my overriding concern since I had first attempted to form opinions of my own? Why can't Graham walk properly, Father? Why is he different?

My hand holding the book was trembling and when Hugh Hadley covered it with both of his I felt an energy rush between us which both excited and confused me.

'Borrow the book,' he said. 'Perhaps that's why you are here tonight, and remember there's more where that came from. It's just a matter of turning on the power.'

'Imagine yourself in a dark room, no light, no apparent way of escape, just four walls with a switch and a closed door!' the dominie had said all those years ago. Of course! The source of hidden power and the door of opportunity! I realized I had been groping in the dark for too long, had been resigning myself to the shadow of reality, settling for less than my intrinsic best.

I looked round the book-crammed room, rich with recorded thoughts, ideas and inspirations of people of all ages, rescued from oblivion by the printed word.

'I think,' interrupted Hugh, 'the lecture is about to begin. Shall we join the others?'

Theresa! I'd forgotten her! At the moment of leaving the library we ran full tilt into Theresa as she headed up the stairs on to the landing. She was accompanied by another woman who became a blur to me as my eyes were transfixed on my old friend and my thoughts became so jumbled by my tumbling emotions that I could only stand in dumb disbelief as I looked at her. Gone was the rotundity of the woman I had known, gone the flamboyant clothes and accessories but as if operated by an invisible switch the familiar face lit into a radiance of remembrance. The large eyes almost popped out of the pleasant face and the arms spread wide.

'Jenny!'

I was wrapped in those welcoming arms, held off, examined, drawn close again and struck dumb with overwhelming gratitude and love.

'This is wonderful,' Theresa was saying as her companion and Hugh Hadley looked on in obvious delight. I knew it was going to be a special day for me but never guessed just how special. Oh, Jenny McLeod, why have you kept your distance for so long.Why did you not answer my letters? Why did you make me think you wanted nothing to do with me any more? You have much to answer for, my friend.'

She was smiling her broad, happy, all-encompassing smile unaware that my own light had suddenly extinguished at the mention of letters I had never answered. I had never received any letters but before I could say anything the companion reminded Theresa gently that her audience was waiting.

'Don't you go away,' Theresa warned hugging me again. 'I see you know Professor Hadley.' She turned to Hugh who acknowledged her attention with a slight incline of the head. 'Don't let this woman run off,' she told him. 'Now that I've found her I've no intention of losing her again. Guard her with your life.' With a bounce in her step she followed her companion to the lecture hall.

'Will I have need of chains?' the professor asked jocularly.

'No way,' I replied feeling awash with excitement and an anticipation I had not experienced for a long time. I pushed the question of the letters onto the back burner. I would have been happy to slip unnoticed into the back but, with a light touch on my arm, the professor led me to the front of the hail where I could feast my eyes and ears on an old friend and share my delight in being with her again with a new friend.

Try as I did, I couldn't concentrate fully on Theresa's lecture. It seemed to be about a comparison of the natal charts of dictators. She demonstrated that Stalin, Hitler and Goering each had Scorpio rising, the sure sign of the dictator, she told us. Churchill too had Scorpio rising but, she went on to explain, the rest of his chart nullified the prevalence of the dictator attributes. Sun in the first house, she told us, gave him dignity and authority and being in Sagittarius it showed ambition, loyalty, generosity and energy whereas with Goering's moon in Uranus with its subconscious instinctive character allied to the animal passion of Scorpio, there was something utterly amoral.

Interesting as this might well be, I began to lose track. I had become conscious of the professor next to me who seemed totally absorbed by Theresa's words. I was aware of a vibrant energy radiating from him which played upon me. His was the first question at the end of the lecture.

'Can you tell us Theresa,' he asked, 'of what practical use is astrology?'

Theresa waited before answering and, although she was responding to the professor's question, her eyes were fixed on me.

'Astrology reveals a person's natural abilities and can offer direction or warn of potential danger. It cannot alter a person's stars but can help in showing the way to make the best of them and warn of the pitfalls.'

Here her eyes seemed to bore into mine and I was uncomfortably reminded of the last time we'd been together when she'd given me a progressive reading and pleaded with me to take heed and not marry Neil.

'It can stop one from being a square peg in a round hole,' she said her eyes now directed at the professor, 'and so avoid lives of wasted energy.'

I wondered if that was what my life had been since then. Had all my efforts to please God and my husband been nothing but years of wasted energy?

'If it is as good as you say it is,' smiled the professor, 'why has it fallen into such disrepute since the days of Chaucer and Shakespeare for instance?

Then, even common people like, for instance, the Wife of Bath seemed to understand it.'

'Like all good things it was at the mercy of charlatans, in this case the so-called "fortune-tellers" and, as scientific methods went from strength to strength, astrology was largely discarded. It is certainly a discipline that challenges credulity.'

'Is it a challenge to your credulity?' I whispered to the professor when Theresa was questioned by another voice in the room.

'Not in the least,' smiled the professor. 'But it's a coat I'm inclined to keep on a hanger in my wardrobe. Now tell me, Jenny,' he in his turn whispered, 'why do you keep looking at your watch?'

I flushed and couldn't disguise my mounting anxiety. 'It's later than I realized,' I whispered. 'I should be going home.'

'Theresa would never forgive me if I let you escape,' he said, keeping his voice light.

'And my husband will never forgive me if I keep indecent hours.' But these words I did not voice.

The lecture came to an end. The chairman duly thanked Theresa for her contribution to the evening. This was followed by announcements.

My desire told me to wait and speak to Theresa but my conscience told me I should leave immediately if I wanted to catch a tram home. Neil had no idea where I was. He would be worried but more pressing for me was the thought of his anger when he learned of the company I'd kept. My defiance was still in its early stages and in many ways untested. Could I hold out against him? Was it worth it? Had I subjugated my own interests for too long now? How much was at stake? Then there was the question of Theresa's letters to me. What had happened to them? Could I tackle Neil about this? So many questions. So much to think about.

'You see,' said the professor to Theresa as she jumped from the platform and came towards us. 'I have not let this little bird fly away but I can feel the draught from fluttering wings. You must catch her now before she escapes.'

'Thank you, my dear professor,' gushed Theresa. 'I am taking her home with me.'

The professor looked from Theresa's excited face to my more troubled one. 'Is that wise?' he asked.

'Wise, perhaps not, but necessary, absolutely.' 'Theresa...' I began.

'No, Jenny. You are coming with me. We will phone your husband from my home and put his mind at rest. I will see that you get safely home by taxi when we've caught up.'

I let my resistance go. I wanted to 'catch up' as she put it and besides I wasn't ready yet for a confrontation with Neil. Not tonight.

'It's settled then,' she concluded. 'Just let me fetch my coat. Can I give you a lift, professor?'

'Thank you, dear lady but no,' the professor replied. 'I have my own transport.'

He turned to me as Theresa dashed off to fetch her coat.

'It has been a pleasure meeting you, Jenny.'

He took an envelope from the inside pocket of his jacket and held it towards me. 'I'd like you to put this in your purse,' he said. 'Read it later after you and Theresa have "caught up". It was intended for the notice-board but I'd like you to have it.'

I pushed it into my handbag and, in the excitement of leaving with Theresa to 'catch up', I immediately forgot about it.

CHAPTER 21

Theresa's flat in Stockbridge was a den of clutter. There were planetary models swinging from the ceiling, posters covering walls and a variety of crystals on cupboard tops and shelves. The table was lost under a litter of papers. She cleared an armchair of books before persuading me into it.

'Sit down, Jenny, and let me get you a drink. After it's warmed you, you can phone Neil.'

Feeling that some Dutch courage wouldn't go amiss I sank thankfully into the wide, high-backed, surprisingly comfortable armchair. It was almost half-past ten. My husband and his housekeeper would still be at their prayers. It wouldn't do to interrupt them. I relaxed.

'Where's Guy?' I asked accepting the glass. Theresa recorked the whisky bottle, set it on the table and seated herself on another armchair opposite.

'Guy's dead.'

Her words stunned me. I struggled to respond.

'It's all right Jenny. It was nearly two years ago. You can talk about it.'

'What happened?' I managed.

'The fool tried to save a woman who'd jumped off a bridge into a river. He hit his head on a submerged rock and was knocked unconscious. By the time help came he'd been washed downstream and drowned. It was the next day when they recovered both bodies.'

'That's terrible.' I had fond memories of Guy Mason.

'Well, there's a lot of water flowed under that same bridge since then,' she replied with a wry smile which didn't fool me for a moment. I remembered their joy together. 'At first I thought it was just the stupid sort of thing he'd do until I did a reading and saw it written in his chart.'

I wanted to ask how that could be possible, not from any desire to be instructed, but from an attitude of disbelief. This, I felt, was taking astrology a step too far, but Theresa spoke with such conviction that I kept my thoughts to myself while I took a gulp of whisky.

'That was when I wrote to you. I thought you might come to the funeral.'

'I never got your letters, Theresa.' I rested my glass on a clear inch of carpet space.

'I know I got the right address because I took great pains to find out Neil's church.'

'I'm sorry Theresa - about everything,' I stammered, struggling with the shock of Guy's death and the awful suspicion of what might have happened to Theresa's letters.

'And so you should be,' said Theresa briskly. 'You have a lot to answer for. First of all, tell me why are you so scared? It's all wrong, you know. It's completely out of character. It makes me angry. You, Jenny McLeod - I'm calling you Jenny McLeod because that's the person I know. I don't know Jenny Fraser yet but you, Jenny McLeod, are needing, to put it crudely, a kick up the backside.'

I settled for another few gulps of whisky. This was a new image for me. I giggled and couldn't stop. Soon I was laughing hysterically. It could have been the whisky or the excitement of the evening or it could have been the first leakage from a buried well of repression but I went on laughing, long and shrill. Theresa, after rescuing my glass, seized me and shook me until I choked on my own hysteria. The demon released, I was left limp and exhausted. She refilled our glasses.

'You'd better begin at the beginning,' she said before collapsing into her chair and waited for me to begin.

So much has happened,' I began.

'Tell me about it.'

Out spilled the whole sorry story of my life with Neil. She heard me out in silence.

'He is a good man really,' I kept reiterating. 'Graham adores him and he is devoted to Graham. He inspires his congregation to raise thousands for the needy, has fought ceaselessly with the powers that be to improve the fabric of the church. He never stints himself in his pastoral duties. He is always there to comfort his flock and relieve their suffering.'

My voice wavered and disappeared into a well of silence. Then Theresa spoke.

'He doesn't know the meaning of suffering,' she said quietly.

We were sitting in the darkness of the night. The only glimmer of light was from a pair of scented candles in the alcove which Theresa had lit during my long confession. I heard the ticking of a clock buried somewhere under the general litter.

'He has spent his life cocooning himself against suffering,' she said while I listened in growing amazement. 'He knows the theory of suffering but he's never been touched by it. He's like someone who's read all the details about a disease and thinks that he knows what it is to suffer from it. Knowing the details gives no appreciation of utter despair, loss of identity or fear of the demon forces outside one's control. Neil Fraser is so hooked on his God and his principles that any threat to their validity must be mercilessly extinguished to the point of paranoia because if his beliefs were shaken enough to weaken his defences it would destroy him. Then he would know what suffering was all about. If everything upon which he'd built his existence were to crumble, what would be left? Pain, despair and suffering.

The far-flung missionaries, the sick and disabled, the poor and the weak, the biddable and easily swayed are no threat. Of course he spares no effort in indulging them. They are all bolsters to his spiritual ego. Only the strong are a threat. You, Jenny McLeod, are his greatest threat. When he made you Jenny Fraser he was convinced he had you where he wanted you - under his control.'

'But why, if I was such a threat, did he marry me?'

'Because,' and here Theresa paused for a moment, 'because,' she repeated, 'he loves you.'

I gasped. 'Loves me!'

'Obsessively. He wants you body and soul.'

'Hardly body,' I mumbled, remembering our wedding night.

'Don't you believe it,' she said. 'But for him to surrender his self-imposed rules for physical satisfaction would be the surest way to lose everything he values. What the fool needs is a good dose of Pluto, the planet of transformation. He needs his fanaticism recycled to the quality of his higher ideals that you're at such pains to point out.'

'For a little while,' I said almost in a whisper, 'before he knew I was pregnant, I thought things might work out. It was becoming more than a "procreation exercise". I was beginning to hope.'

'So long as he could equate intercourse with a biblical edict he could enjoy himself. Once the need for that disappeared he was consumed by guilt.'

'Guilt?'

'Yes, an ugly word is guilt, especially with religious connotations. It's time we refilled.'

Before I could protest, she had emptied what was left of the whisky into our glasses. This, along with the relief of being able to share my turmoil at last offered me a relaxation of body and mind that I had not experienced for a long time.

'He's so good with Graham,' I mused feeling the whisky warm my belly.

'Being good with Graham's no threat. It's a constant reassurance of his own goodness.'

'Tell me Theresa,' I asked, on the brink of intoxication, 'what do you think of reincarnation and karma? Is there anything in it, do you think?'

'More than half the world's population seems to think there is.'

'But not Christianity?'

'It did before the religion became vulgarized. Now we have to read between the lines. "Judge not that ye be not judged, for with what judgement ye judge, ye shall be judged: and with what measure ye mete, it shall be measured to you again" (Matthew seven; one and two). You see, Jenny McLeod, justice must rule.'

'Injustice has always made me angry,' I said. 'It has been my life-long argument with God. I don't think I have ever come to terms with the fact that Graham was born so disabled, through no fault of his own, while Callum had everything to his advantage and yet the same people, if you like "begat" them. It doesn't make sense, but reincarnation offers an explanation for the anomaly of the genius and the degenerate. It makes nonsense of such a limited existence being the only existence.'

'It is a question of choice,' said Theresa. 'Does chance or does justice rule our lives and why, for the love of Jesus and Mary, Mother of God, should human life be an exception to the natural laws of periodicity?'

For a moment we were each lost in our own thoughts, then I pressed her further.

'You talked about guilt. I walk with it. Guilt for despising my husband. Guilt for shutting Graham out from all that is best in me buried somewhere beneath my disillusionment. Guilt for my sister Moira whom I've always ignored and seldom offered a kindly thought. And now guilt that I wasn't there when you wanted me, that I hadn't the courage to defy Neil when he threw that astrology book to the flames.'

'I hope tonight has given you plenty to think about.'

'What I think about mostly is my guilt about Graham.'

'But Jenny, you always adored Graham.'

'I still do in a way, but I can't compete with Neil. He really does care. He spends time with him. I could do more of that. Even Mrs Martin spends more time with him than I do. I've shut him out just as I shut out my baby sister. It's been me, me, me all the way. I see that now.'

'Would you like me to give you another reading?' asked Theresa.

'No, not yet. I have to work this out for myself.'

'Well, you couldn't have found a better place to do it than in the Theosophical Society where the whole emphasis is on just that. No one indoctrinates. No one tells you right from wrong. The divine wisdom of the ages is on its library shelves and cupboard tops, drawers and anywhere there's room for another book. It's the old adage "seek and ye shall find" but wisdom as you well know is not handed out on a platter. It has to be sought after and discovered before it becomes one's own.'

'I shall make it up to Graham,' I vowed.

'And what about Neil?' asked Theresa looking at the clock. 'Are you going to phone?'

I sprang out of my chair. 'Two o'clock in the morning. My God! I forgot all about Neil. He has no idea where I am.'

'I hope he will be worried sick,' said Theresa.

'I'm sure he will be worried and probably raging mad. I must phone at once.'

'Wouldn't it be better to wait till morning?' 'It is morning, for goodness sake.'

'You will stay here till later in the morning then. I can run you home or you could call a taxi if you prefer.'

'Where is your phone?' My agitation was heightening. I had been so uplifted with the evening's events, raised right up from my slough of despondency, that the worry my absence must have caused had totally escaped me. Although I dreaded having to confront Neil at this hour, under these circumstances, I dreaded still more the thought that he might, if he had not already done so, raise a missing person's alarm.

Theresa dug out the telephone from under a mountain of charts and as, with hands trembling, I rang the manse she filled the kettle and opened the lid of the tea caddy.

'Don't bother,' I said as I waited for the connection. 'I must go straight away.'

'You'll have a warm drink first and a slice of toast. It will help soak up all that whisky.'

At last I was connected.

'Hullo. Oh it's you Mrs Martin. This is Mrs Fraser. Could you fetch my husband please? I must speak to him.'

At first I could not take in what she was saying to me.

'He's where?'

As the housekeeper repeated what she had just told me and continued in a stream of vindictive accusation I could feel the blood drain from my veins. I began to shake so much that I could no longer hold the receiver. Theresa rushed to my side in alarm and, grabbing the instrument, began demanding information while I slipped into the chair and unconsciousness. It could only have been for a minute. When I came round Theresa was still talking into the phone. She had grabbed paper and pencil from somewhere and was making notes. When she replaced the receiver she told me to stay where I was, poured a mug of tea which she'd made before the interruption and heaped in a generous helping of sugar.

'Drink this,' she ordered. 'I'll make the toast.'

'I couldn't eat a—'

'You'll have one slice of toast at least. I insist.'

She had taken over. I couldn't resist. Indeed I was thankful for her practicality.

'Is Graham...?' I began.

'Graham has had an accident,' she explained slowly as if spelling out instructions to a child. 'He was knocked down by a car. He is in intensive care and Neil is with him. He hasn't left Graham's side.'

Unprotesting, I accepted the hot, buttered toast. 'Mrs Martin said...' I shook my head in an attempt to clear it of its total and unexpected confusion. 'She said he'd been looking for me.' I felt the toast slip from my fingers. Theresa caught it and returned it to my still-trembling hands.

'Eat this,' she ordered.

Mutely I put it to my lips but an uprush of nausea made me throw it to the ground.

Theresa ignored it and, putting a comforting arm around my shoulder, continued steadily.

'When you didn't come home he was worried. Apparently he went to bed but never slept. He got up, heard the others discuss your disappearance, heard Neil threaten to ring the police. He put on his slippers and dressing-gown, let himself out of the manse and began looking for you. When he was crossing the road a speeding car hit him. At least the driver had the decency to stop and notify the police. It wasn't long before an ambulance arrived. He's in intensive care and everything that can be done for him is being done. Neil's with him.'

'I should be with him,' I said struggling to my feet. 'I must go.'

'We'll go together,' she said collecting her car keys. 'Come!'

CHAPTER 22

Theresa, after throwing the usual collection of books and papers from the passenger seat into the already cluttered back seat, bundled me into her car and silently, breaking every rule of the driving code, drove me to the infirmary.

I was glad of her silence. This was no time for conversation, helpful or otherwise. In my mind I saw Graham as the little brother I had worshipped in that time and land long ago into which we had both been born. I saw his unfailing happiness, his love of nature and his adoration of myself. He had been the brightest star in our heaven then. After my mother's death he had been no less loving and adored but his need of us had become all-consuming and it was a need, I realized now, that little by little I had been glad to relinquish. As my life had become focused on my learning it was my grandfather who had borne the brunt. Neil too, had been particularly generous with his help.

Although I had put up a fight to keep Graham in the family when Neil and his father first revealed their charitable plans for him, in the end I was relieved for him to go. It was Neil who visited him regularly in the 'home'. Neil who took him on jaunts. Neil who grew ever closer to him and I who became more detached, barely appreciative of his blessedly happy nature. Eventually I readily concluded that the bond between us had weakened and had unashamedly felt relief. Graham was not as others, never had been, never would be.

Now suddenly, I was face to face with something else. Graham had, of his own volition, left the security of the manse, left it in secret unbeknown to Neil or Mrs Martin to look for me. He had been worried about me, needed me, wanted me. The fact that I had always made a habit of saying goodnight before he went to his room seemed small comfort now. It had never occurred to me that Graham would be wondering and worrying about my absence. My chief concern was that Neil would be fuelling fires. Now I burned with the need to be with Graham, really with him, bonded again as we once had been. I needed to reassure him of my love.

Theresa steered me through the enquiry desk routine, through a maze of empty tiled corridors and a succession of swing doors until we reached the ward number we had been given. After a quick consultation with the nurse in charge, I was taken to Intensive Care. I was barely aware of Theresa's departure and her whispered promise to be in touch.

When I entered Intensive Care, Neil was with Graham. He rose to his feet, his eyes silently accusing me. I quickly averted my gaze and, pushing past him, took the bedside seat which he had just vacated.

I looked at Graham. His expression was peaceful. His long lashes lay in a curve against the pallor of his skin. His hair, too long, was spread across the crisp cotton of the pillow. His arms lay still on top of the folded sheets.

I reached for his hand, massaging the translucent skin with my thumb. I had to make contact. He had to know of my presence and of my love. I felt I had to make it up to him. There was so much I could have done for him. I pushed Neil's presence from my mind, exerting every ounce of my will to drag Graham from the well of unconsciousness in which he lay.

'Graham, forgive me,' I whispered over and over. Jenny is here and she loves you so much. Can you hear me darling? Forgive me. I understand now. You are going to be all right. I promise.'

I wasn't sure exactly what it was that I understood. I had only so recently been offered a glimpse of cosmic possibilities as to why my brother was as he was. Later I would examine it. But the glimpse had been enough to sustain me now.

Refusing to leave, I sat holding my brother's hand. I waited and watched for the merest glimmer of awareness but he lay immobile, apparently at peace, the slow beat of his pulse beneath my probing fingers the only sign that he was still alive. The nurse came and went. I was aware that Neil had left the room at one stage but he returned and now stood stiffly at the other side of the bed.

'I think you should go home.' His voice was stern, without empathy.

I kept my eyes on Graham. 'No. I shall stay till he comes out of this coma.'

'He may never do that,' Neil warned.

'He will,' I said with utter conviction, allowing myself one upward glance at my husband's stern face.

'He is not going to survive,' he insisted.

'Not the way you think,' I replied, returning my attention to my brother.

'You realize it is because of you that he is in this state.'

I tried to keep my breathing steady and my voice calm.

'This is neither the time nor the place for recriminations.'

'You're right. That can come later.'

There was no escaping the veiled threat.

'I must leave soon,' Neil said. 'I have a wedding at noon.'

He seemed to find nothing absurdly unfitting in the statement. I smiled grimly. 'I shall pray now.' He dropped to his knees on the other side of the bed. I averted my glance.

'Will you join me?'

'Go ahead,' I said. 'I'm listening.'

He waited, expecting me to drop on my knees but tenaciously I held on to Graham's hand and listened. He prayed that Graham's sins would be forgiven and that his soul would have a life of eternal happiness in heaven with Jesus.

His words jarred. Where was the logic? I looked at the shell which housed my brother's soul. What sin had Graham ever committed? Where was that soul now? Where was it going? Where did it come from? How meaningful had his few incapacitated years on earth been in the ocean of eternity? Was that his full entitlement? Surely, that was not enough for the journey of a soul. To listen to Neil's traditional absurdity that a soul was created at a fixed point in time and yet, as he was now saying, end in a heaven of eternal happiness could not be the answer. That a soul should survive the body but not pre-exist it was illogical.

I sat thus as hour followed hour, as one day ended and the next day dawned. I refused to leave, only withdrawing grudgingly into the corridor when the nurses or doctors were tending Graham. At first the hospital staff tried persuasion to send me home. When this proved pointless they tried enlisting my husband but, seeing the hopelessness of that, they left me alone. I was offered the occasional refreshment which I refused.

Neil came and went. There was no doubting his purity of heart and love for Graham. Where we differed was where we located our God. To Neil God was 'out there' in that place called heaven. My God was 'in here' in the centre of my existence. But then who was I to criticize? Wasn't I, in my heart, praying that Graham would awake so that I could relieve myself of my guilt and make it all right for me?

Surely prayer was not for wish-fulfillment. Surely prayer was striving towards one's highest and best. Divine goodness needs no help from me, I decided, nor indeed from Neil. We were one in our desires. Neil needed communion with his 'out there' God. I needed self-communion. Graham needed neither of us, not now, not anymore. His soul was already preparing for its next journey, taking with it what each of us had already given him in our own way, in our own time and leaving behind this empty shell to which, for reasons of its own, it had entered and borne with love and cheerfulness. Why should I try to stop it? It was ready to move on. Why should Neil spoil its launch by thoughts of sin and need for repentance.

It was perhaps symbolic that at that moment of self-revelation the sun illuminated the ward. I released mytension, watched Neil give his priestly blessing and knewwith a quiet certainty that life was never going to be the same for me again.

Almost as if my brother had been waiting for this self-revelatory moment he opened his eyes. I dropped on my knees beside him, not in supplication, but in order to miss nothing of what he might reveal.

'Chenny.'

It was barely audible. I held my breath. That was all but it was enough. Where I had been hoping to comfort I was being comforted. The sunshine penetrated my whole being. Graham's expression was changing, shifting from me to something far out of my understanding, altering his features from the gangly youth he had become to someone departing in wonder and in joy.

When his own earthly light extinguished it was Neil who reached out and closed his eyes and offered his further prayers for the soul's release. I was led gently away by the nurse and later, in a little ante-room given refreshment for my body and well-meant counsel for my soul.

When I reached home I shut myself in my room, crept into bed and slept for twelve hours. Mrs Martin, when hearing I was up and moving around, brought me a tray with tea and hot-buttered toast. I thanked her, accepted her condolences, ignored her obvious curiosity and told her I would stay in my room for a while and did not want to be disturbed.

'The minister wants to know when you are comin downstairs.'

'When I am ready,' I replied shortly.

Sniffing, she withdrew, closing the door behind her.

I settled down in my chair by the window which offered a view of the garden and a corner of the church-: yard. I opened the book I had borrowed from the library and which had been recommended by the professor and, for the best part of the day, sat there gorging my mind with its contents. From being a 'one-life' thinker brought: up in a tradition of 'one-life' thinking which would culminate in eternal bliss or eternal damnation, I was discovering a new horizon, an alternative way of thinking, a new level of being.

Chance or justice? In my 'one-life' theory upbringing, justice had not been seen to be present. Circumstances led one to the hopeless acceptance of chance - chance without choice. Never had I been offered an explanation of the problems of heredity, the anomaly of genius and degenerate. Was this chance or justice?

Those questions had never been satisfactorily explained to me but here, as my eyes greedily engaged in the print before me, there was an explanation - karma and reincarnation.

'Do not regard Karman,' I read, 'as an outside Fate or something which we must put up with against our will. Our Karman is what we have made for ourselves, what we have inbuilt into our own characters. Above all, do not look upon karma as either punishment for sins or reward for virtues doled out by some overruling "Providence". It is the consequence that inevitably follows an action as "the wheel follows the ox".'

How simple, I thought. How fitting an explanation. As a guideline for living for the benefit of mankind and the betterment of self there could be none fitter.

'Those who believe in karma,' I read, 'have to believe in destiny which from birth to death every man is weaving thread by thread around himself as a spider does its cobweb.'

Lowering my book I gazed into the garden recalling my schooldays with the schoolmaster and with Todd. Thought, Archie Ross had told us was the springboard of action and thought breeds act, breeds habit, breeds character which in its turn creates one's destiny. How often had I seen that exemplified without being aware of its crucial importance. Slowly I was appreciating that my idea of a 'one-life' theory was changing. I was finding the idea of a different kind of one-life concept where man was one with all things most attractive. What is death? I pondered. Was it sleep writ large? Sleep was the blessed abeyance of consciousness without which the body could not grow and develop. It was the rest between the day-by-day activities of the body operating in different shapes and sizes throughout a body's lifetime, ever striving, developing, ever evolving. Why is it so difficult I wondered, to accept the concept of death as a long sleep between the activities of the soul operating in different physical bodies throughout a soul's lifetime, ever striving, ever evolving? It made sense to me. I liked the thought. It appealed to my sense of justice and above all it was helping me come to terms with Graham's departure from our lives.

I felt excited and, lowering my eyes once more to my book, continued my reading.

'Do you intend incarcerating yourself in here for ever?'

Startled, the book fell from my hands. I jumped from my chair and turned to face my husband who had entered my bedroom unannounced.

'Graham's funeral has to be discussed,' he said. 'What is there to discuss?'

'The day, the time, the announcement, the order of service.' There was an edge to his voice.

'You can see to that. I will abide by your decisions.'

'A bit late for that now.'

The edge was cutting. I glanced uneasily at my book, still lying on the floor and made no comment.

'We need to talk, Jenny. You can't run away from things forever.'

'Let's leave it till after the funeral,' I said. 'I have a lot to think about.'

'About yourself, no doubt. It's time you thought about other things - and people.'

'I agree and that's just what I intend to do.' I turned from him moving towards the door.

'Typical!' he spat. 'Running away. As soon as things become uncomfortable for you, you up and run. You've learned nothing.'

'We can talk later, after the funeral,' I said wearily. 'We will talk now and you can begin by telling me where you were all night when you should have been at home.'

I wanted to be evasive. I wasn't ready for this conversation but as I hesitated I saw him spot my book lying where it had fallen on the floor. He pounced on it and one glance at the cover sent the blood rushing to his face. I saw the twist of his mouth and the anger blazing from his eyes as he read the title.

'You're at it again! Stuffing your mind with this ... this sinful trash!'

'Is your mind so stuffed that you can't find room for any idea that isn't your own?' I shouted. 'You are a bigot, Neil. You think your religion says it all and you can show nothing but contempt for anyone who may think differently.' I could feel my control slipping and could do nothing to stop it. 'You are prejudiced. You are arrogant, believing that only you can be right and the rest of humanity is wrong. Is that your demonstration of the love of your God?'

'You are damned!' he shouted.

'You're also out of date,' I yelled back, 'because you've kept your mind so closed no light can get in.'

'Damn you!' he choked.

'And the same to you,' I yelled back.

We looked at each other in horror, realizing the enormity of the gap between us which no amount of shouting could ever bridge. I think that we were both ashamed.

'Where were you?' he asked in quieter tones.

'I went to a meeting of the Theosophical Society.'

'And what in God's name is theosophy?'

'Before you say anything, it is not a religion, nor a sect. It has always been there since man could think. Theos - God; Sophia - wisdom, and it's a fount of knowledge from which all religions spring without the superstition and bigotry which generally masquerades as religion. The Theosophical Society does not proselytize. It was formed to remind us of these early teachings. It debars no one. All are welcome - Christians, Jews, atheists. You name it, they are all welcome. All it asks is that you believe in the brotherhood of man and have no prejudice against race, sex or creed.' I didn't add that its third requirement was a willingness to study comparative religions and the powers latent in man, which meant of course the occult. That word, I knew, would immediately conjure in his mind witches, magic and orgies. The finer teachings of occultism would be too subtle for him. He would rubbish my words.

'The book you are holding,' I continued, 'tells us that what we call a life is in reality only one day of many existences. Don't you see, Neil,' I pleaded, 'Graham's death is more the beginning of the next life than the end of this one.'

'Graham is with Jesus and the holy angels.'

'Forever?' I asked, incredulous.

'Forever,' he replied emphatically.

'With his poor twisted half-formed body and mind, forever? What a punishment for his sins!'

'You talk rubbish, as usual,' he said contemptuously, adding, 'It must have been some meeting. Do they usually last into the small hours?'

'The meeting closed at 10 o'clock.' I waited, aware of increasing tension.

'Where were you after 10 o'clock?'

'With a friend. I intended phoning but we got talking and the time flew by and I was indeed sorry when I remembered.'

'Not half as sorry as Graham.' He threw my book on the armchair and moved towards the door.

'I intended to phone.'

He stopped and looked at me. 'This friend who could make you forget your family and responsibilities, was it a man?'

'And if it was?' I felt goaded to reply.

'You Jezebel!' His arm half rose from his side.

I stood rooted, full of disgust and dismay that we were allowing ourselves this ugly confrontation.

'Would it make you feel better if I told you that it was a woman?'

'That woman, that she-devil?' He spat out his words like a dirty taste in the mouth.

'If you mean Theresa, yes it was.'

'She put you up to this rubbish, I suppose.' Pointing dramatically to the book he'd pitched into the armchair.

'I borrowed the book from the theosophical library.'

I could see that his fury had peaked. Beyond striking me there was nothing more he could do and this I knew, tempting as it may have been to him, he would never do.

His shoulders slouched and the life seemed to go out of him. For a moment I felt a great pity for him, for me, for us all.

'All I am doing is learning about man and his history way back, before Jesus. There was a very long time before Jesus, you know, that has to be accounted for Everything doesn't begin and end with the Bible.'

'It does for me.'

I had to shut my ears to his bigotry. I had to get away. I had to learn more. I had to follow this path that had opened up for me.

'Can we leave this for now Neil? Perhaps later, after we bury Graham, we can talk about it. I can try and explain what this means to me.'

'There is nothing to explain that will make any difference to me. You are a sinner. I have tried to save you from yourself but have obviously failed. I shall have to learn to live with that.'

I sighed.

'What hymn shall we have?' he asked coldly.

'Graham loved "What a friend we have in Jesus".' I bit my tongue.

'Wise child.'

He rose and left but not before he muttered, 'Just make sure that she-devil never crosses this threshold.'

I sank into my chair at the window more shaken than I realized. The scene both sickened and angered me. In an effort to calm myself I thought of Graham and his short life. I refused to believe that it had been meaningless.

I recalled some lines from Tennyson from his poem 'By an Evolutionist'. It was a small poem and I was surprised at how the words had stuck in my mind as if they had been secreted there, waiting for this moment of revelation.

'The Lord let the house of a brute to the soul of a man
And the man said "Am I your debtor?"
The Lord - "Not yet, but make it as clean as you can
And then I will let you a better."

I looked at the word 'let'. There was nothing final about let, no suggestion that this house would be forever and ever the only house. Clean it up and you would get a better one. Rubbish it and you will have to balance the cost in the next 'let'. The Lord was not giving. He was letting. I did not realize that I was weeping until I tasted my own tears.

Neil performed the funeral service. I stood at the graveside, my face hidden under my veil, my eyes on the coffin as it was lowered into the space prepared to receive it. I threw in the wild flowers I had picked in the morning and while Neil intoned the burial service I recited more Tennyson to myself.

> 'What is it all, if we all of us end but in being
> our own corpse-coffins at last
> Swallowed in vastness, lost in silence, drowned in
> the deeps of a meaningless past.
> What but a murmur of gnats in the gloom or a
> moment's anger of bees in their hive
> Peace, let it be, for I loved him, and love him for
> ever; the dead are not dead but alive.'

Comforted I left the graveside. Postponing the moment when I would have to return downstairs to see to our guests, I went to my room ostensibly to freshen up. I'll get today over, I thought, then I shall do something. I need to know so much more. There is so much to learn. I remembered the professor and wondered why I hadn't thought of him sooner. He had made such an impression on me. With the recollection came another, of the envelope which he'd given me and which I'd stashed in my handbag. Had I left it in Theresa's flat? Was it downstairs? Had I perhaps lost it? Anxiously I went to my cupboard, relieved to find my handbag on the shelf where I had put it. Yes, the envelope was still there. I sat on the edge of my bed and slit it, extracting the sheet of paper it held. Before reading the contents I took a moment to savour inexplicable excitement. Why was I so sure of its importance? Why so convinced?

'Volunteer', I read, 'most welcome to make order out of chaos with the library of a rather absent-minded professor. No salary offered but anyone with a thirst for knowledge will be amply rewarded.'

I gasped in amazement. SynchronicitY! Was there such a thing? Was this convergence of need and opportunity purely coincidental or were there subtle forces at work here, forces to which my antennae were already attuned? With hope in my heart I made my way downstairs to join my husband and our fellow mourners.

CHAPTER 23

I was determined to seek out the professor the next day but before doing so I had to confront Neil. I knew the meeting would be unpleasant for I was about to plead with a man to understand, when I knew that would be attempting the impossible. Neil was barricaded into a life's pattern of belief structure which allowed no invasion of criticism. He fanatically held forth on his certainties allowing no intrusion of ideas that he did not share. I had little hope of releasing him from his self-imposed prison. I felt justifiable anger that I was being made to put up a fight for my freedom of thought. So, having roused myself into a working resentment, I was not in the best emotional state to sustain a reasoned argument. Knocking briefly on the door of his study I waited for his call.

'I want to talk to you,' I began more timidly than I'd intended.

'Can't it wait?' he replied with ice and arrogance.

'I'm sorry no, it can't.'

'You know I prepare my sermon at this hour and brook no interruption.'

'This is an exception. I'm going out and I want to tell you where and why.' I had lost my timidity.

'That's a change.'

I ignored the sarcasm. Lowering his head, he continued his writing.

'Don't you want to know?' I insisted. 'I've been offered a job.' I had hoped for a bombshell but there was no response. 'Unpaid of course. It is voluntary work - in a library.'

It was as if he hadn't heard but, to emphasize my determination, I seated myself on the chair opposite him which was generally occupied by visiting parishioners.

He placed his pen carefully in its groove and straightening himself in his chair asked, 'Is that it?'

'It is a private library belonging to a professor. I met him at the Theosophical Society meeting.'

I could feel the weight of his disapproval.

'I can be as flexible as I wish.'

'That's nice.' He was leaving it all to me. I realized that my hands were tightly clenched. I relaxed them before continuing.

'You don't mind then?'

'Does that matter?'

'I'd prefer your approval.'

His mood changed abruptly. 'I'll bet you would. Tell me,' he said rising to his feet. 'What sort of books are in this library?'

'A very wide collection - philosophy, science, poetry, essays, health - religion,' I added quickly.

'And reincarnation?'

'That too.'

'And if I said no?'

This was the moment I'd been waiting for.

'I'll go anyway.' I felt no doubt that I would. Indeed as our conversation progressed from bad to worse my determination strengthened.

'Haven't you thought how unseemly it is for a minister's wife to work?'

'It is unpaid work.'

'In another man's establishment, alone with a man who is a stranger. He must be quite something, this professor of yours. I suppose his private library is in his house.'

'I'm not sure, but I think so.'

'Very convenient.' His words were heavy with sarcasm and innuendo.

I didn't need to listen to this. I rose from my chair.

'That remark ill becomes you,' I accused.

He began pacing the floor. 'I take it you are resigning from your other voluntary work - like chairing the Women's Guild, organizing the Youth Club, helping in the Missionary Fund events?'

Say yes I told myself. The thought of continuing in the grooves of parish events held no attraction. I had never felt I fitted in. I had never been able to muster the enthusiasm for jumble sales and craft exhibitions so much the lifeblood of the women of the parish. I had done my duty as the minister's wife but if truth be told had disliked every minute of it. Now with a taste for a whole new other landscape was that likely to change? Say yes I repeated to myself. This too is a moment you've been waiting for. I was forced to turn and face him.

'I ... not right away,' I heard myself stammer.

'That's considerate. Maybe you'd like to stop attending services too?'

There was nothing I wanted more but I kept that thought to myself.

'Where is this library?' he asked.

'In the New Town, somewhere near Charlotte Square.' I looked at my watch.

'You can't wait, can you?'

I heard the bitterness in his voice. I might have been more concerned for his discomfiture if he hadn't then decide to quote the scriptures at me. Taking what I considered a melodramatic stand he confronted me.

"Thus saith the Lord, Stand ye in the ways, and see, and ask for the old paths, where is the good way, and walk therein, and ye shall find rest for your souls. But they said, We will not walk therein."

I sighed, feeling the now familiar ineptitude of widening any discussion with Neil.

'There are other ways, Neil.'

He continued unabashed. "Were they ashamed when they committed abomination? Nay, they were not at all ashamed, neither could they blush."

Then quickly averting from his pulpit manner to his normal tones continued into the attack.

'It is abominable what you are doing, Jenny. Quite deplorable and you have no shame. Neither can you blush.'

'I don't see it that way,' I said wearily.

'No, you only see it the way you want to see it.'

'And can't I feel the same about you? You only see things your way.' I knew that this line of argument would only lead to futile point-scoring.

'You are prepared to forsake your wifely duties to join a strange man in his strange house filling your mind with the strangest of notions when you could be working for the Lord and helping to save souls and clothe the bodies of the needy.'

"Judge not that ye be not judged,"' I retorted, hating myself for saying it.

He sat down heavily at his desk, lifted his pen and, pulling his sheaves of paper towards him, began writing. It seemed the argument was over. I was dismissed and possibly damned.

I left the house feeling more determined than ever. I had to know without a shadow of a doubt what I wanted to do. I had to know the road I must travel. Whether it be with or without Neil could not be decided until I could map out my own journey. I was still unsure where I wanted to go or what I was looking for but I knew that there was no standing still or going back. What did I need? What did I want? What could I not do without and, more importantly, what could I now shed? Fetters? Misconceptions? Timidity? My husband? What should be my new purpose in life?

If I were to find the answers to these questions, the professor and his library of books would be as good a place to start as anywhere.

I found him in a Georgian house in a Georgian street in the Georgian New Town of Edinburgh. It was a house almost identical to the headquarters of the Theosophical Society. It was light, airy and practical with classical charm.

He welcomed me warmly, as I stepped across the threshold into the entrance hall. The hall was large with flock-papered walls and a winding staircase leading up to a glass-domed roof three storeys further on. I had an impression of highly polished furnishings, jardinières topped with foliage plants, heavily framed portraits and a carpet of dated worth.

He opened a door from the hail and, with what was to become a characteristic flourish of arm and half bow, signalled me into his library. Three walls were shelved from high ceiling to floor. Leather-bound volumes seemed to be making a statement of such magnitude to me I couldn't speak. I just stood and gazed in awe. There was a leather-covered armchair on each side of an Adam-style fireplace. The mantel was shining with crystal prisms which looked stunning in the sun's rays. The sash windows were large and framed by velvet curtains. Beside the window was an antique desk. In the centre of the floor, which was covered by a richly coloured oriental carpet, was a table with a crystal bowl of fresh-cut flowers.

The professor, who had given me time to absorb the atmosphere, broke the spell still binding me. He motioned me to sit and took the armchair opposite. I noticed a jade Buddha, serene in lotus position sitting on the hearth among various rocks and stones. The morning light filtering through the window cast a mellowness reflected in the book-lined walls, enriching the leather spines and embossed lettering.

'I'm glad you followed your instinct,' he said with surprising perspicacity.

My eyebrows must have been raised. He went on to explain.

'No wife of a minister of the Church of Scotland wanders into a meeting of the Theosophical Society without being led by her intuition.'

'I'm glad I came,' I said from the heart.

'You're most welcome and much needed,' he said with a smile. 'I've been lax and what order I once had seems to have disintegrated by neglect. Would you like to catalogue my collection on the understanding of course that you can read anything when and where you like?'

I felt if I said or did the wrong thing this vision would vanish. I'd wake up from a dream perhaps or discover some factor that would make the professor think again. I hardly recognized my own voice as the words poured out.

'I'd be honoured, sir. I thirst for the knowledge you can give me. I have so many questions I want to ask, so much I want to straighten out in my mind. I need to find truth and decide the path I must follow.'

The professor remained silent for so long that I almost panicked, convinced I had said too much, disappointed him, perhaps even annoyed him. I'd been too presumptuous.

His voice, when he did speak, was reassuring, his expression kind and understanding.

'It is important,' he began, 'to find our own answers to our questions. You are looking for something?'

He sat straight-backed on his chair, elbows resting on the arms and abstractedly making a fingertip steeple.

'What are we all looking for?' he mused before I could reply. 'Now that is a difficult question to ask oneself. Is it God, truth, immortality, happiness, self-fulfilment - which you never find anyway, because once you think you have it, you immediately want more. Whatever you seek, Jenny, you must find it for yourself. You have so many friends around you now.' He swept an arm in a wide arc to encompass the book-lined walls. 'Get to know them. Listen to what they have to say. They will all say something different. Some may be wrong for you but then again, some may be right.

It will be for you to choose. And if it is truth you are looking for you will find what suits you - the coat that fits, remember? What is truth to you is heresy to another and it is easy to be intolerant of another's truth. The most I can do for you Jenny is to show you the light switches. You must turn them on for yourself.'

His words aroused vivid memories, so vivid that this elderly sage opposite seemed to vanish into thin air to be replaced by the schoolmaster with myself and Todd seated at his feet. I felt that if I stretched out my hand I could touch Todd. The image stirred such a depth of feeling that I wanted to cry out, 'Look at me, Todd! Speak to me!'

The spell was broken by the professor's voice.

'I will give you a list of recommended reading – very wide, very challenging, very stimulating reading - and if you explore it you might find what you are looking for, or you might even find out what it is you want to start looking for.'

He leaned forward, beaming. 'There is something else I can tell you but first we will have some tea and cake. I will just go and tell my housekeeper to fetch it here for us. Then, my dear Jenny,' he whispered as he leaned to my ear, 'I will let you into a secret of mine. Wait here.'

When he'd gone I rose from my chair and wandered alongside the shelves, skimming the many titles, running my fingers gently down the leathered spines. Arundale, Besant, Conan Doyle, Jinarajadasa. The door opened and the professor returned followed by an elderly woman behind a laden tea trolley. That was my first meeting with the kindly Agnes Calder, affectionately known as Aggie, and my first tea ceremony with Professor Hugh Hadley.

It was the first of many things and a relationship which was to develop and span many years of study and research. The many 'friends' to which the professor had referred, nestling between their leather covers, opened door after door of discovery and delight, restoring a joy to my soul which I hungrily embraced. But if I had thought to shed my old responsibilities and wipe out the past with a new perspective on the future, I could not Fbeen more mistaken.

I could not open my mind to the esoteric without familiarizing myself with the ego. The more familiar I became with the ego, the more conscious I became of the sleeping tiger within.

Upon examination of my own ego I began to appreciate its effect on my day-to-day living. It was one thing to refrain from harming others but quite another to be positive in serving others. It was one thing to serve in a preferred cause but quite another to take up the cudgels of one for which there was no personal appeal.

Spiritual endeavour, I discovered to my cost, was not an occupation to be slotted in to my life now and again. It was a day-to-day, indeed hour-to-hour, even moment-bymoment affair with no let up. There was no fall-back, like confession or conciliatory prayer. I was on my own; really on my own. Like an artist, never satisfied with the end results, I kept chiselling at the refinements, opening mind and heart to the subtleties of the demands which offering service to others really meant. A spiritual journey was more like a maze than a mountain climb. An intricately constructed maze meant being constantly faced with choices. This way or that? This way could take me back to where I started. That way I knew would lead to another choice. What this meant in my own life was a complete turn around in my intentions.

What did I need, I asked myself. I discovered that what I needed was exactly what I had. I had responsibilities as the minister's wife. Instead of abandoning them, I had to respect them, transform them and eventually love them.

What could I do without?

Although Neil might remain forever entrenched in his own beliefs and be as adamant as ever in waging wars, I could learn to do without the need to respond.

What could i now shed?

My husband? Could I shed him?

That would be the supreme test of my new commitment. However none of this happened overnight.

CHAPTER 24

On this first of many tea ceremonies with cake deliciously prepared by Aggie Calder I had little conception of the land I found myself in. It was a green and pleasant land. It was interesting and exciting and was eventually to change my life.

Aggie poured the tea, chatting incessantly.

'With a figure like yours you won't be having sugar,' she said. 'Am I not right then?'

'No sugar,' I smiled. 'Nor should I be having cake,' I protested as she poised a knife over a cream sponge.

'Get away with you,' she laughed. 'A wee bittie home baking won't do you any harm. Isn't that right Professor?'

'Absolutely.' Then turning to me, 'Aggie is what Shakespeare described as the "queen of curds and cream",' he rejoined. 'Her cakes are so good that they will melt in your mouth and you will reach for more. Isn't that right Aggie, my lass?'

'Get away wi' ye,' the old woman laughed. After cutting an ample slice for each of us she made to leave.

'You won't forget to tell me when it's siesta time,' said the professor.

'Do I ever?'

'No indeed. You're a guid woman - nearly as guid as your cake.'

'Get away wi' ye!'

The professor tackled his tea and cake with relish. He talked about Aggie and how she had looked after him for thirty years.

'We all want to find happiness and inner security and truth. We go about it in our own way and there's Aggie, happy the whole day, every day, never ill at ease or hassled or careless of tongue, as true blue as you could find them, and you know what, Jenny, she doesn't even have to try. She doesn't know most people need to try. She doesn't know she carries God in her ample bosom. She doesn't spend hour upon hour reading about how to reach enlightenment, as you're planning to do, or experimenting on the routes to nirvana as I'm doing, but she's where we'd all like to be.'

'She reminds me of my grandfather,' I said.

'Tell me about him, and about your dear brother who's just departed from the shackles of this life.'

I found it easy to talk about them. I told him about Strathard and all the happy times because these were the times that were to the fore.

'I feel I know them and love them too,' he replied, regretfully replacing his empty plate on the table, 'and I feel I am getting to know you too. You are going to enjoy many surprises from your leather-jacket "friends",'

he said indicating the bookshelves, 'and perhaps a few shocks. Tell me Jenny, do you remember the third tenet of the Theosophical Society?'

'You mean the one for the sceptics?'

'That's the one,' he grinned. 'To investigate unexplained laws of nature and the powers latent in man.' A blob of cream from Aggie's cake was deposited on his flowing beard as he began stroking it.

'That's a tricky one.' I smiled.

'It's got me by the throat at the moment,' the professor confessed, discovering the blob and removing it with his handkerchief. 'I should be busy on other things but I cannot give up my addiction and I'd like you to help me.'

His words alerted me and I must have looked as puzzled as I felt. He went on to explain.

'You don't have to be dead, you know, to have an out-of-body experience.'

I blinked. 'I've read of people dying—'

'No, not dying or dead people but healthy and fit people like myself.'

'I don't understand,' I said.

'You know that our physical body has a double composed of a subtle form of matter invisible to the physical eye.'

I nodded, noting the change coming over my companion. He was betraying a restlessness uncharacteristic of him and seemed to be having trouble controlling his excitement.

'It's called the astral body and it coincides with the physical body when we are awake, but when sleeping it hovers usually just above it. Now it is possible for a person to will to leave his physical body and travel in his double. This is called astral projection. His astral body is attached to his physical body by a silver cord which acts like a piece of elastic and pulls it back to coincidence.'

I sat up, feeling a shiver of apprehension. This was the last thing I had expected. What on earth was I letting myself in for? Was it my imagination or was this bearded gent with the sparkling eyes and slightly stuck out ears, taking on the likeness of a mischievous goblin? It was scary and I wanted to up and run. Half-rising from my chair I had a vision of my husband hovering behind the professor with a cynical smile on his face, goading me. 'That's right, Jenny. Run away. This is uncomfortable so run, run.'

I pulled myself together and pushed my body further back into the shape of the old chair.

As if assessing my reaction the professor continued.

'What I am going to tell you Jenny, you need not believe. Accept nothing second-hand. You can acknowledge it, investigate but you are never called upon to believe it. What I am going to tell you cannot be proved. You have to experience it. No one is going to believe you. You do not believe me. Why should you?'

'This silver cord?' I mumbled not wishing to appear completely out of tune with his images.

'Or ever the silver cord be loosed, or the golden bowl be broken, or the pitcher be broken at the fountain, or the wheel broken at the cistern.
Then shall the dust return to the earth as it was; and
The spirit shall return unto God who gave it.'

'Ecclesiastes, Chapter 12,' he finished. 'The silver cord,' he added, 'wonderfully fastens together the soul and the body. Through it run vital currents and, when the cord is severed, you die. It is elastic and capable of great extension. One could travel to far-flung horizons if one were experienced enough but for myself I'm happy to stay in my own neighbourhood.'

I gulped, shrinking further back in my chair.

'Don't be afraid, Jenny. If you want to broaden your mind you must give room for all ideas. It doesn't mean you have to accept them or agree with them and certainly you should always be chary of believing them but let them in.'

I understood what he was saying. Hadn't that been my quarrel with Neil for all the years we had known each other? Nevertheless it did not lessen my apprehension. I just felt that it was a step too far. The image of the stout little professor floating above his body, attached to it by a piece of elastic was so far-fetched as to be almost laughable. Again I was horrified when he immediately tuned in my thoughts.

'Most people scoff,' he said matter-of-factly, 'even laugh. I cannot prove to such people that it is an astral projection and not a dream, of which they generally accuse me, but then neither can the sceptic prove that it is a dream and not an astral projection. I experience it, in a small way so far. I have been in every corner of every ceiling in my house. Now I want to go farther - not too far to begin with. The garden will do for a start and that's where I want your help, but not today. You have had enough excitement today and very soon now Aggie will be telling me it's time for my "fiesta", as she calls it. But between you, me and the gatepost, as they say, I don't have a siesta. I prepare myself for astral travel. Tomorrow I will have a little job for you.'

'Professor—'

'Call me Hugh. We are going to be together a great deal. Now let's stroll among our "friends" for a few moments before you take your leave.'

I let him lead me along the library shelves, listening with half my mind to his comments on the various authors lettered on the book spines, of the greatness of Plato, Newton, and Einstein.

'But remember Jenny,' he said as he replaced The Republic on the shelf 'everything you want to know is inside you.'

'That's too deep for me, I'm afraid.'

'You are a westerner, Jenny, brought up in the western tradition of seeing-is-believing.'

'And yet,' I countered, 'we are asked to believe in a virgin birth, a resurrection and a heaven and hell and, of course, Jesus. Why do westerners think he has the answer to everything?'

'Christ was a highly evolved soul who knew more than anyone about God. You are interested in justice Jenny?'

'Ever since I can remember.'

'That was before you opened your mind to a cosmic justice.'

'You mean reincarnation?'

'And karma. Every act and thought has a consequence - you reap what you sow, Jesus said. Cause and effect. Who knows what effect meeting me, for instance, will reap in your life. Good, I hope.'

He smiled saying, 'Take Plato here,' fingering the book he had just replaced, 'and Pythagoras. They knew all about reincarnation.'

I thought of Neil and realized, if what I was considerjing had any credibility, our responsibilities to each other were enormous. It was all very well for me to be concerned with my own soul but how should that affect my relationship with my husband?

My mood was plummeting to depression at the enormity, even I felt absurdity, of the whole complicated setup.

I needed a break. My mind was being stretched to the point of discomfort. Fortunately we were interrupted by the housekeeper.

'Time for fiesta!' she called.

'In a minute,' called the professor.

'Now! Time now!'

'Dinna fash yourself woman,' he roared and I could feel the smile broadening on my face. How long since I'd heard these words.

Aggie was smiling too. You could see she loved the gentle bullying which didn't deter her purpose a jot. She refused to leave us until the professor made tracks for his own room.

'Tomorrow,' he whispered, his eyes twinkling conspiratorially and his body, to my highly charged senses, assuming the mischievous goblin look.

'It's today I'm concerned about,' said Aggie jostling him to the door. 'I'll see the lady out. Be off wi' ye.'

I felt light of head, enjoying the interplay. When the professor was safely out of the way Aggie offered more refreshment which I declined. I wanted to be on my own to sort out my jumbled feelings and, as I closed the front door behind me and walked down the quiet Georgian street, I wasn't sure I'd be back the next day. 'What in the name o' the wee man', as my grandfather would have said, had I let myself in for!

CHAPTER 25

'Have you any idea what you are letting yourself in for, Jenny?'

On impulse I had decided to call on Theresa before going home in the hope of learning her opinion of Hugh Hadley's revelation.

'That's why I've come to you, Theresa. I find the professor's projection business a bit weird and I don't want any part of it.'

'I'm not talking about that. The professor will do nothing that will harm you. He's not going to ask you to grab his silver cord while he tows you around his ceiling. Anyhow, I'm not referring to astral projection. That's not as rare as you might think and to an occultist it's an everyday event. No, what I'm referring to is this spiritual path you've set yourself on.'

'There's no harm in that surely. I'm only doing what any decent Christian should be doing - unto others as they might, you know.'

I moved a few books from the armchair.

'Aren't you forgetting something?'

I raised my brows in question.

'The type of Christian you are referring to does not embrace the notion of believing that he or she is God, that the great mystery is not out there but in here.' Theresa pointed to herself. 'That makes a difference. At least, when calamity strikes, they have the comfort of thinking that it's not their fault. They give themselves someone to bargain with and their belief absolves them of a great deal of responsibility. The way you intend going is to take everything, and I mean everything, upon yourself. God is within you. You are God. God is you and loving everything that lives and harming no one by act - and if you go far enough - even by thought is un-godlike. You are accepting total responsibility for everything that you do or say.'

I sat back in the chair which was now free of clutter, feeling relaxed and even began to tolerate the scented candles which Theresa had lit.

'Is that such a bad thing - being totally responsible for your own actions?'

'Have you thought it through?'

'I feel it's right. It's just and it's good and it's beautiful. In fact, it's an ideal way of life.'

'And what's an ideal way of life?'

'Peace, freedom, justice, service I suppose, to feel worthy, fulfilled, in harmony, of use, unhindered by pride and bigotry and meanness and doubt.'

'Listen to yourself!' screamed Theresa. 'You talk like a holy cow. You only have an ideal way of life when you no longer think of an ideal way of life.'

'Like Aggie Calder?'

'If you like, but you don't get there by taking communion, embracing communism, sitting in the lotus position or joining the Theosophical Society.'

'No, you get there by plodding every step of the way in whatever is your chosen belief,' I said.

'The burden of complete responsibility is an awesome task, Jenny.'

'But not impossible,' I said, frowning.

Theresa shook her head slowly.

'It's at least worth a try,' I said, brightening.

'What about your husband?'

'What about him?' My voice had lost its enthusiasm.

'Isn't all this an attempt to escape from him?'

'An attempt to gain my self-esteem.'

'If you're only seeking insight by half measures, better not bother. It demands your all.'

'You doubt my sincerity?'

'Not for a moment, but I doubt your capability. For a start it will be more difficult coming from your background.'

'And what sort of background should I have?'

'Certainly not Calvinism. A Buddhist is halfway there. His reincarnation and karma are already a part of him. As often as not he's been trained in meditation.'

'Just because Christianity dispensed with reincarnation and karma doesn't mean we can't come to it in other ways, especially when one has a need for it.'

'What you need, my girl, is a good man's love and children.'

'I have a good man in spite of our incompatibility. He's as strong in his beliefs as I am in mine and as for children there is no possibility there.'

'I wonder what would have happened to you if your freedom fighter had stayed at home and married you,' said Theresa eyeing me warily.

'That was a long time ago.' I couldn't keep the annoyance from my voice.

'You've forgotten how you felt?'

I looked at her through a haze of memories. It was some minutes before I answered. She sat waiting.

'No. I could never do that. He made me alive. We sparked each other off. We fitted. I have a suitcase of letters hidden in the attic which I wrote to him over a number of years. I could never post them because I never had an address.'

'Why did you keep them?'

'At first I refused to believe he was dead. I was convinced that he would come back one day and we could read them together. Then as time went on I hadn't the heart to get rid of them; then I simply forgot.'

'Don't you think you should burn them now? If Neil finds them it won't help the harmonizing.'

'I'll get round to it, and talking about Neil I'd best be going. I promised I'd be back for the committee meeting of the Women's Guild which I'm supposed to be chairing.'

'So you think the professor is OK?' I said, rising and collecting my handbag.

'Absolutely. Pity there aren't more like him. He was an engineer in his working life. Surprised?'

'I am a bit. I thought he'd just come out from his ivory tower for a while.'

'Oh Jenny. You have a lot to learn.'

I left Theresa's flat only partially reassured. She had leaped too far ahead for me. All I wanted to do was enjoy life as a good Christian without my mind being offended by dogma and the absurdities which Neil grappled to his soul. That way lay resentment, frustration and intellectual suicide. Neil must learn to accept the new me - or lump it.

Any thought I might have had of discussing my day with Neil was quickly dismissed from my mind when I arrived home.

As soon as I stepped into the house I sensed the atmosphere. It was a field force of animosity. Neil was standing resolute at his study door.

'I was on the point of phoning the secretary of the Guild to offer your apologies, although why I should bother beats me.'

'And me,' I retorted. 'I told you I would be back for the meeting.'

'It's like a lot of things you say. They're always different from what you do.'

'That's unfair. Anyway,' I hastened, 'I'm back now. No harm's done.'

'There is a meal to prepare before then.'

'I expect Mrs Martin will be taking care of that.'

'You expect a great deal.'

'She usually does.'

'Things are different now. Did you bother checking with her?'

'No. I—'

'Well then, don't be surprised if she isn't available.' He turned a cold shoulder and retreated into his office.

The joy went out of me and I wondered why I didn't leave there and then.

Mrs Martin I discovered had just returned from a visit to a friend for afternoon tea. She feigned surprise when I tackled her about the meal preparation - or lack of it.

'You didn't say what you wanted cooked,' she hedged, doffing her hat and stabbing it with a vicious-looking pin.

'I don't usually. You know you've always taken care of that.'

'Ah well, things are different now, aren't they? That's what the minister said.' She hung up her coat then added when I didn't give her the expected response, 'He said that you have a job now and since your hours are fertile we won't always know when you're coming or going. So the best thing is for you to make arrangements for meals and other things yourself.'

207

She was loving every minute of this. I had learned that when it came to split loyalties my husband received the larger portion.

'The word you mean is flexible, Mrs Martin, not fertile. Fertile means productive, rich, fat, diamond-studded.

I'm none of these things. Flexible means adaptable, versatile, capable of dealing with many things and of course I am capable of dealing with my job and my duties here. All it needs is a little chat and deciding on what suits us both.'

'The minister said—'

'Just leave the minister to me, Mrs Martin. I'll let him know what arrangements we make together and I'm sure we will both make sure he does not suffer in any way.' She seemed mollified so I pressed home my advantage. For the first time in our acquaintance I felt I was the one in charge.

'We both have a meeting in an hour's time. Suppose we just have a salad tonight. There should be some ham left. I think, if you agree, we might spend a few minutes every morning discussing household arrangements so that we both benefit.'

'I miss the lad,' she sighed.

'We all do, Mrs Martin, and especially the minister. He was very fond of my brother and spent a lot of time with him - and so did you. It will take time but I'm sure that together we'll help the minister all we can.'

'He never stops helping others,' she said pointedly while donning her pinny. 'He's a good man and awfy well thought of.'

'Indeed he is,' I agreed.

'Are you going to your job tomorrow?' she queried.

'For a few hours but, like I said, we'll make arrangements in the morning.'

'It isn't right that you should be working. What will folk say?'

'Mrs Martin. I'm not working for money. I'm only helping a friend doing something that interests us both.' 'Your place is here,' she muttered.

'I'll make sure this place doesn't suffer,' I said, silently aghast at my words.

As I left Mrs Martin to the salad I asked myself if I really thought I could protect the manse and its occupants from suffering. Could I possibly hope to dissolve Neil's built-in resentment or establish a mutual trust and respect? Could I stop myself from feeling I was constantly being 'got at' or 'put down' and all the bitterness and frustration this would provoke? Was I right in continuing my involvement with the affairs of the church when I had no heart for it? I knew I was not loved, hardly liked. I had never conformed to their satisfaction, was considered superior, not one of them. Because I turned my back on the gossiping groups and especially since I'd lapsed in attending the services I was branded an outsider. Now that I'd found myself a job I had little hope of making any headway. They loved and respected their minister, praised his fund-raising efforts to high heaven and had already decided he was not getting the support from me which he deserved.

Was this what I wanted? Could this constant drain on my energies and restriction of my freedom ever be reconciled to my inner aspirations?

Theresa had a point. I was aiming at the top of a mountain which I could never hope to climb. Was that a good enough reason for not trying? I remembered one of my grandfather's homilies to Callum and myself: 'Aim at the top o' the tree and you're sure to land on one o' the branches.'

I knew I had to get myself off the ground. I'd found a means of transport. I needed Neil's resentment and his congregation's disapproval like I needed a bullet in the brain. One step at a time, I told myself. Let's get this meeting over and done with.

In later years looking back on that Women's Guild meeting I marvel yet again at the inimitability of the law of cause and effect. I don't know how Mrs Martin did it but, with great effect and unexpected consequences, she did.

I opened the meeting, as usual, with welcome and thanks, then began introducing the items on the agenda. The atmosphere was polite. Any light-hearted remarks, the ladies tossed among themselves. I was accorded the deference of one there on sufferance. Somehow I managed to stick a smile on my face but it was unadorned and had no connection at all with my eyes which missed nothing of the smirks and knowing glances being exchanged among the other members of the committee. I was being deliberately excluded from their camaraderie. It hurt.

The matter of most significance was, as always, fundraising. It was generally agreed that they must all pull their weight. The minister was awfully anxious to reach his target for the Missionary Fund, they kept saying. All these poor starving people in Africa and the two teachers who had gone to China to spread the good news and save more souls for Jesus. And not to forget the orphans someone reminded us and the home for the disabled, stealing a glance at me.

I could feel the old Jenny McLeod temper rear its ugly head. In no way, I promised myself, was I going to let this situation continue. Damn them, damn them all. They didn't need me here. They didn't want me. They could find someone else to sneer at. I'd had it. I was worth more than this. Who did they think they were anyhow? All they could think about was how to make more money. They'd had enough jumble sales. Folk had no jumble left. Teas were prohibitive in war-time Scotland. Crafts took time. There was a limit to how many of these they could offer. A garden fête with some sports for adults and children with sponsoring was a possibility.

'I could find a fortune-teller,' I heard myself say in a desperate bid to be included.

There was a deathly hush before meek little Mary Queen whispered.

'I don't think the minister would like that. Would he, Mrs Martin?'

'Indeed he would not. He's agin that sort of thing. Sinful it is,' snorted Mrs Martin.

There were nods of general agreement while I was assigned to the sin bin.

'What we could do...' said Mrs Martin, head thrown back and eyes gazing at the ceiling with a mysterious smirk playing around the corners of her mouth.

'Yes?' Everyone waited with baited breath while I silently voiced that they could all take a run and jump. What mischief was she hatching I wondered.

'We could have a concert.'

There were gasps of delight while bodies swayed and heads nodded and eyes gleamed in anticipation.

'But...' cautioned the spokeswoman, dragging her eyes from the ceiling and looking at everyone in turn, finally resting them on me. 'We will need someone to organize it.'

My spirits sank. Was I going to be forced into an embarrassing confrontation after all? She wasted no time.

'What about you Mrs Fraser? You said yourself, only this afternoon, that you were - now let me see, what was the word again? It wouldn't do to get it wrong now, would it? Och aye, I mind now - versatile. Wasn't that what you said, Mrs Fraser? You are versatile,' and for the benefit of everyone else, explained graciously, 'capable of dealing with many things, your new job and your share o' the housekeeping. Does it stop there or do you think maybe it could stretch to organizing a concert for us - not just for us but for the minister and his funds?'

She had put me nicely in a corner. I had to get out of it without losing face but then could I be any lower in their esteem? Why not just tell them to get lost and get up and go.

Every eye was on me and as I returned look for look something flared in me not altogether unpleasant. I could knock the socks off anyone in the parish in organizing a concert I realized. Why not go out with a bang rather than a whimper? Let them see and learn to appreciate what contribution I could make and not until then would I go and they'd know what they were losing.

'On one condition,' I heard myself saying. They waited open-mouthed. 'I couldn't do it without your support.'

'Of course, of course,' they muttered among themselves. 'You can count on us. Just tell us what you want.'

'Right. I'll organize your concert and now I suggest we adjourn, arrange another meeting when I can bring some ideas for your approval.'

And that's that, I thought as I made my way through the churchyard to the manse, stopping for a brief moment under the oak tree where Callum had carved my daughters name. This was my little piece of sacred ground and something told me I was going to need the strength it seemed to give me in the days ahead.

I'd tackle Neil tonight. At least the housekeeper in her cunning little scheme had given me some bargaining powers.

'Are you listening to what I'm saying?' I asked my husband as he stood, back to me, gazing out of his study window.

He turned, seating himself at his desk.

'I've heard every word you've said - and what you haven't said,' he added.

'And what was that?'

'You said you are going to organize a fund-raising concert.'

'Yes.'

'Why?'

'It's something I think I can do and it will raise much-needed money. I thought you'd be pleased.'

'You're not doing it for me.'

'Then who?'

'For yourself. You've had every opportunity to raise funds for me before, to take a greater interest in the church activities and you've done nothing so far. Why should I think you suddenly want to help me? You're doing this for you for whatever reason.'

'I didn't want to do it, I'll admit, but I am. Doesn't that mean something?'

'So it wasn't your own idea. You were cornered into doing it and you hadn't the courage to decline.'

'But I did have the courage to accept the challenge.'

'You were always keen on a challenge,' he said. 'You accepted I think because of your pride. You couldn't bear to be thought incapable.'

He was showing unusual perspicacity which, without flying in the face of truth, I found it difficult to refute. 'And what have I not said?' I asked.

'That you hate being here, would like nothing better than to go away as far as possible and you don't know how you are going to be able to put up with me for the rest of your life.'

It was true and I wasn't going to deny it.

'You've been very blunt,' I said, pulling another chair to the desk. 'No, don't stop me,' as he made to object. 'We've a lot to say to each other and I'd rather be seated while I say it. That way there's less chance of me running away.'

'We've nothing to say to each other.'

'You've had your say, now I'll have mine. I'll come straight to the point. I want to make a deal with you. Against our better judgement we married each other. I suppose we needed each other then.'

'We don't now?'

I was surprised by the question. 'I have come to realize Neil, without any doubt that what I need above all is freedom. I need the freedom to think what I like, to do what I like, read and speak what I like.'

'What you like?'

'Yes, especially when being denied these rights I feel bereft of identity. When a book I enjoy reading is thrown in the fire,' (there, I'd released that resentment at last) 'friends I want to meet are maligned and personal letters intercepted.'

I was watching him closely and saw the quick flush and tightening jaw. I hurried on. 'You can't deny it. Your face admits your guilt, so hold your anger and let me finish. The only thing you seem to want of me apart from cloning my mind in your image, is a dutiful wife and co-worker, someone who will chair meetings, play the lady hostess to visiting brethren and sit in the family pew. If that's what you want, all that you can have, on condition.'

I paused, expecting the peevish interruption. 'I will fulfil these needs in exchange for my personal freedom. I shall read what I want, see my friends and continue my job in Edinburgh. What I ask from you is recognition of my rights as an individual and a cessation of your persistent animosity to any thought I may have which is inconsistent with your own.'

There was no relaxation of his grim exterior. He rose to his feet, moving purposefully towards the door which he opened and held ajar.

I turned in my chair and looked at him in amazement. 'You've had your say,' he said stiffly. 'I have a sermon to prepare.'

'Can't you even discuss it?'

'There's nothing to discuss.'

'Are we to continue living side by side in this ridiculous fashion? Can't you visualize the mounting misery, the emptiness, the futility of our marriage?'

'You don't have to preach to me about futility, emptiness or...' he hesitated, 'misery.'

He looked so much the picture of every word he uttered that I felt a rushing concern.

'What's wrong Neil?' He looked through me. 'I think it's more than me, than us, that—'

'Elementary psychology is not on your list of duties.' 'I only want to understand. You seem to get little comfort or joy from your faith.'

'It is not comfort or joy I want.'

'Then that is very foolish. We all need comfort and joy. I am dead without it. I crave for comfort at times and I know the difference joy can make to living.'

'I've no doubt you'll get all the comfort you want from your wonderful professor.'

I gasped. Could he possibly be jealous?

I moved closer. 'Neil, I wish, I only wish I could get a little, just a little comfort from you. Perhaps if—'

His hand tightened on the doorknob. 'Leave,' he hissed. 'Leave now. Read what you want, think and say what you want but not to me. I don't want to know. If your inflated pride helps swell the church funds you'll be doing it for God, not for me.'

He might as well have flayed me with a whip. The injustice of his attitude both enraged and dismayed me. I couldn't see the way ahead. I could hardly see my way upstairs to the refuge of my own room. If it was injustice I was set on fighting I needed to look no further than life within these walls. I had declared my freedom whose taste was lost on an arid tongue. How I wished that I could run away from this prison, this surrounding field of negativity, this stifling atmosphere of a loveless marriage.

CHAPTER 26

I spent the rest of the evening contemplating my circumstances. Supposing, I told myself, this is my karma, to be here with Neil, locked in that battle, opposed to each other's attitudes. Bereft of the comfort of physical togetherness, the ground of our marriage compacted and left infertile by mutual dislike. Perhaps we were put here, or had put ourselves here, to dig that ground, find the nature of the lower stratas and discover what the subconscious might reveal. If I were to test-drive my new ideas this would be where I must begin. I needed to start digging, looking for the soft places, exposing them to the surface, tending them, sowing seeds which might root and spread until they could pit their growing strength against the hard upper crust and eventually stretch their way through to the sun.

It was a fantasy but it appealed to my imagination. It was my imagination, I realized. And was imagination a special thought force which could lead to manifestations of hidden strengths? I liked that idea too. Suppose, I told myself, you don't stop at liking the idea but did something about it. Really don the mantle of responsibility, concern yourself entirely with what you do and leave Neil to his own choices without passing judgement and certainly without taking offence. Forget about favours or appreciation. Forget about public approval. Just concentrate on what you can do to soften the ground, to look for cracks that might be explored, gaps that might be filled, terrain that might be cultivated, bridges that might be crossed.

There were things I would have to throw out of my backpack - self-pity, self-righteousness, vanity, arrogance. Oh God! I was beginning to sound like a born-again Christian! You certainly can't dismiss Christianity I told

215

myself - only its dogma, its historical rapes, its abuse, its modern trimmings and commercialized fairy tales. The concept would not go away.

I decided that I had to study and with this thought a magnificent light filled the room. I couldn't contain myself and rising from my chair I began pacing the room. I remembered the wonderful library. Names like Blavatsky, Krishnamurti, Jinarajadawa floated in banner headlines before my eyes. I remembered new 'friends' who offered interest and inspiration. I was actually getting excited. I hadn't felt this way for years.

I sat down again, concentrating my thoughts on Neil and the dearth of communication between us and his condemnation and ridicule of the intrinsic me. Careful, don't dwell on the victim side, I cautioned. You are only a victim if you think yourself a victim. No one, but no one, has the power to diminish you.

Oh God! I repeated, what am I getting at? Where is all this crazy thinking leading me? But I knew. With an intuitive flash I knew. I was donning the mantle of total responsibility for my own destiny, as Theresa, that unerring prophetess had warned I might be crazy enough to do. I was attempting to climb a mountain. But wasn't that better than allowing external forces to suck me into sinking sands?

I had the force I needed, I decided. I had it inside me, in my deepest layers of my subconscious or in the highest reaches of my mind. That was what I must carry in my backpack - the God within me, the beckoning higher self and the only weapon I would need to carry was the faith in myself, in none other. I would be my own arbiter. If I really wanted to climb that mountain I could do it. With the help of my new 'friends'.

The problem was where to begin?

I had to begin with the next step of course, and the next step was waiting for me on my next visit to the professor's library.

'Ah, my dear Jenny. I'm glad you have come. I was allowing for your second thoughts. Your arrival does you credit.'

Heart-warming words. I would take my cue from him. He led the way to the library, calling on Aggie Calder to bring in the coffee. I still felt powered by my new resolutions which helped me to relax.

'I am glad you decided to trust me,' the professor said,

"And trust me not at all, or all in all," as our friend Tennyson proclaimed. But remember Jenny, above all others, trust yourself.'

He smiled at me, not realizing how once again he was hitting the nail on the head. Who was this man? I had no prototype for him either in life or in fiction and yet, on such a short acquaintance, I trusted him.

'What do you require of me?' I asked.

'I am experimenting in my astral travelling and I have become impatient to test its efficacy. I do not heed the warnings. I should not be harbouring this impatience so let us call it excitement, or better still, enthusiasm. That way I shall feel more comfortable,' he twinkled. 'Perhaps, if the experiment is successful I can then settle down to the jobs I have to do on this plane. I have been neglecting them. One should never neglect the important things in life, I remind myself. But more important Jenny, and I want you to remember this, there should be no neglect of the ordinary. Do not neglect the ordinary. It is easy to wander off into the byways and stray from the straight and narrow. I've no doubt your husband regularly warns his flock of this temptation.' He smiled again while I waited.

'After we drink Aggie's delicious coffee I shall leave you here and go to my room to prepare myself for projection. It may come quickly. It may take time. In the meantime...' he rose and walked to the writing desk, tore a page from a notebook and offered it to me with a thick leaded pencil. 'When I am gone you will be here alone. I want you to write a sentence - any sentence. It can be a question or a statement, your own or one borrowed from a "friend",' nodding in the direction of the book shelves. 'Write it very clearly. There will be no hurry. Take your time. When you have finished, leave the paper unfolded and take it with you into the garden.' He walked to the window beckoning me to follow.

'Look. There are trees, shrubs, rocks, seats, a table, a rabbit hutch and a pool. Place the paper wherever you choose, written side up, I think. There is no breeze and the garden is sheltered so it should be safe. You can wait in the garden and make sure that the paper stays exactly where you put it. No one will disturb you. I have told Aggie that on no account must anyone approach you or try to speak to you. You must remain entirely alone with the paper in full view until I call from here. I will raise the window and wave my handkerchief.'

He withdrew a large red handkerchief from his waistcoat pocket and flapped it before me.

'When you see me do this you will return here, bringing your written message with you.'

I was enthralled. It all seemed so harmless and innocent. There was nothing to fear.

'What happens next?' I asked, enjoying the build-up.

'With the breadth of the room between us I will tell you exactly what you have written. I will have joined you in the garden, seen where you placed your message and read it. All this of course in my astral body invisible to the naked eye. You understand?'

I nodded while he raised a finger to his lips as Aggie entered with the coffee. Pleasantries were exchanged and once more we were left alone.

'It is our secret, Jenny. For me, if the experiment should prove successful it will give me courage to walk further in the path I have chosen to explore. For you, it will illustrate the importance of the Theosophical Society's third tenet. "To investigate unexplained laws of nature and the powers latent in man." This should help you trust ever more the power of your own intuitive faculties.'

We sipped our coffee. I was enjoying the life in me. I felt alert and outgoing and in a good condition to absorb the shock of his next question.

'Have you identified any of your karma yet?' Not waiting for an answer he continued. 'Don't be upset by the question. It's no different from one a minister of the church might ask a supplicant. "Have you considered your wrongdoings, my child? Can you think where you might have gone wrong?" He rose suddenly. 'But now I must be off to my room and you must write your message. Take your time.'

He saluted me in his characteristic fashion then left the room.

I had lost all fear. Nor was I in awe. I was merely curious. There had been nothing sinister in the request, eccentric perhaps, but not sinister.

Idly I scrutinized the bookshelves, nothing definite in mind, taking my time as he'd advised. It was a bit like playing a party game. I found myself at the writing desk on which some pamphlets were scattered, some on reincarnation, evolution, meditation and one outlining the values of the Theosophical Society. The Society had a motto which was 'There Is No Religion Higher Than Truth'.

That's it, I thought. It's as good as any and it's a statement which appeals to me. I had a momentary vision of trying to argue the point with my husband which I very quickly banished. Carefully, not being sure of the quality of astral eyesight, I wrote the motto in large formed letters. I made my way downstairs, through the back hall and kitchen and into the garden. Aggie Calder was nowhere in sight. I glanced back at the house, turning my head to see if there was anyone watching from a window. I saw no one. I walked to the farthest boundary of the garden, a fair distance from the house and placed my paper with its message on an upturned flowerpot with the writing towards the large stone wall. I sat on a boulder about 20 feet from the paper and took up watch. My eyes made a continuous survey of garden, wall, house, windows and trees. I saw no one, felt no presence and after fifteen inutes even began to wonder if I was being hoaxed.

'Jenny! Yoo-hoo Jenny!'

It was the professor, leaning out of the window frantically waving his large red handkerchief.

'You can come up now. Bring the paper.'

I caught his excitement and hurried inside, taking the stairs two at a time. Without waiting to knock I burst into the library to be suddenly stopped in my tracks.

'Wait! Stay where you are! Come no nearer. Put the paper behind you.'

I did exactly as requested and stood waiting, surprised to feel my heart pounding.

The professor stood, his back to the window, smiling from ear to ear.

'On your paper you have written these words.' Here he paused, I expect deliberately for better effect. '"There Is No Religion Higher Than Truth".'

I couldn't take in the enormity of this revelation. There was no way he, or anyone else, could have seen what I had written.

'What do you think then, Jenny?' He waited excitedly for my response.

Thoughts flashed through my mind. I'd already experienced his, what I could only take to be, telepathic powers of touching directly on my thoughts, not just once but three or four times. Then again, had he deliberately left that pamphlet where I was sure to see it, making an intuitive guess that the motto would immediately appeal? Or, and the thought was mind-boggling, had he phantomized and read it for himself? I didn't know.

'Well?' he coaxed. 'Have I convinced you?'

'It is so incredible,' I struggled.

'Quite beyond ordinary comprehension,' he added. 'I know, and if you can doubt its veracity how much more the cynics and sceptics.'

'It's not that I doubt.'

He held up his hand. 'You do well to hesitate, Jenny. I think I might have been disappointed if it had been otherwise but you are not dismissing it out of hand.'

'No I—'

'Sit down, my dear. I've already told Aggie to bring us a sandwich and some tea. What I have just managed to do - no small feat,' he added, 'is against all the known laws of nature, but then again, so were voices in the air travelling across the ocean and being heard at the other side once upon a time. So too was electricity. Perhaps one day men will fly to the moon even if at this time it is against the laws of nature. The thing is not to dismiss the ideas out of hand. As our friend Shakespeare says, "There are more things in heaven and earth Horatio, than are dreamt of in your philosophy." Now let me give you a book to read. Come in Aggie,' he yelled as he rose to fetch a book from the shelves.

'Tuck in to these, Jenny lass,' the housekeeper said as she indicated sandwiches, scones, cakes, biscuits and oatcakes and cheese. 'You need to keep up your strength when ye work for this man.'

'Get away wi' ye woman,' the professor said fondly, pretending to shoo her from the room. As Aggie left with a skip and a laugh he placed the book which he had chosen into my hand. I looked at the title The Projection of the Astral Body.

'Let Muldoon and Carrington tell ye a wee bit more about it. Now, let's tuck into Aggie's goodies then I'll leave you to your cataloguing.'

It was an astonishing book. I did no cataloguing that afternoon. I could not put the book down. It described astral catalepsy, astral exteriorization, the crypto-conscious mind, telekinesis, obsession, clairvoyance and much much more. When I finished the book I was no more convinced than before but I was certainly intrigued.

CHAPTER 27

For the next few weeks I concentrated on ideas for the Guild show and the night came when I was to present them for approval. Initially my ideas were received by the ladies of the Guild with alarm. I was faced then with the choice of throwing in the towel or engaging in a battle of coercion. Retreating was unthinkable. I decided to employ every tactic I knew or could devise to get them on my side. It took a great deal of flattery and persuasion, not to mention a lot of patience, to break down their natural reserve. I was surprised at how much I'd absorbed about the members. When I wrote the play I had no problem placing the characters.

I surprised myself by its comic structure. I wrote the funniest part for Mrs Martin which to everyone's glee fitted like a glove. Being, on the surface, the least funny candidate imaginable, the housekeeper was slow to admit her own potential. But, once she experienced its explosive effect on the others, her enthusiasm knew no bounds. She saw herself as the prima donna and her energy became boundless. She took the others with her. It wasn't my show any more. It was theirs.

Once Mrs Martin was converted I could do no wrong. I was up and away. Deciding that, in for a penny, in for a pound, I planned some singing and also choreographed a comic dance. I began to enjoy myself!

All my efforts turned out to be the sure-fire way of getting to know them better and in the months ahead I began the process of re-evaluating them. Once their reserves were broken down we made headway.

Gradually I was accepted into their circle. The talk which I'd previously judged as fickle and without substance became less inhibited, revealing women of more substance than I had given them credit for. I was learning humility. At times the old irritation would surface and barriers would rise again but I had progressed enough to make an immediate effort to knock down these self-defensive mechanisms. Every laugh, every honest effort in drama, music and dance which I managed to coax out of this motley group of serious churchwomen I notched as a victory and it gave me no end of satisfaction.

It became the most important aspect of my life to be considered their friend. Between rehearsals I listened to tales of domestic trials and tribulations or reports of family fortunes. My advice began to be sought, my views heeded. My standing in the community was confirmed.

Even as I exulted in this new freedom I was constantly aware of my shortcomings. I still judged. I was often irritated, lost my temper, was dishonest in my flattery, hasty in my decisions and grudged the time spent when I could be reading, enjoying more time with the professor or Theresa, whom I now met on a regular basis.

Constantly in the background was my husband. We met at meals. I sat in the family pew. I kept him informed of the fund-raising. In parallel with the concert, there were teas, whist and beetle drives, bring-and-buy sales, sponsored walking, swimming and knitting. The proceeds gradually mounted to previously undreamed of targets.

Neil did not interfere. He asked no questions. He made no demands. Only after the show, when even he could not ignore its overwhelming success or be unaware of the good feeling that the effort had engendered among his flock, did he begin to come round.

He made a platform speech of appreciation which delighted everyone, expressed thanks for the financial results and hope that it was the first of many efforts. He smiled in acknowledgement of the furious clapping and stamping of feet.

We still met at meals and we began to converse. He did not interfere but showed interest in my fund-raising activities, seeming genuinely pleased at my popularity. He tried to hide his annoyance at the thriving bonhomie between his housekeeper and myself. He lengthened the grace before evening meal but suspended the ten o'clock devotions. His housekeeper and his wife always seemed to be pressingly engaged in meetings or activities in connection with fund-raising. He did not ask why I was doing so much. I could hardly tell him I was developing the God within. He'd think I'd lost my mind. Yet he was working hard for his God out there and I was learning that we were doing the same thing but differently.

The hard ground was crumbling, not much, but enough to drop in some seeds.

'Seeds of what, for goodness sake?' queried Theresa on one of our dining out evenings in a Royal Mile pub. It had become a regular rendezvous so that we could 'catch up' on each other's news. This was good for both of us. I looked forward to these meetings intensely. Here was a relationship without barriers, without obligations.

'Go on, tell me,' she insisted.

'Seeds of kindness. I use every opportunity I can to sow these.'

She raised her eyes to the ceiling. 'Lord preserve us. You're not getting sloppy, are you?'

'On the contrary, I am being very meticulous, you know, quality conscious.'

'What's worth doing is worth doing well, you mean?' queried Theresa.

'It makes sense. I think kindness is the highest attribute in a marriage, that and loyalty.'

'And what about love?' She raised a quizzical eyebrow, forcing me to look her in the eye.

'That word means different things to different people.

Kindness is specific. You cannot be confused with kindness - and it doesn't hurt.'

'Love does?'

'Oh Theresa! If you are asking me if I love Neil, I don't know. I still wish we were closer but there are too many differences separating us. Our souls are on different route marches but our bodies are within touching distance.'

Another eyebrow shot up.

'No touching,' I said.

'You wish?'

'My feeling body wants to, my mind body won't allow it to give way and my soul yearns for a twinning I seem to have missed.'

'How sad,' she sympathized quietly. 'You have such a capacity for loving. You should have had an adoring husband and lots of children.'

'Sometimes,' I confessed, 'I feel so barren, then I remind myself that it could be a help towards that state of desirelessness which Krishnimurti so recommends and ranks high in the road to enlightenment. Oh don't look at me like that. I know that isn't likely to happen in this incarnation or the next. It's enough just to have the maps charted in this one, to be aware that there are routes to the high ground, difficult, but not impossible.'

'I think you have done wonderfully well, Jenny. Even if you haven't won Neil over to your more liberal way of thinking, you've enriched his flock and of course his charity nest egg. I'll bet you've also overtaken him in popularity.'

'Are you testing my ego?' I laughed but felt cheered by the encouragement. 'I have come to care less that Neil and I differ and more about how we differ. I want him to try to understand me so I must be prepared to try to understand him.'

'And do you? Understand him any better?'

'What I understand is that his truth is his truncheon. It's his battering-ram against anyone else's, especially mine. To Neil his truth is the only truth. His grip on it is tight enough to stunt its growth.'

'You've always known that.'

'True, but theosophy has taught me that it is possible to hold one's own truth lightly but share in that of another.'

'And what can you do about that, Jenny?'

'Perhaps, if I try hard enought, I can help Neil to loosen his grip.'

My husband was changing although I knew that he would be the last to admit it. Just as the seasons changed and the burgeoning, dying and rebirthing of nature continued for another year, I could detect a similar pattern of change in Neil. I liked to think that while a new willingness to accommodate was burgeoning, some of the old diehard attitudes were dissolving to make way for even greater change. Exactly what I was expecting to find at the end of it all I was not sure. It had begun by wanting his tolerance of my way of looking at life. I could hardly expect a complete U-turn. Was I really doing it for him? Or, which seemed more likely, was I doing it for me? If so, how much for me?

Although my spiritual life was richer than it had ever been and I had all the mental stimulation I could deal with, there was an immense gap in the life of my emotions. In spite of all the warning signs which I had raised about the need for complete independence, the dangerous vulnerability of having to depend on another for emotional security, it seemed that my feelings had a life of their own. Was it likely, I kept asking myself, that Neil would ever turn to me for physical comfort? Did I want that? Why, after all, should sexual intimacy ask the price of total affinity? Wasn't a non-aggressive, compatibly sound working and living relationship better than an illusory all or nothing one? Physically Neil did not repel me. He never had. I cherished the moments of closeness we had already shared without any illusion that they indicated more than they had been - comfort.

We continued to meet at meals but now the conversation was expanding and more evenly distributed. My non-parochial activities were still out of conversational bounds but those connected with the Guild, the Youth Club - which I had decided to champion - and especially anything to do with raising money were, one might go as far as to say, enthusiastically entered into. We set aside a time in the week when we could go over the accounts. Only the fact that every penny raised was for the good work of the parish, kept Neil's super-charged interest in the finances from bordering on the indelicate.

I continued my library work unfettered by the need br explanation or oblique apology. I stopped reading in secret. I began leaving my books on side tables where Neil might see them. To begin with I chose to leave books such as In the Steps of Moses the Lawgiver by Louis Golding to which I thought he could take no exception, or The Creed of Christ by Edmond Holmes. From these I progressed to titles such as Key to the Problems of Existence, True Meaning of Christ's Teachings or more daringly, L[e in Freedom by Krishnamurti. And so it continued. I steered clear of leaving any books on astrology lying around because of painful associations. Never once did he comment. He may have read a page or two. If he did, I never knew.

The Guild concert became an established bi-annual event and was extended to the younger sect whose demands kept me on my toes.

'What a full life you're leading,' Theresa would say at one of our pub meetings.

'A double life, more like it,' I corrected. 'Yet, to me they are all part of the same thing. From the professor, my book-bound "friends", yourself and the Theosophical Society I receive my inspiration and a new wisdom. With Neil and my work for his church I try to put into practice the wisdom imbibed. It is an ideal battleground for the developing spirit. A straight path to slog!'

'Then one day Prince Charming will appear, bowl you over and your path will turn all crooked.'

I smiled. 'I'll settle for what I have. You know Theresa, I'm enjoying life. I feel I'm in control now.'

'Jenny?'

'Yes?'

'I've prepared another chart for you.'

'No, Theresa.'

'Why not? Things might have been different if you'd heeded my last one.'

That might not have been such a good idea. Perhaps I needed to choose the way I did. If I hadn't I'd never have met the professor or had so much access to all his "friends".'

'If you had you might not have needed the professor and his so-called "friends". You might have left yourself free to meet your Prince Charming and had pattering little feet around you. Sorry, I forgot. It still hurts, I expect.'

'Not often, but I can never forget and I often wonder what she would have been like.'

'Let me tell you what might yet be,' and before I could stop her she had plucked my hand from the table and held it palm up. 'Your life is going to change in the most dramatic way.'

'Please Theresa.'

'No, let me finish, just the main points. You're going to have to make a crucial choice, something dramatic and you're going to meet someone who will turn your life upside down.'

I frowned and withdrew my hand. 'There will never be any question of leaving Neil. I admit I was on the point of doing just that after Graham died and before I came under the influence of theosophical thinking.'

'That may not be your choice.'

'Theresa, you don't know!'

'Respect my psychic capabilities Jenny - oh I know I've betrayed and abused them at times for easy money but never with the people I love, never with you.'

226

'If you were half as serious about your spirituality as I am you would never have betrayed them to the people you didn't love. They are entitled to the best you can give them every bit as much as the people you love.'

'All right, goody-two-shoes. We won't fall out about it this time but what truth you think you are living now is nothing like the one you are soon going to need. I hope you hold it lightly.'

'I do - to give it scope to grow.'

'You have the slick answers now, haven't you?' There was nothing cynical or unkind in her remark. She was merely taking mental notes of my development.

In the months to follow I had little time to ponder Theresa's claims. Also, I was growing more and more sensitive to the change in Neil. He had taken to questioning Mrs Martin about her sister who lived in the North of England and who was recovering from an operation. He was even, surprisingly, hinting about a wish to go home to Strathard to preach. This idea I firmly scotched. 'When is she hoping to be allowed home?' he asked Mrs Martin.

'Ah weel, that's the trouble. She has no one to look after her at home so she's having to stay in hospital.'

I sensed that there was more to the questioning than polite concern.

'Why don't you go there for a while and look after her?' 'I couldn't leave you here,' she said hesitantly.

'My wife will see that I don't starve,' looking at me.

I nodded, still puzzled at his unexpected concern, then quickly voiced my reassurance.

'Of course,' I said smiling. 'I'm sure your sister would love that and it would put your mind at rest.'

'She couldn't have a better nurse,' added Neil.

'Are you sure you don't mind?' the housekeeper asked me. 'You're always so busy.'

I did mind but I could hardly admit that. I would have to cut down my library visits. I looked shrewdly at Neil. Was this his intention? Was it a way of punishing? Did he want me tied so much to duties here so that I could see less of the professor? Or was I being unfair?

The following day, after Mrs Martin had packed her case and caught a train for Carlisle, Neil returned from driving her to the station to seek me out in the kitchen.

'I can take over a few kitchen chores,' he offered watching me slice cucumber for the salad.

'That's all right.'

'I insist. I don't want this to interfere with your other interests.'

'All of them?' I asked, turning to shake the lettuce I had just washed.

'Yes, all of them,' he said quietly.

I felt he was about to say more but rising, he looked at the kitchen clock and muttered some reason for having to leave in haste.

I continued preparing the salad, my mind in a whirl. He was up to something. Why did he want Mrs Martin out of the house? My earlier assumption was wrong. He didn't seem to object to my library visits? How little I really knew my husband I thought, checking the casserole which Mrs Martin had prepared and left ready for heating. What I did know was so ingrained I found the knowledge difficult to shift. He was entirely motivated by his religious beliefs and had not given me any reason to suspect that these might have changed. True, I reflected, his sermons were gradually being based more on the New Testament. There was less pulpit thumping and less use of the word sinner but that could mean anything or nothing. He was keeping to his side of the bargain and was making no attempt to interfere with my chosen lifestyle, but that was in line with his principles. He would never barter his principles. Apparently then I was wrong to suspect a weakening there as his offer of help had just testified. What then?

I was not to find out until the middle of the night. I had been asleep when suddenly I woke immediately conscious of some kind of disturbance. My heart was thumping and I could feel beads of sweat on my brow. Perhaps I'd been having a nightmare but I had no images, only a highly charged feeling of expectancy. I was lying on my side, my face to the window. The blackness of the night was being gently eased by the faintest light of dawn. There was a soft sound behind, like an indrawn breath. Opening my eyes I turned my head slowly and saw Neil, on his knees, head bowed, by the side of my bed. He was not aware of my stirring. His eyes were closed. I felt relief, but was also amazed and puzzled. Was he sleepwalking? I wondered but as his eyes opened they met mine. Intuitively I read their message. The horror of a great longing and a great doubt were naked for me to see. I felt an upsurge of compassion. His shoulders drooped. His lips moved but he couldn't voice what he wanted to say. He was wrestling with himself or perhaps, I thought, with his God whose protection seemed to have deserted him.

We looked at each other and whatever feelings we were experiencing it was my maternally protective ones that took over.

'It's cold,' I whispered, throwing back the bedclothes and shifting my body to make room. 'Come in and get warm.'

With a muffled moan he joined me. I held him in my arms, cradling his head on my breast, massaging the smooth skin on his back as my hand crept under his pyjama jacket. We lay thus for a long time, his face buried in my bosom, my hands soothing, comforting, understanding. Only when I felt his limbs gradually relax and his breathing steady did I lower my fondling, undo his pyjama trousers and both stimulate and free his torment. For the first time in our coupling his sex was uninhibited. He was wild in his hunger, greedy in his demands and when his climax came his ecstatic yells were like the baying of an animal.

Even as I held him, guiding him slowly back to earth, back to awareness of what had just happened I wondered what would be the cost exacted for this rapturous indulgence. His religious scruples were without the protection of his 'procreation justification' theory. He had just violated one of the main tenets of his individual truth. Now, as I released him and watched him leave my bed to hurry into his pyjama trousers I realized he had an account of greater import than the Church Fabric Account to balance with his conscience.

His leave taking was abrupt. I made no claims, felt no personal affinity with the soul. My body basked in the comforting aftermath of intercourse but I was conscious of the aching emptiness of all the other factors which had not been there. It would appear that the more my physical body enjoyed its sexual satisfaction, the more aware I was of a deeper, greater loss.

CHAPTER 28

The next morning Neil left the manse before I came downstairs. The kettle was still warm. I resisted the temptation to walk across the garden into the church. I was afraid of finding him on his knees and didn't relish the thought of having to deal with his moral burden as well as my own uncertainty. In the light of day my feelings were mixed and I knew they needed sorting before I came face to face with him again. I needed to make a new assessment of our relationship and what it was going to mean to us.

It was a comfort to know that I was spared the illusion of 'being in love' and all the painful experiences created by such an obsession. If Neil and I never made love again I would not be resentful or hurt and yet, I wondered why I could enjoy our intimacy without any feeling of revulsion. I was fortunate that my body could respond so comfortably to sex without feeling enslaved by its passions. Neil was a man with a built-in sexual urge which for so long now had been self-constrained. If his self-imposed celibacy had suddenly become too much for him, so much that in spite of his strength of will and religious beliefs he had lost control, then he had a problem. I could think of no other reason. It could not have been for love of me or he would not have forced himself upon me.

But had he forced himself? He might well be blaming me for taking advantage of his moment of weakness. Had I been right in succouring his needs? Was my motivation really as pure as I'd given myself credit for last night? Had I not benefited? Yes, but alas in spite of the pleasure it had given me it only emphasized my sense of loss.

Neil, I decided, was wrestling with an illusory devil. I would know the outcome soon enough. I was wrestling with reality. I had no illusions about my marriage. I had never been in love with my husband. I had no misconceptions about the reasons for our marrying. I had needed the security marrying him provided and I had looked upon our union as a way to spiritual growth. The security had become a prison and the spirit, far from growing, had been constantly under threat.

Could I possibly continue in our marriage accommodating Neil's sexual needs while compromising my deepest yearnings? Last night had taken me by surprise. Any more demands would require a more considered response on my part.

Would it have been different with anyone else? I wondered. Someone to whom I was more attuned. Perhaps if Todd had not left when he did. But then Todd was special. Still, when I thought of him, I could feel a poignancy difficult to dismiss. Who knows what might have happened if Lady Catriona had not become involved with McGreegor, which led to Tam's death and Todd leaving Strathard when he did.

How far back did one have to go in the laws of causality to find a reason?

Thinking of Todd reminded me of the suitcase of letters in the attic, which reminded me of Theresa's suggestion of Neil's likely objection to these, which only brought me back again to my present situation.

What had prompted Neil's surprise behaviour last night? A need for me, a build-up of hormone pressure or a need for me in order to manifest his love? One thing was certain. The ball was now at his feet. Meanwhile I would spend the rest of the day at the library with the professor and my gilt-edged 'friends'.

When Aggie opened the door in response to my knock she didn't seem to be quite her cheerful self. Her smile was as wide and welcoming as ever. Her immediate promise to bring a 'wee cuppa' to help me get started was delivered with customary cheer but my developing sensitivity to this environment picked up unhappy vibes.

While she went to make the 'cuppa' I sat at the writing desk by the window where the professor had left a carton of books for me to catalogue. I began sorting them into the various categories. Esoteric Single Eye Essays on the Mystic Point of View by Arthur Gray, I mumbled; Rational Mysticism by Wm. Kingsland; a growing number on astrology and channelling; an interesting looking 1)00k entitled Eastern Studies: Sufism of Omar Khayyam and E. Fitzgerald by Laurence Hope; a few on meditation; some novels, and the largest pile of all regarded theosophical literature, authors such as Annie Besant, Clara Codd, Blavatsky herself and many more.

Seeing the title The Universality of Truth by George S. Arundale I picked up the book and wandered to the armchair by the fire. As I began reading my senses quickened, realizing yet again that when I was in this library the information I needed almost always seemed ready to hand. According to Arundale, once an individual found the truth he sought, the question arose as to what he was to do with it.

'If there is to be any acid test as to the value of any particular truth to the individual', he began '...then he might very well look to see the influence and effect the truths he holds have upon the life he leads.' Then the words which seemed to say it all; '...if there is any negation of truth whatever, it is when that truth is held as a weapon of attack on somebody else's beliefs, no matter how crude they may seem to the wielder of the weapon.' These were words I needed to hear.

I looked around me, treasuring the atmosphere of the tastefully elegant room, the shelves of books, sparkling crystal, old and cared-for furniture, the colour-rich carpet, the serene Buddha on the hearth, flowers and freedom, and I knew then what that freedom was doing for me.

I held no grudge against Neil for holding his truths but could not understand why he grasped them so tenaciously. I could only pity him that they were not big enough to encompass the veracity of my own. By living my truth among the folk of his congregation and serving their needs, I had learned to live their truths and understand the strength they received from them. I could only wish that they were able to open their minds wide enough to see what my horizons had on offer. I remembered my grandfather and valued how he had grasped his truth and how generous he had been in sharing it with others who thought differently.

Todd had given his life for his truth. What more could anyone do? The professor generated his truth and, by his book collection, was passing it on to others who might benefit if they should so desire. Aggie, like Graham just lived her truth and I could only envy her. I might have spent my day musing if Aggie had not arrived with the tea tray.

Usually the professor joined me at this ceremony but before I could comment Aggie said, 'I don't think the professor will be having his tea this morning, but I've brought his cup just in case he decides to come after all.'

'Is he all right?' I asked moving the books on the table to make room for the tray. She sighed as if from her boots which was so unlike her that I couldn't keep from asking if something was wrong.

'A dinna ken lass. I just dinna ken but I'm right worried.'

'Look,' I suggested, 'if you don't think the professor's coming why don't you join me in a cup and you can tell me what's worrying you?'

There was another sigh and an unconvincing hesitation.

'Please,' I gently urged, aware of her genuine distress. 'Maybe I will. I'll have to speak to somebody and you're a guid friend o' his.'

I stirred my tea and waited while she sat and composed herself. After a few sips she placed her cup and saucer carefully on the low table and looked at me with mute appeal in her soft blue eyes.

'What is it Aggie?' I gently encouraged.

'He's acting all queer,' she said.

'The professor?'

'Aye. He goes off to bed at a' hours of the day. He's there now with the curtains drawn and the door locked. He won't let me in to his room, not even to clean it. He's no eatin', he never answers the telephone and you should see his desk in his study. There are piles of letters he hasna even opened. Some of them are weeks old. Some are marked Urgent and some have a' they foreign stamps on them. I just dinna ken what's wrong wi' the man. It isna like him. I tell you Jenny lass, I'm fair worried.'

'How long has this been going on Aggie?'

'Since you came.'

She seemed totally unaware that there could be a hidden rebuke in this remark. I knew it was a time notch in her mind, nothing more.

'Have you consulted a doctor?'

'I couldna do that,' she gasped qualifying her remark after a minute's reflection, 'at least no yet.'

'Is his doctor a friend? Do you know him well?'

'Oh aye, young Jamie Robertson. We ken him fine. A fine lad. I'm sure he'd be understandin',' she mused.

'Well then.' But my remark was cut short by the lively entrance of the professor himself, a bit tousled, a bit flushed and excited but sounding as lively and as cheerful as ever.

'What's this then?' he exclaimed in exaggerated amazement. He tweaked Aggie's cheek playfully croaking, 'Who's been sitting in my chair? Who's been drinking my tea?'

"A' right. A' right,' she replied rising quickly. 'Behave yourself,' she admonished as he began nibbling her ear.'Stop your nonsense man. I thought you weren't coming. I was just having a friendly chinwag wi' Jenny here.' The professor straightened himself and turned to me.

'Ah Jenny, my friend. It is good to see you.'

His voice was too hearty, his face too flushed. Before I could reply he spoke again, his words knocking the breath from me.

'How's your new truth fitting then? Pinching a wee bit here and there, eh?'

He was doing it again. Uncannily he was plucking my newest and ripest thoughts straight from my head. Suddenly I felt naked. What power did this man have that he could read my mind so aptly and so often? It was more than coincidence.

I caught his flippancy and threw it back at him. 'I'm still trying it for size,' I replied when I'd found my voice.

Aggie was already halfway to the door and for once the professor let her leave without a teasing.

'You are wearing it well, Jenny. Your health is much improved I see but why do you still carry around those tiresome doubts of your truth upon your shoulders?'

'The doubts are not of my truth, Professor, but of my ability to wear it.'

'Ah. Better some days than others eh?'

'That isn't enough surely?'

'No. Every step of the journey, I'm afraid and,' he began pacing the room, his hands deep in the pockets of his jacket, 'that is something few are able to achieve.'

He was now at the far end of the library and had stopped to run his fingers lovingly along some of the books. He did not speak for some time, taking a book, opening it, mumbling some extract to himself, returning it to the shelf, doing the same with another, then another. I began to think he had forgotten me and did not speak. He was different in some subtle way. I began to understand Aggie's concern. I suspected that the reason for spending so long in bed with the door locked was his craze for astral projection. I remembered from the time I had been given proof of this strange occult power he possessed that Aggie had not been a party to it. But the rest of her worry, his unopened letters, unanswered phone calls - that didn't sound like the professor. On the point of beginning some cataloguing he rushed towards me and began talking where we had left off.

'Every step of the way, Jenny. Can you do it?'

'I doubt—'

'No doubts. Think big. Think out. Think away from yourself to the universal. Keep above yourself, detached, outside yourself and you can do it.'

He walked round me, his eyes penetrating but impersonal.

'Your colours are good!' he suddenly exclaimed with what seemed like joy. 'You can do anything you want, Jenny. What you need is a challenge. You will always respond to a challenge, the bigger the better.'

He stopped suddenly and looked in an abstracted manner towards the ceiling. I was by now distinctly uncomfortable and wanted to leave him to his eccentricity. Then he gave a little whoop of delight, danced a few steps round me chanting, 'A challenge! That's all that's needed! Your colours are right. Now I must leave you for my siesta. Where is that woman? She should have reminded me. Aggie!' he yelled. 'Where the devil are you woman?'

He left me without another glance and it was all I could do to walk the few steps needed to sit down. I didn't like this one bit. He must be ill. He was obviously too much involved with the occult. Why otherwise would he be acting irresponsibly with his regular duties and bringing misery to his beloved Aggie. It didn't make sense. There was no way I could settle to work. I waited until I thought he'd gone to his room and began tiptoeing my way downstairs to the kitchen. I put my ears to the door but could hear nothing. With the lightest of taps I turned the handle then peeped in.

Aggie was sitting at the plain deal kitchen table. She seemed to be gazing at nothing in particular. She looked so sad and lonely and lost. She hadn't heard me. I spoke her name softly so as not to alarm her.

'Oh Jenny lass. What am I to do?'

I pulled a chair and sat with her taking one of her hands in mine.

'You must speak to the doctor,' I said, 'as a friend. Let him advise you and, if he's as nice as you say he is, he will understand your worry and keep your confidence.'

'You see what I mean, don't you?'

I squeezed her hand. 'Well, we both know he's different from most folk - a wee bit unusual, wouldn't you say?'

She didn't seem able to say anything but just shook her head.

'He works very hard,' I suggested but she wouldn't buy that. She snorted.

'Locked up in his room all day, not bothering to open his letters. You call that working?'

I stayed with her, accepting her offer of lunch, more to make sure she had some herself than for my own needs. I had lost my appetite.

I made her promise to speak to Jamie Robertson, her trusted doctor, and promised in my turn to come back the following afternoon.

On impulse I walked to Theresa's flat. We hadn't been in touch for a few weeks. Perhaps she would be able to throw some light on the professor's behaviour. I found her packing a suitcase.

'Going away?'

'A sudden invitation for a series of lectures in Holland.'

'For long?' I couldn't hide my disappointment.

'A few weeks. I thought I'd look up some friends while I'm there. You look worried. Has something happened?'

'This isn't the time,' I began apologetically.

'Nonsense. I'm not leaving till tomorrow. There's time
for tea if you can stay and if you don't mind cold meat and salad.'

I thought of Neil probably expecting me home for tea. With no Mrs Martin there he'd either be waiting for me to organize the evening meal or perhaps already be preparing it for us both.

'May I ring Neil before we begin?' I asked.

With raised brows she nodded in the direction of the telephone, as usual almost hidden under a pile of papers.

Neil made no attempt to hide his disappointment, explaining he'd put a small roast in the oven, the vegetables were prepared and he was just about to open a tin of fruit.

I had a pang of misgiving but made a quick assessment of my priorities.

'I'm sorry Neil. It's unexpected. There's something wrong with the professor and I need Theresa's advice. She's leaving for Holland tomorrow and I've only just arrived.'

I could feel the drop in temperature but I ignored his silence, noting that he showed no concern for the professor. Hardly surprising, I suppose. If he was converting he would not do it overnight.

I was conscious of Theresa's silent criticism. I had half-considered confiding in her about Neil's apparent change of direction but now decided against it. Anyway, I had enough on my plate at the moment with the professor.

'I'm not surprised,' she said when I'd put her in the picture. 'He's made the paranormal his special study. It's one thing to study it and quite another to become actively involved. That business with you and his astral projection left a niggle in my mind.'

'Is it dangerous?'

'Shouldn't be to him if he keeps his balance, but from what you say he's very much off balance and wants to watch. It's powerful stuff.'

'What can we do?'

'Nothing. He's weaving his own web. We can hardly stick our fingers in. The whole matter is much too delicate and I'm sure he knows the dangers.'

'Poor Aggie. I hope I did the right thing in advising. the doctor's help.'

'Jamie Robertson's OK. He's keen on the holistic approach to medicine. At least he can keep his eye on Aggie even if he can't interfere with the professor's paranormal experiments.'

'So you think it is that which is making the professor act strangely?'

'Sure to be. He'll come to his senses soon. You'll see. Before you know it he'll be lifting up the threads of ordinary life again.'

'What about my colours which he says are so good?' I asked summoning a smile.

'He's reading your aura.'

'So?'

'Its colours reveal your inner conditions - the state of your fields - astral, etheric, the alignment of your chakras. All that sort of thing. Not my speciality.'

Conscious of her half-packed suitcase I helped clear up after our meal and left for home. Only then did I remember the possible awkwardness of coming face to face with Neil and the consequences of his particular drama.

CHAPTER 29

He was in the parlour reading, having finished his meal. He made no reference to my day, did not ask about the professor or if I had eaten. Yet I sensed no hidden disapproval. He was just not interested in my life away from the manse. He tolerated it now but still divorced himself from it. At one time I might have resented this, used it as a weapon in an ego war but now I saw it for what it was - a mood of his I had no intention of fuelling, emotional baggage I could do without. I would pick up any ball he happened to pass to me but I would not chase or tackle. That was a game he could play by himself.

'I had a long talk with the moderator.'

'That's good.'

'He was most impressed by your money-raising efforts. In fact, he went as far as to ask me to pass on his personal congratulations.'

I was astonished.

'I'm very proud of you, Jenny.'

'For raising money?'

'For caring so much about the needy. There is so much poverty and misery in the heathen countries, every effort we make here on their behalf is a victory for Jesus.'

'God help me,' I thought and made a quick decision.

'You should realize, Neil, that my efforts were more directed at improving personal relationships in your own parish. If the heathens benefited, well and good. And, I might add, much of my motivation was to improve my own standing in the community.'

But his admiration was not to be thwarted.

'You say that.'

'Because I mean that. I made a big discovery when I involved myself with the ladies of the parish. I discovered that the more I became involved, the more I enjoyed it and the more I gave to them, the more they gave in return. Frankly, I hadn't a thought for the heathen poor.'

He remained silent for so long that I wondered if I'd blown it.

'I'm sorry, Neil, if that shocks you but the motivation should be as accountable as the deed itself.'

'No, don't be sorry, Jenny.' A long pause and then, almost inaudibly, 'About anything. I'm not.'

I caught his meaning immediately, held my breath and waited, forcing him to continue.

'Last night,' he said gruffly. 'I've sorted it out. I had a long talk with the moderator. He showed me the situation in a different light. I've come to terms with my weakness. I see it differently now. I see marriage differently. My commitment is redirected.'

I! I! I! No words of love or concern for my feelings or my way of thinking. I felt immense relief. I didn't want the complication of Neil loving me. Needing me for sexual satisfaction I could cope with. To me that was a deal healthier than what had been going on for so long. Loving me for myself would be much more difficult but there was little danger of that. We were living our lives in different arenas.

'Marriage is a two-way commitment,' I ventured.

'You can rest assured I shall be diligent in my commitment.'

I had to stifle a cruel little laugh. The language was almost as bad as it was on the first night of our marriage when he had explained that intercourse was for procreation only. That was obviously different now but I determined to establish the ground rules this time.

'I would like you to sleep in my bed, Jenny.'

'Every step of the way,' a little voice was repeating in my head. 'Stand outside yourself, Jenny,' the professor was whispering in my ear. I had it seemed already worked out a plan for just such a moment.

'It is going to be a big change for us both, Neil. I am your wife so of course I will share your bed if you so wish but I would like to keep my own room and my own bed for such times as I may desire some solitude. I'm sure you understand that and will take no offence if I should on occasion wish to sleep by myself' I was sounding like a wronged heroine in a 19th-century novel. Ordinary conversation with Neil had never been easy. Our marital problems had not helped. Again I felt immeasurable relief that my own longings were not tied up in his nonconformist attitudes to our relationship. Ironically I had made my bed and I must lie in it, something my grandfather might have said.

Our routine changed and surprisingly created little havoc. He was less demanding than I had expected and made no objection on the nights when I preferred my own company in my own bed. I established this right quickly but as the weeks went on felt less inclined to leave the comfort of a warm body beside me. Things could be worse, I told myself, and for the first time was deeply grateful for my inability to conceive. Sexual activity I could put in perspective. Shared parenting with Neil would have been something quite different.

As Theresa had predicted, the professor became earthbound again and, according to Aggie, gradually excavated his mountain of unanswered mail. He was spending more time with me in the library gently guiding me through my work and my studies. He never answered a question directly. Indeed he'd made it clear from the beginning that one had to find one's own answer. Yet somehow, by anticipating my needs in that uncanny way, my questions were always answered. Advice was delivered obliquely. Once when I let my enthusiasm for analytical reasoning run away with me, he quoted for my amusement and no doubt instruction:

> 'The centipede was happy, quite,
> Until a toad in fun said,
> "Pray, which leg goes after which?"
> This worked his mind to such a pitch,
> He lay distracted in a ditch
> Considering how to run!'

I laughed and reset my thinking levels and Aggie arrived with the tea trolley.

As a horticulturist might tend his plants and exclaim at their beauty or a potter feel the creation of life under his hands as his wheel turned and the clay responded to his touch, I felt a similar delight in the professor's esoteric library. Myths, legends, grail seekers, truth seekers, the Zen of the Bhuddists, the Tao, the I Ching and the Four Horsemen of the Apocalypse became more absorbing than the daily newspaper.

I was constantly amazed at the pictures conjured of life before Christ, ancient civilizations which rose and fell and are still relevant in our thinking today.

All week I'd fill my head to bursting point with new thoughts and on Sundays I'd listen to Neil's sermons. The story of Jesus could move me to tears but sometimes I wanted to push my husband out of the pulpit and offer a fuller conception, more profound than the immaculate one constantly on offer by the church.

Jesus said,' I would say to the congregation, "Know ye not that ye are the temple of the living divinity and that the spirit divine dwelleth within you?" Jesus's words, not mine.'

I could fly with the wings of my imagination as could the professor on his extended silver cord. What he garnered on his flights I did not know but what I discovered were the ideas and inspirations to help balance a way of living which by wriggling gradually and some times painfully from the garb of self could feel the grace of serving a wider and growing community.

I was as happy as I felt I could be under the circumstances. I had stopped running away. I was useful and enjoyed the satisfaction of seeing my husband relax more, accept that some human satisfactions could border on the divine. It was not love, but commitment that gave me the means to do this. Besides giving freely of my body, I gave generously of my time and effort for his fund-raising in which he exulted. He really believed he was feeding Africa and educating China.

One evening I was in the kitchen preparing the meal when the doorbell rang. I heard the study door open and Neil's footsteps cross the hall. Knowing he was answering I paid no more attention until I realized that the doorstep conversation seemed to be going on a bit. This was unusual. Neil was fairly welcoming to calling parishioners of whom there were many. Knife in hand and arm poised for slicing onions I thought I recognised something familiar in the voice. It was raining hard and I had a vision of the hail carpet being saturated. I replaced the knife on the chopping board, gave my hands a quick wipe on the kitchen towel and went into the hail to satisfy my curiosity.

Neil was filling the door-frame with his bulk but over his shoulder I saw Theresa's animated face. Seeing me approach she hailed me, attempting to squeeze past Neil who firmly stood his ground.

'Jenny. Will you please tell this husband of yours to let me in? I've tried to reassure him that I've left my broomstick and familiar behind but he obviously doesn't trust me.'

I saw Neil's glower and remembered his previous instruction that the she-devil would never cross his threshold. However I was more alarmed at Theresa's unexpected call than Neil's typical intransigence.

'I must speak with Jenny,' Theresa insisted.

'Come into the kitchen, Theresa,' I said. Neil stood aside, albeit reluctantly, but he'd allowed the she-devil access to his domain.

I felt that whatever Theresa had to say, Neil should hear it too. My alarm bells were ringing.

'It's bad news, I'm afraid.'

'Please, come into the kitchen.'

She glanced quickly from me to Neil then back, holding my gaze.

'The professor is dead.'

Neil who had been about to turn on his heels stood still, looking at me. They were both looking at me, waiting for my reaction.

'Please, come into the kitchen,' I repeated shaking my head at Neil who appeared uncertain.

'Not if you don't want to,' I said.

He hesitated, uncertain, then without speaking left us standing on the carpet while he sought the seclusion of his study.

I led the way into the kitchen waving Theresa to a chair by the smouldering embers of a slow-backed fire. Theresa comforted me into the other fireside chair.

'What happened?' I eventually managed to ask.

'He died in his bed, fully clothed with the door locked.' We looked at each other.

'I think so,' she said. 'I think he made one journey too far.'

'How's Aggie taking it?'

'Need you ask. She's at my place just now because she has nowhere else to go but there just isn't room for the two of us. I was wondering Jenny if—'

'Come here, you mean?'

She nodded.

'As far as I'm concerned she's very welcome. As you know Mrs Martin is with her sister and, from what we can gather from broad hints in her letters, she isn't likely to be coming back.'

'And Neil?' asked Theresa.

'Let's ask him.'

In the end Neil agreed as an act of Christian charity, to accept Aggie into our household.

'He's changing,' said Theresa.'

'Yes,' I agreed but left it at that.

The professor's death hit me hard. Not only was he a dear friend and guru but without him I would lose access to much of my freedom and inspiration.

I knew then how much the library meant to me. With the professor and his 'friends' I could slay the dragons and tame the tigers who lurked in the darkness or walked unbidden by my side. Without them I would be easy prey to all those doubts and uncertainties that were in the dark recesses of my mind.

Theresa was talking to me.

'You haven't really lost him, Jenny.'

'Already I am desolate.'

'He'll be there for you, you'll see.'

'I no sooner seem to have something wonderful when I lose it. It's always been like that. Why should it be any different now?'

'The professor would be the first to say every obstacle was a challenge, every setback an opportunity.'

'The problem is not in appreciating that sentiment. Millions do. The problem is in living it. Very few do.'

'And you've set your sights on that - still?'

'I thought I had. Already I'm wallowing in self-pity.'

"Then don't. It's destructive.'

'You're right. When can I expect Aggie?'

'Today?'

'I'll get her room ready.' Life, it seemed, must go on.

'She'll never fit in here,' grumbled Neil when we discussed the matter later.

'Then we'll have to fit in with her,' I answered.

He looked at me and for the next few weeks I felt he went on looking at me for signs of I didn't know what. Not once did he mention the professor. I attended the funeral and he kept his silence. I mourned my friend.

He showed no sign of understanding. He avoided Aggie as much as possible but was always courteous.

Aggie did fit in wherever she happened to be because all her energies were bent on giving and never sparing a thought to what she might be receiving in return. Not for her the long face or self-pity. Her goodness was as much a part of her as her body. There were no dragons or tigers on her spiritual path it seemed.

In the weeks ahead I had to fight constant battles with myself. Some I won, some I lost and I felt the gloom of my new reality creep up on me. I now resented what others expected of me. Mrs Martin had decided to move in with her sister and Aggie took over managing the household, relieving us of domestic chores.

Neil's enthusiasm for the Missionary Society was, I felt, getting out of proportion. He was no longer grateful for my efforts and just took them for granted.

Every weapon in the devil's armoury was being thrown at me - feelings of resentment, injured pride, self-righteousness, a sense of injustice and a longing to cry again that it wasn't fair, compounded by the fact that any conversation about my feelings or wishes did not exist.

I stopped attending the Theosophical Society meetings. Theresa was in America at a convention. I could feel my lofty aspirations floating away from me like the down of a dandelion clock. Neil had never looked happier and never more so than the day I returned from the office of an Edinburgh solicitor to which Aggie and I had been summoned by a very brief, very formal invitation on expensively headed notepaper. Neil had guessed the reason. It wasn't difficult. The professor had made a will and Aggie and I were beneficiaries.

When he learned that I had inherited the professor's library of some 6,000 leather-bound books, the furrow between his eyes deepened.

'What the deuce can you do with 6,000 books and where are you going to keep them?'

I didn't answer because I'd given the matter no thought. The impact of the rest of my inheritance had left little room for 6,000 books.

'I've also been left money,' I said.

'Oh,' he responded, adding, 'I'd have thought Aggie would be more in need of money.'

'Aggie's well provided for. She'll never need to worry about money.' I paused then plunged. 'The professor has left me a million pounds.'

I watched as his jaw dropped and wondered if I had looked like that when I'd been told.

He couldn't seem to find his voice. He sat heavily on a chair opposite while we looked at each other.

'There is a condition,' I told him. 'It is not for my pleasure or comfort. The only way I can spend it is for the good of humanity. The way in which I spend it is up to me just as long as it is for the benefit of humanity.'

I sat back and waited. It didn't take long. The furrow between the eyes disappeared. Gone was the veiled antagonism, the rising suspicion, the fear.

'That's wonderful,' he said on a long ecstatic breath. 'You must see just how wonderful.'

He didn't hear my barely audible, 'Must I?' His mind had already travelled from me and the manse and his congregation halfway to Africa to distribute the professor's million pounds. Perhaps a fairish share for China, I thought unkindly.

I was totally unkind. To me his magnanimity with the professor's money was obscene, his disregard of my feelings and possible wishes uncharitable.

I left him without a word, collected my few belongings kept in his bedroom and took them to my own.

The next morning I told him I was going to Strathard for a few days to give the matter some thought.

'Strathard! You've often said you had no desire to go back there.'

'It's more a case of needing to,' I said. 'I've telephoned a reservation at the hotel. I leave tomorrow.'

He didn't have to voice his thoughts. They were there in familiar presentation. He thought I'd taken leave of my senses. Perhaps I had. All I knew was that I was following my other sense, my intuition, which I had decided in the quiet of the night, was impossible to ignore.

CHAPTER 30

I had come full circle. Here I was in a Strathard Castle bedroom, perhaps once inhabited by Miss Catriona herself. It was certainly grand enough, making my few drab belongings look out of place. I had rushed here to flee my resentment and to reach a decision.

The professor had carried this burden through most of his adult life. It had been his solemn task to do what he had now willed me to do but he had failed. He'd strayed from the path. Addicted to his paranormal powers he'd neglected the ordinary, that is, if you could call nobly disposing of a million pounds ordinary. If he had failed, what chance had I?

I supposed I could forget my resentment towards Neil and go along with his simplistic idea but I dismissed this notion. It was too simplistic. I wanted a solution that I thought was important and that was certainly not the short-term alleviation of problems for some randomly selected individuals.

I wanted an idea that was different but not impossible. Anything I was likely to come up with, of course, would be shot down before it had taken wing. The world was full of sceptics and critics with their guns primed and their powder dry. Cynicism was fashionable. It was easier to be cynical than sympathetic.

One step at a time the professor had said. What he'd forgotten to say was that for every step forward be prepared to slide three back. Theresa had been right. I was crazy to work so hard on spiritual development. I was probably doing it for all the wrong reasons anyway. And yet to me my aspirations were not eccentric or antisocial or plain stupid. They were compelling. The hardest part to come to terms with was that, to be effective, they had to be lived. Theory was not enough. The highest aspirations such as taught by Jesus and Buddha were worthless unless lived, day by day, hour by hour, moment by moment.

So help me God! I've set my feet on this path of enlightenment and I'm finding I can't leave it because then I would be lost in a fog of meaningless nothings.

'Mrs Fraser!'

It was Flora's voice and she was knocking on my bedroom door.

'Your husband is on the telephone.'

I rose, following Flora downstairs to the one telephone at reception.

'I'm coming to Strathard tomorrow,' he said without preamble.

A bolt from the blue! 'Why the urgency?'

'I could bring you home. Save you hassle on the train.'

'You don't have to come.'

'I know I don't have to but I want to. Won't that do for now?'

I couldn't stop myself. 'Suppose I'm not ready to return with you?'

'Just try to be. There's a lot to be done here.' Perplexed, I replaced the receiver. Flora had got the gist of the conversation and was waiting for me.

'Good job you're in a double room already, Mrs Fraser,' she said with a cheeky smile. 'Save changing.'

I curbed my irritation and decided I needed a stiff drink. It was less than an hour until dinner. I bathed, changed, made my way to the lounge and rang for service. So slack was business that it was Flora who answered my summons.

'I knew you'd be wanting this,' she said presenting a whisky on a salver.

'A real five-star hotel,' I said, smiling my thanks.

'It could be if some folk would stay put long enough,' she replied. 'I've news for you. Your husband isn't the only one coming tomorrow. The owners will be here come dinner time.' She was signalling agitation.

'Are you worried?' I asked, pushing my nose in the glass and drowning in the comfort of the alcoholic fumes.

'Why should I be? I know everything isn't done that's supposed to be but I'll tell you this. They won't even notice. They're not a bit interested in Strathard. You must have seen that for yourself.'

'It is a bit rundown, I admit.'

'A bit!' she shrieked. 'If it wasn't for Jock and me this place would've gone to the dogs long ago.' She flounced off leaving me to the comfort of my drink.

It was a long evening. I had lost all desire to revisit any more childhood haunts. I decided to make one more visit to the cemetery before Neil arrived. Perhaps, if I sat near Grandpa's grave some idea would come to me. From somewhere in the collective unconscious I'd receive the motivation I needed. I must believe that.

After dinner I settled down in my room to read, hoping it might induce sleep, but it was well after midnight when I resigned myself to the fact that sleep was going to be impossible. So now was as good a time as any, I decided, to visit the cemetery. Instead of undressing I decided to try and slip out of the hotel unnoticed. With my shoes in hand I tiptoed downstairs and escaped through a servants' door which I'd already discovered was left unlocked. There was a bright moon occasionally dimmed by cloud. No one around.

Why was I here? I wondered as I passed the church and made my way to the family graves. I didn't need to come here to remember my grandfather. He was someone I carried around with me wherever I went. Why come here? Only because tradition had conditioned me to believe that visiting the grave of a loved one brought that loved one closer. Stuff and nonsense. No loved one could be closer to me than my grandfather wherever I happened to be.

Nevertheless it was with a feeling of near reverence that I approached my family burial sites. At that moment the clouds parted and the moon shone in all her splendour upon the mound of my grandfather's grave. What I saw lying there froze me solid. Something lay on the grass below the headstone and that something was a bunch of wild flowers. Someone had placed it there. To say I was disturbed would be like describing a force-ten gale as a gentle zephyr. I felt blitzed and it made things no easier when I spied a similar offering on the adjoining mound of my mother's grave. I began some deep breathing and only when the panic passed and my limbs stopped shaking did I dare look around.

Fearfully I scanned the graveyard but there was nothing to disturb its tranquility. I summoned enough courage to stroll round the perimeter, bound on one side by the church wall, two sides by mixed borders of shrubs and the remaining side by a drystone dyke beyond which the land rolled to the village and beyond to the moors. Panic returned when I spied a similar bouquet on another grave. I knew the grave. I'd knelt there on my previous visit. Something strange and perhaps wonderful was happening. Dare I open my mind to the possibility? Don't even think it, I cautioned myself.

I lifted the flowers from young Tam McGreegor's grave and buried my face in their loveliness. Then I waited, every nerve quickened and senses alert. I felt the presence first moving from the shrubbery, then raising my eyes I watched the tall dark shadow approach. It moved slowly but without hesitation. I waited until it was within striking distance then, my breath trapped in my throat, I managed the one word hammering in my brain.

'Todd?'

Like magic he whipped off that absurd wide-brimmed hat, made a slight obeisance and replied in a strong voice.

Jenny.'

Then the heavens rent. Todd who was dead, was alive. Todd who had been a memory was a reality. Todd of my dreams was flesh and blood and my heart was full of joy.

I was riveted to his eyes, those wide, wicked, winsome eyes. Now they were waiting. My knight of old had returned from battle. The bright moonlight revealed his sorry scars which he did nothing to hide. His trophy was his presence and this he laid bare for my response.

It all rushed back to me, that other time, that other moon but the same moon, the same time.

'Have you the feeling of déjà-vu?' I whispered in a voice that trembled.

'Aye, but last time I came to say goodbye. This time is to say hello.' His voice was music to my ears.

I held out both hands which he took in his and the pain of his tightening grasp was exquisite.

'Has anyone,' I breathed, 'ever died of sheer unadulterated joy?'

'Don't you dare pass out on me, Jenny McLeod. I haven't come this far to mourn at your funeral.'

He was laughing. I was laughing. He took me in the circle of his arms and we both wept.

'Hey, this'll never do,' he said huskily. 'Surely we can do better than blurb.'

'Why didn't you let me know years ago?' I wailed, my face pressed to his chest.

'How was I to know you were growing a halo. I was more inclined to think you would have recoiled before disowning me and who could have blamed you.'

'You should have known me better than that.' I raised my head and looked at him.

'Aye, maybe I should. It seemed best at the time.'

'Why now and why all this cloak and dagger stuff and scaring the living daylights out of the natives?' My voice was stronger now and I strove to keep it light.

He laughed. 'I've been disguising myself for so many years it seems to come naturally. The cloak and hat have got me out of many a scrape.'

'Those scrapes. I want to hear about them.' He did not turn away from my scrutiny.

'And you? Have you had any scrapes?'

'Too many.' I shrugged them off as of no further significance.

'I want to hear about them.'

'I want to hear about everything that's happened to you since you deserted me.'

'I want to know about everything you've been getting up to since you, since you...'

'I never deserted you, Todd McGreegor. I wrote to you every day for years after you, after you...'

'Deserted?'

'No. I don't think you ever did.'

'I've thought of you consistently since...'

'Since this?' I asked raising my hand and gently touching the malformed nose, the scarred and sunken cheek, the broken and bruised chin.

I felt him tense then slacken, then tremble but he never flinched. He let me explore and I kept my fingers light and tender. Our eyes locked and I sighed in bliss.

'Your eyes are just as I remember them.'

'And your hair is still as red as carrots. I've still to find out about the temper.'

'I'm a reformed woman.'

'Not too much, I hope,' he said. 'And how do we begin to bridge a gap of nearly thirty years?'

'As long as that?' I whispered.

'Centuries longer, I'd say,' he said softly.

Carefully we brought our feet back down to earth. 'We can hardly stay here,' I breathed, releasing myself from his arms.

'Come with me,' he said, offering his hand.

I followed without question, happy to walk into the sea with him or jump off a cliff together or, as it turned out step with him quietly back to the castle grounds and on to the Square. He led me to the stables where a handsome stallion began to nuzzle Todd's shoulder.

'No one ever comes here now,' he whispered adding, 'except for the odd visitor from the past.'

'So it was you and your horse that night I was prowling.'

'I was the one prowling,' he laughed. 'I very nearly pounced.'

He led his horse along the cobbled yard before veering off to the birchwood path.

'He'll carry us both,' he said as he helped me mount. 'I won't ask where we're going.'

'You will soon guess when we're underway.'

Whatever woes and worries I may have suffered in the past were more than compensated for by that wild gallop over the moors of Strathard with my arms tight around Todd's waist, my hair loosened and lifting from my scalp like a flag at half mast, the stars and flooding moonlight casting a spell on the landscape. I felt like Scott's fair Ellen, whisked from the side of her bridegroom by her daring, dashing knight. Only it wasn't a bridegroom but a husband, I thought, not too soberly. The thumping rhythm of the horse's gallop drummed out some long-remembered lines from the poem.

'0, young Lochinvar is come out of the west,
Through all the wide Border his steed was the best.'

I held close to my gallant. There may have been no bridal gown, measured dance or cup of wine but the stars were my jewels and the moon my gold.

     'So faithful in love, and so dauntless in war
     There never was knight like the young Lochinvar.'

The horse had the bit between the teeth and I gave my excitement unbridled rein as I almost shouted the next remembered line.

     'She is won! We are gone, over bank, bush, and scaur;'

On we galloped leaving the village far behind and heading for what I now guessed would be the Shooting Lodge where the old laird had lived out his last days in loneliness. Was ever a woman more blessed!

As we entered deer country where once we'd watched the stags having guts removed, and being skinned and quartered on the spot, I had a quick vision of Callum eating too much of the nice-tasting liver and coming up in spots while the flesh around his eyes swelled up affording him a month off school. On we galloped, past the ruins of labourers' cottage once inhabited by sturdy lads.

But all that was a long time ago. I was with Todd. The horse's hooves thundered in my ears, my blood thundered through my veins, knock, knock, knocking at my heart and hammering on my brain. I held tight, never wanting this flight from reality to come to an end. But of course it did and as the ruin of a one-time idyllic hunting lodge came into view Todd slackened the reins and slowed his steed to a trot. The world belonged to us.

He helped me dismount and waited, quietly supporting me, until I regained control of my breath and limbs.

'You're out of condition, Jenny McLeod.'

'I admit I haven't made a habit of galloping over the moors in the wee sma' hours of the morning.' I had never known such happiness.

Taking my hand he led both horse and me up the overgrown approach drive to the waiting ruin.

'Are you hungry?' he asked.

'I could eat a horse,' I quipped.

'I'm afraid we'll need Tipsy to take you back but crusty bread and cheese and a bottle of wine is on offer.'

I had never felt so alive and at one with the universe.

Tethering his horse he led me towards the gawping caverns of the windows but ignoring their easy entry he opened the heavy oak door, miraculously preserved. He guided me into the stone-floored hall, austere in its emptiness, towards the crumbling wooden staircase and showed me the best means of reaching the top in safety. In contrast to the sad emptiness of the entrance hall, this upstairs attic showed all the evidence of a careful tenant. There was a palliasse on the floor and a spirit stove on an upturned wooden box. Other boxes served as chair, table and shelves holding tinned food and a few eating utensils such as tin mugs, some horn spoons and wooden bowls. These should have given me a clue.

In a corner alcove stood a bench of sorts housing basin and water-jug and a rough towel hanging on a nail.

'I'll be back. I must see to Tipsy.'

He left me, wide-eyed and wondering and already impatient for his return.

Only Todd McGreegor could do this I thought. There was moonlight enough to examine this strangest of lodging. Everything spoke of an ordered, self-sufficient being, sure in purpose if lacking in comfort.

My heart began thumping again. Todd is alive! Todd is here! Todd is with me! We are together, alone in the world. No one else, nothing! Just us! Todd and me.

I heard him cross the stone-floored hall, climb the rickety wooden stairs and watched him enter the room, hatless, cloakiess and brandishing a bottle of wine.

'Straight from the cellar,' he said, 'which is a carefully chosen hole in the ground, left there this morning by Tam Tamson along with these which I found in Tipsy's quarters.'

He emptied a sack of provisions on to the 'table' - bread, cheese, butter, a tin of bully beef and two apples.

'Tam Tamson?' I was beginning to feel intoxicated and not all due to the whisky I'd had earlier.

'The resident tinker of the day. There's a family of them in the valley camped about a mile from here, near the river. He sniffed me out early on and introduced himself. His offer to valet solved a few problems.'

'Of course, that accounts for the kitchenware,' I said nodding towards the tin, wood and horn utensils.

'And the horse,' said Todd beginning to organize our banquet. 'In fact he provides whatever I need.'

'Your needs are few,' I said making a gesture of help, immediately waved away, and instead I was invited to sit on a box retrieved from inside another box.

'I've been minimalist for a long time now.'

He opened the wine, filled two 'tinnies', offered me one while watching me with those long-remembered, twinkling eyes.

'To the good life,' he said.

We raised our mugs and drank.

'Not too tired, I hope?'

I returned his smile. 'I've never been more alive.' The wine was firing my belly. We ate and drank and talked.

'What's it to be?' Todd began when we'd eaten all we could manage. 'The broad brush canvas or the pen and ink etching?'

'The broad brush,' I replied. 'You begin.'

His brush strokes were too broad for my liking. I hungered for every detail of his life but I bit back the multitude of questions whirling in my mind, listened again to his deaf-mute experiences, his escape to France and short flying career which ended when his plane was shot down.

'Was that when...' I began, half-raising my hand towards his face.

'No,' he said halting my intent by refilling my tinny. 'That was much later. I found myself involved in the French resistance and the involvement escalated till it filled my life. First it was helping Jews and gypsies and other free-thinking, so-called heretics being hunted by the Gestapo. The work was finding safe houses, papers, some form of transport and when that wasn't going on I was helping to print and secretly distribute leaflets which the dominie was writing.'

'The dominie?' I interrupted. 'What—'

'He's dead. When war was declared we thought we could do more where we were than returning home. Anyhow by that time we were too deeply involved.'

'How did he die, Todd?' I asked, remembering my unkind thoughts of our old friend.

'Shot. I don't know the details. We'd separated by then but not before I asked him to write you and my folk that I was dead. That was probably the last thing he did and it probably cost him a great deal. He was in a bad way when we parted. We both were.'

I silently hoped that Archie Ross's spirit would understand my earlier grievance.

Aloud I said, 'But why, Todd? If you weren't dead why...'

'I believed it was only a matter of time. Look at me!' he said defiantly forcing his face in my view.

'I'm looking.' My eyes never wavered from his face. 'What do you see, Jenny? Eh?'

I controlled my breathing and my urge to envelop him in my over-brimming sympathy and love.

'Two bright and discriminating eyes mirroring a brave soul.'

'Ugh!'

'How *did* it happen, Todd?'

'Humanity at its lowest!' he said flatly.

I held my breath.

'I was betrayed while helping some Jews flee the country and captured by the Gestapo, then taken to a concentration camp.' He looked searchingly at me before continuing. 'Are you ready for a bruiser of a brush stroke?'

I nodded dumbly.

'I don't think they liked my good looks.'

His eyes softened for a moment as he reached and caught my hand.

'My face annoyed them so they tried to remodel it. The trouble was they couldn't agree among themselves as to what model they liked best and kept on experimenting.' He was silent for a moment then smiled grimly. 'At least they saved my eyes so that I could enjoy the finished effect, I suppose. Pretty artistic, eh?'

'I'm glad they saved your eyes,' I said gently. I dared to touch him and he did not stop me. 'There are some wonderful surgeons.'

'Never.' Then more quietly. 'This new model has served me well, Jenny. It has taught me values I never dreamed of.'

Our reunion had taken on the quality of a strange dream.

'Why then have you come back here to Strathard?' I asked refusing to relinquish my hand.

'To find you.' He was not laughing, not even smiling. 'Did you really expect to find me here?'

'Yes.'

'But it's sheer chance I'm here at all,' I gasped.

'Chance? Do you really think so?'

I shivered, not with cold but with the stirrings of a new joy that told me I wasn't alone any more on this relentless journey I had chosen for myself. We were speaking the same language, building the same thought force, trying to penetrate the same mystery.

Misinterpreting my shiver he was all concern.

'You're cold.' He rose and held out his hand. 'Come, we will lie on the palliasse and I can keep you warm while you start painting your picture. We can watch the sunrise together.'

The wine had made me heady and when Todd raised me to my feet I swayed and would have fallen had he not caught me. I felt I had been lifted right outside myself and was heading fast for some strange and unknown destination. It was with relief that I stretched myself on the comfortable straw bed.

As the stars in the sky above sent us light, stars of a different kind were sending mixed messages to my body and my soul. Todd gathered me in his arms and we cuddled close. When I had stopped shivering he groped for my hand and slowly turned the wedding ring on my finger.

'Now your brush strokes, Jenny,' he said gently.

'I'll begin from Grandpa's death,' I said into his chest, 'because everything of significance before that, and I mean everything, is in my letters to you in a huge suitcase in my attic. You can read them at your leisure. They will tell you all that happened in Strathard from the hour you left in secret till the hour I left in despair.'

'I should like to read them.'

'You will,' adding with a half-laugh, half-sob, 'so long as you don't expect me to stamp and post them. It would bankrupt me.'

He held me close. 'Go on then, I'm waiting.'

I painted my picture, leaving nothing out. Although I tried to keep my brush strokes bold there were times I had to use more delicate lines especially when explaining my marriage to Neil. When I had finished we lay together in silence until I asked tentatively, 'Are you surprised I married Neil Fraser?'

'Yes,' then after a pause, 'but I think it was probably meant to be.'

'My karma?'

'That's one way of looking at it.'

'Is there another way that makes as much sense?'

'It is your way and to you it makes sense. That's good.' 'Some choices are difficult,' I mumbled.

'Only our thoughts make them difficult. If we are clear-minded about what we want there is no difficulty.'

At that moment I was finding it difficult to be clear-minded about anything. Far from shivering I was becoming overheated and not just by our combined body temperatures. So recently and so earnestly I had sworn to cultivate a state of desirelessness but now all I felt was desire. Every nerve was alive with it. With our bodies wrapped together mine was responding as it had been biologically programmed to do. Only my thoughts were getting in the way. Was Todd feeling likewise? If he was showing remarkable restraint but my instinct told me that I wouldn't be lying in his arms like this if he felt nothing.

I had to know. My love was yearning to extend itself. It was as if the peak of a mighty mountain beckoned me. All my clear-thinking about the state of desirelessness, so much appreciated on a different canvas, no longer mattered. This was one mountain I had to climb and I had to climb it with Todd. Whether I would be excited by new horizons when I reached the summit or perhaps appalled at the dangerous route back down to the foothills did not matter. There was only one way I wanted to go and if Todd were to take me I had to let him know. This was my choice. I'd offer him his.

I moved against him. I needed no words. I let my body do the speaking. It spoke the oldest language in the world and it was a language Todd understood. I heard his indrawn breath, felt his body tense.

'Are you sure about this Jenny?'

'Yes. I want to scale the heights with you Todd.' My voice was rough. My language was clumsy and a poor vehicle for my feelings.

'It could be dangerous.'

'Yes.'

'We might find the return journey hazardous.' 'Yes.'

'You might not like the view.'

'I will.'

'Others may be troubled about us.'

'It is my choice, Todd.'

'Close your eyes.'

With absolute trust and certainty I closed my eyes.

I abandoned myself to the physical pleasure of Todd's hands on my body, exploring, caressing, rousing my sexual appetite. My thoughts were drowned in a heaving flood of emotion. I reached for him, sliding my hands down his body and discovering, to my horror, that my fingers were tracing a network of laceration - ridges, furrows, scars, the hoof marks of the Gestapo! Everything changed. My passion which had been riding high became in an instant a weapon against the seal of satanic evil which I imagined was embedded in Todd's flesh.

With a frenzied wail I thought that with my ardour I could exorcize the evil force I sensed there. I felt that every kiss and caress I bestowed on Todd's wounds could act like a crucifix and expunge that evil.

When my hands discovered his manhood still intact my spirits soared but, not until I heard my lover's pleasured gasps on consummation, did I let my vexation fully abate in an aftermath of euphoria. If ever there was a moment when the act of sexual intercourse could transcend the physical and experience a spiritual dimension, it was surely that moment. It was as if all my life's personal battles against injustice and all my quarrels with God had been a preparation for just this moment.

Passion spent, we lay, our bodies spooned together, Todd's hands cupping my breasts and I wondered at their gentleness, their passion and their pleasure-giving. For a while we lay thus in silence, our loving having effectively killed off language. There was nothing words could add to how we felt. We watched the first crack of dawn and then, for a little while, we slept. When I woke I was still curved into Todd's body, his hands still cupped my breasts. My thoughts were still. I was, for a brief moment of eternity, just glad to be.

I felt him move and then the old familiar, good-humoured voice whispered in my ear.

'I'm glad your hair is still a flaming red.'

I turned and snuggled my face into his chest, my arm lying loosely across his waist.

'It's what kept me sane,' he said. 'When I felt I needed reinforcements I thought of Jenny McLeod's caurry fist and carroty hair. That's what gave me the gumption to stay alive.'

'And what gave you the gumption to keep free of bitterness?' I asked.

'Free of bitterness! Don't you believe it.'

'I don't detect any bitterness now.'

'When I was eventually freed I sought help at a Zen Buddhist Sitzen. I came across one in my travels. That's where I began to learn the meaning of patience and the lesson that some things take a long time - like effectively ridding oneself of bitterness.'

'I like what I've read of Buddhism,' I said, 'especially their belief in reincarnation and karma.'

'I detect you've been ploughing some deep thought furrows,' he said, stroking my hair.

I could feel him smiling. I sniffed his scent and could happily have roused him again but the first thin crack of dawn had widened into daylight. It was time to make the descent to the foothills. Divining my thoughts Todd spoke.

'Are you ready for the journey back?'

'I don't want to leave,' I said. 'Not now, not yet, not ever.'

'Nothing can ever take this time together away from us,' he said which to me in my heightened sensitivity, seemed to carry an ominous message.

'So little,' I whispered. 'So short.'

'So much quality,' he replied. 'And it is ours, only ours, Jenny.'

'This is beginning to sound like the time of reckoning,' I said trying to veil my despair with a smile.

'Not reckoning,' he answered, 'but time for concentrating.'

I hoped I didn't look as perplexed as I felt.

'On what?'

'On how you are going to spend a million pounds for the good of humanity.'

'I don't know, Todd. I just don't know.'

'Then we must work it out. First of all, forget about changing the world. You never could. Forget about saying souls. That's not your job. There are countless people already trying to do that. But remember humanity is a broad spectrum.'

'So what am I to do? It would seem I will have failed before I even make a start. Perhaps I should donate the money to Neil's Missionary Fund after all.'

'That's not the answer.'

'Then tell me.'

'No one can tell you the answer to your problem, Jenny. You must decide for yourself.'

I could not hide my exasperation. 'You sound exactly like the professor. That's the sort of advice he usually gave.' 'We have to be realistic.'

'Reality is such a harsh word.'

'It is kinder in the end than romanticism or sentimentality. It is where we see things as they are, not how we would like them to be and seeing things as they are and accepting them is the best starting point. We can operate outwards from there.'

We had left our bed as we spoke and had begun to dress.

'At the bottom of the mountain,' I replied, zipping my skirt, 'the reality is that I have a husband who is going to join me in Strathard later today and who expects me to tell him what I have decided.'

'Then let's start from there,' smiled Todd. 'Tell me one thing, Jenny.'

He was now fully dressed and lighting the primus stove. I looked at him, hoping for something specific.

'What, in your experience, has been the most important influence in your life? What, not who.'

It did not take long.

'I believe that what I rank highest is a broad and open mind and the opportunity to fill it.'

Todd grinned. 'There you have it,' he said. 'You've answered your question. Work on that.'

I laughed. 'Spend a million on opening and broadening minds and providing opportunities to fill them?'

'You've got it. Now how are minds broadened?'

'Considering alternative viewpoints.'

'And how can they be opened?'

'By providing attractive incentives perhaps?'

'And filled?'

'Providing information, lots and lots of information?' I accepted the tinny, cupping it in my hands for comforting warmth.

Todd nodded and in spite of myself I felt excited.

'Do you remember the dominie's favourite word without which no effort, presentation, even idea was worth a candle?' he asked as we wandered to the window and gazed on the breathtaking moorland scenery beyond.

'Do I not! Quality. "Your work must have quality, children. It isn't worth a cock's feather to a hen if it doesn't have quality."'

We turned to each other, laughing, then hastily averted our eyes. The rolling moors may have been an outside attraction but it was the giddy heights of the mountain we had climbed within that beckoned again. The moment passed and with it temptation.

'We could form a nucleus to provide quality information,' said Todd, 'and dispense it in a variety of ways - publishing, broadcasting, lectures, interactive courses designed to open closed minds and teach discrimination. That would be one way of utilizing your inheritance for the good of humanity.'

'Todd!' I stopped him in his tracks. 'You said we. Does that mean we?'

'As in we, the two of us. Of course. Now I know what all that leaflet distribution was leading up to and, of course, I have many useful contacts - quality contacts. I know good and gifted people who would gladly devote themselves to this ideal. It would mean a trip to Europe but I could muster a worthy team for you.'

'For us,' I reminded him then watched in wonder at the transformation as his sudden smile played kindly with his face. The room seemed suddenly full of light.

'I like it, Todd, but who will want it? Won't it be a grain of sand in the desert?'

'Ah, but it will be a quality grain of sand and the people who will want it will be the people who are searching for it. We're not converting. We're offering and,' he continued, 'we would have to find a centre of activity.'

'That won't be easy,' I said, experiencing a stab of pain as I watched his preparations for departure.

'The tinkers carry more than tinnies in their backpacks,' he said as he packed the food that was left for restoring. 'They pick up rumours as surely as they gather kindling for their fires. There is a rumour that the castle is going to be put up for sale.'

'I wouldn't be a bit surprised,' I said, drinking in the sight of him and silently railing against the importunities of time. 'The owners have no interest.' Then it hit me like a thunderbolt.

'Todd!' My voice rose decibels. 'Are you thinking what I'm thinking?'

'I expect so.' His eyes were twinkling.

'Would that be possible?' My legs were melting and I had to lean against the wall for support.

'With a million pounds a great deal is possible.' He took my hands, pulling me towards him. 'We have a long way to travel, Jenny, and our first journey is over the moors to Strathard and all that awaits you there.'

His words had an effect like a headlong free fall from a precipice.

'Hold on,' he whispered, willing me to calm. He waited until I took a grip on myself then said he'd go ahead and saddle Tipsy.

k'But first I must say this. I've merely mapped some bearings. I hope they help but the rest is up to you. You have much to think about and difficult decisions to make but only you can make them. As life seems already to have taught you, you are responsible for your actions. The choice is yours.'

This was not a warning, nor lecture but a reminder of the grim face of reality. It seemed all a question of choice.

'Wait, Todd,' I said as he prepared to go ahead. He turned and looked me steadily in the eyes.

'Neil will be with me in a few hours. His train is due early in the afternoon. Will you come to the hotel and meet him?'

I held his gaze and my breath.

'I'll be there,' he replied.

'And will you come as you are - no cloak, no hat?' 'I'll do that. Now let's go. We should make it before the village wakes up to a new day.'

Not a word was spoken on the ride back. My thoughts raced through my mind at the speed of Tipsy's mad gallop. Todd bent low over the stallion's neck. I held tight, chasing my galloping thoughts. We were back in the plain country, in the ordinary, in the real world. My first and most important task was to get back to my bedroom unobserved. I concentrated my mental energies on how that could best be done.

I dismounted on the edge of the birchwood and by silent consent Todd and I parted without another word. I reached the back door unobserved. I took off my shoes and prepared to travel the last few yards to my room on tiptoe. The door was still unlocked.

So far so good, I thought, as I cautiously let myself into the back hail. Holding my breath I left the back premises and tiptoed my way across reception towards the staircase and safety. No one was astir, or so I believed until, my foot on the first step, the lounge door opened and Flora appeared. On seeing me she yelled in top voice.

'Mrs Fraser! You're alive! Oh, the Lord be praised. We thought something must have happened to you. Where have you been? Were you kidnapped? Was it Him - the Devil? Oh your husband will be relieved. Mr Fraser!' she yelled. 'Your wife's safe. She's here.'

She hadn't stopped to draw breath and as I stood rooted, listening in horror to her words a door above opened, crashed shut and my husband came hurtling down the stairs towards me.

CHAPTER 31

'Thank God you're safe,' he said in obvious relief.

'Another five minutes and I was going to call the police.'

'When did you arrive?' I asked, trying to keep my voice steady.

'Half an hour ago. I had the opportunity of a lift to Inverness and took a taxi from there. I thought I'd surprise you.'

'You've done that,' I said, conscious of Flora still hovering in the background.

'I must say, Jenny, that I feel more shocked than surprised by you. Your bed hasn't been slept in. You've been out all night. We've been demented since we found out. Where have you been?'

'I can explain,' I said playing for time.

'I think you owe us an explanation. This poor woman,' indicating Flora, 'was convinced that you had been abducted by some monster who has been roaming the district for some time now with evil intent.'

'He is no monster and yes, I have been with him all night.'

There was a stunned silence while the words were absorbed and immediately translated into horror, 'accusation and condemnation. Flora stopped hovering and open-mouthed joined us.

'What did you do?' she gasped, 'all night with Him - the Devil?'

'Stop calling him that ridiculous name, Flora. You know nothing about him.'

'I know everyone in Strathard is afraid of him and I did warn you. I did warn her, Mr Fraser.'

'Yes, yes you did,' I replied, turning my attention to my husband who, I could sense, had run over every possible scenario in his mind and settled on the worst.

'Were you willingly in his company?' he asked. Now he really did look worried, far more worried than when he'd said he had been worried.

'Yes, I was willingly in his company.'

Here a dramatic indrawn breath from Flora. They were waiting for me to continue.

'We know him, Neil,' and including Flora in my explanation I continued. 'He is an old friend who used to live here, Flora. In fact we all used to live here. I was born in the Stable Square, which you now call the outhouses. My husband was born in the manse where his father was the minister and the Devil, as you so readily call him, was born in the gamekeeper's cottage in the wood which is no longer there. He went off to the Spanish Civil War and we all thought he was dead.'

My attention was back on my husband. 'He isn't dead. He's very much alive and will be coming here this afternoon to meet you all.'

Neil's face was ageing before me. If I'd been carried home a corpse he couldn't have looked worse.

Flora had collapsed on to the bottom step of the staircase. Neil said nothing, being caught up in the whirling of his own thoughts. With remarkable composure he addressed Flora.

'Perhaps you would be good enough to make us some breakfast and bring it to our room ... I'm sure my wife must be tired and will want to rest. Come Jenny.'

I was tired. Yes, I wanted sleep but I knew that couldn't happen until I'd given a 'proper' explanation to my husband. Todd had given me my bearings and I fastened my sights on these.

'If I tell you how I have decided to use the professor's inheritance I think you will understand why I stayed out all night.'

'It's going to take some understanding,' was the grim retort.

'I appreciate that and I'll do my best.'

I explained that I hadn't left the hotel until after midnight, meaning only a last farewell visit to my family's graves, and how it was only then that I met Todd and made the discovery that he was still alive. I skimmed over his war experiences saying nothing about the concentration camp.

'There was so much to talk about,' I said. 'He wanted to know all about me and my family and all our old friends and acquaintances in Strathard and when I told him we'd got married he wanted to know how you were, where your church was, how I liked living in Edinburgh. There was so much we both wanted to know and somehow before we realized it was well into the early hours. We knew we would be leaving Strathard soon and I suppose wanted to catch up on everything before then.'

'Why is he here at all?'

'He'd already tried to find his parents in Aberdeen but they both died and he'd come to Tam's grave. That's why he was in the cemetery.'

I outlined my plans for a centre of distribution of information for broadening people's minds only I didn't put it quite like that and I didn't use those words.

'You want to broaden and open wide their spirit of love and God,' I said warming to my approach. 'I want to enlarge their vision about the countless ways this can be done, is already being done. "In my Father's house there are many mansions,"' I quoted.

'Where is my help expected?'

'The calling here is empty. You keep telling me you'd like to come back. I didn't encourage you because I couldn't see it working for us.'

'You do now?'

'Yes. Strathard Castle is coming up for sale. I want to buy it and make this the centre for our work. I could form a trust and establish\a team who could make it work. We could broadcast, publish and bring to people's notice what we are trying to do. We could offer philosophical thinking, insights to comparative religion and beauty in the arts. In other words, present only the true, the good and the beautiful.'

'I've never in my life heard such arrogance, not even from you.'

I ignored the personal attack. 'There are different ways of finding God.'

I was dog-tired. I wanted to crawl into bed and oblivion but knew this was one argument I had to win without appearing to win it.

'I'm glad you've decided to bring God into your plans,' he said. 'I thought you'd finished with him.'

'I've always wanted God but it it has taken so long to find him.'

'And you've found him now?'

'What I have found is another way of looking at him, a way that suits me.'

'Oh yes, everything has to suit Jenny. It'll never work. It's cock-eyed, not thought through. You'll be a laughing stock and a million pounds will have been frittered away with nothing to show for it. The money might have clothed, fed and housed the poor. But oh no! That isn't good enough for you. Not a big enough challenge perhaps. Nothing short of saving the world for you.'

'Please Neil, try to understand.'

'What I understand is that someone has put you up to this and it isn't too difficult to guess who.'

'It isn't my intention to try to save the world,' I said, hoping to steer his thoughts away from Todd. 'I only want to make available information that some people don't even know is there and might be subconsciously looking for.'

'You haven't answered my question. Is Todd McGreegor likely to be mixed up in this crazy scheme of yours?'

'There's a good possibility. He has many contacts.'

'I thought as much. Why didn't he stay in Spain? He caused enough trouble here in the past and seems set on causing more now. Have you slept?' he suddenly demanded.

'We talked and talked and still didn't cover all of the last thirty years. I wanted to hear what had happened to him and he wanted to know what I'd been doing,' I said lamely.

'I'm sure he did...'

There was a timid knock at the door. It was Flora with our breakfast.

'I must have some sleep,' I said as Neil set the tray of tea, toast, scrambled egg and tomatoes on the bedside table. We ate in silence. At least Neil ate. I merely picked at the food but we were both silent, wrapped in our own thoughts. I could see that Neil was brooding and guessed it was the reappearance of Todd into my life which bothered him more than my decision about the money.

When we'd finished Neil carried the tray and the remnants of our meal to the kitchen, mumbling something, as he left the room, about going to take a look at the church. I undressed to my underwear, crawled between the sheets and must have been asleep before he'd reached the hall.

I slept long and deep and on waking I panicked. I had to be downstairs when Todd arrived. I had to be there when Neil and he met. I hastily washed and dressed.

On reaching reception I was horrified to see the gathering. Besides Neil and Flora, there was Jock ostensibly straightening pictures on the wall. The gardener had arrived with a truck of vegetables. The cook was consulting Flora about the menu. The few guests that were there were drifting around between lounge and dining room. Maids were scurrying with dustpans.

'Must be spick and span for the owners' arrival,' was Flora's excuse for the audience. She had wasted no time in spreading the gossip. I could feel Neil's antagonism before I joined him.

'The sooner we're out of here and back home the better,' he grumbled.

The owners are expected to arrive for dinner,' I said. 'I will have to stay until I have spoken to them about a possible sale and I could hardly do that as soon as they get here.'

'You are quite determined then to continue with this hare-brained idea?'

'Neil. You must realize I'm not seeking a career, nor targeting a goal or fulfilling an ambition. I only want to fulfill the responsibility thrust upon me the best way I know how and it has to be my decision.'

'Even if I refuse to agree?'

'I'm hoping it won't come to that.'

'There's more to this than you care to admit. It seems strange to me that as soon as Todd McGreegor comes on the scene you want to come back here and yet when I wanted you to come you wouldn't even consider it. You might as well know that as long as Todd McGreegor is here and a part of your life I won't ever consider it.'

There was a stir outside where two of the maids were polishing brasses. They had spotted Todd's arrival. I could feel my heart race and my legs were shaky as I moved towards the door. I was wondering if it had been wise to ask Todd to come. What could Neil and he say to each other? What silly move would Flora, already goggle-eyed and eager, make to push spokes in what I hoped would be a moving wheel.

I went outside to meet Todd. He arrived on foot saying he'd tethered Tipsy on the edge of the Birchwood.

'Why am I here, Jenny?' he asked as we climbed the steps to the portico.

There was no time to answer. We were inside, watched by eyes at first curious then gradually turning to a kind of transfixed horror. Flora gasped and rushed to Jock, whose normally genial features were frozen in disbelief. The cook dropped her menu plans which fluttered at Todd's feet. Leaving them there she made a hasty retreat to the kitchen. The gardener leaned heavily on the reception counter, gazing in open curiosity at Todd. I turned to Neil whose eyes were wide with astonishment and some other expression difficult to fathom.

Todd bent to retrieve the scattered menu sheets then placed them neatly on the counter. Turning, he stood quite still, hatless, cloakiess, facing the silenced onlookers. I looked at their fears and uncertainties. I looked at Todd's chipped and battered face. I could feel my anger rise but knew I must not let it take root. I must not give it credence. By doing so I would endanger my own feelings for Todd. Instead I must try to understand their reactions.

I knew this man. I knew the higher reaches of his mind and his worth. I knew his 'quality'. They did not. They saw an abnormal face and did not even wait to wonder why it was so. They couldn't handle the situation. I loved this man unconditionally. They did not. That was the difference. I understood. Todd understood. The others did not. To me he was a hero. To them he was a freak.

Todd was still and centred but his eyes were observing his fellow men. He had already been where they were now. He'd seen it all, felt it, suffered it and finally understood and accepted it. They cowered. He dominated.

Neil advanced with outstretched hand. I was surprised by his apparent ease. There was no sign of the reluctance or suspicion I had feared. The others too had by now recovered. Jock, after a none-too-friendly glare exited with the gardener who nodded in Todd's direction as he passed. The maids scuttled. Flora became immersed with the pages of the hotel register while Neil, Todd and I retired to the lounge.

I felt I was sitting on a time bomb waiting for the moment Neil would either begin asking awkward questions or pour words of scorn on my intention to buy the hotel. He did neither. I didn't chance my luck. Apart from telling Todd that we were considering the plans we had conceived, I said nothing about Neil's initial response. To give him credit, neither did Neil. I didn't know whether this was a good or a bad sign.

I concentrated my mind on trying to think of a way I could see Todd on his own. Fortunately Neil decided that he wanted to make a telephone call to his parish and excused himself for a few minutes.

'Well, Jenny?' enquired Todd when we were alone, leaving me to guess the question behind the question.

'I know that what we have planned is right, Todd. We will find the ways and means. It is a splendid vision.' 'It is only a vision,' he cautioned.

'Everything begins with a vision, a thought, remember?' We smiled into the depths of each other.

'And Neil?' he asked.

'He wants the incumbency. You are the stumbling block.'

'And how big a stumbling block am I, Jenny?'

His eyes were boring into mine and I could not look away.

'I need you, Todd. I could not do this without you. Is there some way we can talk again before we leave tomorrow? I'll have spoken to the owners by then and, hopefully, Neil will be persuaded.'

'And if he isn't?'

There was no time to reply. Neil was approaching. Todd had only time to say that he'd find a way to see me before I left, and I knew that he would. I was finding that there were no uncertainties with Todd.

When Todd left, Neil did not return with me to our room, saying he was going for a long walk.

'I expect you're still tired,' he said with surprising concern. 'I'll be back before dinner.'

He left me at the foot of the staircase. I went to my room. I wasn't tired, at least not body tired. I was mind weary. I'd been given so much to deal with. It needed sorting out.

Automatically I lifted a book. Was this my comfort? I wondered. I settled in the armchair and began skimming for - what? Solace? Guidance? Inspiration? I needed them all but, I soon realized, what I wanted was my friend Theresa.

'Have you any idea what you are letting yourself in for?' she'd asked. 'The way you are going,' she'd said, 'is to take everything upon yourself. With your God within you are accepting total responsibility for everything that happens to you.' And I had thought she was making a meal of something really straightforward!

'It's an awesome task Jenny,' she had said. 'You will not be able to shed the responsibility of creating harmony where none exists, of being unselfish in complying with his needs, of serving him above yourself. He will demand your all.' That's what she had said and she had been referring to my husband, Neil.

I gazed unseeingly at the printed word while I pondered the significance of her words. All that had been before Todd, before desire asserted itself as it never had before and swept me off my feet, right off this oh so noble path. It had swept me into a delight beyond my wildest dreams, swept me into the arms of the love of my life. Where was this noble path now? How could I find it again? Did I want to find it again? It had seemed at the time of my awareness the way, the truth and the life. It had seemed so right then. Was it right for me now?

The more I thought about this the more confused I became. Was I perhaps out of step with modern thinking? After all, had I not merely been finding a way to sublimate my desire for something else?

Theresa again. 'What you need, my girl, is a good man's love and children.' Was that it? Had all this noble talk and high aspiration been merely a comfort strategy for not having a good man's love and children? I dismissed that idea. It might be a psychologist's conclusion but I knew it went much deeper. I wanted to be free of strife, pettiness, meanness, cruelty and injustice. I wanted to be able to live my life with equanimity, to handle things well, to be centred.

During my short stay here, recapturing my past, considering my present and contemplating my future I had recognized a pattern and in this pattern there was the stuff of destiny. By today's standards I'd be considered crazy, stupid, possibly arrogant in the extreme. 'The only way to make effort effective is to put it to the universal good' someone had said. 'Only that way will it cease to be effort and become love.'

I rose from my chair and silently paced the floor. There must be others, like myself, who kept asking questions, wanting to understand more, wanting to live in the high lands of the mind, free from the cul-de-sacs of the crowded regions.

To the people of early history, when the world was discovered to be spherical and not flat, everything changed. And yet, nothing changed! To the people of today who tenaciously hold on to their belief system as the only belief system and then discover there are other belief systems equally valid, everything could change. And yet, everything would be exactly the same! Would the way be open then for the end of prejudice and the beginning of unity? Surely that would be for the good of humanity.

I knew it wasn't as simple as that. I had only my own intuition and philosophical platitudes to support me. The reality was that I was as full of carnal desire as I ever was. I was proving resistant to the thought of subjugating my personality with all its demands to the greater good of universal love. My reason dictated that it was the only way, that the power of Jesus was based on this self-denial, that he'd considered it important that even the lowliest on earth should hear of this and more importantly that he had considered it within their power to understand and act upon it. That was the difference Jesus had made to the world.

I believed this. In that respect I could call myself a Christian. Neil preached this gospel. Why were we incompatible? Why was our relationship difficult when we fundamentally believed the same thing? And why, for that matter, were Todd and I soulmates? Todd and I believed in the need to keep our minds open to the flood of change and differences, trusting in the current to carry us to the sea. Neil had found his loadstone but had fenced it off from threatening infiltration. Todd and I were free to roam. Neil had imprisoned himself.

He did not appear for dinner. I asked to have mine in my room, a safeguard against Flora's unquenchable curiosity. I tried again to read but this time it was thoughts of his possible whereabouts which made this impossible. There was more sound of activity from the hall than usual. Then I remembered the owners should be here by now. Would they be selling? If Neil decided to stay put in Edinburgh, would I want to buy? Where was he?

The hotel had settled into its customary silence when he eventually returned. I could hear his footsteps slowly approach the door. The clock struck eleven. I felt apprehensive. I knew him better than I'd realized. I was afraid of what he was going to reveal. I felt its inevitability and it was something I didn't want to hear. I had not previously taken this into my calculations.

My first sight of him confirmed my growing fear. He sat down on the bed, hands clasped and dangling between his legs, head bowed, silent. I waited with a sinking heart.

'Jenny.'

I said nothing. I was sitting by the window. My book had slipped from my hands and lay at my feet. He knelt by my chair, one hand on my knee repeating my name.

'Jenny. Look at me.'

I looked.

'Forgive me. I was wrong. I have always been wrong. I've been wrestling with God and told Him how wrong I've been. I plead your forgiveness.' He was not looking at me but at my hand which he was holding like a lifeline.

I still said nothing, suffering the discomfort of his grip.

'I've always considered I loved you,' he continued. 'I know now that what I wanted was to possess you. I realize my love has been consumed by jealousy. I've been jealous of your strength, your convictions, your courage, your relationships. I was jealous of your professor, your friend Theresa. God forgive me, I've even felt jealous of Callum. I've always felt you were out of my reach and that only fuelled my jealousy. You deserved better than that. I think I've always known it but never felt able to admit it, never knew how to deal with it.'

He looked up then and I returned his gaze, unsmiling. There was a long silence. I sat immobilized, feeling the cold begin on the back of my neck and creep up and over my scalp. I managed to free my hand and, as if from a distance, I heard my own voice.

'And now, Neil?'

He continued, his voice sounding strangled by his emotion and as if he hadn't heard my question.

'Most of all I was jealous of your relationship with Todd - alive and dead.'

My hands were like ice and in the effort to continue I had to unclench my teeth.

'And now that he is alive again?'

'I know I have nothing to fear. Poor man, he is a total wreck. I was almost out of my mind with jealousy when you told me that he was alive and you had been together through the long night. I've never felt so threatened.'

I had to force the words from my tongue. 'And you don't feel threatened now?'

'Seeing Todd's ugliness made me realize that I was so wrong about you staying out all night. Indeed I have nothing but admiration that you were able to withold your horror for his sake. I am glad you exposed him to the community. Given time, people will come to pity him rather than recoil.'

I sat immobilized. I thought of the glory of unconditional love and pitied my husband. He was talking again and what he said made no sense to me but his intensity did nothing to relieve my creeping cold.

Never had he been prompted to come so close to me and never had I felt further apart from him.

'I love you Jenny, truly, truly love you and all I want to do is make it up to you. When I returned from my walk I met the owners who were most friendly and communicative. Such was my desire to please you that I was emboldened enough to ask, in the politest possible way of course, if it was in their minds to sell the hotel. Do you know what they said?'

'What did they say?'

'Just try and stop us. And do you know what I said?'

'Tell me.'

'Don't look any further than here. My wife and I are very interested.'

Another long silence while I gauged the weight of my cross.

'I wanted to atone,' he finished lamely. 'I've decided that I'll join you here. As you know it has long been my dream to return. We could do a good job here, each in our own way. You can run your centre from here. I'll operate once again from Strathard pulpit and we'll modernize the manse.'

I forced myself. 'You are no longer jealous?'

'Not a shred.'

'So if Todd decides to live here and help me in my venture you will raise no objection?'

'You have nothing to fear.'

'I wanted to be sure.'

There was nothing left but to go to bed. I pleaded a great weariness and expressed a wish to sit up a little and finish my book which I explained would help calm me. I would join him shortly.

My grief was barely containable. I had found the path again and been made aware of its tortuous route. I must not think of the end of that route which had once been my source of inspiration. I must only think of each step and try to make it an end in itself rather than the means to an end.

While Neil slept immediately his head touched the pillow, I retrieved my book, opened it and read:

'...nothing shall ever turn you, even for a moment, from the path upon which you have entered. No temptations, no worldly pleasures, no worldly affections even, must ever draw you aside. For you yourself must become one with the path; it must be so much part of your nature that you follow it without needing to think of it, and cannot turn aside. You, the monad have decided it; to break away from it would be to break away from yourself.'

I closed the book and remembered Sunday School texts learned under duress.

'Whatsoever ye do, do it heartily, as to the Lord, and not unto men.'

I rose and prepared for bed thinking of Todd and looking at my husband. It was all a question of choice. Or was it?

Printed in the United States
By Bookmasters